ADVENTURES ON THE GO

# ADVENTURES ON THE GO

offbeat Reads

Always adventure in a book.

# ADVENTURES ON THE GO

**VOLUME 1**      **BOOK 4**

## SUMMER, 2022

## ISBN: (PAPERBACK) 978-1-950464-12-8
## ISBN: (EBOOK) 978-1-950464-13-5

Photo: Ishantrivedi, CC BY-SA 3.0 <https://creativecommons.org/licenses/by-sa/3.0>, via Wikimedia Commons. (No Changes.)

Photo: Palmer, A. T., photographer. (1943) Operating a hand drill at Vultee-Nashville, woman is working on a "Vengeance" dive bomber, Tennessee. Tennessee United States Nashville, 1943. Feb. [Photograph] Retrieved from the Library of Congress, https://www.loc.gov/item/2017878546/.

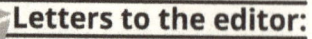

**Letters to the editor:**

Comments/Questions are accepted. Put *Letter to Editor* in Subject and send to: OffBeatReads@pm.me
*Email content could be published in future Adventures on the Go.*

offbeat **Reads**
Always adventure in a book.

**WWW.OFFBEATREADS.COM**

# EDITOR'S NOTE

Welcome to the fourth issue of *Adventures on the Go*. Before I introduce the content, OffBeatReads (the publisher of this rag) wishes to make a proclamation:

We support freedom and rights for the smallest minority—the individual.

It is unfortunate in today's culture, despite the virtue-signaling cries for tolerance, that a popular attitude is to shut out differing views. But right off, let's be clear about something: though times and circumstances change, what is *just* does not. (Postmodernist cringe is duly noted.) So rationally speaking, words do not equal violence. Some words may be rude, inappropriate, harsh, even *unacceptable*—but a happy and peaceful society can never be if any speech in a culture must be innocuous. Freedom of speech exists for many valid reasons. Among those reasons is the obvious fact: it inhibits the need for aggression. If people cannot talk things out, if people cannot push the envelope of ideas, if people cannot be themselves, what is left? Aggression.

The will to silence any outlier or opposing viewpoint is itself totalitarian. This is because inevitably a ruler is needed to determine what is acceptable and what is not. You don't need to be a historian to know what that means for groups of people who are the hated ones. (And they are hated only because they can be used by the corrupt in power.) We see it today. Using various tactics, those in powerful positions gain influence over a selected collective of citizens. They then need one last thing: for that same collective of citizens to be just large enough, angry enough, and loud enough to help them enforce their political end. There is nothing moral or virtuous about that.

If each and every single person is valued and respected—in other words, an individual does not need to be labeled or attached to a group to be important—then we are all free... free because the powerful can no longer spin the collective steering wheel (attached to the collective mind) to corral our feelings and energies.

I think the world would be better for all if we would not look at people to determine what we do not like about them. We don't need to categorize, we can be better. What about recognizing that someone is different (and we can with civility debate those differences), but at the end of the day we are free to live according to our own conscience. I remember a country like that. Some don't, and some never will. None of us can expect rights or freedom if we won't afford the same to others, even if we don't like the life they choose for themselves.

*Above: Mary Pickford in 1918, same year as Stella Maris Film Release. Below: Mary at home (from the April 10, 1920 Exhibitors Herald). Bottom: Stella Maris Film Lobby card from 1918.*

On that note, this issue of *Adventures...* introduces *Southwest Scenarios*, an editorial sure to make you ponder, maybe cause a rise in blood pressure.

Miranda Maples provides for us a new and original story, *Ghosts and Heartbeats in the Rain*. *Two Old Lovers* touches the heart; *Don't Look Now* is a SciFi offering that may prove martians now lurk among us.

In our efforts to provide as much entertainment in an issue as possible, there is more. Dragon-Wrangler Savannah J. Goins gives us insight in an exclusive interview—oh—she's also an author and writing coach. (Authors: see the Fun Page for discount information on Savannah's unparalleled coaching services.)

## WE ARE HONORED TO HAVE MARY PICKFORD ON THE COVER.

Like others, I was once guilty of attributing silliness, exaggerated acting and slap-stick humor to silent films. This can be true, but an honest thrust into these silent works of art soon shows a different picture.

Early films mostly relied on the unadulterated combination of story and talent; and film aficionados tend to agree: there is a raw attraction to the black and white.

Without a doubt, one of the standout films from this era is *Stella Maris* (1918 version) in which Mary Pickford plays two parts. Mary Pickford was a known flapper of the era, and a very savvy businesswoman. After a young start in Vaudeville, she grew to be a popular actress known as, "The Queen of the Movies". Pickford also co-founded United Artists. Her life is interesting beyond these few words and worth research.

We are pleased to be able to include the original story *Stella Maris* by British novelist Willian John Locke. *Stella Maris* is a wonderful drama with an unforeseeable climax. We ask one thing: that you overlook minor errors that may exist. In reproducing the original text, errors such as an extra space (or others) may remain. However, this does not affect the readability, and the complete story is included as authored. Thank you serious bibliophiles who understand.

Enjoy your reading adventures!

*Robert Kimbrell*

Robert Kimbrell

*A New, Original Story*

## GHOSTS AND HEARTBEATS

# IN THE RAIN
*by Miranda Maples*

*This story is dedicated to my mother, who took me to my first Noir movie, Blade Runner.*

*Miss you, Mom.*

"These warehouses, lots of weird things happen at night," said the driver. He shook his head back and forth in a what-has-this-world-come-to way.

I was busy looking at the cityscape of Los Angeles. The sun was setting, and I had never seen anything like it. The sky was a palette of electric violet and red, like God was having an art exhibit.

Just a few minutes ago, I had maneuvered through LAX, swept up in the excitement of the crowds and the noise. Coming out of the sliding glass doors, the city and the incoming night inhabited me. I stood outside smoking a cigarette, taken aback by the population: every race and nationality seemed to have converged in this one place on earth. A guy bummed a smoke and offered me a dollar for it.

"No, don't worry about it," I said. He seemed surprised and said thanks have a goodnight. I felt like we could have been friends.

But the driver's words had caught my attention. "What weird things?" I prodded.

"Damned fools dress up as animals and go to these clubs, some wear these old costumes, like from the pre-talkie era, get into all kinds of weird shit," he said and chuckled. He sped through the never-ending traffic, unbothered, fluidly weaving in and out of the lanes and somehow avoiding near collisions.

I didn't say anything, not certain if he was truly scandalized, or just trying to make fun of me. I had that look: naïve and most definitely a girl who had never been to LA before. I didn't care either way. Still, I looked more closely at the warehouses lining both sides of La Cienega Boulevard.

I paid the driver and went to check in. After showering and changing into fresh clothes, I pulled back the heavy curtains of the window and saw a small patio area. I walked out and sat and

smoked, marveling again at the feel of this place. Every town has a vibe, but this city had a pulse; and for some reason, I wondered what this spot, right now, had looked like a million years ago.

What gave a place a heartbeat? What imbued it with the energy of a living organism? The inhabitants, or was it the place itself that gave forth the life force? Maybe a special beam of light from a star long gone had mingled with the bacteria and it was still swimming around in the great Pacific, like a benefic mutation that gives a human the skill of singing or being able to figure out how to harness lightning into electricity to power the earth.

My stomach rumbled; I had not eaten in over seven hours. I got an Uber and gave the girl the address for a place on Sunset in West Hollywood. I goggled at the size of the city, at the buildings touching the silky sky. The moon was a crescent, on her way to being full. I paid the driver and stepped onto the sidewalk. The restaurant was lined with fairy lights and green vines climbed the archway of the entrance.

The bar was a study in gold and gleaming wood, and the inside of the place was dark, the only lighting came from small candles and more fairy lights. I ordered an expensive beer and some even more expensive crab pasta, which at that moment was worth it. I sipped another beer and soaked in the people and the beautiful restaurant. I was not being noticed by anyone, back where I came from, some people might have looked askance at me, like who's this dateless freak out to dinner alone on a Friday night? But here, no one cared.

After dinner, I walked for a while on Sunset, and I saw a club that was advertising a band. I checked the time on my phone, and realized I had to be up early the next morning. There was a liquor store close to The Viper Room, all I knew about The Viper Room was it was where River Phoenix had died. I was standing right outside the door where it might have happened, and I quickly walked away. The liquor store was an overpriced tourist trap, but I wanted to sit outside with a couple more beers before bed.

Back at my hotel, I was sitting in the shaded alcove patio staring at the moon. I looked across the street at the warehouses: still nothing going on, maybe all the action happened farther down out of my line of sight. Someone came around the corner, a man perhaps in his mid-fifties.

"Spare a smoke, sweetheart?" he asked.

I nodded and handed him one and my lighter. He began to cough.

"You okay?" I asked.

"Fine just fine, just been a while since I had one of these" he said and took another drag. "Just gotta numb the vigilant, hardworking cilia," he said. I just now realized he was wearing a fedora and a shabby dark suit, his tie undone.

I noticed I didn't feel on edge around this man, alone in the dark so far from home. I must have been too buzzed and tired; I felt completely drained, wanting to sleep. Suddenly it got darker. I looked up and sinister clouds were rolling in, and it began to sprinkle.

"It never rains in LA, but when it does, it gets even more hot, the rain comes down hard, not used to being here, not gentle or pleasant, the heat rises up from the baked asphalt and mean concrete, and you feel like you're being cooked by your own steam," he said.

He pulled his fedora down slightly, and threw his butt down, stomping it out with his patent leather shoe, sparks rising like demonic fireflies. He coughed again, and his shoulders hunched against the incoming rain, which was indeed mean and hard like he said.

"Thanks for the smoke, kid, but you ought to kick those things, don't you know they targeted women back in the day to think smoking was glamourous? Don't be a sheep," he said and walked off.

I watched him walk off, and I put my already wet cigarette into the tall ashtray and got up, following him, but he was gone, swallowed by the shadows. I stood in the rain, looking around, and sure enough, I began to sweat in the August heat. I went into my room and showered and crawled into bed, so tired I didn't even dream, which was strange for me.

The next morning, I was sitting across from the development duo named Chris and Lee who were painfully younger than me. They seemed to be carved from the same block of pristine marble, both flawless and crisp, and they were talking very fast, but they would check their phones every few minutes.

"We love this script, I can see why it won the contest, it's so... original, and its message is so relevant," said Chris.

"Thank you," I said. I was picking at my nails and put them in my lap. I had not had a cigarette since last night with my odd visitor.

"So relevant!" said Lee, nodding in approval, then she checked her phone typing at light speed.

"How so?" I asked.

"Well, I mean you clearly are remarking on patriarchal imagery in a male-centric era of film," said Chris.

"Oh, no I wasn't trying to, um, convey any messages, I just love Raymond Chandler," I said.

Lee stopped typing, and they exchanged a look.

"But, if people take messages from my screenplay, that's great," I said smiling widely. It wasn't great, not in this case, but I was tired of not having money, I had been poor my whole life, and writing was the only thing I loved, the only thing I was truly good at doing, and I wanted to start being paid for it for a change. I wagered they had both gone to private universities, and never had to worry about such pedestrian things. I also wondered what cosmic fluke had landed me here in this office, groveling before these impeccably dressed privileged dolts.

"Who's Raymond Chandler?" asked Chris.

I blinked. "The main character in my script is based off of Phillip Marlowe, the character created by the writer Raymond Chandler, and of course mixed with Hammett's Sam Spade," I said. I touched the foil packet of my nicotine gum in my blazer pocket.

They were looking at me like I was speaking a foreign language.

"You know, Humphrey Bogart," I said.

"Oh, Casablanca! I love that movie!" said Lee smiling as bright as the sun.

"Me too," I lied. It was my least favorite Bogart film.

"Well, here's the thing, we want you to revise and write a treatment set in present day and give us a list of actors who you think could play the lead," said Chris. Chris looked down at my script. "The main character, Arche Forge, the detective, he needs to be younger, someone more modern and relatable," said Chris as if he were imparting great wisdom upon me.

"I'm thinking Cody Maguire or Jay Turner," said Lee.

"No, but the thing is, my script is set in the 1940s, and Arch Forge is a seasoned detective, older and street-smart, the whole narrative revolves around that..." I began.

They sat back in their seats and nodded, pretending to appear commiserating. *Shit.*

"But, sure, I'm open to revising it with a more modern feel, of course, why didn't I think of that" I said. My heart sank down to my feet. The rain pattered against the large window. I tried to picture Arche Forge being played by a young shiny-faced actor. Had they not read my script? Did they not know about Arche's handsome but menacing mug? That sexy frown line that popped up between his eyebrows when he was looking over a crime scene? The intense eyes that have seen way too much but could charm a dame with one glance?

Instead of asking them these burning questions, I stood up and we all shook hands, and I walked out of the office before I shoved their phones down their throats, their muffled screams and gurgling like a balm for my anger. I popped more gum in the elevator. It helped a little.

That night after I was done revising my precious screenplay, I felt like a fraud, a traitor to my art. I got an Uber to take me to a nightclub. I wanted a cigarette more than anything, but I settled for the synthetic chewy square instead; it had been almost twenty-four hours without a smoke. There was no way I could drink at a bar and not have a cigarette; I recalled how a cigarette tastes after a drink, like a smoky campfire smore being fed intravenously into your body. *Don't be a sheep*, Fedora's deep melodic voice echoed in my mind.

I walked into the dark club; the walls were painted a bold shade of burgundy, and the floors were old wood, and they creaked as I walked to the small bar. The place was lit only by small lamps on the round tables, and it was the right amount of bleak and cozy. A jazz singer was crooning on stage, and I ordered a bourbon, feeling very much like an adult. It was still raining, and even hotter than today. I looked at my empty glass, and as if I summoned him with my urge, the bartender refilled it silently.

The booze was working, but my nerves sizzled, desperately wanting a cigarette. I put another piece of the nicotine gum in my other cheek. I looked around the club; the room had a fog of cigarette smoke hanging in the air. I saw a woman light up a fresh stick, and I downed my bourbon, blown away that something had such a grip on my soul. I paid for my drinks and walked out, slightly listing, and I felt like I was on a ship in the ocean; I could actually hear the creaking of the boat and smell the dank ocean. I was drunk.

It was raining even harder, and I realized I left my umbrella in the bar. I turned to go back inside to retrieve it, and suddenly from behind me I heard successive loud bangs: the unmistakable sounds of crunching metal and shattering glass. I turned and saw a three-car pile-up on Sunset. Suddenly someone ran right into me, knocking me off my feet, and I landed on the wet sidewalk, somehow avoiding falling on my face, catching myself with my hands.

My hand slid in the grease and grime, and then I tasted the sidewalk slime and dirty runoff water on my lips, and I choked on the city rain, and the heat from the concrete went into my mouth, and I vomited right there. I got to my feet and leaned against a pole. I heard sirens and saw oncoming flashing red lights, and there was a crowd in front of me.

The crowd was pressed against me, I felt the heat from their bodies, almost as hot as the night, I could hear their collective hearts beating, circulating adrenaline-spiked blood. I could also hear the other heartbeats, the ones in those mangled cars, weak as dying kittens. I squeezed past them and walked towards my hotel. I found a cab about a mile up, and the driver peered at me for a minute, and said he would charge extra since I was drenched.

Back in my room. I put my wet clothes in a pile on the bathroom floor, my new blazer I had bought at the local mall for the meeting was stained and ruined. I showered and then brushed my teeth and tongue, getting the wretched silt out of my mouth. I sat on the bed and opened more nicotine gum, dropped it. I got down on all fours, looking frantically for the piece, and found it under the bed. I felt something else. I turned on the lamp and looked under the bed. It was a box. I chewed the gum furiously, debating.

Finally, I slid the box out from under the bed. It was shoe box, dusty with age, and a brand name I had never heard of. I looked at it. How had this been left here? What was inside? A fetus, a murder weapon? Drugs? Did someone take a shit in here and leave it as a welcome gift? Instead of a mint on the pillow, enjoy this crap in a box? It would be fitting with how this lousy trip was shaping up.

I decided to open the dusty box. Inside were newspaper clippings. I looked at the dates: August through October 1936. The newspaper articles were stories about a young woman whose body had been found on the docks, stabbed to death. She was an aspiring actress from Tennessee who had moved to Los Angeles named Arabelle Fenton, but her stage name was Victoria Caine. She had been in one film, a role as a cigarette girl named Lucy Shaw who becomes involved with a crime boss. The movie, titled *A Taxi at Midnight*, was about how Lucy Shaw, a wannabe showgirl, gets involved with the sleazy owner of the Club Bella Fortuna, also a ruthless but suave crime lord, named Jake Scar. The most recent article went on to state that Victoria Caine was slated to star as the lead in a movie called *A Smart Blonde*. '*This would have made Caine's career, but alas fate had other ideas for the silver-screen stunner!*' the article read like a cheap tabloid and was degrading to say the least. Her murder was never solved, and some other articles alluded to her involvement with drug dealers and even ties to the mob.

I had never heard the name Victoria Caine, and I had seen all the old films, knew all the famous and more obscure stars of that long-forgotten era. I stared at the name: Arabelle, that was my first name, but I went by my middle name. I remember being told it was a family name. I looked at the small headshot of her above the article. She had bleached blond hair, and a dreamy look, her lips were full and pouty, and she was smiling in a way that was somewhat naïve yet seductive. She wasn't beautiful, but she had a quality about her that made you want to keep staring at her, what they called magnetism.

I sat down with my laptop and saw an email from the contest representative with whom I was working. She said the dynamic development duo were liasoning with a production company for possible option and they would be in touch, and furthermore I needed to get an agent. Liasoning, whatever that meant. It meant this trip, footed by the company, was over and I had to go home. I wondered why they had even bothered. I Googled the names Arabelle Fenton and Victoria Caine but came up with nothing. When I got home, I would visit the library for birth records, or try to access the archives of LA newspapers.

It was 2:30 am. I looked out my window; it had stopped raining. I walked out and sat in the patio area, waiting for my man in the fedora to come back, but he didn't so I went back to my room. I fell asleep on top of the blankets, and then the dreams came. I guess they were dreams; I'm still not convinced they weren't real.

The fedora man came back, my Arche Forge. He shook his head at me, lighting a cigarette in the darkness, the streetlights illuminating his chiseled jaw in the shadows. I heard a dreary saxophone off in the distance. His eyes glowed with neon and black streets.

"You got a real problem kid, you don't know how good you got it," he said. The smell of the smoke reached through my senses, lighting up my pleasure centers like a practiced lover.

"They made me butcher my writing, like those poor souls on the street, like the unknown actress they found on the docks" I said. "Arche Forge isn't meant for this time and place, he's a hardboiled cynic, world-weary and smart as a whip, he's black and white, and lonely streets at night," I whined.

"You're in LA, how long have ya wanted to be here, alive in this city, an actual screenwriter in LA? I remember how you daydreamed, and night dreamed about being here, far away from the small town, from the people who don't dream, who don't want something more. Now you're here and you're blowing it, and for what, standards?" he asked.

"You said don't be a sheep, I just keep being led around, compromising myself, my work, if it even gets made, it won't even resemble what it was supposed to be," I said. "I'm just another blip on the radar, no one will remember me," I said, and I began to cry.

"That's the thing, isn't it, we all are eventually forgotten, and I know you're gonna say what about Shakespeare, or the other literary greats, well someday, they might be too, who knows, but the story, that will never die, come with me," said Arche.

Somehow, we were walking down Hollywood Boulevard, the streets were slick and black, but there were the stars, smaller than I thought they would be. We walked and looked at all of them, eventually we got to the names I didn't recognize, so many of them.

"In time, we all will be forgotten, but the forgotten always remember," said Arche. He stared down at the stars, I stared at that frown line between his perfectly shaped eyebrows. I wanted to kiss him. Instead, I stood with him, looking at the rows of names.

"So many of them, they all came here and were on the big screen larger than life and we marveled. Am I a ghost too? How are you here? I made you up, but here we are, and here they are," I said.

"You don't get all the answers when you want them, it doesn't work that way," said Arche. He took of his fedora and put his arms around me.

"How lucky are you, huh?" and he smiled a charming, crooked smile and I wrapped my arms around my hero, on the streets of Hollywood at night with all these stars. They danced around us, ghost celluloid black and white, their eyes glowing and eventually they leapt up and were hovering over the City of Angels. I saw Victoria Caine go gliding along the boulevard, her arms open dancing with the city, in love.

"Are they angels or ghosts?" I asked Arche.

"Whatever you want them to be, doll," he winked at me. My knees almost buckled.

"You smell the way the Taj Mahal looks by moonlight," Arche said. And we kissed among the stars.

I left the next day, but before I did, I went on a tour of the Hollywood Hills. It was something else. I looked over the city one last time, took pictures of the Hollywood sign. The sun was bright, and the air was dry and arid, it was as if the rain had never happened. The "dreams" I had with Arche Forge, walking at night on Hollywood Boulevard seemed like they had never happened in the bright morning light.

I was already starting to forget, and wasn't that the damnable irony of it all? But the newspaper clippings in the dusty box in my suitcase were very real. Blanketed by smog, the city was like a dragon in heat, ready to either receive or devour you, and the thing was, you didn't care which one she picked.

*Not bad, kid, keep working on those.*

Later, as the plane took off, I watched the city disappear from me, knowing I'd be back. I felt empty and I wanted nothing more than to stay, to be close to the heartbeat of that place, and feel alive. Sometimes empty was good, it meant there was room for more.

I would figure out a way to keep parts of me here, but I finally realized we can't stay in the past, eventually we must get chummy with the time and place in which the Great Boss in the sky plopped us into. But you can always visit, and dance with those ghosts, just don't become one of them before its your time. And isn't that what we're all looking for, kid? Even the dead yearn for greatness, but more than that, sometimes they need answers. They help us, we help them.

The skyline of LA disappeared, and I was among the clouds. I knew someone had left that dusty box under the bed for me, and now I wondered why. I suddenly felt it was more than just a warning, it was an invitation. What if the ones who were gone somehow came through as characters we just thought we had made up? Maybe that's one way the dead come back, brought to life again by our imagination? Time was not a straight line, we only think it is, but the reality could be stranger. Maybe the ones who haunt are haunted too. Maybe Arche is haunted by Victoria Caines' cold case, and he needs my help. Maybe I needed to find out why.

That was a lot of maybes, but so what? I popped a piece of gum, opened my laptop, and typed two of my favorite words:

Fade In.

What a town. A place so alive that the dead never left; they were always near, whispering, walking right beside you. But to hear and see them, you had to get your ass knocked down onto the cruel, hot pavement, on a rare rainy night in the City of Angels.

*An East Tennessee native, Miranda Loves writing about the mysterious and the supernatural, the beautiful and the grotesque. Among other things, she loves high-end beer, Gothic and Greek revival homes, Carl Jung, baking, and back roads.*

*For more about the author and her upcoming novel, visit MirandaMaples.com.*

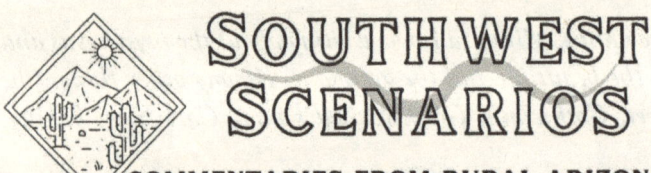

# SOUTHWEST SCENARIOS

## COMMENTARIES FROM RURAL ARIZONA
### BY DARRYLE PURCELL

Because humankind fails to learn from past lessons, we find that many circumstances from yesteryear are repeating themselves yet again. The commentaries that follow here and in future issues were originally published by *The Mohave Valley Daily News between 1993 & 2013*--and in many ways they apply to today.
We are grateful to republish these commentaries written by Darryle Purcell in full and unedited. His own brand of humor and style can deliver insight, provoke thought, and even boil blood.

# INTRODUCTION

Arizona is a special place. Individuals from all over the United States, Mexico and Canada come here to work, play and live in this land of diverse culture and climate.

One has to look closely to find a commonality among this mass immigration of unique personalities. The same qualities that brought the original settlers to America, first to the east coast, then westward across the country, brought our growing population to Arizona. That would be the quest for freedom from thought control, which has been known throughout the late $20^{TH}$ and early $21^{ST}$ centuries as political correctness.

One of the deciding factors that brought me to Arizona was the openness of the residents to discuss popular and unpopular subjects, something that, at the time of my immigration, was beginning to vanish in my prior home of southern California. Having been a conservative, newspaper editorial cartoonist in the Golden State, I had always enjoyed open political discourse, including the many letters, both pro and con, that I received at my office every day. In the 1980s and early '90s, there was no Internet, no e-mail and no Twitter. People had to sit down at their desks or kitchen tables and write letters. And I appreciated the correspondence no matter how the writers felt about my editorial stance. Expressing a political position had yet to become offensive. People didn't demand that opposing views be silenced—not yet.

But, by the early 1990s, many southern California daily newspapers had been purchased by large national and multi-national publishing corporations. With that came an amalgamation of accepted editorial viewpoints that wouldn't outrage special-interest activists. In other words, newspaper publishers were replacing local editorial writers and cartoonists with syndicated columnists and artists whose work had little effect on local issues and advertisers. That kind of pandering was the beginning of a trend that has, at this point in time, led to my reference to my former home state as the People's Republic of California.

Today, like California, many other states tout their acceptance of diversity—as long as one agrees completely with their version of that philosophy. And state officials, Hollywood activists and a variety of movers and shakers often silence individuals who may have other points of view. One only needs to remember that in the late 1940s and early 1950s, Sen. Joseph McCarthy was the leader of political correctness. The song and the singers may have changed, but the pressure for all of us to carry the same tune is still there. Just ask anyone who has been shunned by today's cartel of social media platforms.

Now don't get me wrong. There is just as much political and social silliness going on in Arizona, which you will notice in the following pages, as any other state. The difference is, in Arizona we are still free to be critical of the social order without fear of reprisals. Yes, some city, county and state officials threaten reprisals, but those actions are seldom carried out as there are still a couple of news publications that are not in the pockets of elected officials, activists or back-room political bosses.

Arizona is truly a diverse state in that there are many philosophies professed and many discussions and arguments held both in the legislative world and the world of private citizens and business. And since so many of our residents have come from areas where they had experienced pressure from the "majority," or from those in social power, they are thankful for their Arizona rights to be themselves. Of course, ex-Californians like me would probably not be welcomed back to our former state.

Southwest Scenarios is a look back at some local and national issues during a time of change in America. Most of the following essays appeared in a small daily newspaper along the Colorado River in Arizona where I served as managing editor from 1993 until 2005. A few of them were published in some Arizona weeklies in more recent years and dealt with topics not necessarily widely criticized by the mainstream (usual suspects) media. And although not all of them involve politics, most of them probably would not appear in today's newspapers from other (more PC) states. And as far as Left-Coast techies are concerned, Twitter hearts would probably go all-aflutter as they co-conspire with Google and Facebook to turn banning into an art form. The columns are quite facetious—"smart ass"—according to one of my former publishers. They are my opinions, at the time of publication, and not those of anyone else including (especially) the management of that publication.

Although readers probably will not recognize most of the local Arizona characters in these opinion articles, they will probably be familiar with public officials and activists in their own communities who might just fit the bill. Of course, most of the national politicos and entertainers mentioned are still either famous, or infamous, today.

Most of the following columns include the date of publication. Some, by today's standards, seem naive while others come off as angry or caustic. All are views over the last few decades through a time-specific window of a rural Arizona newspaper editor, smartass cartoonist, neo-pulp writer and grumpy old man.

I am thankful to the people of Arizona for the prevalent acceptance of individualism. I am truly thankful for the freedom that gives us all the right to be wrong.

## CALIFORNIA BIRDBRAINS
# TAKE A DIVE
*Originally Published July 15, 2004*

E ver since Charles Darwin communicated the Law of Natural Selection, there have been those who have attempted to repeal it.

During the last 20 years we have heard a lot about spotted owls, desert tortoises, razorback chubs and a variety of snail-darting minnows, gnat-catching mud suckers and cross-dressing root rats. I'd swear that some "rare" species are being created just so a group of otherwise out-of-work bureaucrats will have something to protect.

Darwin's theory is that some species are better adapted to survive than others. For instance, a desert tortoise won't do too well in the Antarctic region, and penguins are quite scarce in Arizona. They are both well designed to survive in their respective neighborhoods.

Humans have an advantage on other species in that most of us possess the intelligence to come in out of the rain, put on a jacket in cold weather and grab a chilled brewsky when it's hot. This places us at the top of the evolutionary scale—even with "Lite" beer.

But the attempt to keep some species with us may just be a lost cause.

The *Mohave Valley Daily News* printed an Associated Press story out of Phoenix Sunday headlined "Endangered pelicans mistaking Arizona asphalt for lakes."

According to the article, some endangered brown pelicans have come to Arizona looking for fish (first sign that these creatures may be too stupid to survive) and are mistaking mirages, created over hot asphalt, as lakes. This can cause an incredible road-rash problem for the big-beaked Bozos.

California environmentalists should be alarmed, since the birds are native to the People's Republic of Santa Monica and other Left-coast hubs of enlightenment. Those folks can't afford to allow a single endangered species to leave as government restrictions and taxpayer-funded programs depend on keeping the creatures local.

Perhaps they should print flyers warning the birds against the Republican state of Arizona and its desert asphalt traps. Of course it would be hard to distribute the flyers to the birds because that would be littering. It would also be quite expensive since, in California, government flyers have to be printed in several languages.

Another possibility would be to build pelican helmets with tinted goggles so the birds wouldn't be bothered by the mirages, and, if they were, the helmets would protect them from birdbrain damage. This program could create a lot of government jobs in the Golden State—pelican helmet manufacturers and distributors—and may just be a major part of John Kerry's job growth plan.

And then maybe Darwin had it right and it should be up to Mother Nature as to the survivability of some creatures. Pacific Coast brown pelicans that fly into the desert looking for fish and kamikaze dive into highways and parking lots are not necessarily a benefit to the rest of us. They could be looked at as dinner from heaven for Arizona transients hanging around parking lots. But for the rest of us, those creatures are showing signs of terminal stupidity and don't deserve protection.

And in the same category, there are Hollywood "entertainers" who demand we put our tails between our legs and surrender in the Mideast. They consider Americans to be the barbarians and offer only love and acceptance to the terrorists.

The brown pelicans are smarter than that.

---

*Darryle Purcell has had a variety of jobs during his lifetime—including soldier, illustrator, editorial cartoonist, newspaper managing editor and government flack. He currently writes and illustrates the Hollywood Cowboy Detectives, Man of the Mist and Vermin pulp adventures from his home in rural Arizona, where he lives with his wife Patricia.*

# DON'T LOOK NOW
*by Henry Kuttner*

*Originally published in Startling Stories, March, 1948

*That man beside you may be a Martian.
They own our world, but only a few wise
and far-seeing men like Lyman know it!*

The man in the brown suit was looking at himself in the mirror behind the bar. The reflection seemed to interest him even more deeply than the drink between his hands. He was paying only perfunctory attention to Lyman's attempts at conversation. This had been going on for perhaps fifteen minutes before he finally lifted his glass and took a deep swallow.

"Don't look now," Lyman said.

The brown man slid his eyes sidewise toward Lyman; tilted his glass higher, and took another swig. Ice-cubes slipped down toward his mouth. He put the glass back on the red-brown wood and signaled for a refill. Finally he took a deep breath and looked at Lyman.

"Don't look at what?" he asked.

"There was one sitting right beside you," Lyman said, blinking rather glazed eyes. "He just went out. You mean you couldn't see him?"

The brown man finished paying for his fresh drink before he answered. "See who?" he asked, with a fine mixture of boredom, distaste and reluctant interest. "Who went out?"

"What have I been telling you for the last ten minutes? Weren't you listening?"

"Certainly I was listening. That is—certainly. You were talking about —bathtubs. Radios. Orson—"

"Not Orson. H. G. Herbert George. With Orson it was just a gag. H. G. *knew*—or suspected. I wonder if it was simply intuition with him? He couldn't have had any proof—but he did stop writing science-fiction rather suddenly, didn't he? I'll bet he knew once, though."

"Knew what?"

"About the Martians. All this won't do us a bit of good if you don't listen. It may not anyway. The trick is to jump the gun—with proof. Convincing evidence. Nobody's ever been allowed to produce the evidence before. You *are* a reporter, aren't you?"

Holding his glass, the man in the brown suit nodded reluctantly.

"Then you ought to be taking it all down on a piece of folded paper. I want everybody to know. The whole world. It's important. Terribly important. It explains everything. My life won't be safe unless I can pass along the information and make people believe it."

"Why won't your life be safe?"

"Because of the Martians, you fool. They own the world."

The brown man sighed. "Then they own my newspaper, too," he objected, "so I can't print anything they don't like."

"I never thought of that," Lyman said, considering the bottom of his glass, where two ice-cubes had fused into a cold, immutable union. "They're not omnipotent, though. I'm sure they're vulnerable, or why have they always kept under cover? They're afraid of being found out. If the world had convincing evidence—look, people always believe what they read in the newspapers. Couldn't you—"

"Ha," said the brown man with deep significance.

Lyman drummed sadly on the bar and murmured, "There must be some way. Perhaps if I had another drink...."

The brown suited man tasted his collins, which seemed to stimulate him. "Just what is all this about Martians?" he asked Lyman. "Suppose you start at the beginning and tell me again. Or can't you remember?"

"Of course I can remember. I've got practically total recall. It's something new. Very new. I never could do it before. I can even remember my last conversation with the Martians." Lyman favored the brown man with a glance of triumph.

"When was that?"

"This morning."

"I can even remember conversations I had last week," the brown man said mildly. "So what?"

"You don't understand. They make us forget, you see. They tell us what to do and we forget about the conversation—it's post-hypnotic suggestion, I expect—but we follow their orders just the same. There's the compulsion, though we think we're making our own decisions. Oh, they own the world, all right, but nobody knows it except me."

"And how did you find out?"

"Well, I got my brain scrambled, in a way. I've been fooling around with supersonic detergents, trying to work out something marketable, you know. The gadget went wrong—from some standpoints. High-frequency waves, it was. They went through and through me. Should have been inaudible, but I could hear them, or rather—well, actually I could see them. That's what I mean about my brain being scrambled. And after that, I could see and hear the Martians. They've geared themselves so they work efficiently on ordinary brains, and mine isn't ordinary any more. They can't hypnotize me, either. They can command me, but I needn't obey—now. I hope they don't suspect. Maybe they do. Yes, I guess they do."

"How can you tell?"

"The way they look at me."

"How do they look at you?" asked the brown man, as he began to reach for a pencil and then changed his mind. He took a drink instead. "Well? What are they like?"

"I'm not sure. I can see them, all right, but only when they're dressed up."

"Okay, okay," the brown man said patiently. "How do they look, dressed up?"

"Just like anybody, almost. They dress up in—in human skins. Oh, not real ones, imitations. Like the Katzenjammer Kids zipped into crocodile suits. Undressed—I don't know. I've never seen one. Maybe they're invisible even to me, then, or maybe they're just camouflaged. Ants or owls or rats or bats or—"

"Or anything," the brown man said hastily.

"Thanks. Or anything, of course. But when they're dressed up like humans—like that one who was sitting next to you awhile ago, when I told you not to look—"

"That one was invisible, I gather?"

"Most of the time they are, to everybody. But once in a while, for some reason, they—"

"Wait," the brown man objected. "Make sense, will you? They dress up in human skins and then sit around invisible?"

"Only now and then. The human skins are perfectly good imitations. Nobody can tell the difference. It's that third eye that gives them away. When they keep it closed, you'd never guess it was there. When they want to open it, they go invisible—like *that*. Fast. When I see somebody with a third eye, right in the middle of his forehead, I know he's a Martian and invisible, and I pretend not to notice him."

"Uh-huh," the brown man said. "Then for all you know, I'm one of your visible Martians."

"Oh, I hope not!" Lyman regarded him anxiously. "Drunk as I am, I don't think so. I've been trailing you all day, making sure. It's a risk I have to take, of course. They'll go to any length—any length at all—to make a man give himself away. I realize that. I can't really trust anybody. But I had to find someone to talk to, and I—" He paused. There was a brief silence. "I could be wrong," Lyman said presently. "When the third eye's closed, I can't tell if it's there. Would you mind opening your third eye for me?" He fixed a dim gaze on the brown man's forehead.

"Sorry," the reporter said. "Some other time. Besides, I don't know you. So you want me to splash this across the front page, I gather? Why didn't you go to see the managing editor? My stories have to get past the desk and rewrite."

"I want to give my secret to the world," Lyman said stubbornly. "The question is, how far will I get? You'd expect they'd have killed me the minute I opened my mouth to you—except that I didn't say anything while they were here. I don't believe they take us very seriously, you know. This must have been going on since the dawn of history, and by now they've had time to get careless. They let Fort go pretty far before they cracked down on him. But you notice they were careful never to let Fort get hold of genuine proof that would convince people."

❖

The brown man said something under his breath about a human interest story in a box. He asked, "What do the Martians do, besides hang around bars all dressed up?"

"I'm still working on that," Lyman said. "It isn't easy to understand. They run the world, of course, but why?" He wrinkled his brow and stared appealingly at the brown man. "Why?"

"If they do run it, they've got a lot to explain."

"That's what I mean. From our viewpoint, there's no sense to it. We do things illogically, but only because they tell us to. Everything we do, almost, is pure illogic. Poe's *Imp of the Perverse*—you could give it another name beginning with M. Martian, I mean. It's all very well for psychologists to explain why a murderer wants to confess, but it's still an illogical reaction. Unless a Martian commands him to."

"You can't be hypnotized into doing anything that violates your moral sense," the brown man said triumphantly.

Lyman frowned. "Not by another human, but you can by a Martian. I expect they got the upper hand when we didn't have more than ape-brains, and they've kept it ever since. They evolved as we did, and kept a step ahead. Like the sparrow on the eagle's back who hitch-hiked till the eagle reached his ceiling, and then took off and broke the altitude record. They conquered the world, but nobody ever knew it. And they've been ruling ever since."

"But—"

"Take houses, for example. Uncomfortable things. Ugly, inconvenient, dirty, everything wrong with them. But when men like Frank Lloyd Wright slip out from under the Martians' thumb long enough to suggest something better, look how the people react. They hate the thought. That's their Martians, giving them orders."

"Look. Why should the Martians care what kind of houses we live in? Tell me that."

Lyman frowned. "I don't like the note of skepticism I detect creeping into this conversation," he announced. "They care, all right. No doubt about it. They *live* in our houses. We don't build for our convenience, we build, under order, for the Martians, the way they want it. They're very much concerned with everything we do. And the more senseless, the more concern.

"Take wars. Wars don't make sense from any human viewpoint.

Nobody really wants wars. But we go right on having them. From the Martian viewpoint, they're useful. They give us a spurt in technology, and they reduce the excess population. And there are lots of other results, too. Colonization, for one thing. But mainly technology. In peace time, if a guy invents jet-propulsion, it's too expensive to develop commercially. In war-time, though, it's got to be developed. Then the Martians can use it whenever they want. They use us the way they'd use tools or—or limbs. And nobody ever really wins a war—except the Martians."

The man in the brown suit chuckled. "That makes sense," he said. "It must be nice to be a Martian."

"Why not? Up till now, no race ever successfully conquered and ruled another. The underdog could revolt or absorb. If you know you're being ruled, then the ruler's vulnerable. But if the world doesn't know—and it doesn't—

"Take radios," Lyman continued, going off at a tangent. "There's no earthly reason why a sane human should listen to a radio. But the Martians make us do it. They like it. Take bathtubs. Nobody contends bathtubs are comfortable—for us. But they're fine for Martians. All the impractical things we keep on using, even though we know they're impractical—"

"Typewriter ribbons," the brown man said, struck by the thought. "But not even a Martian could enjoy changing a typewriter ribbon."

Lyman seemed to find that flippant. He said that he knew all about the Martians except for one thing—their psychology.

"I don't know *why* they act as they do. It looks illogical sometimes, but I feel perfectly sure they've got sound motives for every move they make. Until I get that worked out I'm pretty much at a standstill. Until I get evidence—proof—and help. I've got to stay under cover till then. And I've been doing that. I do what they tell me, so they won't suspect, and I pretend to forget what they tell me to forget."

"Then you've got nothing much to worry about."

Lyman paid no attention. He was off again on a list of his grievances.

"When I hear the water running in the tub and a Martian splashing around, I pretend I don't hear a thing. My bed's too short and I tried last week to order a special length, but the Martian that sleeps there told me not to. He's a runt, like most of them. That is, I think they're runts. I have to deduce, because you never see them undressed. But it goes on like that constantly. By the way, how's your Martian?"

The man in the brown suit set down his glass rather suddenly.

"My Martian?"

"Now listen. I may be just a little bit drunk, but my logic remains unimpaired. I can still put two and two together. Either you know about the Martians, or you don't. If you do, there's no point in giving me that, 'What, *my* Martian?' routine. I know you have a Martian. Your Martian knows you have a Martian. My Martian knows. The point is, do *you* know? Think hard," Lyman urged solicitously.

"No, I haven't got a Martian," the reporter said, taking a quick drink. The edge of the glass clicked against his teeth.

"Nervous, I see," Lyman remarked. "Of course you *have* got a Martian. I suspect you know it."

"What would I be doing with a Martian?" the brown man asked with dogged dogmatism.

"What would you be doing without one? I imagine it's illegal. If they caught you running around without one they'd probably put you in a pound or something until claimed. Oh, you've got one, all right. So have I. So has he, and he, and he—and the bartender." Lyman enumerated the other barflies with a wavering forefinger.

"Of course they have," the brown man said. "But they'll all go back to Mars tomorrow and then you can see a good doctor. You'd better have another dri—"

He was turning toward the bartender when Lyman, apparently by accident, leaned close to him and whispered urgently, "*Don't look now!*"

The brown man glanced at Lyman's white face reflected in the mirror before them.

"It's all right," he said. "There aren't any Mar—"

Lyman gave him a fierce, quick kick under the edge of the bar.

"Shut up! One just came in!"

And then he caught the brown man's gaze and with elaborate unconcern said, "—so naturally, there was nothing for me to do but climb out on the roof after it. Took me ten minutes to get it down the ladder, and just as we reached the bottom it gave one bound, climbed up my face, sprang from the top of my head, and there it was again on the roof, screaming for me to get it down."

"*What?*" the brown man demanded with pardonable curiosity.

"My cat, of course. What did you think? No, never mind, don't answer that." Lyman's face was turned to the brown man's, but from the corners of his eyes he was watching an invisible progress down the length of the bar toward a booth at the very back.

"Now why did he come in?" he murmured. "I don't like this. Is he anyone you know?"

"Is who—?"

"That Martian. Yours, by any chance? No, I suppose not. Yours was probably the one who went out a while ago. I wonder if he went to make a report, and sent this one in? It's possible. It could be. You can talk now, but keep your voice low, and stop squirming. Want him to notice we can see him?"

"I can't see him. Don't drag me into this. You and your Martians can fight it out together. You're making me nervous. I've got to go, anyway." But he didn't move to get off the stool. Across Lyman's shoulder he was stealing glances toward the back of the bar, and now and then he looked at Lyman's face.

"Stop watching me," Lyman said. "Stop watching him. Anybody'd think you were a cat."

"Why a cat? Why should anybody—do I look like a cat?"

"We were talking about cats, weren't we? Cats can see them, quite clearly. Even undressed, I believe. They don't like them."

"Who doesn't like who?"

"Whom. Neither likes the other. Cats can see Martians—sh-h!—but they pretend not to, and that makes the Martians mad. I have a theory that cats ruled the world before Martians came. Never mind. Forget about cats. This may be more serious than you think. I happen to know my Martian's taking tonight off, and I'm pretty sure that was your Martian who went out some time ago. And have you noticed that nobody else in here has his Martian with him? Do you suppose—" His voice sank. "Do you suppose they could be *waiting for us outside*?"

"Oh, Lord," the brown man said. "In the alley with the cats, I suppose."

"Why don't you stop this yammer about cats and be serious for a moment?" Lyman demanded, and then paused, paled, and reeled slightly on his stool. He hastily took a drink to cover his confusion.

"What's the matter now?" the brown man asked.

"Nothing." Gulp. "Nothing. It was just that—he *looked* at me. With—you know."

"Let me get this straight. I take it the Martian is dressed in—is dressed like a human?"

"Naturally."

"But he's invisible to all eyes but yours?"

"Yes. He doesn't want to be visible, just now. Besides—" Lyman paused cunningly. He gave the brown man a furtive glance and then looked quickly down at his drink. "Besides, you know, I rather think you can see him—a little, anyway."

The brown man was perfectly silent for about thirty seconds. He sat quite motionless, not even the ice in the drink he held clinking. One might have thought he did not even breathe. Certainly he did not blink.

"What makes you think that?" he asked in a normal voice, after the thirty seconds had run out.

"I—did I say anything? I wasn't listening." Lyman put down his drink abruptly. "I think I'll go now."

"No, you won't," the brown man said, closing his fingers around Lyman's wrist. "Not yet you won't. Come back here. Sit down. Now. What was the idea? Where were you going?"

Lyman nodded dumbly toward the back of the bar, indicating either a juke-box or a door marked MEN.

"I don't feel so good. Maybe I've had too much to drink. I guess I'll—"

"You're all right. I don't trust you back there with that—that invisible man of yours. You'll stay right here until he leaves."

"He's going now," Lyman said brightly. His eyes moved with great briskness along the line of an invisible but rapid progress toward the front door. "See, he's gone. Now let me loose, will you?"

The brown man glanced toward the back booth.

"No," he said, "He isn't gone. Sit right where you are."

It was Lyman's turn to remain quite still, in a stricken sort of way, for a perceptible while. The ice in *his* drink, however, clinked audibly. Presently he spoke. His voice was soft, and rather soberer than before.

"You're right. He's still there. You can see him, can't you?"

The brown man said, "Has he got his back to us?"

"You *can* see him, then. Better than I can maybe. Maybe there are more of them here than I thought. They could be anywhere. They could be sitting beside you anywhere you go, and you wouldn't even guess, until—" He shook his head a little. "They'd want to be *sure*," he said, mostly to himself. "They can give you orders and make you forget, but there must be limits to what they can force you to do. They can't make a man betray himself. They'd have to lead him on—until they were sure."

He lifted his drink and tipped it steeply above his face. The ice ran down the slope and bumped coldly against his lip, but he held it until the last of the pale, bubbling amber had drained into his mouth. He set the glass on the bar and faced the brown man.

"Well?" he said.

The brown man looked up and down the bar.

"It's getting late," he said. "Not many people left. We'll wait."

"Wait for what?"

The brown man looked toward the back booth and looked away again quickly.

"I have something to show you. I don't want anyone else to see."

Lyman surveyed the narrow, smoky room. As he looked the last customer beside themselves at the bar began groping in his pocket, tossed some change on the mahogany, and went out slowly.

They sat in silence. The bartender eyed them with stolid disinterest. Presently a couple in the front booth got up and departed, quarreling in undertones.

"Is there anyone left?" the brown man asked in a voice that did not carry down the bar to the man in the apron.

"Only—" Lyman did not finish, but he nodded gently toward the back of the room. "He isn't looking. Let's get this over with. What do you want to show me?"

The brown man took off his wrist-watch and pried up the metal case. Two small, glossy photograph prints slid out. The brown man separated them with a finger.

"I just want to make sure of something," he said. "First—why did you pick me out? Quite a while ago, you said you'd been trailing me all day, making sure. I haven't forgotten that. And you knew I was a reporter. Suppose you tell me the truth, now?"

Squirming on his stool, Lyman scowled. "It was the way you looked at things," he murmured. "On the subway this morning—I'd never seen you before in my life, but I kept noticing the way you looked at things— the wrong things, things that weren't there, the way a cat does—and then you'd always look away—I got the idea you could see the Martians too."

"Go on," the brown man said quietly.

"I followed you. All day. I kept hoping you'd turn out to be—somebody I could talk to. Because if I could *know* that I wasn't the only one who could see them, then I'd know there was still some hope left. It's been worse than solitary confinement. I've been able to see them for three years now. Three years. And I've managed to keep my power a secret even from them. And, somehow, I've managed to keep from killing myself, too."

"Three years?" the brown man said. He shivered.

"There was always a little hope. I knew nobody would believe—not without proof. And how can you get proof? It was only that I—I kept telling myself that maybe you could see them too, and if you could, maybe there were others—lots of others—enough so we might get together and work out some way of proving to the world—"

The brown man's fingers were moving. In silence he pushed a photograph across the mahogany. Lyman picked it up unsteadily.

"Moonlight?" he asked after a moment. It was a landscape under a deep, dark sky with white clouds in it. Trees stood white and lacy against the darkness. The grass was white as if with moonlight, and the shadows blurry.

"No, not moonlight," the brown man said. "Infra-red. I'm strictly an amateur, but lately I've been experimenting with infra-red film. And I got some very odd results."

Lyman stared at the film.

"You see, I live near—" The brown man's finger tapped a certain quite common object that appeared in the photograph. "—and something funny keeps showing up now and then against it. But only with infra-red film. Now I know chlorophyll reflects so much infra-red light that grass and leaves photograph white. The sky comes out black, like this. There are tricks to using this kind of film. Photograph a tree against a cloud, and you can't tell them apart in the print. But you can photograph through a haze and pick out distant objects the ordinary film wouldn't catch. And sometimes, when you focus on something like this—" He tapped the image of the very common object again, "you get a very odd image on the film. Like that. A man with three eyes."

Lyman held the print up to the light. In silence he took the other one from the bar and studied it. When he laid them down he was smiling.

"You know," Lyman said in a conversational whisper, "a professor of astrophysics at one of the more important universities had a very interesting little item in the *Times* the other Sunday. Name of Spitzer, I think. He said that, if there were life on Mars, and if Martians had ever visited earth, there'd be no way to prove it. Nobody would believe the few men who saw them. Not, he said, unless the Martians happened to be photographed...."

Lyman looked at the brown man thoughtfully.

"Well," he said, "it's happened. You've photographed them."

The brown man nodded. He took up the prints and returned them to his watch-case. "I thought so, too. Only until tonight I couldn't be sure. I'd never seen one—fully—as you have. It isn't so much a matter of what you call getting your brain scrambled with supersonics as it is of just knowing where to look. But I've been seeing *part* of them all my life, and so has everybody. It's that little suggestion of movement you never catch except just at the edge of your vision, just out of the corner of your eye. Something that's *almost* there—and when you look fully at it, there's nothing. These photographs showed me the way. It's not easy to learn, but it can be done. We're conditioned to look directly at a thing—the particular thing we want to see clearly, whatever it is. Perhaps the Martians gave us that conditioning. When we see a movement at the edge of our range of vision, it's almost irresistible not to look directly at it. So it vanishes."

"Then they can be seen—by anybody?"

"I've learned a lot in a few days," the brown man said. "Since I took those photographs. You have to train yourself. It's like seeing a trick picture—one that's really a composite, after you study it. Camouflage. You just have to learn how. Otherwise we can look at them all our lives and never see them."

"The camera does, though."

"Yes, the camera does. I've wondered why nobody ever caught them this way before. Once you see them on film, they're unmistakable—that third eye."

"Infra-red film's comparatively new, isn't it? And then I'll bet you have to catch them against that one particular background—you know—or they won't show on the film. Like trees against clouds. It's tricky. You must have had just the right lighting that day, and exactly the right focus, and the lens stopped down just right. A kind of minor miracle. It might never happen again exactly that way. But... don't look now."

They were silent. Furtively, they watched the mirror. Their eyes slid along toward the open door of the tavern.

And then there was a long, breathless silence.

"He looked back at us," Lyman said very quietly. "He looked at us... that third eye!"

The brown man was motionless again. When he moved, it was to swallow the rest of his drink.

"I don't think that they're suspicious yet," he said. "The trick will be to keep under cover until we can blow this thing wide open. There's got to be some way to do it—some way that will convince people."

"There's proof. The photographs. A competent cameraman ought to be able to figure out just how you caught that Martian on film and duplicate the conditions. It's evidence."

"Evidence can cut both ways," the brown man said. "What I'm hoping is that the Martians don't really like to kill—unless they have to. I'm hoping they won't kill without proof. But—" He tapped his wrist-watch.

"There's two of us now, though," Lyman said. "We've got to stick together. Both of us have broken the big rule—*don't look now*—"

The bartender was at the back, disconnecting the juke-box. The brown man said, "We'd better not be seen together unnecessarily. But if we both come to this bar tomorrow night at nine for a drink—that wouldn't look suspicious, even to them."

"Suppose—" Lyman hesitated. "May I have one of those photographs?"

"Why?"

"If one of us had—an accident—the other one would still have the proof. Enough, maybe, to convince the right people."

The brown man hesitated, nodded shortly, and opened his watch-case again. He gave Lyman one of the pictures.

"Hide it," he said. "It's—evidence. I'll see you here tomorrow. Meanwhile, be careful. Remember to play safe."

They shook hands firmly, facing each other in an endless second of final, decisive silence. Then the brown man turned abruptly and walked out of the bar.

Lyman sat there. Between two wrinkles in his forehead there was a stir and a flicker of lashes unfurling. The third eye opened slowly and looked after the brown man.

END

# MOMENT IN HISTORY

*A "Vengeance" dive bomber is getting the drill treatment at Vultee Aircraft Corporation in Tennessee; 1943.*

## Four Questions With Savannah J. Goins

*Adventures:* It's an absolute pleasure to have this interview with you, and from your various social media it's evident you keep very busy. Can you tell readers, what keeps you busy, and who is Savannah J. Goins?

*SJG:* Hello! Thank you so much for interviewing me for the Off Beat Reads July Edition. Yes, I do keep very busy! I am a full-time writer and spend a lot of my time creating non-fiction content for my clients. The rest of my writing time goes to writing my YA fantasy books. I am working hard to flip this balance so that fiction writing is my primary income, but I have a ways to go to get there. When I'm not writing, I like to run through the woods near my country home to get some exercise, drink coffee with my friends, and of course, wrangle dragons.

*Adventures:* Yes, your Instagram bio states you are a Dragon Wrangler, so I can't imagine anything getting in your way! But, if anything, what has been your biggest obstacle to your own success?

*SJG:* One of the biggest obstacles to my success would be a lack of disposable income, especially in the early days, to invest in my fiction writing business. I've been writing seriously since 2015 and published a novel in 2017, 2019, and 2021, but all my money went into investing in quality covers, editing, and formatting for the books themselves and I've barely experimented with ads or newsletters or any other paid marketing strategies. When I left my regular full-time job last year and moved to reduce my living expenses, that changed and I've had a little more wiggle room to invest in my publishing and marketing education so that I am better equipped to invest in these things now and in the coming months.

When it comes to the success I'm experiencing now though, I have to credit one of the biggest failures of my life for getting me here. My parents chose to homeschool me growing up, and they had great reasons to do so and did a good job with my education. But the other teenagers I knew during my high school years made me feel like I was socially and intellectually behind. I desperately hoped to prove myself in college and vet school after that, but I started the whole experience out by missing the full-ride scholarship to IUPUI by a hair—just the worth of a single SAT question.

I was crushed. I thought that everyone was right about me and that I'd never be anything or do anything worth being proud of. But, when there's no obligation to take advantage of a full-ride scholarship, you can more easily change your mind about your career path. I hated having no time for creative activities between college and working, and I couldn't imagine spending 10 years - undergrad, vet school, and 2+ years to specialize in reptiles - in school with no time to write or sketch or paint.

So I left IUPUI after a year, got my degree in veterinary technology instead in 2 years, worked my first dream job as an exotic animal vet tech (where wrangled all manner of real dragons), and kept writing in my spare time. After publishing three novels and learning how to write non-fiction like I do for my clients now, I left my first dream and am now pursuing my second. And if I had gotten that scholarship, I would still be in vet school with no time to enjoy my creativity and so much debt that it would be a lot harder for me to be able to work full-time for myself doing what I love.

So sometimes, the most embarrassing, crushing failure is really just a blessing in disguise.

*Adventures:* You are also a Writing Journey Coach. What can you help others with, and is there any single issue you see as being a constant challenge to authors? How might an author overcome that challenge?

*SJG:* Right now, my coaching and consulting clients are usually writers who need help deciding which publishing route (independent publishing, traditional big house, or traditional small press) is the best choice for them based on what they most want from the experience. In those cases, I think the biggest challenge is the overwhelming amount of advice from so many people online. Some of it is great advice for everyone, but a lot is only good advice for an author with a specific goal or in a specific circumstance.

I've damaged my career in the past by following excellent advice for many indies that was not beneficial to me at the stage I was in. Now that I've been writing seriously for nearly 7 years, I'm able to shed some light on which strategies and priorities are really ideal for their specific circumstances and desires so that they can get a headstart on their writing journey and save time they might otherwise have lost on the wrong advice.

*Adventures:* Whoever did the cover art for your books nailed them! They make me want to read what's inside. Can you briefly explain to readers what The Gwythienian & The Crivabanian are about? What can fans and new readers look forward to from you in the future?

*SJG:* Thank you! My cover artist is Ingrid Nordli, and she is a completely self-taught digital artist. We're currently working on the covers for my next series and I cannot wait to share her incredible handiwork with everyone!

My YA fantasy trilogy is about a teenage girl named Enzi who discovers that an old family heirloom has the power to give her what she wants more than anything else: invisibility. She can finally hide from the bullies and name-callers. But just when she realizes this, someone from another world finds out that she has it. He's been looking for this relic for years and needs it to restore his family's good name in the world he came from, but since Enzi touched it first, he can't use it without her permission.

When a dangerous dragon arrives in our world to steal it from Enzi and harm her in the process, they're forced into a quest to protect this magical artifact from those who would use it for ill, and to find the other artifacts before its too late.

Enzi struggles with her self-image and past abuse. But throughout this story, she makes better friends and learns to love herself as she is, and maybe even to let a little love in from outside. But finding true love doesn't just fix everything for her. When it comes to the danger no human or dragon can save her from, she finally rolls up her sleeves and takes it on herself.

My next series, The Castors of Wrynford, is a five-book saga that takes place in another world with all new characters. This Pokemon meets the Hunger Games story takes place in a world where your childhood and teenage years are spent choosing a type of weapon, honing your fighting skills with it, and then crafting your own for the Casting Ceremony. During the ceremony, you'll officially become an adult when you call your castling - an animal familiar who is the embodiment of the other side of yourself - from that casting weapon.

But sixteen-year-old Mella Yarinelle fails to produce a castling from her carefully honed scythe and, an outcast from society now, seeks to comfort herself by playing an illegal musical instrument that reminds her of her mother. When she accidentally calls her castling from this contraband instrument of music instead of her instrument of war, Mella's life gets even more complicated. She strives to pass her castling off as normal and reenter society, but if they get caught, her castling will be sentenced to death by shattering. With the help of some other new castors, a mean girl, and some spiked punch, Mella seems to be pulling it off—at least for now.

---

*You really don't want to miss The Gwythienian Trilogy. Connect with Savannah on Twitter and Instagram: @savannahjgoins and on Facebook: @thegwythienian*

# TWO OLD LOVERS

*by Mary E. Wilkins Freeman*

*Two Old Lovers* first appeared in Harper's Bazaar
(March, 1883).

Leyden was emphatically a village of cottages, and each of them built after one of two patterns: either the front door was on the right side, in the corner of a little piazza extending a third of the length of the house, with the main roof jutting over it, or the piazza stretched across the front, and the door was in the center.

The cottages were painted uniformly white, and had blinds of a bright spring-green color. There was a little flower garden in front of each; the beds were laid out artistically in triangles, hearts, and rounds, and edged with box; boys'-love, sweet williams, and pinks were the fashionable and prevailing flowers.

There was a general air of cheerful though humble prosperity about the place, which it owed, and indeed its very existence also, to the three old weather-beaten boot-and-shoe factories which rose stanchly and importantly in the very midst of the natty little white cottages.

Years before, when one Hiram Strong put up his three factories for the manufacture of the rough shoe which the workingman of America wears, he hardly thought he was also gaining for himself the honor of founding Leyden. He chose the site for his buildings mainly because they would be easily accessible to the railway which stretched to the city, sixty miles distant. At first the workmen came on the cars from the neighboring towns, but after a while they became tired of that, and one after another built for himself a cottage, and established his family and his household belongings near the scene of his daily labors. So gradually Leyden grew. A built his cottage like C, and B built his like D. They painted them white, and hung the green blinds, and laid out their flower beds in front and their vegetable beds at the back. By and by came a church and a store and a post office to pass, and Leyden was a full-fledged town.

That was a long time ago. The shoe factories had long passed out of the hands of Hiram Strong's heirs; he himself was only a memory on the earth. The business was not quite as wide-awake and vigorous as when in its first youth; it droned a little now; there was not quite so much bustle and hurry as formerly. The factories were never lighted up of an evening on account of overwork, and the workmen found plenty of time for pleasant and salutary gossip over their cutting and pegging. But this did not detract in the least from the general cheerfulness and prosperity of Leyden. The inhabitants still had all the work they needed to supply the means necessary for their small comforts, and they were contented. They too had begun to drone a little like the factories. "As slow as Leyden," was the saying among the faster-going towns adjoining theirs. Every morning at seven the old men, young men, and boys, in their calico shirt sleeves, their faces a little pale—perhaps from their indoor life—filed unquestioningly out of the back doors of the white cottages, treading still deeper the well-worn footpaths stretching around the sides of the houses, and entered the factories. They were great, ugly wooden buildings, with wings which they had grown in their youth jutting clumsily from their lumbering shoulders. Their outer walls were black and grimy, streaked and splashed and patched with red paint in every variety of shade, according as the original hue was tempered with smoke or the beatings of the storms of many years.

The men worked peacefully and evenly in the shoe shops all day; and the women stayed at home and kept the little white cottages tidy, cooked the meals, and washed the clothes, and did the sewing. For recreation the men sat on the piazza in front of Barker's store of an evening, and gossiped or discussed politics; and the women talked over their neighbors' fences, or took their sewing into their neighbors' of an afternoon.

People died in Leyden as elsewhere; and here and there was a little white cottage whose narrow footpath leading round to its back door its master would never tread again.

In one of these lived Widow Martha Brewster and her daughter Maria. Their cottage was one of those which had its piazza across the front. Every summer they trained morning-glories over it, and planted their little garden with the flower seeds popular in Leyden. There was not a cottage in the whole place whose surroundings were neater and gayer than theirs, for all they were only two women, and two old women at that; for Widow Martha Brewster was in the neighborhood of eighty, and her daughter, Maria Brewster, near sixty. The two had lived alone since Jacob Brewster died and stopped going to the factory, some fifteen years ago. He had left them this particular white cottage, and a snug little sum in the savings bank besides, for the whole Brewster family had worked and economized all their long lives. The women had corded boots at home, while the man had worked in the shop and never spent a cent without thinking of it overnight.

Leyden folks all thought that David Emmons would marry Maria Brewster when her father died. "David can rent his house and go to live with Maria and her mother," said they, with an affectionate readiness to arrange matters for them. But he did not. Every Sunday night at eight o'clock punctually the form of David Emmons, arrayed in his best clothes, with his stiff white dickey, and a nosegay in his buttonhole, was seen to advance up the road toward Maria Brewster's, as he had been seen to advance every Sunday night for the last twenty-five years, but that was all. He manifested not the slightest intention of carrying out people's judicious plans for his welfare and Maria's.

She did not seem to pine with hope deferred; people could not honestly think there was any occasion to pity her for her lover's tardiness. A cheerier woman never lived. She was literally bubbling over with jollity. Round-faced and black-eyed, with a funny little bounce of her whole body when she walked, she was the merry feature of the whole place.

Her mother was now too feeble, but Maria still corded boots for the factories as of old. David Emmons, who was quite sixty, worked in them, as he had from his youth. He was a slender, mild-faced old man, with a fringe of gray-yellow beard around his chin; his head was quite bald. Years ago he had been handsome, they said, but somehow people had always laughed at him a little, although they all liked him. "The slowest of all the slow Leydenites," outsiders called him, and even the "slow Leydenites" poked fun at this exaggeration of themselves. It was an old and well-worn remark that it took David Emmons an hour to go courting, and that he was always obliged to leave his own home at seven in order to reach Maria's at eight, and there was a standing joke that the meeting house passed him one morning on his way to the shop.

David heard the chaffing, of course—there is very little delicacy in matters of this kind among country people—but he took in all in good part. He would laugh at himself with the rest, but there was something touching in his deprecatory way of saying sometimes: "Well, I don't know how 'tis, but it don't seem to be in my natur' to do any other way. I suppose I was born without the faculty of gittin' along quick in this world. You'll have to git behind and push me a leetle, I reckon."

He owned his little cottage, which was one of the kind which had the piazza on the right side. He lived entirely alone. There was a half acre or so of land beside his house, which he used for a vegetable garden. After and before shop hours, in the dewy evenings and mornings, he dug and weeded assiduously between the green ranks of corn and beans. If David Emmons was slow, his vegetables were not. None of the gardens in Leyden surpassed his in luxuriant growth. His corn tasselled out and his potato patch was white with blossoms as soon as anybody's.

He was almost a vegetarian in his diet; the products of his garden spot were his staple articles of food. Early in the morning would the gentle old bachelor set his pot of green things boiling, and dine gratefully at noon, like mild Robert Herrick, on pulse and herbs. His garden supplied also his sweetheart and her mother with all the vegetables they could use. Many times in the course of a week could David have been seen slowly moving toward the Brewster cottage with a basket on his arm well stocked with the materials for an innocent and delicious repast.

But Maria was not to be outdone by her old lover in kindly deeds. Not a Saturday but a goodly share of her weekly baking was deposited, neatly covered with a white crash towel, on David's little kitchen table. The surreptitious air with which the back-door key was taken from its hiding place (which she well knew) under the kitchen blind, the door unlocked and entered, and the good things deposited, was charming, although highly ineffectual. "There goes Maria with David's baking," said the women, peering out of their windows as she bounced, rather more gently and cautiously than usual, down the street. And David himself knew well the ministering angel to whom these benefits were due when he lifted the towel and discovered with tearful eyes the brown loaves and flaky pies—the proofs of his Maria's love and culinary skill.

Among the young and more irrevent portions of the community there was considerable speculation as to the mode of courtship of these old lovers of twenty-five years' standing. Was there ever a kiss, a tender clasp of the hand, those usual expressions of affection between sweethearts?

Some of the more daring spirits had even gone so far as to commit the manifest impropriety of peeping in Maria's parlor windows; but they had only seen David sitting quiet and prim on the little slippery horsehair sofa, and Maria by the table, rocking slowly in her little cane-seated rocker. Did Maria ever leave her rocker and sit on that slippery horsehair sofa by David's side? They never knew; but she never did. There was something laughable, and at the same time rather pathetic, about Maria's and David's courting. All the outward appurtenances of "keeping company" were as rigidly observed as they had been twenty-five years ago, when David Emmons first cast his mild blue eyes shyly and lovingly on red-cheeked, quiet-spoken Maria Brewster. Every Sunday evening, in the winter, there was a fire kindled in the parlor, the parlor lamp was lit at dusk all the year round, and Maria's mother retired early, that the young people might "sit up." The "sitting up" was no very formidable affair now, whatever it might have been in the first stages of the courtship. The need of sleep over-balanced sentiment in those old lovers, and by ten o'clock at the latest Maria's lamp was out and David had wended his solitary way to his own home.

Leyden people had a great curiosity to know if David had ever actually popped the question to Maria, or if his natural slowness was at fault in this as in other things. Their curiosity had been long exercised in vain, but Widow Brewster, as she waxed older, grew loquacious, and one day told a neighbor, who had called in her daughter's absence, that "David had never reely come to the p'int. She supposed he would some time; for her part, she thought he had better; but then, after all, she knowed Maria didn't care, and maybe 'twas jest as well as 'twas, only sometimes she was afeard she should never live to see the weddin' if they wasn't spry." Then there had been hints concerning a certain pearl-colored silk which Maria, having a good chance to get at a bargain, had purchased some twenty years ago, when she thought, from sundry remarks, that David was coming to the point; and it was further intimated that the silk had been privately made up ten years since, when Maria had again surmised that the point was about being reached. The neighbor went home in a state of great delight, having by skillful maneuvering actually obtained a glimpse of the pearl-colored silk.

It was perfectly true that Maria did not lay David's tardiness in putting the important question very much to heart. She was too cheerful, too busy, and too much interested in her daily duties to fret much about anything. There was never at any time much of the sentimental element in her composition, and her feeling for David was eminently practical in its nature. She, although the woman, had the stronger character of the two, and there was something rather motherlike than loverlike in her affection for him. It was through the protecting care which chiefly characterized her love that the only pain to her came from their long courtship and postponement of marriage. It was true that, years ago, when David had led her to think, from certain hesitating words spoken at parting one Sunday night, that he would certainly ask the momentous question soon, her heart had gone into a happy flutter. She had bought the pearl-colored silk then.

Years after, her heart had fluttered again, but a little less wildly this time. David almost asked her another Sunday night. Then she had made up the pearl-colored silk. She used to go and look at it fondly and admiringly from time to time; once in a while she would try it on and survey herself in the glass, and imagine herself David's bride—a faded bride, but a happy and beloved one.

She looked at the dress occasionally now, but a little sadly, as the conviction that she should never wear it was forcing itself upon her more and more. But the sadness was always more for David's sake than her own. She saw him growing an old man, and the lonely, uncared-for life that he led filled her heart with tender pity and sorrow for him. She did not confine her kind offices to the Saturday baking. Every week his little house was tidied and set to rights, and his mending looked after.

Once, on a Sunday night, when she spied a rip in his coat, that had grown long from the want of womanly fingers constantly at hand, she had a good cry after he had left and she had gone into her room. There was something more pitiful to her, something that touched her heart more deeply, in that rip in her lover's Sunday coat than in all her long years of waiting.

As the years went on, it was sometimes with a sad heart that Maria stood and watched the poor lonely old figure moving slower than ever down the street to his lonely home; but the heart was sad for him always, and never for herself. She used to wonder at him a little sometimes, though always with the most loyal tenderness, that he should choose to lead the solitary, cheerless life that he did, to go back to his dark, voiceless home, when he might be so sheltered and cared for in his old age. She firmly believed that it was only owing to her lover's incorrigible slowness, in this as in everything else. She never doubted for an instant that he loved her. Some women might have tried hastening matters a little themselves, but Maria, with the delicacy which is sometimes more inherent in a steady, practical nature like hers than in a more ardent one, would have lost her self-respect forever if she had done such a thing.

So she lived cheerfully along, corded her boots, though her fingers were getting stiff, humored her mother, who was getting feebler and more childish every year, and did the best she could for her poor, foolish old lover.

When David was seventy, and she sixty-eight, she gave away the pearl-colored silk to a cousin's daughter who was going to be married. The girl was young and pretty and happy, but she was poor, and the silk would make over into a grander wedding dress for her than she could hope to obtain in any other way.

Poor old Maria smoothed the lustrous folds fondly with her withered hands before sending it away, and cried a little, with a patient pity for David and herself. But when a tear splashed directly on to the shining surface of the silk, she stopped crying at once, and her sorrowful expression changed into one of careful scrutiny as she wiped the salt drop away with her handkerchief, and held the dress up to the light to be sure that it was not spotted. A practical nature like Maria's is sometimes a great boon to its possessor. It is doubtful if anything else can dry a tear so quickly.

Somehow Maria always felt a little differently toward David after she had given away her wedding dress. There had always been a little tingle of consciousness in her manner toward him, a little reserve and caution before people. But after the wedding dress had gone, all question of marriage had disappeared so entirely from her mind, that the delicate considerations born of it vanished. She was uncommonly hale and hearty for a woman of her age; there was apparently much more than two years' difference between her and her lover. It was not only the Saturday's bread and pie that she carried now and deposited on David's little kitchen table, but, openly and boldly, not caring who should see her, many a warm dinner. Every day, after her own housework was done, David's house was set to rights. He should have all the comforts he needed in his last years, she determined. That they were his last years was evident. He coughed, and now walked so slowly from feebleness and weakness that it was a matter of doubt to observers whether he could reach Maria Brewster's before Monday evening.

One Sunday night he stayed a little longer than usual—the clock struck ten before he started. Then he rose and said, as he had done every Sunday evening for so many years, "Well, Maria, I guess it's about time for me to be goin'."

She helped him on with his coat and tied on his tippet. Contrary to his usual habit, he stood in the door and hesitated a minute—there seemed to be something he wanted to say.

"Maria."

"Well, David?"

"I'm gittin' to be an old man, you know, an' I've allus been slow-goin'; I couldn't seem to help it. There has been a good many things I haven't got around to." The old cracked voice quavered painfully.

"Yes, I know, David, all about it; you couldn't help it. I wouldn't worry a bit about it if I were you."

"You don't lay up anything ag'in me, Maria?"

"No, David."

"Good night, Maria."

"Good night, David. I will fetch you over some boiled dinner tomorrow."

She held the lamp at the door till the patient, tottering old figure was out of sight. She had to wipe the tears from her spectacles in order to see to read her Bible when she went in.

❖

Next morning she was hurrying up her housework to go over to David's —somehow she felt a little anxious about him this morning—when there came a loud knock at her door. When she opened it a boy stood there, panting for breath; he was David's next neighbor's son.

"Mr. Emmons is sick," he said, "an' wants you. I was goin' for milk, when he rapped on the window. Father an' mother's in thar, an' the doctor. Mother said, tell you to hurry."

The news had spread rapidly; people knew what it meant when they saw Maria hurrying down the street, without her bonnet, her gray hair flying. One woman cried when she saw her. "Poor thing!" she sobbed. "Poor thing!"

A crowd was around David's cottage when Maria reached it. She went straight in through the kitchen to his little bedroom, and up to his side. The doctor was in the room, and several neighbors. When he saw Maria, poor old David held out his hand to her and smiled feebly. Then he looked imploringly at the doctor, then at the others in the room. The doctor understood, and said a word to them, and they filed silently out. Then he turned to Maria. "Be quick," he whispered.

She leaned over him. "Dear David," she said, her wrinkled face quivering, her gray hair straying over her cheeks.

He looked up at her with a strange wonder in his glazing eyes. "Maria" —a thin, husky voice, that was more like a wind through dry cornstalks, said—"Maria, I'm—dyin', an'—I allers meant to—have asked you—to—marry me."

END

# FUN PAGE!
Recharge for the next ADVENTURE.

## BEHIND THE SCENES BATTLES FOUGHT BY THE BRAVE.
# PULP AVENGERS

"Real courage is when you know you're licked before you begin, but you begin anyway and see it through no matter what."
-In *To Kill a Mockingbird*; by Harper Lee

# SUDOKU

|   |   | 6 | 8 |   |   | 7 | 5 |   |
|---|---|---|---|---|---|---|---|---|
| 7 | 9 |   |   |   | 4 |   |   | 1 |
|   |   |   |   |   | 5 | 9 |   | 4 |
|   |   |   | 1 |   | 6 |   | 4 |   |
| 5 |   |   |   |   |   | 6 | 1 |   |
| 8 |   |   | 2 |   |   |   |   |   |
| 9 | 5 | 4 |   |   | 7 |   |   |   |
|   | 6 | 1 |   |   |   | 8 |   |   |

(MEDIUM DIFFICULTY; ANSWERS IN BACK OF BOOK)

# UNSCRAMBLE:

### plebbiiolkt

(Word definition: A book thief)

quick
2 out of 3 with someone near.

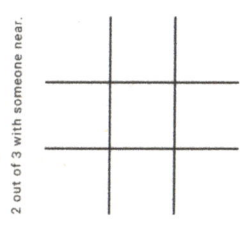
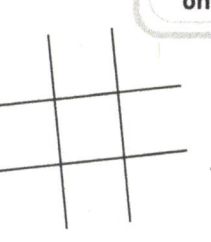
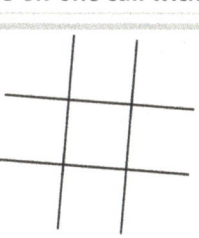

# STELLA MARIS

*By William J. Locke*

# CHAPTER I

S TELLA MARIS—Star of the Sea!
    That was not her real name. No one could have christened an inoffensive babe so absurdly. Her mother had, indeed, through the agency of godfathers and godmothers, called her Stella after a rich old maiden aunt, thereby showing her wisdom; for the maiden aunt died gratefully a year after the child was born, and bequeathed to her a comfortable fortune. Her father had given her the respectable patronymic of Blount, which, as all the world knows, or ought to know, is not pronounced as it is spelled.

It is not pronounced "Maris," however, as, in view of the many vagaries of British nomenclature, it might very well be, but "Blunt." It was Walter Herold, the fantastic, who tacked on the Maris to her Christian name, and ran the two words together so that to all and sundry the poor child became Stellamaris, and to herself a baptismal puzzle, never being quite certain whether Stella was not a pert diminutive, and whether she ought to subscribe herself in formal documents as "Stellamaris Blount."

The invention of this title must not be regarded as the supreme effort of the imagination of Walter Herold. It would have been obvious to anybody with a bowing acquaintance with the Latin tongue.

Her name was Stella, and she passed her life by the sea—passed it away up on top of a cliff on the South coast; passed it in one big, beautiful room that had big windows south and west; passed it in bed, flat on her back, with never an outlook on the outside world save sea and sky. And the curtains of the room were never drawn, and in the darkness a lamp always shone in the western window; so that Walter Herold, at the foot of the cliff, one night of storm and dashing spray, seeing the light burning steadily like a star, may be excused for a bit of confusion of thought when he gripped his friend John Risca's arm with one hand and, pointing with the other, cried:

"Stella Maris! What a name for her!"

And when he saw her the next morning—she was twelve years old at the time and had worked out only a short term of her long imprisonment —he called her Stellamaris to her face, and she laughed in a sweet, elfin way, and Herold being the Great High Favourite of her little court (a title conferred by herself), she issued an edict that by that style and quality was it her pleasure henceforth to be designated. John Risca, in his capacity of Great High Belovedest, obeyed the ukase without question; and so did His Great High Excellency, her uncle, Sir Oliver Blount, and Her Most Exquisite Auntship, Lady Blount, his wife and first cousin to John Risca.

The events in the life of Stella Blount which this chronicle will attempt to record did not take place when she was a child of twelve. But we meet her thus, at this age, ruling to a certain extent the lives of grown-up men and women by means of a charm, a mystery, a personality essentially gay and frank, yet, owing to the circumstances of her life, invested with a morbid, almost supernatural atmosphere. The trouble in the upper part of her spine, pronounced incurable by the faculty, compelled a position rigidly supine. Her bed, ingeniously castored, could be wheeled about the great room. Sometimes she lay enthroned in the centre; more often it was brought up close to one of the two windows, so that she could look out to sea and feed her fancy on the waves, and the ships passing up and down the Channel, and the white sea-gulls flashing their wings in mid air. But only this unvibrating movement was permitted. For all the splints and ambulance contrivances in the world, she could not be carried into another room, or into the pleasant, sloping garden of the Channel House, for a jar would have been fatal. The one room, full of air and sunlight and sweet odours and exquisite appointments, was the material kingdom in which she ruled with sweet autocracy; the welter of sea and sky was her kingdom, too, the gulls and spring and autumn flights of migratory birds were her subjects, the merchants and princes traversing the deep in ships, her tributaries.

But this was a kingdom of Faerie, over which she ruled by the aid of Ariels and Nereids and other such elemental and intangible ministers. The latter had a continuous history, dreamy and romantic, episodes of which she would in rare moments relate to her Great High Belovedest and her Great High Favourite; but ordinarily the two young men were admitted only into the material kingdom, where, however, they bent the knee with curious humility. To them, all she seemed to have of human semblance was a pair of frail arms, a daintily curved neck, a haunting face, and a mass of dark hair encircling it on the pillow like a nimbus. The face was small, delicately featured, but the strong sea air maintained a tinge of colour in it; her mouth, made for smiles and kisses, justified in practice its formation; her eyes, large and round and of deepest brown, sometimes glowed with the laughter of the child, sometimes seemed to hold in their depths holy mysteries, gleams of things hidden and divine, unsealed revelations of another world, before which the two young men, each sensitive in his peculiar fashion, bowed their young and impressionable heads. When they came down to commonplace, it was her serene happiness that mystified them. She gave absolute acceptance to the conditions of her existence, as though no other conditions were desirable or acceptable. She was delicate joyousness just incarnate and no more—"the music from the hyacinth bell," said Herold. In the early days of his acquaintance with Stellamaris, Herold was young, fresh from the university, practising every one of the arts with feverish simultaneousness and mimetic in each; so when he waxed poetical, he made use of Shelley.

Stella was an orphan, both her parents having died before the obscure spinal disease manifested itself. To the child they were vague, far-off memories. In loco parentium, and trustees of her fortune, were the uncle and aunt above mentioned. Sir Oliver, as a young man, had distinguished himself so far in the colonial service as to obtain his K.C.M.G. As a man nearing middle age, he had so played the fool with a governorship as to be recalled and permanently shelved. To the end of his days Sir Oliver was a man with a grievance. His wife, publicly siding with him, and privately resentful against him, was a woman with two grievances. Now, one grievance on one side and two on the other, instead of making three, according to the rules of arithmetic, made legion, according to the law of the multiplication of grievances. Even Herold, the Optimist, introduced by his college friend John Risca into the intimacies of the household, could not call them a happy couple. In company they treated each other with chilling courtesy; before the servants they bickered very slightly; when they wanted to quarrel, they retired, with true British decorum, to their respective apartments and quarreled over the house telephone.

There was one spot on the earth, however, which by common consent they regarded as a sanctuary,—on whose threshold grievances and differences and bickerings and curses (his imperial career had given Sir Oliver an imperial vocabulary) and tears and quarrelings were left like the earth-stained shoes of the Faithful on the threshold of a mosque,—and that was the wide sea-chamber of Stellamaris. That threshold crossed, Sir Oliver became bluff and hearty; on Julia, Lady Blount, fell a mantle of tender womanhood. They "my-deared" and "my-darlinged" each other until the very dog (the Lord High Constable), a Great Dane, of vast affection and courage, but of limited intelligence, whose post of duty was beside Stella's couch, would raise his head for a disgusted second and sniff and snort from his deep lungs. But dogs are dogs, and in their doggy way see a lot of the world which is a sealed book to humans, especially to those who pass their lives in a room on the top of a cliff overlooking the sea.

It was the unwritten law of the house: Stella's room was sacrosanct. An invisible spirit guarded the threshold and forbade entrance to anything evil or mean or sordid or even sorrowful, and had inscribed on the portal in unseen, but compelling, characters

*Never harm nor spell nor charm*

*Come our lovely lady nigh.*

Whence came the spirit, from Stella herself or from the divine lingering in the faulty folks who made her world, who can tell? There never was an invisible spirit guarding doors and opening hearts, since the earth began, who had not a human genesis. From man alone, in this myriad-faceted cosmos, can a compassionate God, in the form of angels and ministering spirits, he reflected. Perhaps the radiant spirit of the child herself, triumphing over disastrous circumstances, instilled a sacred awe in those who surrounded her; perhaps the pathos of her lifelong condemnation stirred unusual depths of pity. At all events, the unwritten law was irrefragable. Outside Stella's door the wicked must cast their evil thoughts, the gloomy shed their cloak of cloud, and the wretched unpack their burden of suffering. Whether it was for the ultimate welfare of Stellamaris to live in this land of illusion is another matter.

"Save her from knowledge of pain and from suspicion of evil," John Risca would cry, when discussing the matter. "Let us make sure of one perfect flower in this poisonous fungus garden of a world."

"Great High Belovedest," Stellamaris would say when they were alone together, "what about the palace to-day?"

And the light would break upon the young man's grim face, and he would tell her of the palace in which he dwelt in the magic city of London.

"I have got a beautiful new Persian carpet," he would say, "with blues in it like that band of sea over there, for the marble floor of the vestibule."

"I hope it matches the Gobelin tapestry."

"You couldn't have chosen it better yourself, Stellamaris."

The great eyes looked at him in humorous dubiety. He was wearing a faded mauve shirt and a flagrantly blue tie.

"I am not so sure of your eye for colour, Great High Belovedest, and it would be a pity to have the beautiful palace spoiled."

"I assure you that East and West in this instance are blended in perfect harmony."

"And how are Lilias and Niphetos?"

Lilias and Niphetos were two imaginary Angora cats, nearly the size of the Lord High Constable, who generally sat on the newel-posts of the great marble staircase. They were fed on chickens' livers and Devonshire cream.

"Arachne," he replied gravely, referring to a mythical attendant of Circassian beauty—"Arachne thought they were suffering from ennui, and so she brought them some white mice—and what do you think happened?"

"Why, they gobbled them up, of course."

"That's where you 're wrong, Stellamaris. Those aristocratic cats turned up their noses at them. They looked at each other pityingly, as if to say, 'Does the foolish woman really think we can be amused by white mice?'"

Stella laughed. "Don't they ever have any kittens?"

"My dear," said Risca, "they would die if I suggested such a thing to them."

It had been begun long ago, this fabulous history of the palace, and the beauty and luxury with which he was surrounded; and Stella knew it all to its tiniest detail—the names of the roses in his gardens, the pictures on his walls, the shapes and sizes of the ornaments on his marquetry writing-table; and as her memory was tenacious and he dared not be caught tripping, his wonder-house gradually crystallized in his mind to the startling definiteness of a material creation. Its suites of apartments and corridors, the decoration and furniture of each room, became as vividly familiar as the dreary abode in which he really had his being. He could wander about through house and grounds with unerring certainty of plan. The phantom creatures with whom he had peopled the domain had become invested with clear-cut personalities; he had visualized them until he could conjure up their faces at will.

He had begun the building of the dream palace first with the mere object of amusing a sick child and hiding from her things forlorn and drab; gradually, in the course of years, it had grown to be almost a refuge for the man himself. When the child developed into the young girl he did not undeceive her. More and more was it necessary, if their sweet comradeship was to last, that he should extend the boundaries of her Land of Illusion; for the high ambitions which had made him laugh at poverty remained unsatisfied, the promise of life had been hopelessly broken, and he saw before him nothing but a stretch of dull, laborious years unlit by a gleam of joy. Only in the sea-chamber of Stellamaris was life transformed into a glowing romance. Only there could he inhabit a palace and walk the sweet, music-haunted, fragrant streets of an apocalyptic London, where all women were fair and true, and all men were generous, and all work, even his own slavery at the press, was noble and inspired by pure ideals.

"What exactly is your work, Belovedest?" she asked one day.

He replied: "I teach the great and good men who are the King's ministers of state how to govern the country. I show philanthropists how to spend their money. I read many books and tell people how beautiful and wise the books are, so that people should read them and become beautiful and wise, too. Sometimes I preach to foreign sovereigns on the way in which their countries should be ruled. I am what is called a journalist, dear."

"It must be the most wonderful work in the world," cried Stella, aglow with enthusiasm, "and they must pay you lots and lots of money."

"Lots and lots."

"And how you must love it—the work, I mean!"

"Every hour spent in the newspaper-office is a dream of delight," said Risca.

Walter Herold, who happened to be present during this conversation, remarked, with a shake of his head, as soon as they had left the room:

"God forgive you, John, for an amazing liar!"

Risca shrugged his round, thick shoulders.

"He will," said he, "if He has a sense of humour." Then he turned upon his friend somewhat roughly. "What would you have me tell the child?"

"My dear fellow," said Herold, "if you would only give the world at large some of the imaginative effort you expend in that room, you would not need to wear your soul to shreds in a newspaper-office."

"What is the good of telling me that?" growled Risca, the deep lines of care returning to his dark, loose-featured face. "Don't I know it already? It's just the irony of things. There's an artist somewhere about me. If there was n't, why should I have wanted to write novels and plays and poetry ever since I was a boy? It's a question of outlet. There are women I know who can't do a blessed thing except write letters; there they find their artistic outlet. I can find my artistic outlet only in telling lies to Stella. Would you deny me that?"

"Not at all," said Herold, with a gay laugh. "The strain of having to remember another fellow's lies, in addition to one's own, is heavy, I admit, but for friendship's sake I can bear it. Only the next time you add on a new wing to that infernal house and fill it with majolica vases, for Heaven's sake tell me."

For Herold, being Risca's intimate, had, for corroborative purposes, to be familiar with the dream palace, and when Risca made important additions or alterations without informing him, was apt to be sore beset with perplexities during his next interview with Stellamaris. But being an actor by profession (at the same time being an amateur in all other arts), he was quick to interpret another man's dream, and once, being rather at a loss, improved on his author and interpolated a billiard-room, much to Risca's disgust. Where the deuce, he asked, in angry and childlike seriousness, was there a place for a billiard-room in his palace? Did n't he know the whole lay-out of the thing by this time? It was inexcusable impertinence!

"Then why did n't you tell me about the music-room?" cried Herold, hotly, on this particular occasion. "How should I guess that an unmusical dog like you would want a music-room? In order not to give you away, I had to invent the billiard-room. A rotten house without a billiard-room!"

"I suppose you think it's a commodious mansion, with five reception-rooms, fourteen bedrooms and baths, hot and cold."

The two men nearly quarreled.

But no hard words followed the discussion of Risca's rose-coloured and woefully ironical description of his work. Herold knew what pains of hell had got round about the man he loved, and strove to mitigate them with gaiety and affection. And while the Great High Belovedest and the Great High Favourite were grappling together with a tragedy not referred to in speech between them, and as remote from Stella's purview of life as the Lupanaria of Hong-Kong, she, with her white hand on the head of the blue Great Dane, who regarded her with patient, topaz eyes, looked out from her western window, over the channel, on the gold and crimson lake and royal purple of the sunset, and built out of the masses of gloried cloud and streaks of lapis lazuli and daffodil gem a castle of dreams compared with which poor John Risca's trumpery palace, with its Arachnes and Liliases and Niphetoses, was only a vulgar hotel in a new and perky town.

# CHAPTER II

THE judge pronounced sentence: three years' penal servitude. The condemned woman, ashen-cheeked, thin-lipped, gave never a glance to right or left, and disappeared from the dock like a ghost.

John Risca, the woman's husband, who had been sitting at the solicitor's table, rose, watched her disappear, and then, the object of all curious eyes, with black brow and square jaw strode out of the court. Walter Herold, following him, joined him in the corridor, and took his arm in a protective way and guided him down the great staircase into the indifferent street. Then he hailed a cab.

"'May I come with you?"

Risca nodded assent. It was a comfort to feel by his side something human in this pandemonium of a world.

"Eighty-four Fenton Square, Westminster." Herold gave the address of Risca's lodgings, and entered the cab. During the journey through the wide thoroughfares hurrying with London's afternoon traffic neither spoke. There are ghastly tragedies in life for which words, however sympathetic and comprehending, are ludicrously inadequate. Now and then Herold glanced at the heavy, set face of the man who was dear to him and cursed below his breath. Of course nothing but morbid pig-headedness in the first fatal instance had brought him to this disaster. But, after all, is pig-headedness a crime meriting so overwhelming a punishment? Why should fortune favour some, like himself, who just danced lightly upon life, and take a diabolical delight in breaking others upon her wheel? Was it because John Risca could dance no better than a bull, and, like a bull, charged through life insensately, with lowered horns and blundering hoofs? This lunatic marriage, six years ago, when Risca was three and twenty, with a common landlady's commoner pretty vixen of a daughter, he himself had done his best to prevent. He had pleaded with the tongue of an angel and vituperated in the vocabulary of a bargee. He might as well have played "Home, Sweet Home," on the flute or recited Bishop

Ernulphus's curse to the charging bull. But still, however unconsidered, honourable marriage ought not of itself to bring down from heaven the doom of the house of Atreus. This particular union was bound to be unhappy; but why should it have been Æschylean in its catastrophe?

As Risca uttered no word, Herold, with the ultimate wisdom of despair, held his peace.

At last they arrived at the old-world, dilapidated square, where Risca lodged. Children, mostly dirty-faced, those of the well-to-do being distinguished at this post-tea hour of the afternoon by a circle of treacle encrusting like gems the circumambient grime about their little mouths, squabbled shrilly on the pavement. Torn oilcloth and the smell of the sprats fried the night before last for the landlord's supper greeted him who entered the house. Risca, the aristocrat of the establishment, rented the drawing-room floor. Herold, sensitive artist, successful actor, appreciated by dramatic authors and managers and the public as a Meissonier of small parts, and therefore seldom out of an engagement, who had created for himself a Queen Anne gem of a tiny house in Kensington, could never enter Risca's home without a shiver. To him it was horror incarnate, the last word of unpenurious squalor. There were material shapes to sit down upon, to sit at, it is true, things on the walls (terribilia visu) to look upon, such as "The Hunter's Return," and early portraits of Queen Victoria and the Prince Consort, and the floor was covered with a red-and-green imitation Oriental carpet; but there was no furniture, as Herold understood the word, nothing to soothe or to please. One of the chairs was of moth-eaten saddle-bag, another of rusty leather. A splotch of grease, the trace left by a far-distant storm of gravy that had occurred on a super-imposed white cloth, and a splotch of ink gave variety to a faded old table-cover. A litter of books and papers and unemptied ash-trays and pipes and slippers disfigured the room. The place suggested chaos coated with mildew.

"Ugh!" said Herold, on entering, "it 's as cold as charity. Do you mind if I light the fire?"

It was a raw day in March, and the draughts from the staircase and windows played spitefully about the furniture. Risca nodded, threw his hat on a leather couch against the wall, and flung himself into his writing-chair. Hot or cold, what did it matter to him? What would anything in the world matter to him in the future? He sat, elbows on table, his hands clutching his coarse, black hair, his eyes set in a great agony. And there he stayed for a long time, silent and motionless, while Herold lit the fire, and, moving noiselessly about the room, gave to its disarray some semblance of comfort. He was twenty-nine. It was the end of his career, the end of his life. No mortal man could win through such devastating shame. It was a bath of vitriol eating through nerve and fibre to the heart itself. He was a dead man—dead to all the vital things of life at nine-and-twenty. An added torture was his powerlessness to feel pity for the woman. For the crime of which she had been convicted, the satiating of the lust of cruelty, mankind finds no extenuation. She had taken into her house, as a slut of all work, a helpless child from an orphanage. Tales had been told in that court at which men grew physically sick and women fainted. Her counsel's plea of insanity had failed. She was as sane as any creature with such a lust could be. She was condemned to three years' penal servitude.

It was his wife, the woman whom he, John Risca, had married six years before, the woman whom, in his passionate, obstinate, growling way, he had thought he loved. They had been parted for over four years, it is true, for she had termagant qualities that would have driven away any partner of her life who had not a morbid craving for Phlegethon as a perpetual environment; but she bore his name, an honoured one (he thanked God she had given him no child to bear it, too), and now that name was held up to the execration of all humanity. For the name's sake, when the unimagined horror had first broken over him, he had done his utmost to shield her. He had met her in the prison, for the first time since their parting, and she had regarded him with implacable hatred, though she accepted the legal assistance he provided, as she had accepted the home from which he had been driven and the half of his poor earnings.

Murder, clean and final, would have been more easily borne than this, the deliberate, systematically planned torture of a child. There is some sort of tragic dignity in murder. It is generally preceded by conflict, and the instinct of mankind recognizing in conflict, no matter how squalid and sordid, the essence of drama, very often finds sympathy with the protagonist of the tragedy, the slayer himself. How otherwise to account for the petitions for the reprieve of a popular murderer, a curious phenomenon not to be fully explained by the comforting word hysteria? But in devilish cruelty, unpreceded by conflict; there is no drama, there is nothing to touch the imagination; it is perhaps the only wickedness with which men have no lingering sympathy. It transcends all others in horror.

"Murder would have been better than this," he said aloud, opening and shutting his powerful fists. "My soul has been dragged through a sewer."

He rose and flung the window open and breathed the raw air with full lungs. A news-urchin's cry caused him to look down into the street. The boy, expectant, held out a paper, and pointed with it to the yellow bill which he carried apronwise in front of him. On the bill was printed in large capitals: "The Risca Torture Case. Verdict and Sentence." Risca beckoned Herold to the window, and clutched him heavily on the shoulder.

"Look!" said he. "That is to be seen this afternoon in every street in London. To-night the news will be flashed all round the world. To-morrow the civilized press will reek with it. Come away!" He dragged Herold back, and brought down the window with a crash. "It's blazing hell!" he said.

"Every man has to pass through it at least once in his life," said Herold, glad that the relief of speech had come to his friend. "That is, if he 's to be any good in the world."

Risca uttered a grim sound in the nature of a mirthless laugh. " 'As gold is tried by the fire, so souls are tried by pain,' " he quoted with a sneer. Was ever a man consoled by such drivelling maxims? And they are lies. No man can be better for having gone through hell. It blasts everything that is good in one. Besides, what do you know? You've never been through it."

Herold, standing by the fire, broke a black mass of coal with the heel of his boot. The flames sprang up, and in the gathering twilight threw strange gleams over his thin, eager face.

"I shall, one of these days," said he—"a very bad hell."

"Good God! Wallie," cried Risca, "are you in trouble, too?"

"Not yet," Herold replied, with a smile, for he saw that the instinct of friendship, at any rate, had not been consumed. "I 've walked on roses all my life. That 's why I 've never done anything great. But my hell is before me. How can I escape it?" The smile faded from his face, and he looked far away into the gray sky. "Sometimes my mother's Celtic nature seems to speak and prophesy within me. It tells me that my roses shall turn into red-hot ploughshares and my soul shall be on fire. The curtains of the future are opened for an elusive fraction of a second—" He broke off suddenly. "I'm talking rot, John. At least it's not all rot. I was only thinking that in my bad time I should have a great, strong friend to stand by my side."

"If you mean me," said Risca, "you know I shall. But, in the meanwhile I pray to God to spare you a hell like mine. Sometimes I wonder," he continued after a gloomy pause, "whether this would have happened if I had stuck by her. I could have seen which way things were tending, and I would have stepped in. After all, I am strong enough to have borne it."

"You were talking about murder just now," said Herold. "If you had stayed with her, there would have been murder done or something precious near it."

Risca sighed. He was a big, burly man, with a heavy, intellectual face, prematurely furrowed, and a sigh shook his loose frame somewhat oddly. "I don't know," said he, after a lumbering turn or so up and down the room. "How can any man know? She was impossible enough, but I never dreamed of such developments. And now that I reflect, I remember signs. Once we had a little dog—no, I have no right to tell you. Damn it! man," he cried fiercely, "I have no right to keep you here in this revolting atmosphere." He picked up Herold's hat. "Go away, Wallie, and leave me to myself. You 're good and kind and all that, but I 've no right to make your life a burden to you."

Herold rescued his hat and deliberately put it down. "Oh, yes, you have," said he, with smiling seriousness. "You have every right. Have you ever considered the ethics of friendship? Few people do consider them nowadays. Existence has grown so complicated that such a simple, primitive thing as friendship is apt to be neglected in the practical philosophy of life. Our friendship, John, is something I could no more tear out of me than I could tear out my heart itself. It's one of the few vital, real things —indeed, it's perhaps the only tremendous thing in my damfool of a life. I believe in friendship. If a man hath not a friend, let him quit the stage. Old Bacon had sense: a man has every right over his friend, every claim upon him, except the right of betrayal. My purse is yours, your purse is mine. My time is yours, and yours mine. My joys and sorrows are yours, and yours mine. But a friend may not supplant a friend either in material ambition or in the love of a woman. That is the unforgivable sin, high treason against friendship. Don't talk folly about having no right."

He lit with nervous fingers the cigarette he was about to light when he began his harangue. Risca gripped him by the arm.

"God knows I don't want you to go. I 'm pretty tough, and I 'm not going to cave in, but it's God's comfort to have you here. If I'm not a merry companion to you, what the devil do you think I am to myself?"

He walked up and down the dreary room, on which the dark of evening had fallen. At last he paused by his writing-table, and then a sudden thought flashing on him, he smote his temples with his hands.

"I must send you away, Wallie. It's necessary. I have my column to write for The Herald. It must be in by eleven. I had forgotten all about it. They won't want my name,—it would damn the paper,—but I suppose they 're counting on the column, and I don't want to leave them in the lurch."

"They don't want your column this week, at any rate," said Herold. "Oh, don't begin to bellow. I went to see Ferguson yesterday. He's as kind as can be, and of course wants you to go on as usual. But no one except a raving idiot would expect stuff from you to-day. And as for your silly old column, I've written it myself. I suggested it to Ferguson, and he jumped at it."

"You wrote my column?" said Risca, in a softened voice.

"Of course I did, and a devilish good column, too. Do you think I can only paint my face and grin through a horse-collar?"

"What made you think of it? I did n't."

"That's precisely why I did," said Herold.

Risca sat down, calmer in mood, and lit a pipe. Herold, the sensitive, accepted this action as an implication of thanks. Risca puffed his tobacco for a few moments in silence, apparently absorbed in enjoyment of the fragrant subtleties of the mixture of honeydew and birdseye and latakia and the suspicion of soolook that gives mystery to a blend. At last he spoke.

"I shall arrange to keep on that house in Smith Street, and put in a caretaker, so that she shall have a home when she comes out. What will happen then, God Almighty knows. Perhaps she will have changed. We need n't discuss it. But, at any rate, while I 'm away, I want you to see to it for me. It's a ghastly task, but some one must undertake it. Will you?"

"Of course," said Herold. "But what do you mean by being 'away'?"

"I am going to Australia," said Risca.

"For how long?"

"For the rest of my life," said Risca.

Herold leaped from his chair and threw his cigarette into the fire. It was only John Risca who, without giving warning, would lower his head and charge at life in that fashion.

"This is madness."

"It's my only chance of sanity," said Risca. "Here I am a dead man. The flames are too much for me. Perhaps in another country, where I 'm not known, some kind of a phoenix called John Smith or Robinson may rise out of the ashes. Here it can't. Here the ashes would leave a stench that would asphyxiate any bird, however fabulous. It's my one chance—to begin again."

"What will you do?"

"The same as here. If I can make a fair living in London, I ought n't to starve in Melbourne."

"It's monstrous!" cried Herold. "It's not to be thought of."

"Just so," replied Risca. "It's got to be done."

Herold glanced at the gloomy face, and threw up his hands in despair. When John Risca spoke in that stubborn way there was no moving him. He had taken it into his head to go to Australia, and to Australia he would go despite all arguments and beseechings. Yet Herold argued and besought. It was monstrous that a man of John's brilliant attainments and deeply rooted ambitions should surrender the position in London which he had so hardly won. London was generous, London was just; in the eyes of London he was pure and blameless. Not an editor would refuse him work, not an acquaintance would refuse him the right hand of fellowship. The heart of every friend was open to him. As for the agony of his soul, he would carry that about with him wherever he went. He could not escape from it by going to the antipodes. It was more likely to be conjured away in England by the love of those about him.

"I'm aware of all that, but I 'm going to Melbourne," said Risca, doggedly. "If I stay here, I'm dead."

"When do you propose to start?"

"I shall take my ticket to-morrow on the first available boat."

Herold laid his nervous hand on the other's burly shoulder.

"Is it fair in this reckless way to spring such a tremendous decision on those who care for you?"

"Who on God's earth really cares for me except yourself? It will be a wrench parting from you, but it has to be."

"You've forgotten Stellamaris," said Herold.

"I have n't," replied Risca, morosely; "but she 's only a child. She looks upon me as a creature out of a fairy-tale. Realities, thank God! have no place in that room of hers. I 'll soon fade out of her mind."

"Stella is fifteen, not five," said Herold.

"Age makes no difference, I'm not going to see her again," said he.

"What explanation is to be given her?"

"I'll write the necessary fairy-story."

"You are not going to see her before you sail?"

"No," said Risca.

"Then you 'll be doing a damnably cowardly thing," cried Herold, with flashing eyes.

Risca rose and glared at his friend.

"You fool! Do you suppose I don't care for her? Do you suppose I would n't cut off my hand to save her pain?"

"Then cut off some of your infernal selfishness and save her the pain she's going to feel if you don't bid her good-bye."

Risca clenched his fists, and turned to the window, and stood with his back to the room.

"Take care what you 're saying. It 's dangerous to quarrel with me to-day."

"Danger be hanged!" said Herold. "I tell you it will be selfish and cowardly not to see her."

There was a long silence. At last Risca wheeled round abruptly.

"I'm neither selfish nor cowardly. You don't seem to realize what I 've gone through. I 'm not fit to enter her presence. I 'm polluted. I 'm a walking pestilence. I told you my soul had been dragged through a sewer."

"Then go and purify it in the sea-wind that blows through Stella's window, John," said Herold, seeing that he had subdued his anger. "I am not such a fool as to ask you to give up your wretched idea of exile for the sake of our friendship; but this trivial point, in the name of our friendship, I ask you to concede to me. Just grant me this, and I 'll let you go to Melbourne or Trincomalee or any other Hades you choose without worrying you."

"Why do you insist upon it? How can a sick child's fancies count to a man in such a position?"

His dark eyes glowered at Herold from beneath lowering brows. Herold met the gaze steadily, and with his unclouded vision he saw far deeper into Risca than Risca saw into him. He did not answer the question, for he penetrated, through the fuliginous vapours whence it proceeded, into the crystal regions of the man's spirit. It was he, after a while, who held Risca with his eyes, and it was all that was beautiful and spiritual in Risca that was held. And then Herold reached out his hand slowly and touched him.

"We go down to Southcliff together."

Risca drew a deep breath.

"Let us go this evening," said he.

A few hours afterward when the open cab taking them from the station to the Channel House came by the sharp turn of the road abruptly to the foot of the cliff, and the gusty southwest wind brought the haunting smell of the seaweed into his nostrils, and he saw the beacon-light in the high west window shining like a star, a gossamer feather from the wings of Peace fell upon the man's tortured soul.

# CHAPTER III

I T will be remembered that Stellamaris was a young person of bountiful fortune. She had stocks and shares and mortgages and landed property faithfully administered under a deed of trust. The Channel House and all that therein was, except Sir Oliver and Lady Blount's grievances, belonged to her. She knew it; she had known it almost since infancy. The sense of ownership in which she had grown up had its effect on her character, giving her the equipoise of a young reigning princess, calm and serene in her undisputed position. In her childish days her material kingdom was limited to the walls of her sea-chamber but as the child expanded into the young girl, so expanded her conception of the limits of her kingdom. And with this widening view came gradually and curiously the consciousness that though her uncle and aunt were exquisitely honoured and beloved agents who looked to the welfare of her realm, yet they could not relieve her of certain gracious responsibilities. Instinctively, and with imperceptible gradations, she began to make her influence felt in the house itself. But it was an influence in the spiritual and not material sense of the word; the hovering presence and not the controlling hand.

When, shortly after the arrival of the two men, Walter Herold went up to his room, he found a great vase of daffodils on his dressing-table and a pencilled note from Stella in her unformed handwriting, for one cannot learn to write copper-plate when one lies forever on the flat of one's back.

Great High Favourite: Here are some daffodils, because they laugh and dance like you. Stellamaris.

And on his dressing-table John Risca found a mass of snowdrops and a note:

Great High Belovedest: A beautiful white silver cloud came to my window to-day, and I wished I could tear it in half and save you a bit for the palace. But snowdrops are the nearest things I could think of instead. Your telegram was a joy. Love. S.

Beside the bowl of flowers was another note:

I heard the wheels of your chariot, but Her Serene High-and-Mightiness [her trained nurse] says I am tucked up for the night and can have no receptions, levees, or interviews. I tell her she will lose her title and become the Kommon Kat; but she does n't seem to mind. Oh, it's just lovely to feel that you 're in the house again. S.

Risca looked round the dainty room, his whenever he chose to occupy it, and knew how much, especially of late, it held of Stellamaris. It had been redecorated a short while before, and the colours and the patterns and all had been her choice and specification.

The castle architect, a young and fervent soul called Wratislaw, a member of the Art Workers' Guild, and a friend of Herold's, who had settled in Southcliff-on-Sea, and was building, for the sake of a precarious livelihood, hideous bungalows which made his own heart sick, but his clients' hearts rejoice, had been called in to advise. With Stellamaris, sovereign lady of the house, aged fifteen, he had spent hours of stupefied and aesthetic delight. He had brought her armfuls of designs, cartloads of illustrated books; and the result of it all was that, with certain other redecorations in the house with which for the moment we have no concern, Risca's room was transformed from late-Victorian solidity into early-Georgian elegance. The Adam Brothers reigned in ceiling and cornice, and the authentic spirit of Sheraton, thanks to the infatuated enterprise of Wratislaw, pervaded the furniture. Yet, despite Wratislaw, although through him she had spoken, the presence of Stellamaris pervaded the room. On the writing-table lay a leather-covered blotter, with his initials, J. R., stamped in gold. In desperate answer to a childish question long ago, he had described the bedspread on his Parian marble bed in the palace as a thing of rosebuds and crinkly ribbons tied up in true-lovers' knots. On his bed in Stella's house lay a spread exquisitely Louis XV in design.

Risca looked about the room. Yes, everything was Stella. And behold there was one new thing, essentially Stella, which he had not noticed before. Surely it had been put there since his last visit.

In her own bedroom had hung since her imprisonment a fine reproduction of Watt's "Hope," and, child though she was, she had divined, in a child's unformulative way, the simple yet poignant symbolism of the blindfold figure seated on this orb of land and sea, with meek head bowed over a broken lyre, and with ear strained to the vibration of the one remaining string. She loved the picture, and with unconscious intuition and without consultation with Wratislaw, who would have been horrified at its domination of his Adam room, had ordained that a similar copy should be hung on the wall facing the pillow of her Great High Belovedest's bed.

The application of the allegory to his present state of being was startlingly obvious. Risca knitted a puzzled brow. The new thing was essentially Stella, yet why had she caused it to be put in his room this day of all disastrous days? Was it not rather his cousin Julia's doing? But such delicate conveyance of sympathy was scarcely Julia's way. A sudden dread stabbed him. Had Stella herself heard rumours of the tragedy? He summoned Herold, who had a prescriptive right to the adjoining room.

"If any senseless fools have told her, I 'll murder them," he cried.

"The creatures of the sunset told her—at least as much as it was good for her to know," said Herold.

"Do you mean that she did it in pure ignorance?"

"In the vulgar acceptance of the word, yes," smiled Herold. "Do you think that the human brain is always aware of the working of the divine spirit?"

"If it's as you say, it's uncanny," said Risca, unconvinced.

Yet when Sir Oliver and Julia both assured him that Stella never doubted his luxurious happiness, and that the ordering of the picture was due to no subtle suggestion, he had to believe them.

"You always make the mistake, John, of thinking Stellamaris mortal," said Herold, at the supper-table, for, on receipt of the young men's telegram, the Blounts had deferred their dinner to the later hour of supper. "You are utterly wrong," said he. "How can she be mortal when she talks all day to winds and clouds and the sea-children in their cups of foam? She's as elemental as Ariel. When she sleeps, she's really away on a sea-gull's back to the Isles of Magic. That's why she laughs at the dull, clumsy old world from which she is cut off in her mortal guise. What are railway-trains and omnibuses to her? What would they be to you, John, if you could have a sea-gull's back whenever you wanted to go anywhere? And she goes to places worth going to, by George! What could she want with Charing Cross or the Boulevard des Italians? Fancy the nymph Syrinx at a woman writers' dinner!"

"I don't know what you 're talking about, Walter," said Lady Blount, whose mind was practical.

"Syrinx," said Sir Oliver, oracularly (he was a little, shrivelled man, to whose weak face a white moustache and an imperial gave a false air of distinction)—"Syrinx," said he, "was a nymph beloved of Pan,—it's a common legend in Greek mythology,—and Pan turned her into a reed."

"And then cut the reed up into Pan-pipes," cried Herold, eagerly, "and made immortal music out of them—just as he makes immortal music out of Stellamaris. You see, John, it all comes to the same thing. Whether you call her Ariel, or Syrinx, or a Sprite of the Sea, or a Wunderkind whose original trail of glory-cloud has not faded into the light of common day, she belongs to the Other People. You must believe in the Other People, Julia; you can't help it."

Lady Blount turned to him severely. Despite her affection for him, she more than suspected him of a pagan pantheism, which she termed atheistical. His talk about belief in spirits and hobgoblins irritated her. She kept a limited intelligence together by means of formulas, as she kept her scanty reddish-gray hair together by means of a rigid false front.

"I believe in God the Father, God the Son, and God the Holy Ghost," she said, with an air of cutting reproof.

Sir Oliver pushed his plate from him, but not the fraction of a millimetre beyond that caused by the impatient push sanctioned by good manners.

"Don't be a fool, Julia!"

"I don't see how a Christian woman declaring the elements of her faith can be a fool," said Lady Blount, drawing herself up.

"There are times and seasons for everything," said Sir Oliver. "If you were having a political argument, and any one asked you whether you believed in tariff reform, and you glared at him and said, I believe in Pontius Pilate,' you'd be professing Christianity, but showing yourself an idiot."

"But I don't believe in Pontius Pilate," retorted Lady Blount.

"Oh, don't you?" cried Sir Oliver, in sinister exultation. "Then your whole historical fabric of the Crucifixion must fall to the ground."

"I don't see why you need be irreverent and blasphemous," said Lady Blount.

Herold laid his hand on Lady Blount's and looked at her, with his head on one side.

"But do you believe in Stellamaris, Julia."

His smile was so winning, with its touch of mockery, that she grew mollified.

"I believe she has bewitched all of us," she said.

Which shows how any woman may be made to eat her words just by a little kindness.

So the talk went back to Stella and her ways and her oddities, and the question of faith in Pontius Pilate being necessary for salvation was forgotten. A maid, Stella's own maid, came in with a message. Miss Stella's compliments, and were Mr. Risca and Mr. Herold having a good supper? She herself was about to drink her egg beaten up in sherry, and would be glad if the gentlemen would take a glass of wine with her. The young men, accordingly, raised their glasses toward the ceiling and drank to Stella, in the presence of the maid, and gave her appropriate messages to take back to her mistress.

It was a customary little ceremony, but in Risca's eyes it never lost its grace and charm. To-night it seemed to have a deeper significance, bringing Stella with her elfin charm into the midst of them, and thus exorcising the spirits of evil that held him in their torturing grip. He spoke but little at the meal, content to listen to the talk about Stella, and curiously impatient when the conversation drifted into other channels. Of his own tragedy no one spoke. On his arrival, Lady Blount, with unwonted demonstration of affection, had thrown her arms round his neck, and Sir Oliver had wrung his hand and mumbled the stiff Briton's incoherences of sympathy. He had not yet told them of his decision to go to Australia.

He broke the news later, in the drawing-room, abruptly and apropos of nothing, as was his manner, firing his bombshell with the defiant air of one who says, "There, what do you think of it?"

"I'm going to Australia next week, never to come back again," said he.

There was a discussion. Sir Oliver commended him. The great dependencies of the empire were the finest field in the world for a young man, provided he kept himself outside the radius of the venomous blight of the Colonial Office. To that atrophied branch of the imperial service the white administrator was merely a pigeon-holed automaton; the native, black or bronze or yellow, a lion-hearted human creature. All the murder, riot, rapine, arson, and other heterogeneous devilry that the latter cared to indulge in proceeded naturally from the noble indignation of his generous nature. If the sensible man who was appointed by the Government to rule over this scum of the planet called out the military and wiped out a few dozen of them for the greater glory and safety of the empire, the pusillanimous ineptitudes in second-rate purple and cheap linen of the Colonial Office, for the sake of currying favour with Labour members and Socialists and Radicals and Methodists and Anti-vivisectionists and Vegetarians and other miserable Little-Englanders, denounced him as a Turk, an assassin, a seventeenth-century Spanish conquistador of the bloodiest type, and held him up to popular execration, and recalled him, and put him on a beggarly pension years before he had reached his age limit. He could tell them stories which seemed (and in truth deserved to be) incredible.

"John," said Lady Blount, "has heard all this a thousand times,"—as indeed he had,—"and must be sick to death of it. He is not going out to Australia as governor-general."

"Who said he was, my dear?" said Sir Oliver.

"If you did n't imply it, you were talking nonsense, Oliver," Lady Blount retorted.

"Anyhow, Oliver, do you think John is taking a wise step?" Herold hastily interposed.

"I do," said he; "a very wise step."

"I don't agree with you at all," said Lady Blount, with a snap of finality.

"Your remark, my dear," replied Sir Oliver, "does not impress me in the least. When did you ever agree with me?"

"Never, my dear Oliver," said Lady Blount, with the facial smile of the secretly hostile fencer. "And I thank Heaven for it. I may not be a brilliant woman, but I am endowed with common sense."

Sir Oliver looked at her for a moment, with lips parted, as if to speak; but finding nothing epigrammatic enough to say—and an epigram alone would have saved the situation—he planted a carefully cut cigar between the parted lips aforesaid, and deliberately struck a match.

"Your idea, John," said Lady Blount, aware of victory, "is preposterous. What would Stella do without you?"

"Yes," said Sir Oliver, after lighting his cigar; "Stella has to be considered before everything."

Risca frowned on the unblushing turncoat. Stella! Stella! Everything was Stella. Here were three ordinary, sane, grown-up people seriously putting forward the proposition that he had no right to go and mend his own broken life in his own fashion because he happened to be the favored playmate of a little invalid girl!

On the one side was the driving force of Furies of a myriad hell-power, and on the other the disappointment of Stella Blount. It was ludicrous. Even Walter Herold, who had a sense of humour, did not see the grotesque incongruity. Risca frowned upon each in turn—upon three serene faces smilingly aware of the absurd. Was it worth while trying to convince them?

"Our dear friends are quite right, John," said Herold. "What would become of Stella if you went away?"

"None of you seems to consider what would happen to me if I stayed," said John, in the quiet tone of a man who is talking to charming but unreasonable children. "It will go to my heart to leave Stella, more than any of you can realize; but to Australia I go, and there's an end of it."

Lady Blount sighed. What with imperial governments that wrecked the career of men for shooting a few murderous and fire-raising blacks, and with lowborn vixens of women who ruined men's careers in other ways, life was a desperate puzzle. She was fond of her cousin John Risca. She, too, before she married Sir Oliver, had borne the name, and the disgrace that had fallen upon it affected her deeply. It was horrible to think of John's wife, locked up that night in the stone cell of a gaol. She leaned back in her chair in silence while the men talked—Sir Oliver, by way of giving Risca hints on the conduct of life in Melbourne, was narrating his experiences of forty years ago in the West Indies—and stared into the fire. Her face, beneath the front of red hair that accused so pitifully the reddish gray that was her own, looked very old and faded. What was a prison like? She shuddered. As governor's wife, she had once or twice had occasion to visit a colonial prison. But the captives were black, and they grinned cheerily; their raiment, save for the unæsthetic decoration of the black arrow, was not so very different from that which they wore in a state of freedom; neither were food, bedding, and surroundings so very different; and the place was flooded with air and blazing sunshine. She could never realize that it was a real prison. It might have been a prison of musical comedy. But an English prison was the real, unimaginable abode of grim, gray horror. She had heard of the prison taint. She conceived it as a smell—that of mingled quicklime and the corruption it was to destroy —which lingered physically forever after about the persons of those who had been confined within prison-walls. A gaol was a place of eternal twilight, eternal chill, eternal degradation for the white man or woman; and a white woman, the wife of one of her own race, was there. It was almost as if the taint hung about her own lavender-scented self. She shivered, and drew her chair a few inches nearer the fire.

Was it so preposterous, after all, on John Risca's part to fly from the shame into a wider, purer air? Her cry had been unthinking, instinctive, almost a cry for help. She was growing old and soured and worn by perpetual conjugal wranglings. John, her kinsman, counted for a great deal in a life none too rich. John and Stella were nearest to her in the world—first Stella, naturally, then John. To the woman of over fifty the man of under thirty is still a boy. For many years she had nursed the two together in her heart. And now he was going from her. What would she, what would Stella, do without him? Her husband's direct interpellation aroused her from her reverie.

"Julia, what was the name of the chap we met in St. Kitts who had been sheep-farming in Queensland?"

They had sailed away from St. Kitts in 1878. Lady Blount reminded him tartly of the fact while professing her oblivion of the man from Queensland. They sparred for a few moments. Then she rose wearily and said she was going to bed. Sir Oliver looked at his watch.

"Nearly twelve. Time for us all to go."

"As soon as I' ve written my morning letter to Stellamaris," said Herold.

"I must write, too," said Risca.

For it was a rule of the house that every visitor should write Stellamaris a note overnight, to be delivered into her hands the first thing in the morning. The origin of the rule was wrapped in the mists of history.

So John Risca sat down at Sir Oliver's study-table in order to indite his letter to Stellamaris. But for a long time he stared at the white paper. He, the practised journalist, who could dash off his thousand words on any subject as fast as pen could travel, no matter what torture burned his brain, could not find a foolish message for a sick child. At last he wrote like a school-boy:

Darling: The flowers were beautiful, and so is the new picture, and I want to see you early in the morning. I hope you are well. John Risca.

And he had to tear the letter out of its envelope and put it into a fresh one because he had omitted to add the magic initials "G. H. B." to his name. Compared with his usual imaginative feats of correspondence, this was a poverty-stricken epistle. She would wonder at the change. Perhaps his demand for an immediate interview would startle her, and shocks were dangerous. He tore up the letter and envelope, and went to his own room. It was past two o'clock when he crept downstairs again to lay his letter on the hall table.

At the sight of him the next morning the color deepened in the delicate cheeks of Stellamaris, and her dark eyes grew bright. She held out a welcoming hand.

"Ah, Belovedest, I 've been longing to see you ever since dawn. I woke up then and could n't go to sleep again because I was so excited."

He took the chair by her bedside, and her fingers tapped affectionately on the back of the great hand that lay on the coverlid.

"I suppose I was excited, too," said he, "for I was awake at dawn."

"Did you look out of window?"

"Yes," said John.

"Then we both saw the light creeping over the sea like a monstrous ghost. And it all lay so pallid and still,—did n't it?—as if it were a sea in a land of death. And then a cheeky little thrush began to twitter."

"I heard the thrush," replied John. "He said, 'Any old thing! Any old thing!'"

He mimicked the bird's note. Stella laughed. "That's just what he said —as though a sea in a land of death or the English Channel was all the same to him. I suppose it was."

"It must be good to be a thrush," said Risca. "There 's a je m'en fich'isme about his philosophy which must be very consoling."

"I know what that is in English," cried Stellamaris. "It is 'don't-care-a-damativeness.' " Her lips rounded roguishly over the naughty syllable.

"Where did you learn that?"

"Walter told me."

"Walter must be clapped into irons, and fed on bread and water, and seriously spoken to."

Unconsciously he had drifted into his usual manner of speech with her. She laughed with a child's easy gaiety.

"It's delightful to be wicked, is n't it?"

"Why?" he asked.

"It must be such an adventure. It must make you hold your breath and your heart beat."

John wondered grimly whether a certain doer of wickedness had felt this ecstatic rapture. She, too, must have seen the gray dawn, but creeping through prison-bars into her cell. God of Inscrutability! Was it possible that these two co-watchers of the dawn, both so dominant in his life, were of the same race of beings? If the one was a woman born of woman, what in the name of mystery was Stellamaris?

"Don't look so grave, Great High Belovedest," she said, squeezing a finger. "I only spoke in fun. It must really be horrid to be wicked. When I was little I had a book about Cruel Frederick—I think it belonged to grandmama. It had awful pictures, and there were rhymes—

He tore the wings off little flies,

And then poked out their little eyes.

And there was a picture of his doing so. I used to think him a detestable boy. It made me unhappy and kept me awake when I was quite small, but now I know it's all nonsense. People don't do such things, do they?"

Risca twisted his glum face into a smile, remembering the Unwritten Law. "Of course not, Stellamaris," said he. "Cruel Frederick is just as much of a mythical personage as the Giant Fee-fo-fum, who said:

I smell the blood of an Englishman,

And be he alive or be he dead,

I 'll grind his bones to make my bread."

"Why do people frighten children with stories of ogres and wicked fairies and all the rest of it, when the real world they live in is so beautiful?"

"Pure cussedness," answered John, unable otherwise to give a satisfactory explanation.

"Cussedness is silly," said Stellamaris.

There was a little pause. Then she put both her hands on his and pressed it.

"Oh, it's lovely to have you here again, Great High Belovedest; and I have n't thanked you for your letter. It's the most heavenly one you've ever written to me."

It might well have been. He had taken two hours to write it.

# CHAPTER IV

"$T$HE most heavenly of all letters," Stellamaris repeated, as Risca made no reply. "I loved it because it showed me you were very happy."

"Have you ever doubted it?" he asked.

The Great Dane, the Lord High Constable, who was stretched out on his side, with relaxed, enormous limbs, on the hearth-rug, lifted his massive head for a second and glanced at John. Then with a half-grunt, half-sigh, he dropped his head, and twitched his limbs and went to sleep again.

"Now and then when you 're not looking at me," said Stellamaris, "there is a strange look in your eyes: it is when you 're not speaking and you stare out of window without seeming to see anything."

For a moment Risca was assailed by a temptation to break the Unwritten Law and tell her something of his misery. She, with her superfine intelligence, would understand, and her sympathy would be sweet. But he put the temptation roughly from him.

"I am the happiest fellow in the world, Stellamaris," said he.

"It would be difficult not to be happy in such a world."

She pointed out to sea. The blustering wind of the day before had fallen, and a light breeze shook the tips of the waves to the morning sunshine, which turned them into diamonds. The sails of the fishing-fleet of the tiny port flashed merrily against the kindly blue. On the horizon a great steamer was visible steaming up Channel. The salt air came in through the open windows. The laughter of fishermen's children rose faintly from the beach far below.

"And there's spring, too, dancing over everything," she said. "Don't you feel it?"

He acknowledged the vernal influence, and, careful lest his eyes should betray him, talked of the many things she loved. He had not seen her for a fortnight, so there were the apocryphal doings of Lilias and Niphetos to record,—Cleopatras of cats, whom age could not wither, and whose infinite variety custom could not stale,—and there was the approaching marriage of Arachne with a duke to report. And he told her of his gay, bright life in London and of the beautiful Belinda Molyneux, an imaginary Egeria, who sometimes lunched with the queen. The effort of artistic creation absorbed him, as it always had done, under the spell of Stellamaris's shining eyes. The foolish world of his imagination became real, and for the moment hung like a veil before his actual world of tragedy. It was in the nature of a shock to him when Stella's maid entered and asked him if he could speak to Mr. Herold outside the door..

"Tell him to come in," said Stellamaris.

"He says he will, Miss, after he has seen Mr. Risca."

Risca found Herold on the landing.

"Well?"

"Well?" said John.

"What has happened? How did she take it?"

John looked away, and thrust his hands into his pockets.

"I 've not told her yet."

Walter drew a breath. "But you 're going to?"

"Of course," said John. "Do you think it 's so damned easy?"

"You had better be quick, if you 're coming back to town with me. I'm due at rehearsal at twelve."

"I'll go and tell her now," said John.

"Let me just say how d' ye do to her first. I won't stay a minute."

The two men entered the sea-chamber together. Stella welcomed her Great High Favourite and chatted gaily for a while. Then she commanded him to sit down.

"I 'm afraid I can't stay, Stellamaris. I have to go back to London."

Stella glanced at the clock. "Your train doesn't go for an hour." She was jealously learned in trains.

"I think John wants to talk to you."

"He has been talking to me quite beautifully for a long time," said Stella, "and I want to talk to you."

"He has something very particular to say, Stellamaris."

"What is it, Belovedest?" Her eyes sparkled, and she clasped her hands over her childish bosom. "You are not going to marry Belinda Molyneux?"

"No, dear," said John; "I'm not going to marry anybody."

"I'm so glad." She turned to Herold. "Are you going to get married?"

"No," smiled Herold.

Stella laughed. "What a relief! People do get married, you know, and I suppose both of you will have to one of these days, when you get older; but I don't like to think of it."

"I don't believe I shall ever marry, Stellamaris," said Herold.

"Why?"

Herold looked out to sea for a wistful instant. "Because one can't marry a dream, my dear."

"I've married hundreds," said Stella, softly.

If they had been alone together, they would have talked dreams and visions and starshine and moonshine, and their conversation would have been about as sensible and as satisfactory to each other and as intelligible to a third party as that of a couple of elves sitting on adjacent toadstools; but elves don't talk in the presence of a third party, even though he be John Risca and Great High Belovedest. And Stellamaris, recognizing this instinctively, turned her eyes quickly to Risca.

"And you, dear—will you ever marry?"

"Never, by Heaven!" cried John, with startling fervency.

Stella reached out both her hands to the two men who incorporated the all in all of her little life, and each man took a hand and kissed it.

"I don't want to be horrid and selfish," she said; "but if I lost either of you, I think it would break my heart."

The men exchanged glances. John repeated his query: "Do you think it's so damned easy?"

"Tell us why you say that, Stellamaris," said Herold.

John rose suddenly and stood by the west window, which was closed. Stella's high bed had been drawn next to the window open to the south. The room was warm, for a great fire blazed in the tall chimneypiece. He rose to hide his eyes from Stella, confounding Herold for a marplot. Was this the way to make his task easier? He heard Stella say in her sweet contralto:

"Do you imagine it 's just for silly foolishness I call you Great High Belovedest and Great High Favourite? You see, Walter dear, I gave John his title before I knew you, so I had to make some difference in yours. But they mean everything to me. I live in the sky such a lot, and it's a beautiful life; but I know there 's another life in the great world—a beautiful life, too." She wrinkled her forehead. "Oh, it 's so difficult to explain!

It's so hard to talk about feelings, because the moment you begin to talk about them, the feelings become so vague. It's like trying to tell any one the shape of a sunset." She paused for a moment or two; Herold smiled at her and nodded encouragingly. Presently she went on: "I 'll try to put it this way. Often a gull, you see, comes hovering outside here and looks in at me, oh, for a long time, with his round, yellow eyes; and my heart beats, and I love him, for he tells me all about the sea and sky and clouds, where I'll never go,—not really,—and I live the sky life through him, and more than ever since you sent me that poem—I know it by heart—about the sea-gull. Who wrote it?"

"Swinburne," said Herold.

"Did he write anything else?"

"One or two other little things," replied Herold, judiciously. "I 'll copy them out and bring them to you. But go on."

"Well," she said, "yesterday afternoon a little bird—I don't know what kind of bird it was—came and sat on the window-sill, and turned his head this way and looked at me, and turned his head that way and looked at me, and I did n't move hand or foot, and I said, 'Cheep, cheep!' And he hopped on the bed and stayed there such a long time. And I talked to him, and he hopped about and looked at me and seemed to tell me all sorts of wonderful things. But he did n't somehow, although he came from the sky, and was a perfect dear. He must have known all about it, but he did n't know how to tell me. Now, you and John come from the beautiful world and tell me wonderful things about it; and I shall never go there really, but I can live in it through you."

Constable, the Great Dane, known by this abbreviated title in familiar life, rose, stretched himself, and went and snuggled his head beneath John's arm. John turned, his arm round the hound's neck.

"But you can live in it through anybody, dear," said he—"your Uncle Oliver, your Aunt Julia, or anybody who comes to see you."

Stellamaris looked at Herold for a characteristically sympathetic moment, and then at John. She sighed.

"I told you it was hard to explain. But don't you see, Belovedest? You and Walter are like my gull. Everybody else is like the little bird. You know how to tell me and make me live. The others are darlings, but they don't seem to know how to do it."

John scratched his head.

"I see what you mean," said he.

"I should hope so," said Herold.

He looked at his watch and jumped to his feet. "Star of the Sea," said he, "to talk with you is the most fascinating occupation on earth; but managers are desperate fellows, and I 'll get into boiling water if I miss my rehearsal." He turned to John. "I don't see how you are going to catch this train."

"Neither do I," said John. "I shall go by the one after."

Herold took his leave, promising to run down for the week-end. Constable accompanied him to the door in a dignified way, and this ceremony of politeness accomplished, stalked back to the hearth-rug, where he threw himself down, his head on his paws, and his faithful eyes fixed on his mistress. John sat down again by the bedside. There was a short silence during which Stellamaris smiled at him and he smiled at Stellamaris.

"Does n't the Great High Belovedest want to smoke?"

"Badly," said John.

She held out her hand for the pipe and tobacco-pouch. He gave them to her, and she filled the pipe. For a while he smoked peacefully. From where he sat all he could see of the outside world was the waste of sun-kissed waters stretching away and melting into a band of pearly cloud on the horizon. He might have been out at sea. Possibly this time next week he would be, and the salt air would be playing, as now, about his head. But on board that ship would be no spacious sea-chamber like this, so gracious in its appointments—its old oak and silver, its bright chintzes, its quiet old engravings, its dainty dressing-table covered with fairy-like toilet-articles, its blue delft bowls full of flowers, its atmosphere so dearly English, yet English of the days when Sir Bedivere threw Excalibur into the mere. In no other spot on the globe could be found such a sea-chamber, with its high bed, on which lay the sweet, elfin face, half child's, half woman's, framed in the soft, brown hair.

Risca smoked on, and Stellamaris, seeing him disinclined to talk, gazed happily out to her beloved Channel, and dreamed her dreams. They had often sat like this for an hour together, both feeling that they were talking to each other all the time; and often Stella would break the silence by telling him to listen. At such times, so people said, an angel was passing. And he would listen, but could not hear. He remembered Walter Herold once agreeing with her, and saying:

"There's a special little angel told off to come here every day and beat his wings about the room so as to clear the air of all troubling things."

In no other spot on the globe could be found such a sea-chamber, wing-swept, spirit-haunted, where pain ceased magically and the burden of intolerable suffering grew light. No other haven along all the coasts of the earth was a haven of rest such as this.

And the Furies were driving him from it! But here the Furies ceased from driving. Here he had delicious ease. Here a pair of ridiculously frail hands held him a lotus-fed prisoner. He smoked on. At last he resisted the spell. The whole thing was nonsensical. His pipe, only lightly packed by the frail hands, went out. He stuffed it in his pocket, and cleared his throat. He would say then and there what he had come to say.

Stellamaris turned her head and laughed; and when Stellamaris laughed, the sea outside and the flowers in the delft bowl laughed, too.

"The angel has been having a good time."

John cleared his throat again.

"My dear," said he, and then he stopped short. All the carefully prepared exordiums went out of his head. How now to break the news to her he did not know.

"Are you very tired?" she asked.

"Not a bit," said John.

"Then be a dear, and read me something. Read me 'Elaine.' "

The elevated and sophisticated and very highly educated may learn with surprise that "The Idylls of the King" still appeal to ingenuous fifteen. Thank God there are yet remaining also some sentimentalists of fifty who can read them with pleasure and profit!

"But that is so sad, Stellamaris," said John. "You don't want to be sad this beautiful spring morning."

Which was a very inconsistent remark to make, seeing that he was about to dash the young sun from her sky altogether.

"I like being sad sometimes, especially when the world is bright. And Lancelot was such a dear,"—here spoke ingenuous fifteen,—"and Elaine —oh, do read it!"

So John, secretly glad of a respite, drew from the bookcase which held her scrupulously selected and daintily bound library the volume of Tennyson and read aloud the idyll of Lancelot and Elaine. And the sea-wind blew about his head and fluttered the brown hair on the pillow, and the log-fire blazed in the chimney, and the great dog slept, and a noontide hush was over all things. And Risca read the simple poem with the heart of the girl of fifteen, and forgot everything else in the world.

When he had finished, the foolish eyes of both were moist. "The dead oar'd by the dumb," with the lily in her hand,—dead for the love of Lancelot,—affected them both profoundly.

"I think I should die, too, like that, Great High; Belovedest," said Stellamaris, "if any one I loved left me."

"But what Lancelot is going to leave you, dear?" said John.

She shook the thistledown of sadness from her brow and laughed.

"You and Walter are the only Lancelots I've got."

"The devil's in the child to-day," said Risca to himself.

There was a short pause. Then Stella said:

"Belovedest dear, what was the particular thing that Walter said you had to tell me?"

"It's of no consequence," said John. "It will do to-morrow or the day after."

Stella started joyously,—as much as the rigid discipline of years would allow her,—and great gladness lit her face.

"Darling! Are you going to stay here to-day and to-morrow and the next day?"

"My dear," said John, "I've got to get up to town this morning."

"You won't do that," said Stella. "Look at the clock."

It was a quarter to one. He had spent the whole morning with her, and the hours had flown by like minutes.

"Why did n't you tell me that I ought to be catching my train?"

She regarded him in demure mischief.

"I had no object in making you catch your train."

And then Her Serene High-and-Mightiness, the nurse (who had been called in for Stella when first she was put to bed in the sea-chamber, and, falling under her spell, had stayed on until she had grown as much involved in the web of her life as Sir Oliver and Lady Julia and Constable and Herold and Risca), came into the room and decreed the end of the morning interview.

❖

Risca went down-stairs, his purpose unaccomplished. He walked about the garden and argued with himself. Now, when a man argues with himself, he, being only the extraneous eidolon of himself, invariably gets the worst of the argument, and this makes him angry. John was angry; to such a point that, coming across Sir Oliver, who had just returned from an inexplicably disastrous game of golf and began to pour a story of bunkered gloom into his ear, he gnashed his teeth and tore his hair and told Sir Oliver to go to the devil with his lugubrious and rotten game, and dashed away to the solitude of the beach until the luncheon-bell summoned him back.

"I'm going by the 3:50," said he at the luncheon-table.

At three o'clock Stella was free to see him again. He went up to her room distinctly determined to shut his heart against folly. The sun had crept round toward the west and flooded the head and shoulders of Stellamaris and the dainty bedspread with pale gold, just as it flooded the now still and smiling sea. Again paralysis fell upon John. The words he was to speak were to him, as well as to her, the words of doom, and he could not utter them. They talked of vain, childish things. Then Stellamaris's clock chimed the three-quarters. There are some chimes that are brutal, others ironic; but Stellamaris's chimes (the clock was a gift from John himself) were soft, and pealed a soothing mystery, like a bell swung in a deep sea-cave.

It was a quarter to four, and he had missed his train once more. Well, the train could go to—to London, as good a synonym for Tophet as any other. So he stayed, recklessly surrendering himself to the pale, sunlit peace of the sea-chamber, till he was dislodged by Lady Blount.

An attempt to catch a six o'clock train was equally unsuccessful. He did not return to town that night. Why should a sorely bruised man reject the balm that healed? To-morrow he would be stronger and more serene, abler to control the driving force of the Furies, and therefore fitted to announce in gentler wise the decrees of destiny. So Risca went to bed and slept easier, and the room which Stellamaris had made for him became the enchanted bower of a Fair Lady of All Mercy.

In their simple human way Sir Oliver and Lady Blount besought him to stay for his health's sake in the fresh sea-air; and when he yielded, they prided themselves, after the manner of humans, on their own powers of persuasion. One morning Sir Oliver asked him point-blank:

"When are you going to Australia?"

"I don't know," said John. "There's no immediate hurry."

"I hope, dear," said Julia, "you'll give up the idea altogether."

"Haven't I told you that I've made up my mind?" said John, in his gruff tone of finality.

"When are you going to break the news to Stella?" asked Sir Oliver.

"Now," said John, who had begun to loathe the mention of the doomful subject; and he stalked away—the three were strolling in the garden after breakfast—and went to Stella's room, and of course made no mention of it whatsoever.

Then Herold came down for the week-end, and when he heard of Risca's pusillanimity he threw back his head and laughed for joy; for he knew that John would never go to Australia without telling Stellamaris, and also that if he could not tell Stellamaris in the first madness of his agony, he would never be able to tell her at all.

And so, in fact, the fantastically absurd prevailed. Before the Unwritten Law, mainly promulgated and enforced by Risca himself, which guarded the sea-chamber against pain and sorrow, the driving Furies slunk with limp wing and nerveless claw. And one day Risca was surprised at finding himself undriven. Indeed, he was somewhat disconcerted. He fell into a bad temper. The Furies are highly aristocratic divinities who don't worry about Tom, Dick, or Harry, but choose an Orestes at least for their tormenting; so that, when they give up their pursuit of a Risca, he may excusably regard it as a personal slight. It was the morose and gloomy nature of the man.

"I know I'm a fool," he said to Herold, when every one had gone to bed, "but I can't help it. Any normal person would regard me as insane if I told him I was stopped from saving the wreck of my career by consideration for the temporary comfort of a bedridden chit of a girl half my age, who is absolutely nothing to me in the world (her uncle married my first cousin. If that is anything of a family tie, I'm weak on family feeling); but that's God's truth. I'm tied by her to this accursed country. She just holds me down in the hell of London, and I can't wriggle away. It's senseless, I know it is. Sometimes when I'm away from her, walking on the beach, I feel I'd like to throw the whole of this confounded house into the sea; and then I look up and see the light in her room, and—I—I just begin to wonder whether she 's asleep and what she's dreaming of. There 's some infernal witchcraft about the child."

"There is," said Herold.

"Rot!" said Risca, his pugnacious instincts awakened by the check on his dithyrambics. "The whole truth of the matter is that I'm simply a sentimental fool."

"All honour to you, John," said Herold.

"If you talk like that, I 'll wring your neck," said Risca, pausing for a second in his walk up and down Sir Oliver's library, and glaring down at his friend, who reclined on the sofa and regarded him with a smile exasperatingly wise. "You know I'm a fool, and why can't you say it? A man at my time of life! Do you realize that I am twice her age?"

And he went on, inveighing now against the pitifully human conventions that restrained him from hurting the chit of a child, and now against the sorcery with which she contrived to invest the chamber wherein she dwelt.

"And at my age, too, when I've run the whole gamut of human misery, the whole discordant thing—toute la lyre—when I've finished with the blighting illusion that men call life; when, confound it! I 'm thirty."

Sir Oliver, unable to sleep, came into the room in dressing-gown and slippers. He looked very fragile and broken.

"Here 's John," laughed Herold, "saying that he 's thirty, and an old, withered man, and he 's not thirty. He 's nine-and-twenty."

Sir Oliver looked at John, as only age, with awful wistfulness, can look at youth, and came and laid his hand upon the young man's broad shoulders.

"My lad," said he, "you've had a bad time; but you 're young. You've the whole of your life before you. Time, my dear boy, is a marvellous solvent of human perplexity. Once in a new world, once in that astonishing continent of Australia—"

John threw a half-finished cigar angrily into the fire.

"I'm not going to the damned continent," said he.

# CHAPTER V

THUS it came to pass that, for the sake of Stellamaris, Risca remained in London and fought with beasts in Fenton Square. Sometimes he got the better of the beasts, and sometimes the beasts got the better of him. On the former occasions he celebrated the victory by doing an extra turn of work; on the latter he sat idly growling at defeat.

At this period of his career he was assistant-editor of a weekly review, in charge of the book-column of an evening newspaper, the contributor of a signed weekly article on general subjects to the "Daily Herald," and of a weekly London letter to an American syndicate. From this it will be seen that for a man not yet thirty he had achieved a position in journalism envied by many who had grown gray-headed in the game. But as Risca had written three or four novels which had all been rejected by all the publishers in London, he chose to regard himself as a man foiled in his ambitions. He saw himself doomed to failure. For him was the eternal toil of ploughing the sand; the Garden of Delight cultivated by the happy Blest—such as Fawcus of the club, who boasted of making over a thousand pounds for every novel he wrote, and of being able to take as much holiday as he chose—had its gilded gates closed against him forever. That the man of nine-and-twenty should grow embittered because he was not accepted by the world as a brilliant novelist is a matter for the derision of the middle-aged and for the pitying smile of the hoary; but it is a matter of woeful concern to twenty-nine, especially if twenty-nine be a young man of a saturnine temperament whom fate has driven to take himself seriously. In Risca's life there were misfortunes the reality of the pain of which was independent of age; others which were relative, as inseparable from youth as the tears for a bumped head are inseparable from childhood. Yet to the man they were all equally absolute. It is only in after-years, when one looks back down the vista, that one can differentiate.

For all that he ought to have given himself another decade before crying himself a failure, yet a brilliant young journalist who has not found a publisher for one of four novels has reasonable excuse for serious cogitation. There are scores of brilliant young journalists who have published masterpieces of fiction before they are thirty, and at forty have gone on their knees and thanked kind, gentle Time for his effacing fingers; yet the novels have had some quality of the novel warranting their publication. At any rate, the brilliant young journalists have believed in them. They have looked upon their Creation and found that it was good. But Risca, looking on his Creation, found that it was wood. His people were as wooden as Mr. and Mrs. Ham in a Noah's Ark; his scenery was as wooden as the trees and mountain in a toy Swiss village; his dialogue as wooden as the conversation-blocks used by the philosophers of Laputa. He had said, in an outburst of wrathful resentment, that he found his one artistic outlet in aiding to create Stella's Land of Illusion; and he was right. He was despairingly aware of the lack of the quick fancy; the power of visualization; the sublimated faculty of the child's make-believe, creating out of trumpery bits and pieces a glowing world of romance; the keen, instinctive knowledge of the general motives of human action; the uncanny insight into the hearts and feelings of beings of a sex, class, or type different from his own; the gift of evolving from a tiny broken bone of fact a perfect creature indisputably real, colouring it with the hues of actuality and breathing into it the breath of life—the lack, indeed, of all the essential qualities, artistic and therefore usually instinctive, that go to the making of a novelist. Yet Risca was doggedly determined to be a novelist and a poet. It was pathetic. How can a man who cannot distinguish between "God Save the King" and "Yankee Doodle" hope to write a world-shaking sonata? Risca knew that he was crying for the moon, and it is only because he cried so hard for it that he deserved any serious commiseration.

When he did come to death-grapple with the absolute, the beasts above mentioned, he stood out a tragic young figure, fiercely alone in the arena, save for Herold.

His name, uncommon and arresting, had one connotation in London —the Case, the appalling and abominable Case. Even Ferguson of the "Daily Herald," who had evinced such sympathy for him at first, shrank from the name at the head of the weekly column and suggested the temporary use of a pseudonym. Had it not been for Herold's intervention, Risca would have told Ferguson to go to the devil and would have refused to work for his Philistine paper. He swallowed the insult, which did him no good. He refused to carry the accursed name into the haunts of men.

"Come to the club, at any rate," Herold urged. "Every man there is loyal to you."

"And every man as he looks at me will have on his retina not a picture of me, but a picture of what went on in that house in Smith Street."

"Oh, go and buy a serviceable epidermis," cried Herold. Argument was useless.

So Risca worked like a mole at anonymous journalism in his shabby lodgings where Lilias and Niphetos were suggested only by a mangy tabby who occasionally prowled into his sitting-room, and Arachne presided, indeed, but in the cobwebs about the ceiling in the guise which she had been compelled to take by the angry god when the world was young. Only when his attendance at the office of the weekly review was necessary, such as on the day when it went to press, did he mingle with the busy world.

"If you go on in this way," said Herold, "you 'll soon have as much idea of what's going on in London as a lonely dog tied up in a kennel."

"What does it matter," growled John, "to any of the besotted fools who read newspapers, provided I bark loud enough?"

There was one thing going on in London, however, in which he took a grim interest, and that was the convalescence of the little maid-of-all-work who had been taken back, a maimed lamb, to the cheerless fold where she had been reared. Thither he went to make inquiries as soon as he returned from Southcliff-on-Sea. He found the Orphanage of St. Martha at Willesden, a poverty-stricken building, a hopeless parallelogram of dingy, yellow brick, standing within a walled inclosure. There were no trees or flowers, for the yard was paved. His ring at the front door was answered by an orphan in a light print dress, her meagre hair clutched up tight in a knob at the back. He asked for the superintendent and handed his card. The orphan conducted him to a depressing parlour, and vanished. Presently appeared a thin, weary woman, dressed in the black robes of a Sister of Mercy, who, holding the card tight in nervous fingers, regarded him with an air of mingled fright and defiance.

"Your business?" she asked.

Despite the torture of it all, John could not help smiling. If he had been armed with a knout, his reception could not have been more hostile.

"I must beg of you to believe," said he, "that I come as a friend and not as an enemy."

She pointed to a straight-backed chair.

"Will you be seated?"

"It is only human," said he, "to call and see you, and ask after that unhappy child."

"She is getting on," said the Sister superintendent, frostily, "as well as can be expected."

"Which means? Please tell me. I am here to know."

"She will take some time to recover from her injuries, and of course her nerve is broken."

"I'm afraid," said John, "your institution can't afford many invalid's luxuries."

"None at all," replied the weary-faced woman. "She gets proper care and attention, however."

John drew out a five-pound note. "Can you buy her any little things with this? When you have spent it, if you will tell me, I 'll send you another."

"It's against our rules," said the Sister, eying the money. "If you like to give it as a subscription to the general funds, I will accept it."

"Are you badly off?" asked John.

"We are very slenderly endowed."

John pushed the note across the small table near which they were sitting.

"In return," said he, "I hope you will allow me to send in some jellies and fruits, or appliances, or whatever may be of pleasure or comfort to the child."

"Whatever you send her that is practical shall be applied to her use," said the Sister superintendent.

She was cold, unemotional; no smile, no ghost even of departed smiles, seemed ever to visit the tired, gray eyes or the corners of the rigid mouth; coif and face and thin hands were spotless. She did not even thank him for his forced gift to the orphanage.

"I should like to know," said John, regarding her beneath frowning brows, "whether any one here loves the unhappy little wretch."

"These children," replied the Sister superintendent, "have naturally a hard battle to fight when they go from here into the world. They come mostly from vicious classes. Their training is uniformly kind, but it has to be austere."

John rose. "I will bring what things I can think of to-morrow."

The Sister superintendent rose, too, and bowed icily. "You are at liberty to do so, Mr. Risca; but I assure you there is no reason for your putting yourself to the trouble. In the circumstances I can readily understand your solicitude; but again I say you have no cause for it."

"Madam," said he, "I see that I have more cause than ever."

The next day he drove to the orphanage in a cab, with a hamper of delicacies and a down pillow. The latter the Sister superintendent rejected. Generally, it was against the regulations and, particularly, it was injudicious. Down pillows would not be a factor in Unity Blake's after-life.

"Besides," she remarked, "she is not the only orphan in the infirmary."

"Why not call it a sick-room or sick-ward instead of that prison term?" asked John.

"It's the name given to it by the governing body," she replied.

After this John became a regular visitor. Every time he kicked his heels for ten minutes in the shabby and depressing parlour and every time he was received with glacial politeness by the Sister superintendent. By blunt questioning he learned the history of the institution. The Sisterhood of Saint Martha was an Angelican body with headquarters in Kent, which existed for meditation and not for philanthropic purposes. The creation and conduct of the orphanage had been thrust upon the sisterhood by the will of a member long since deceased. It was unpopular with the sisterhood, who resented it as an excrescence, but bore it as an affliction decreed by divine Providence. Among the cloistered inmates of the Kentish manor-house there was no fanatical impulse towards Willesden.

They were good, religious women; but they craved retirement, and not action, for the satisfying of their spiritual needs. Otherwise they would have joined some other sisterhood in which noble lives are spent in deeds of charity and love. But there are angels of wrath, angels of mercy, and mere angels. These were mere angels. The possibility of being chosen by the Mother Superior to go out into the world again and take charge of the education, health, and morals of twenty sturdy and squalid little female orphans lived an abiding terror in their gentle breasts. A shipwrecked crew casting lots for the next occupant of the kettle could suffer no greater pangs of apprehension than did the Sisters of Saint Martha on the imminence of an appointment to the orphanage. They had taken vows of obedience. The Mother Superior's selection was final. The unfortunate nominee had to pack up her slender belongings and go to Willesden. Being a faulty human being (and none but a faulty, unpractical, unsympathetic human being can want, in these days of enlightenment, to shut herself up in a nunnery for the rest of her life, with the avowed intention of never doing a hand's turn for any one of God's creatures until the day of her death), she invariably regarded herself as a holy martyr and ruled the poor little devils of orphans for the greater glory of God (magnified entirely, be it understood, by her own martyrdom) than for the greater happiness of the poor little devils.

Sister Theophila—in entering into religion the Protestant Sisters changed the names by which they were known in the world, according to the time-honoured tradition of an alien church—Sister Theophila, with the temperament of the recluse, had been thrust into this position of responsibility against her will. She performed her duties with scrupulous exactitude and pious resignation. Her ideal of life was the ascetic, and to this ideal the twenty orphans had to conform. She did not love the orphans.

Her staff consisted of one matron, a married woman of a much humbler class than her own. Possibly she might have loved the orphans had she not seen such a succession of them, and her own work been less harassing. Twenty female London orphans from disreputable homes are a tough handful. When you insist on their conformity with the ascetic ideal, they become tougher. They will not allow themselves to be loved.

"And ungrateful!" exclaimed the matron, one day when she was taking Risca round the institution. He had expressed to Sister Theophila his desire to visit it, and she, finding him entirely unsympathetic, had handed him over to her subordinate. "None of them know what gratitude is. As soon as they get out of here, they forget everything that has been done for them; and as for coming back to pay their respects, or writing a letter even, they never think of it."

Kitchen, utensils, floors, walls, dormitory, orphans—all were spotlessly clean, the orphans sluiced and scrubbed from morning to night; but of things that might give a little hint of the joy of life there was no sign.

"This is the infirmary," said the matron, with her hand on the door-knob.

"I should like to see it," said John.

They entered. An almost full-grown orphan, doing duty as nurse, rose from her task of plain sewing and bobbed a curtsy. The room was clean, comfortless, dark, and cold. Two pictures, prints of the Crucifixion and the Martyrdom of St. Stephen, hung on the walls. There were three narrow, hard beds, two of which were occupied. Some grapes on a chair beside one of them marked the patient in whom he was interested. John noticed angrily that some flowers which he had sent the day before had been confiscated.

"This is the gentleman who has been so kind to you," said the matron.

Unity Blake looked wonderingly into the dark, rugged face of the man who stood over her and regarded her with mingled pain and pity. They had not told her his name. This, then, was the unknown benefactor whose image, like that of some elusive Apollo, Giver of Things Beautiful, had haunted her poor dreams.

"Can't you say, 'Thank you?' " said the matron.

"Thank you, sir," said Unity Blake.

Even in those three words her accent was unmistakably cockney—as unmistakably cockney as the coarse-featured, snub-nosed, common little face. In happier, freer conditions she would have done her skimpy hair up in patent curlers and worn a hat with a purple feather, and joined heartily in the raucous merriment of her comrades at the pickle-factory. Here, however, she was lying, poor little devil, thought Risca, warped from childhood by the ascetic ideal, and wrecked body and spirit by unutterable cruelty. In her eyes flickered the patient apprehension of the ill-treated dog.

"I hope you will soon get better," he said, with sickening knowledge of that which lay hidden beneath the rough bedclothes.

"Yes, sir," said Unity.

"It 's chiefly her nerves now," said the matron. "She hollers out of nights, so she can't be put into the dormitory."

"Do you like the things I send you?" asked John.

"Yes, sir."

"Is there anything special you'd like to have?"

"No, sir."

But he caught a certain wistfulness in her glance.

"She does n't want anything at all," said the matron, and the girl's eyelids fluttered. "She's being spoiled too much as it is already."

John bent his heavy brows on the woman. She spoke not shrewishly, not unkindly, merely with lack of love and understanding. He repressed the bitter retort that rose to his lips. But at the same time a picture rose before him of another sick-room, a dainty sea-chamber open to sun and sky, where pillows of down were not forbidden, where flowers and exquisite colours and shapes gladdened the eye, where Love, great and warm and fulfilling, hovered over the bed. No gulls with round, yellow eyes came to the windows of this whitewashed prison with messages from the world of air and sea; no Exquisite Auntship, no Great High Favourite, no Lord High Constable, executed their high appointed functions; no clock with chimes like a bell swung in a sea-cave told the hours to this orphan child of misery. He realized in an odd way that Stellamaris, too, was an orphan. And he remembered, from the awful evidence, that this child was just over fifteen—Stella's age. Again rose the picture of the cherished one in her daintily ribboned dressing-jacket, as filmy and unsubstantial as if made of sea-foam, with her pure, happy face, her mysterious, brown pools of eyes, her hair lovingly brushed to caressing softness; and he looked down on Unity Blake. Man though he was, the bit of clean sailcloth that did duty as a nightgown moved his compassion.

He did his best to talk with her awhile; but it was a one-sided conversation, as the child could reply only in monosyllables. The matron fidgeted impatiently, and he said good-bye. Her wistful glance followed him to the door. Outside he turned.

"There is just one thing I want to say to her."

He left the matron and darted back into the room.

"I'm sure there must be something you would like me to bring you," he whispered. "Don't be afraid. Any mortal thing."

The child's lips twitched and she looked nervously from side to side.

"What is it? Tell me."

"Oh, sir," she pleaded breathlessly, "might I have some peppermint bull's-eyes."

When Herold returned to his dressing-room after the first act,—the piece for which he had been rehearsing had started a successful career,— he found Risca sitting in a straight-backed chair and smoking a pipe.

"Hallo, John! I did n't know you were in front. Why did n't you tell me? It's going splendidly, is n't it?"

He glowed with the actor's excited delight in an audience's enthusiastic reception of a new play. His glow sat rather oddly upon him, for he was made up as a decrepit old man, with bald wig, and heavy, blue patches beneath his eyes.

"No, I'm not in front," said John.

"I see now," smiled Herold, glancing at his friend's loose tweed suit. No clothes morning or evening ever fitted Risca. Herold called him "The Tailors' Terror."

"I want to talk to you, Wallie," said he.

"Have a drink? No? I sha' n't want anything, Perkins," said he to the waiting dresser. "Call me when I 'm on in the second act. I don't change," he explained.

"I know," said John. "That 's why I 've come now."

"What's the matter?" Herold asked, sitting in the chair before the dressing-table, bright with mirrors and electric lights and sticks of grease paint and silver-topped pots and other paraphernalia.

"Nothing particular. Only hell, just as usual. I saw that child to-day."

Herold lit a cigarette.

"Have you ever speculated on what becomes of the victims in cases of this kind?" asked John.

"Not particularly," said Herold, seeing that John wanted to talk.

"What do you think can become of a human creature in the circumstances of this poor little wretch? Her childhood is one vista of bleak ugliness. Never a toy, never a kiss, not even the freedom of the gutter. Unless you 've been there, you can't conceive the soul-crushing despair of that infernal orphanage. She leaves it and goes into the world. She goes out of a kind of dreary Greek hades into a Christian hell. It lasted for months. She was too ignorant and spiritless to complain, and to whom was she to complain? Now she's sent back again, just like a sick animal, to hades. Fancy, they would n't let her have a few flowers in' the room! It makes me mad to think of it. And when she gets well again, she 'll have to earn her living as a little slave in some squalid Household. But what's going to become of that human creature morally and spiritually? That's what I want to know."

"It's an interesting problem," said Herold. "She may be either a benumbed half-idiot or a vicious, vindictive she-brute."

"Just so," said John. "That is, if she goes to slave in some squalid household. But suppose she were transferred to different surroundings altogether? Suppose she had ease of life, loving care, and all the rest of it?"

The senile travesty of Herold laughed.

"You want me to say that she may develop into some sort of flower of womanhood."

"Do you think she might?" John asked seriously. "My dear fellow," said Herold, "there are Heaven knows how many hundred million human beings on the face of the earth, and every one of them is different from the others. How can one tell what any particular young woman whom one does n't know might or might not do in given circumstances? But if you want me to say whether I think it right for you to step in and look after the poor little devil's future, then I do say it's right. It 's stunning of you. It's the very best thing you can do. It will give the poor little wretch a chance, at any rate, and will give you something outside yourself to think of."

"I was going to do it whether you thought it right or not," said Risca.

Herold laughed again. "For a great, hulking bull of a man you 're sometimes very feminine, John."

"I wanted to tell you about it, that 's all," said Risca. "I made up my mind this afternoon. The only thing is what the deuce am I to do with a child of fifteen in Fenton Square?"

"Is she pretty?"

"Lord, no. Coarse, undersized little cockney, ugly as sin."

"Anyhow," said Herold, extinguishing his cigarette in the ash-tray, "it's out of the question." He rose from his chair. "Look here," he cried with an air of inspiration, "why not send her down to The Channel House?"

"I'm not going to shift responsibilities on to other people's shoulders," John growled in his obstinate way. "This child 's my responsibility. I 'm going to see her through somehow. As to Southcliff, you must be crazy to suggest it. What's to prevent her, one fine day, from getting into Stella's room and talking? My God! it would be appalling!"

Herold agreed. He had spoken thoughtlessly.

"I should just think so," said Risca. "The idea of such a tale of horror being told in that room—"

The dresser entered. "Miss Mercier has just gone on, sir."

"Well, just think out something else till I come back," said Herold. "At any rate, Fenton Square won't do."

He left John to smoke and meditate among the clothes hanging up on pegs and the framed photographs on the walls and the array of grease paints on the dressing-table. John walked up and down the narrow space in great perplexity of mind. Herold was right. He could not introduce Unity Blake into lodgings, saying that he had adopted her. Landladies would not stand it. Even if they would, what in the world could he do with her? Could he move into a house or a flat and persuade a registry-office to provide him with a paragon of a housekeeper? That would be more practicable. But, even then, what did he know of the training, moral and spiritual, necessary for a girl of fifteen? He was not going to employ her as a servant. On that he was decided. What sort of a position she should have he did not know; but her floor-scrubbing, dish-scraping days were over. She should have ease of life and loving care—his own phrase stuck in his head—especially loving care; and he was the only person in the world who could see that she got it. She must live under his roof. That was indisputable. But how? In lodgings or a flat? He went angrily round and round the vicious circle.

When Herold returned, he dragged him round and round, too, until Perkins appeared to help him to change for the third act. Then John had to stop. He clapped on his hat. He must go and work.

"And you have n't a single suggestion to make?" he asked.

"I have one," said Herold, fastening his shirt-studs while Perkins was buttoning his boots. "But it's so commonplace and unromantic that you 'd wreck the dressing-room if I made it."

"Well, what is it?" He stood, his hand on the door-knob.

"You 've got a maiden aunt somewhere, have n't you?"

"Oh, don't talk rot!" said John. "I'm dead serious."

And he went out and banged the door behind him. He walked the streets furiously angry with Herold. He had gone to consult him on a baf-fling problem. Herold had suggested a maiden aunt as a solution. He had but one, his mother's sister. Her name was Gladys. What was a woman of over fifty doing with such an idiot name? His Aunt Gladys lived at Croydon and spent her time solving puzzles and following the newspaper accounts of the doings of the royal family. She knew nothing. He remem-bered when he was a boy at school coming home for the holidays cock-a-whoop at having won the high jump in the school athletics sports. His Aunt Gladys, while professing great interest, had said, "But what I don't understand, dear, is—what do you get on to jump down from?" He had smiled and explained, but he had felt cold in the pit of his stomach. A futile lady. His opinion of her had not changed. In these days John was rather an intolerant fellow.

Chance willed it, however, that when he reached Fenton Square he found a letter which began "My dearest John" and ended "Your loving Aunt Gladys." And it was the letter of a very sweet-natured gentlewoman.

John sat down at his desk to work, but ideas would not come. At last he lit his pipe, threw himself into a chair in front of the fire, and smoked till past midnight, with his heavy brows knitted in a tremendous frown.

# CHAPTER VI

THE same frown darkened Risca's brow the next day as he waited for admittance at his Aunt Gladys's door. It was such a futile little door to such a futile little house; he could have smashed in the former with a blow of his fist, and he could have jumped into the latter through the first-floor windows. With his great bulk he felt himself absurdly out of scale. The tragedy looming huge in his mind was also absurdly out of scale with his errand. The house was one of a row of twenty perky, gabled, two-storied little villas, each coyly shrinking to the farthermost limit of its tiny front garden, and each guarding the privacy of its interior by means of muslin curtains at the windows, tied back by ribbons, the resultant triangle of transparency being obscured by a fat-leafed plant. The terrace bore the name of "Tregarthion Villas," and the one inhabited by Miss Lindon was called "The Oaks." It was a sham little terrace full of sham little gentilities. John hated it. What could have induced his mother's sister to inhabit such a sphere of flimsiness?

Flimsiness, also, met him inside, when he was shown through a bamboo-furnished passage into a gimcrack little drawing-room. He tried several chairs dubiously with his hand, shook his head, and seated himself on a couch. Everything in the room seemed flimsy and futile. He had the impression that everything save a sham spinning-wheel and a half-solved jig-saw puzzle on the little table was draped in muslin and tied up with pink ribbons. A decrepit black-and-tan terrier, disturbed in his slumbers in front of the fire, barked violently. A canary in a cage by the window sang in discordant emulation. John poised his hat and stick on the curved and slippery satin-covered couch, and they fell with a clatter to the floor. The frown deepened on his brow. Why had he come to this distracting abode of mindlessness? He wished he had brought Herold gyved and manacled. What with the dog and the canary and the doll's-house furniture, the sensitive and fastidious one would have gone mad. He would have gloated over his ravings. It would have served him right.

The door opened suddenly, the draught blowing down a fan and a photograph-frame, and Miss Lindon entered.

"My dear John, how good of you to come and see me!"

She was a fat, dumpy woman of fifty, lymphatic and, at first sight, characterless. She lacked colour. Her eyes were light, but neither blue nor green nor hazel; her straight hair was of the nondescript hue of light-brown hair turning gray. Her face was fleshy and sallow, marked by singularly few lines. She had lived a contented life, unscarred by care and unruffled by desire. Her dreams of the possibilities of existence did not pierce beyond the gimcrackeries of Tregarthion Villas. As for the doings of the great world,—wars, politics, art, social upheavals,—she bestowed on them, when they were obtruded on her notice, the same polite and unintelligent interest as she had bestowed on her nephew's athletic feats in the days gone by.

However, she smiled very amiably at John, and reached up to kiss him on both cheeks, her flabby, white hands lightly resting on each coat-sleeve. Having done this, she caught up the barking dog, who continued to growl from the soft shelter of arm and bosom with the vindictiveness of pampered old age.

"Naughty Dandy! I hope you were n't frightened at him, John. He never really does bite."

"What does he do then? Sting?" John asked with gruff sarcasm.

"Oh, no," said Miss Lindon, round-eyed; "he 's quite harmless, I assure you. Don't you remember Dandy? But it's a long time since you 've been to see me, John. It must be three or four years. What have you been doing all this time?"

Her complacency irritated him. The canary never ceased his ear-splitting noise. The canary is a beautiful, gentle bird—stuffed; alive, he is pestilence made vocal. Risca lost his temper.

"Surely you must know, Aunt Gladys. I 've been wandering through hell with a pack of little devils at my heels."

Startled, she lifted up her arms and dropped Dandy, who slithered down her dress and sought a morose shelter under the table.

"My dear John!" she exclaimed.

"I'm very sorry; I did n't mean to use strong language," said he, putting his hands to his ears. "It's all that infernal canary."

"Oh, poor Dickie! Don't you like to hear Dickie sing? He sings so beautifully. The gas-man was here the other day and said that, if I liked, he would enter him for a competition, and he was sure he would get first prize. But if you don't like to hear him, dear—though I really can't understand why—I can easily make him stop." She drew a white napkin from the drawer of the table on which the cage was placed and threw it over the top. The feathered steam-whistle swallowed his din in an angry gurgle or two and became silent "Poor Dickie, he thinks it 's a snowstorm! What were we talking about, John? Do sit down."

John resumed his seat on the slippery couch, and Miss Lindon, having snatched Dandy from his lair, sat by his side, depositing the dog between them.

"You asked me what I had been doing for the last few years," said he.

"Ah, yes. That 's why I wrote to you yesterday, dear."

She had written to him, in fact, every month for many years, long, foolish letters in which everything was futile save the genuine affection underlying them, and more often than not John had taken them as read and pitched them into the waste-paper basket. His few perfunctory replies, however, had been treasured and neatly docketed and pigeon-holed in the bureau in her bedroom, together with the rest of her family archives and other precious documents. Among them was a famous recipe for taking mulberry stains out of satin. That she prized inordinately.

"I should n't like to drift apart from dear Ellen's boy," she said with a smile.

"And I should n't like to lose touch with you, my dear aunt," said John, with more graciousness. "And that is why I've come to see you to-day. I've had rather a bad time lately."

"I know—that awful case in the papers." She shivered. "Don't let us talk of it. You must try to forget it. I wrote to you how shocked I was. I asked you to come and stay with me, and said I would do what I could to comfort you. I believe in the ties of kinship, my dear, and I did n't like to think of you bearing your trouble alone."

"That was very kind indeed of you," said John, who had missed the invitation hidden away in the wilderness of the hastily scanned sixteen-page letter. He flushed beneath his dark skin, aware of rudeness. After all, when a lady invites you to her house, it is boorish to ignore the offered hospitality. It is a slight for which one can scarcely apologize. But she evidently bore him no malice.

"It was only natural on my part," she said amiably. "I shall never forget when poor Flossie died. You remember Flossie, don't you? She used to look so pretty, with her blue bow in her hair, and no one will ever persuade me that she was n't poisoned by the people next door; they were dreadful people. I wish I could remember their name; it was something like Blunks. Anyhow, I was inconsolable, and Mrs. Tawley asked me to stay with her to get over it. I shall never forget how grateful I was. I'm sure you 're looking quite poorly, John," she added in her inconsequent way. "Let me get you a cup of tea. It will do you good."

John declined. He wanted to accomplish his errand, but the longer he remained in the company of this lady devoid of the sense of values, the more absurd did that errand seem. A less obstinate man than he would have abandoned it, but John had made up his mind to act on Herold's suggestion, although he mentally bespattered the suggester with varied malediction. He rose and, making his way between the flimsy chairs and tables, stood on the hearth-rug, his hands in his pockets. Unconsciously he scowled at his placid and smiling aunt, who remained seated on the couch, her helpless hands loosely folded on her lap.

"Did you ever hear of a child called Unity Blake?"

"Was that the girl—"

"Yes."

"What an outlandish name! I often wonder how people come to give such names to children."

"Never mind her name, my dear aunt," said John, gruffly. "I want to tell you about her."

He told her—he told her all he knew. She listened, horror-stricken, regarding him with open mouth and streaming eyes.

"And what do you think is my duty?" asked John, abruptly.

Miss Lindon shook her head. "I 'm sure I don't know what to advise you, dear. I 'll try to find out some kind Christian people who want a servant."

"I don't want any kind Christian people at all," said John. "I'm going to make up in ease and happiness for all the wrongs that humanity has inflicted on her. I am going to adopt her, educate her, fill her up with the good things of life."

"That's very fine of you, John," said Miss Lindon. "Some people are as fond of their adopted children as of their own. I remember Miss Engleshaw adopted a little child. She was four, if I remember right, and she used to dress her so prettily. I used to go and help her choose frocks. Really they were quite expensive. Now I come to think of it, John, I could help you that way with little Unity. I don't think gentlemen have much experience in choosing little girls' frocks. How old is she?"

"Nearly sixteen," said John.

"That's rather old," said Miss Lindon, from whose mind this new interest seemed to have driven the tragic side of the question. "It's a pity you could n't have begun when she was four."

"It is," said John.

"Only if you had begun with her at four, you would n't be wanting to adopt her now," said Miss Lindon, with an illuminating flash of logic.

"Quite so," replied John.

There was a span of silence. John mechanically drew his pipe from his pocket, eyed it with longing, and replaced it. Miss Lindon took the aged black-and-tan terrier in her arms and whispered to it in baby language. She was a million leagues from divining the object of her nephew's visit. John looked at her despairingly. Had she not a single grain of common sense? At last he strode across the room, a Gulliver in a new Lilliput, and sat down again by her side.

"Look here, 'Aunt Gladys," he said desperately, "if I adopt a young woman of sixteen, I must have another woman in the house—a lady, one of my own family. I could n't have people saying horrid things about her and me."

Miss Lindon assented to the proposition. John was far too young and good-looking ("Oh, Lord!" cried John)—yes, he was—to pose as the father of a pretty, grown-up young woman.

"The poor child is n't pretty," said he.

"It does n't matter," replied Miss Lindon. "Beauty is only skin deep, and I've known plain people who are quite fascinating. There was Captain Brownlow's wife—do you remember the Brownlows? Your poor mother was so fond of them—"

"Yes, yes," said John, impatiently. "He had wet hands, and used to mess my face about when I was a kid. I hated it. The question is, however, whom am I going to get to help me with Unity Blake?"

"Ah, yes, to be sure. Poor little Unity! You must bring her to see me sometimes. Give me notice, and I 'll make her some of my cream-puffs.

Children are always so fond of them. You ought to remember my cream-puffs."

"Good heavens!" he cried, with a gesture that set the dog barking. "There's no question of cream-puffs. Can't you see what I'm driving at? I want you to come and keep house for me and help me to look after the child."

He rose, and his great form towered so threateningly over her that Dandy barked at him with a toy terrier's furious and impotent rage.

"I come and live with you?" gasped Miss Lindon.

"Yes," said John, turning away and lumbering back to the fireplace. The dog, perceiving that he had struck terror into the heart of his enemy, dismissed him with a scornful snarl, and curled himself up by the side of his stupefied mistress.

It was done; the proposal had been made, according to the demands of his pig-headedness. Now that he had made it, he realized its insanity. He contrasted this home of flim-flammeries and its lap-dogs and canaries and old-maidish futilities with his own tobacco-saturated and paper-littered den; this life of trivialities with his own fighting career; this incapacity to grasp essentials with his own realization of the conflict of world-forces. The ludicrous incongruity of a partnership between the two of them in so fateful a business as the healing of a human soul appealed to his somewhat dull sense of humour. The whole idea was preposterous. In his saturnine way he laughed.

"It's rather a mad notion, is n't it?"

"I don't think so at all," replied Miss Lindon in a most disconcertingly matter-of-fact tone. "The only thing is that since poor papa died I've had so little to do with gentlemen, and have forgotten their ways. You see, dear, you have put me quite in a flutter. How do I know, for instance, what you would like to have for breakfast? Your dear grandpapa used to have only one egg boiled for two minutes—he was most particular— and a piece of dry toast; whereas I well remember Mrs. Brownlow telling me that her husband used to eat a hearty meal of porridge and eggs and bacon, with an underdone beefsteak to follow. So you see, dear, I have no rule which I could follow; you would have to tell me."

"That's quite a detail," said John, rather touched by her unselfish, if tangential, dealing with the proposal. "The main point is," said he, moving a step or two forward, "would you care to come and play propriety for me and this daughter of misery?"

"Do you really want me to?"

"Naturally, since I've asked you."

She rose and came up to him. "My dear boy," she said with wet eyes, "I know I'm not a clever woman, and often when clever people like you talk, I don't in the least understand what they're talking about; but I did love your dear mother with all my heart, and I would do anything in the wide world for her son."

John took her hand and looked down into her foolish, kind face, which wore for the moment the dignity of love. "I'm afraid it will mean an uprooting of all your habits," said he, in a softened voice.

She smiled. "I can bring them with me," she said cheerfully. "You won't mind Dandy, will you? He'll soon get used to you. And as for Dickie," she added, with a touch of wistfulness, "I'm sure I can find a nice home for him."

John put his arm round her shoulder and gave her the kiss of a shy bear.

"My good soul," he cried, "bring fifty million Dickies if you like." He laughed. "There's nothing like the song of birds for the humanizing of the cockney child."

He looked around and beheld the little, gimcrack room with a new vision. After all, it was as much an expression of her individuality, and as genuine in the eyes of the high gods, as Herold's exquisitely furnished abode was of Herold's, or the untidy jumble of the room in Fenton Square was of his own. And all she had to live upon was a hundred and fifty pounds a year, and no artistic instincts or antecedents whatsoever.

"I feel a brute in asking you to give up this little place now that you've made it so pretty," he said.

Her face brightened at the praise. "It is pretty, is n't it?" Then she sighed as her eyes rested fondly on her possessions. "I suppose it would be too tiny for us all to live here."

"I'm afraid it would," said John. "Besides, we must live in London, on account of my work."

"In London?"

Miss Lindon's heart sank. She had lived in suburbs all her life, and found Croydon—the Lord knows why—the most delectable of them all. She had sat under Mr. Moneyfeather of Saint Michael's for many years

—such a dear, good man who preached such eloquent sermons! You could always understand him, too, which was a great comfort. And the church was just round the corner. In London folks had to go to church by omnibus, a most unpleasant and possibly irreverent prelude to divine worship. Besides, when you did get to the sacred edifice, you found yourself in a confusing land where all the clergy, even to the humblest deacon, were austere and remote strangers, who looked at members of their congregation with glassy and unsympathetic eyes when they passed them in the street. Here, in Croydon, on the contrary, when she met Mr. Moneyfeather in public places, he held her hand and patted it and inquired affectionately after Dandy's health. With a London vicar she could not conceive the possibility of such privileged terms of intimacy. London, where you did not know your next-door neighbor, and where you took no interest in the births of babies over the way; where no one ran in for a gossip in the mornings; where every street was a clashing, dashing High Street.

But though her face pictured her dismay, she was too generous to translate it into words. John never guessed her sacrifice.

"We'll go somewhere quiet," said he, after a while.

"We'll go wherever you like, dear," replied Miss Lindon, meekly, and she rang the bell for tea.

The main point decided, they proceeded to discuss the details of the scheme, the minds of each suffused in a misty wonder. If John had told the simple lady that she could serve him by taking command of a cavalry regiment, she would have agreed in her unselfish fashion, but she would have been not a whit more perplexed at the prospect. As for John he had the sensation of living in a fantastic dream. A child of six would have been a more practical ally. In the course of befogged conversation, however, it was arranged that Miss Lindon should transfer to the new house her worldly belongings, of which she was to give him an inventory, including Dandy and Dickie and her maid Phoebe, a most respectable girl of Baptist upbringing, who had been cruelly jilted by a prosperous undertaker in the neighborhood, whom, if you had seen him conducting a funeral, you would have thought as serious and God-fearing a man as the clergyman himself; which showed how hypocritical men could be, and how you ought never to trust to appearances. It was also settled that, as soon as Unity could be rescued from the guardianship of the orphanage authorities and comfortably installed in a convalescent home by the seaside, Miss Lindon would journey thither in order to make her ward's acquaintance. In the meanwhile John would go house-hunting.

"Walter Herold will help me," said John.

"That's your friend who acts, is n't it?" said Miss Lindon. "I have n't any objection to theatres myself. In fact, I often used to go to see Irving when I was young. You meet quite a nice class of people in the dress-circle. But I don't think ladies ought to go on the stage. I hope Mr. Herold won't put such an idea into Unity's head."

"I don't think he will," said John.

"Young girls are sometimes so flighty. My old friend Mrs. Willcox had a daughter who went on the stage, and she married an actor, and now has twelve children, and lives in Cheshire. I was hearing about her only the other day. I suppose Unity will have to be taught music and drawing and French like any other young lady."

"We might begin," replied John, "with more elementary accomplishments."

"I could teach her botany," said Miss Lindon, pensively. "I got first prize for it at school. I still have the book in a cupboard, and I could read it up. And I'm so glad I have kept my two volumes of pressed flowers. It's quite easy to learn, I assure you."

"I'm afraid, my dear," said John, "you 'll first have to teach her to eat and drink like a Christian, and blow her nose, and keep her face clean."

"Ah, that reminds me. My head's in a maze, and I can't think of everything at once, like some clever people. What kind of soap do gentlemen use? I 'll have to know, so as to supply you with what you like."

"Any old stuff that will make a lather," said John, rising.

"But some soaps are so bad for the skin," she objected anxiously.

"Vitriol would n't hurt my rhinoceros hide."

He laughed, and held out his hand. Further discussion was useless.

Miss Lindon accompanied him to the front gate and watched him stride down the perky terrace until he disappeared round the corner. Then she went slowly into the house and uncovered the canary, who blinked at her in oblique sullenness, and did not respond to her friendly "cheep" and the scratching of her finger against the rails of his cage. She turned to Dandy, who, snoring loud, was equally unresponsive. Feeling lonely and upset, she rang the bell.

"Phoebe," she said, when the angular and jilted maid appeared, "we are going to keep house for my nephew, Mr. Risca, and a young lady whom he has adopted. Will you tell me one thing? Is the lady of the house supposed to clean the gentlemen's pipes?"

"My father is a non-smoker, as well as a teetotaler, miss," replied Phoebe.

"Dear me!" murmured Miss Lindon. "It's going to be a great puzzle."

# CHAPTER VII

I T was a puzzle to John as much as to the palpitating lady, and in the maze of his puzzledom the gleam of humour that visited him during their interview lost its way. Walter Herold's eyes, however, twinkled maliciously when he heard John's account at once rueful and pig-headed. Then he grew serious.

"It will be comic opera all the time. It can't be done."

"It 's going to be done," said John, obstinately. "There's nothing else to do. If I were a rich man, I could work wonders with a scratch in my cheque-book. I could hire an unexceptionable colonel's or clergyman's widow to do the business. But I'm not. How I'm going to get the house together, as it is, I don't know. Besides," he added, turning with some savageness on his friend, "if you think it a comic-opera idea, kindly remember it was you who started it."

Though Herold was silenced for the moment, to the back of his mind still clung the first suggestion he had made. It was the common-sense idea that, given a knowledge of John's relations with the Southcliff household, would have occurred to anybody. John had it in his power to befriend the unhappy child without trying the rash experiment of raising her social status. Wherein lay the advantage of bringing her up as a lady? A pampered maid in a luxurious home does not drag out the existence of a downtrodden slave. Such have been known to smile and sing, even to bless their stars, and finally to marry a prince in grocer's disguise, and to live happy ever afterwards. With John's description of the girl's dog-like eyes in his memory, Herold pictured her as a devoted handmaiden to Stellamaris, a romantic, mediaeval appanage of the sea-chamber. What more amazingly exquisite destiny could await not only one bred in the gutter, but any damsel far more highly born? Her silence as to the past could be insured under ghastly penalties which would have no need of imagination for their appeal. That of course would be an ultimate measure. He felt certain that a couple of months' probation in the atmosphere of the Channel House would compel any human being not a devil incarnate to unthinking obedience to the Unwritten Law. By following this scheme, Unity would achieve salvation, Stellamaris acquire a new interest in life, and John himself be saved not only from financial worries, but from grotesquely figuring in comic opera. As for Miss Lindon, he felt certain that she would fall down on her knees and offer up thanksgivings to the God of her grandmothers.

But of this scheme John would hear no word. He bellowed his disapproval like an angry bull, rushed out, as it were, with lowered head, into the thick of house-agents, and before Herold could catch him in a milder humour he had signed the lease of a little house in Kilburn, overlooking the Paddington Recreation Ground. By the time it was put in order and decorated, he declared, Unity would be in a fit condition to take up her abode there with Miss Lindon and himself.

"Where is this convalescent home you 're going to send her to?" asked Herold.

John did not know. A man could not attend to everything at once. But there were thousands. He would find one. Then, it being the end of the week, he went down to the Channel House, where, by the midnight train on Saturday, Herold joined him.

It was Herold who laid John's rash project before Sir Oliver and Lady Blount.

"Why in the world," cried the latter, checking the hospitable flow of tea from the teapot and poising it in mid air—they were at breakfast— "why in the world does n't he send the child to us?"

John, in desperation, went over his arguments. The discussion grew heated. Sir Oliver, with a twirl of his white moustache, gave him to understand that to take folks out of the station to which it had pleased God to call them was an act of impiety to which he, Sir Oliver, would not be a party. His wife, irritated by her husband's dictatorial manner, demurred to the proposition. John had every right to do as he liked. If you adopted a child, you brought it up as a matter of course in your own rank in life. Why adopt it? Why not? They bickered as usual. At last John got up in a fume and went to cool his head in the garden. It was outrageous that he should never be allowed to mismanage his own affairs. There was the same quarreling interference when he proposed to go to Australia. He lit his pipe and puffed at it furiously. After a while Lady Blount joined him.

She declared herself to be on his side; but, as in most sublunary things, there was a compromise.

"At any rate, my dear John, give your friends a little chance of helping you," she said. "If you set your face against Walter's plan, at least you can send the child down here to recuperate. Nurse Holroyd will keep a trained eye on her, and she can play about the garden and on the beach as much as she likes. I do understand what you 're afraid of with regard to Stella—"

"Oliver and Walter are wooden-headed dolts," cried John.

She smiled wifely agreement. "There need be no danger, I assure you. We can give the child a room in the other wing, and forbid her the use of Stella's side of the house. Stella's room will be guarded. You may trust me. Have I ever failed yet? And Stella need never know of her presence in the place. After all," she continued, touching his coat-sleeve, "I think I am a bit nearer to your life than your Aunt Gladys."

John laughed at the flash of jealousy.

"If you put it that way, it's very hard to refuse."

"Then you 'll send her?"

He knocked the ashes out of his pipe against the heel of his boot, thus hiding the annoyance on his face, but he yielded. "For her convalescence only."

The touch on his arm deepened into a squeeze.

"If you had said no, I should have been so hurt, dear."

"I only want to do what's decently right," said he.

"I think you 're acting nobly," she said.

"My dear Julia," said he, "I'm not going to listen to infatuated rubbish."

He cast off her hand somewhat roughly, but continued to walk with her up and down the terrace, talking intimately of his plans concerning the adopted child and the psychological problem she presented. No man, in his vain heart of hearts, really resents a woman calling him a noble fellow, be she ten years old or his great-great-grandmother. They parted soon afterward, Lady Blount to prepare herself for church, which Sir Oliver and she attended with official regularity, and John to worship in his own way—one equally acceptable, I should imagine, to the Almighty—in the sea-chamber of Stellamaris.

He found Herold there, in the midst of a dramatic entertainment, with Stellamaris and Constable for audience. How familiar and unchanging was the scene! The great, bright room, the wood fire blazing merrily up the chimney, the huge dog lifting his eyes and stirring his tail in welcome, and against the background of sea and sky the fairy head on its low pillow. Stella smiled, put a finger to her lips, and pointed to a chair.

"Go on," she said to Herold.

"We're in the middle of the first act, just before my exit," said the latter.

John became aware, as he listened, that Herold was sketching the piece in which he was playing, a fragrant comedy full of delicate sentiment and humour. His own scenes he acted in full, taking all the parts. Stella lay entranced, and fixed on him glorious eyes of wonder. How could he do it? At one astonishing moment he was a young girl, at another her sailor sweetheart, at another a palsied, mumbling old man. And when, as the old man, he took the weeping girl under his arm and hobbled away on his stick, leaving the young fellow baffled and disappointed, it seemed an optical illusion, so vivid was the picture. He recrossed the room, smiling, the real Walter Herold again; Stella clapped her hands.

"Isn't he perfectly lovely!"

"Stunning," said John, who had often witnessed similar histrionic exhibitions in that room, and had always been impressed with their exquisite art. "I wish you could see the real thing, dear."

Stella glanced out to sea for a moment and glanced back at him.

"I don't think I do," she said. "It would be too real."

"What do you mean by that?"

Herold clapped John on the shoulder. "Can't you see what a subtle little artistic soul she has?" he cried enthusiastically. "She has evolved for herself the fundamental truth, the vital essence of all art—suggestion. She means that, in order that the proper harmony should be established between the artist and the person to whom he is making his appeal, the latter must go a certain way to meet him. He must exercise his imagination, too, on the same lines. The measure of your appreciation, say, of Turner, is the length of the imaginative journey you make toward him. When a thing needs no imaginative effort to get hold of it, it's not a work of art. You haven't got to go half way to the housemaid to realize a slice of bread and butter. That's where so-called realism fails. Stella's afraid that if she saw us all in flesh and blood on the stage, nothing would be left to her imagination. She's right in essence."

Stella smiled on him gratefully. "That's exactly how I feel, but I could n't have expressed it. How do you manage to know all these funny things that go on inside me?"

"I wish I did," said Herold, with a touch of wistfulness.

"But you do." She turned to John. "Does n't he, Belovedest?"

Herold glanced at the clock. "I must run. I promised Sir Oliver to go to church. We 'll have the rest of the play this afternoon."

"Why don't you go to church, too?" Stella asked when Herold had gone.

"I 'm not so good as Walter," he replied.

"You are," she cried warmly.

He shook his head. He knew that Herold's churchgoing was not an act of great spiritual devotion; for the Southcliff service was dull, and the vicar, good, limited man, immeasurably duller. It was an act of characteristic unselfishness: he went so as to be a buffer between Sir Oliver and his wife, who invariably quarreled during their sedate, official walk to and from morning service, and on this particular occasion, with fresh contentious matter imported from the outside, were likely to hold discourse with each other more than usually acrimonious.

"Walter's a sort of saint," said he, "who can hear the music of the spheres. I can't. I just jog along the ground and listen to barrel-organs.",

They argued the point for a while, then drifted back to Herold's acting, thence to the story of the play.

"I wonder what 's going to happen," said Stellamaris. "If Dorothy does n't marry her sailor, I shall never get over it."

John laughed. "Suppose the sailor turns out to be a dark, double-dyed, awful villain?"

"Oh, he can't; he's young and beautiful."

"Don't you believe that beautiful people can be villains?"

"No," said Stella; "it 's silly." She looked for a while out to her familiar sea, the source of all her inspiration, and her brows were delicately knitted. "I may as well tell you," she said at last with great solemnity, "a conclusion I've come to after lots of thought—yes, dear Belovedest, I lie here and think lots and lots—I don't believe the Bible is true."

"My dear Stella!" he cried, scandalized. He himself did not believe in the Jonah and whale story or in many other things contained in Holy Writ, and did not go to church, and was sceptical as to existence of anthropomorphous angels; but he held the truly British conviction of the necessity of faith in the young and innocent. Stella having been bred in the unquestioning calm of Anglican orthodoxy, her atheistical pronouncement was staggering. "My dear Stella!" he cried. "The Bible not true?"

She flushed. "Oh, I believe it's all true as far as it goes," she exclaimed quickly. "But it 's not true about people to-day. All those dreadful things that are told in it—the cruelty of Joseph's brethren, for instance—did happen; but they happened so long, long ago. People have had lots and lots of time to grow better. Have n't they?"

"They certainly have, my dear," said John.

"And then Christ came to wash away everybody's sins."

"He did," said John.

"So it seems to me we can disregard a great deal of religion. It does n't affect us. We are n't good like the angels, I know," she remarked with the seriousness of a young disputant in the school of Duns Scotus; "but men don't kill each other, or rob each other, or be cruel to the weak, and nobody tells horrible lies, do they?"

"I think we 've improved during the last few thousand years," said John.

"So," said Stellamaris, continuing her argument, "as the fathers have no particular sins, they can't be visited much on the children. And if there are no wicked people to go to hell, hell must be empty, and therefore useless. So it's no good believing in it."

"Not the slightest good in the world," said John, fervently.

"And now that everybody loves God," she went on, "I don't see what's the good of religion. I love you, Great High Belovedest, but there's no need for me to get a form of words to say 'I love you,' 'I love you,' all day long. One's heart says it."

"What 's your idea of God, Stella dear?" he asked in a curiously husky voice.

She beckoned to him. He drew his chair nearer and bent toward her. She waved her fragile arms bare to the elbow.

"I think we breathe God," she said.

John Risca went back to Fenton Square and breathed the ghosts of the night-before-last's sprats, and he journeyed to the Orphanage of Saint Martha at Willesden and breathed the prison taint of that abode of hopelessness, and he wrote hard at night in a tiny room breathing the hot, electric atmosphere of a newspaper-office; and ever horribly dominant in his mind was the woman whom once he had held in his arms, who now performed degrading tasks in shameful outward investiture, and inwardly lashed at him with malignant hatred through the distorted prism of her soul, and he breathed the clammy dungeon atmosphere of his own despair; and sitting at his writing-table one night, after having spent the day in court listening to the loathsome details of a sickening murder, a crime passionnel, with the shock of which the wide world was ringing, —his American syndicate insisted on a vivid story, and he had to earn the journalist's daily bread,—the ignorant, fanciful words of Stellamaris flashed through his mind—"I think we breathe God." He threw back his head and laughed aloud, and then let it drop upon his arms, folded over his wet page of copy, and sobbed in a man's dry-eyed agony of spirit.

And as the prophet Elijah, when sore beset, found the Lord neither in the wind nor in the earthquake nor in the fire, so did John Risca find Him not in all these daily things through which he had passed. Life was fierce, inhuman, a devastating medley of blind forces, making human effort a vain thing, human aspiration a derision, faith in mankind a grotesque savage Ju-ju superstition. There was no God, no beneficent influence making order out of chaos; for it was all chaos. Jezebel and her lusts and cruelties ruled the world—this cloaca of a world. Man argues ever from particular to general, instinctively flying to the illogic on which the acceptance of human life is based. To Risca, at nine and twenty, his pain translated itself into terms of the world-pain; and so will it happen to all generations of all the sons and daughters of men.

After a while, as he sat there motionless, he grew aware of something delicately soft touching his ear and hair. For a moment he had the absurd fancy that Stellamaris stood beside him with caressing fingers. It became so insistent that he dallied with it, persuaded himself that she was there; he would have only to turn to see her in her childish grace. He heard a sound as of murmured speech. She seemed to whisper of quiet, far-off things. And then he seemed to hear the words: "The door is open. Go out into the wide spaces under heaven." He roused himself with a start, and, looking about him, perceived that the door of his sitting-room was indeed ajar, the ill-fitting old lock having slipped, thus causing a draught, which poured over his head and shoulders. He rose and clapped on his hat and went down-stairs. A ten-minutes' trudge on the pavements would clear his head for the work that had to be accomplished. But on his doorstep he halted. Away above the housetops on the other side of the dingy square sailed the full moon, casting a wake of splendour along the edge of a rack of cloud. And below it swam a single star.

He caught himself repeating stupidly, "Stella Maris, Star of the Sea." With an impatient shake of the shoulders he went his way through the narrow streets and emerged upon the broad and quiet thoroughfares about the Abbey and the Houses of Parliament. On Westminster Bridge the startling silver of the moonlit river brought him to a stand. The same glory was overspreading the mild sea below the windows of the Channel House. Perhaps Stella even then lay awake, as she often did of nights, and was watching it and was "breathing God." A great longing arose within him to stand on the beach beneath her window in the wide spaces under heaven. So he walked on, thinking vaguely of Stellamaris and her ways and mysteries, and reached his home again in a chastened mood. Like Elijah, he had found God neither in the wind nor in the earthquake nor in the fire; but who can tell whether he had not been brought into touch with something of the divine by the still, small voice that came through the draught of the crazy door?

# CHAPTER VIII

THINGS happened as John and Lady Blount had planned them. Sister Theophila, having satisfied herself that Unity Blake was not a second time being thrown to the wolves—Lady Blount herself undertook the negotiations—surrendered her without many regretful pangs. Unity Blake, fatalistic child of circumstance, surrendered herself without coherent thought. World authorities, vague in their nature, but irresistibly compelling in their force, had governed her life from her earliest years. The possibility of revolt, of assertion of her own individuality, was undreamed of in her narrow philosophy. She had the outlook on life of the slave; not the slave of the mettlesome temperament depicted by the late Mrs. Harriet Beecher Stowe and the late Mr. Longfellow, but the unaspiring deaf-mute of a barbaric harem. It is true that Lady Blount asked her whether she would like to go away to a nice house by the seaside, and afterward live for ever and ever with the kind gentleman who gave her peppermint bull's-eyes and the kind lady who had visited her one day, bringing her a pair of woollen mittens, and that Unity, after the manner of her class, had said, "Yes, ma'am"; but the consultation of Unity's wishes had been a pure formality. She had no idea of what the seaside meant, having never seen the sea or speculated on its nature. She could form no notion of her future life with the kind lady and gentleman, save perhaps that the pokers of the establishment might have other uses than as instruments of chastisement and that, at any rate, they might be applied cold and not red-hot. If they had taken her up without a word, and put her in an open coffin, and lowered her into an open grave, and left her there, Unity would have made no complaint, having at once no standard whereby to assess the right and wrong done to her, and no tribunal to which she could appeal higher than the vague world authorities above mentioned. The instinctive animal might have clambered out of the pit and wandered about the country-side in search of food and shelter, but that would have been all. The fervent human soul would have played but a small part.

So one day the matron came and dressed her in the parody of attire which she had worn during her lamentable excursion into the world, and men carried her, a creature of no volition, down-stairs, and put her into a cab with Lady Blount, and the two journeyed in a train for an hour or so, Unity lying flat on her back along one side of the carriage, and the lady sitting opposite, reading a magazine. The jolting of the train hurt her, but that was not the lady's fault. Sometimes the lady spoke to her, and she said, "Yes, ma'am," and, "No, ma'am," as she had been taught to do at the orphanage; but what the lady was saying she did not very well understand. She grasped, however, the lady's kindness of intention; and now and then the lady, looking up from her magazine, smiled and nodded encouragingly, an unfathomably mysterious proceeding, but curiously comforting. On the opposite side of the compartment was the most beautiful picture she had ever seen—lovely ladies in gorgeous raiment and handsome gentlemen sitting at little lamp-lit tables, eating a meal which chiefly consisted of scarlet birds; and there were other gentlemen, not quite so handsome, hovering about with dishes and bottles of wine; and the pillars of the hall were of pure marble, and the tops of them gold, and the ceiling was golden, too. In the foreground sat a peculiarly lovely lady in a red, low-cut frock, and an entrancingly handsome gentleman, and they were bending over the table and he held a wine-glass in his hand. Below she read the legend, "Supper at the Coliseum Hotel." She could scarcely keep her eyes off the picture. Lady Blount, noticing her rapt gaze, questioned her, and from her answers it was obvious that it was only the details that attracted her—the lovely ladies, the handsome men, the glitter and colour of the preposterously gaudy scene. The essence of it she did not grasp; her spirit was not transported into the shoddy fairy-land; her imagination was untouched by the potentialities of life which to a mind a little, a very little, more awakened it might, with all its vulgar crudity, have suggested.

After the railway journey she was lifted into another cab, and taken into a big house with wonderfully soft carpets and pictures on the walls. They carried her into a pretty room that looked like a bower of roses,—it had a rose-pattern wall-paper,—and from the window she could see trees and a great rolling expanse of country. She wondered why the place had no streets. They undressed her. A maid-servant, so trim and spruce that she addressed her as "ma'am," pointed to the heap of poor garments and asked:

"What are we to do with these, my lady?"

"Bury them," said Lady Blount.

"Ain't I never going out again, ma'am?" Unity inquired humbly.

"Of course, child. But we'll give you some decent clothes," said Lady Blount.

They put her in a bath and washed her. The soap smelled so good that surreptitiously she got hold of the cake and nosed it like a young dog. They dried her in warm towels, and slipped a night-dress over her meagre shoulders. It was then, perhaps, that fingering the gossamer thing, taking up a bunch of stuff in her fist and slowly letting it go, in a dreamy wonder, she first began to realize that she was on the threshold of a new life. Not even the soft bed or the delicious chicken-broth that was brought later eclipsed the effect produced by the night-dress. It had embroidery and all sorts of blue ribbons—an epoch-making garment.

Some time later, the maid, having drawn the curtains and smoothed her pillow and tucked her in, said:

"If you want anything in the night, just touch that bell, and I'll come to you."

Unity looked at her half comprehendingly. "Ring a bell? I should n't dare."

"Why?"

"It's only missuses that ring bells."

"Those are Lady Blount's orders, anyway," laughed the maid. "'Ere," said Unity, with a beckoning finger. "What are they treating me like this for?"

So might a succulently fed sailor have suspiciously interrogated one of a cannibal tribe.

"How else would you want them to treat you?" asked the unpercipient maid. "You 've come down here to get well, have n't you?" She bent down and tied a loosened ribbon in a bow. "I declare if you have n't got on one of Miss Stella's nighties!"

"Who is Miss Stella?" asked Unity.

"Miss Stella?" The maid stared. To be in the Channel House and not know who Miss Stella was! "Miss Stella?" she repeated blankly. "Why, Miss Stella, of course."

The days passed quickly, and in the pure, strong air and under the generous treatment Unity began to mend. She also began to form a dim conception of Miss Stella. It was gradually borne in upon her mind that not only the household, but the whole cosmic scheme, revolved round Miss Stella. Sometimes they called her by another name, Stellamaris, which sounded queer, like the names of princesses in the fairy-tales they had given her to read. Perhaps this Miss Stella was a fairy-princess. Why not? Thus it came to pass that even in the darkened mind of this child of wretchedness Stellamaris began to shine with a lambent glow of mystery.

Now and then the kind gentleman came to visit her, with gifts of chocolates (as became her new estate), which she accepted meekly, though in her heart she regretted the peppermint bull's-eyes of fuller and more satisfying flavour. She learned in course of time that he was the husband of the woman whose image still brought sweating fright into her dreams. To save her from waking terror, Lady Blount spent much time and tact, enlisting her sympathy for John by convincing her that he himself had received barbarous usage from the same abhorred hands. Unity, whose habit of mind was to translate conceptions into terms of the objective, wondered what form of physical torture was applied to John. She pitied him immensely, but consoled herself by the reflection that as he was very big and strong, his probable sufferings were not inordinate. That so big and strong a man, however, should have suffered unresistingly she could not understand.

"Why did n't he wipe her over the 'ed, m' lady?" she asked simply. The "m' lady" was the result of the maid's instructions.

Lady Blount administered the necessary linguistic corrections, and, proceeding to the sociological side, informed her that gentlemen never struck women, no matter how great the provocation. Unity was quick to apply the proposition personally.

"Then Mr. Risca will never beat me, even if I do wrong?"

"Good Heavens! no, child," cried Lady Blount, horrified. "Mr. Risca is as gentle as a kitten. You should see him with Miss Stella."

"Miss Stella loves him very much, m' lady?"

"Of course she does."

"And he loves her, too?"

"Everybody loves her," said Lady Blount, tenderly. The next time that John came to Southcliff he found a convalescent Unity. Dressmakers and other fabricators of feminine raiment had been at work, and she was clad in blouse and short serge skirt and her scanty, brown hair, instead of being screwed up in a diminutive bun at the back of her head, was combed and brushed and secured, after the manner of hair of young persons of sixteen, with bows of ribbon. She stood gawkily before him, confused in her own metamorphosis. At the orphanage she had worn the same uniform from early childhood. During her excursion into the world she had masqueraded as the grown woman. In the conventional attire of the English school-girl she did not recognize herself. Her coarse hands, scarcely refined by illness, hung awkwardly by her side. An appeal for mercy hovered at the back of her dull and patient eyes. Despite the trim dress and hair, she looked hopelessly unprepossessing, with her snub nose, wide mouth, weak chin, and bulgy and shiny forehead. Scragginess, too, had marked her for its own.

"Well, Unity," said John, "so you 're up at last. Have you been in the garden?"

She made the bob taught at the orphanage.

"Yes, sir."

"And you 're feeling well and strong?"

"Yes, sir."

"And don't you think it's a very lovely place?"

"Yes, sir," said Unity.

They were always shy in each other's company, question and answer being the form of their conversation. John, who could talk all day long to Stella, felt curiously constrained in the presence of this unfamiliar type of humanity; and Unity, regarding him at the same time as a god who had delivered her out of the House of Bondage and as a fellow-victim at the hands of the Unspeakable, scarcely found breath for the utterance of her monosyllables.

"Sit down and go on with your work," said he. He had come upon her as she sat by the window of her room sewing some household linen. She obeyed meekly. He watched her busy, skilful fingers for some time.

"Do you like sewing?"

"Yes, sir; can sew beautiful."

John lounged about the rose-covered room. What could he say next. On previous visits he had discoursed on their proposed life together, and she had been singularly unresponsive. He had also plugged her mind full, as he hoped, of moral precepts which should be of great value hereafter. But being no original aphorist, he had exhausted his ready-made stock. He thrust his hands into his pockets and looked out of the window. The little town of Southcliff lay hidden below the bluff, and all that he saw was the Sussex weald lit by the May sunshine and rolling lazily in pasture and woodland into the hazy distance. Within, the monotonous scrabble of the needle going in and out of stiff material alone broke the silence.

Presently the maid came in.

"Miss Stella's compliments, sir, and if you 're disengaged, she would like to speak to you for a minute."

She had a habit of summoning thus politely, but autocratically, her high ministers of state.

"I will come to Miss Stella immediately," said John. He turned to Unity. "Now that you can get about again, I suppose Lady Blount has told you not to go to the other side of the house."

"Yes, sir."

"Do you understand why?"

She raised her eyebrows. Having lived under the despotism of the world authorities, she had never dreamed of questioning the why and wherefore of any ordinance.

"It 's forbidden, sir."

"No one goes there without express invitation from Miss Stella," said John, indiscreetly. "If any one did, I don't know what would happen to him."

He left her with a new idea in her confused little brain. Mr. Risca was obviously speaking the truth, as he himself had just been summoned by the mysterious princess. Unity knew that she was very beautiful and lay all her life on a bed looking out to sea; that she was an angel of goodness; that she was worshipped by the whole household, even by the humbler members of the servants' hall, who had never seen her. A kitchen-maid summoned into the presence for the first time—it was a question of the carriage of coal—decked herself out in her trimmest and cleanest and departed on her errand with the beating heart of one who approaches royalty. There was a tradition, too, that Miss Stella was magically endowed with a knowledge of everything that went on in the house and that nothing was done without her bidding and guidance. Special flowers in the garden were grown for Miss Stella. Special fowls in the poultry-yard laid eggs exclusively for Miss Stella. A day was bright because Miss Stella had requested the sun to shine. Unity knew all this, and when John went out, her heart began to flutter with a wild hope. She laid her sewing in her lap and pictured the scene: the maid would open the door. "Unity, Miss Stella desires to see you." The fairy-books said that you kissed a princess's hand. I think this must have been Unity Blake's first day-dream. It was a sign of a spirit's emancipation.

The days passed, however, without the dream coming true. But she was very humble. Why should Miss Stella want to see any one so ugly and unimportant? Besides, the garden, with its walks and lawns and shrubberies and great, green trees; the unimagined sea rolling from, the purple rim far away, to dash itself in spray upon the shingle of the beach; the almost terrifying freedom; the young animal's unconscious exultation in returning health; the feminine, instinctive delight in tasteful dress; the singular absence of harsh, cold speech; the curious privilege of satiating her young hunger at every meal—all these new joys combined to protect her from disappointment. There was Constable, too. At her first meeting with the great dog in the garden, she was paralyzed with fright. He stood some way off, watching her with pricked-up ears; then he walked slowly up to her, and smelled her all over with awful gravity. She felt his cold nose touch her cheek. She could not run. Every instant she expected him to open his huge mouth and devour her. But after an eternity he turned away with a sniff, and suddenly began to roll on his back, writhing his neck and body in odd contortions and throwing up his great feet in the air. A gardener appeared from a shrubbery close by, and Unity made a wild rush for his protection. The man saw that she was frightened and reassured her. Constable had only wanted to make certain that she was not a wicked person come with intent to harm Miss Stella. He was Miss Stella's own dog, her bodyguard, who saw to it that no unauthorized person came into her presence.

"He would be fierce then?" she asked.

The gardener was amused. "He 'd gobble you up like winking." He called the dog, who rose in a dignified way from his gambol.

"Just pat him on the head, and don't look afraid," counselled the gardener.

So Unity, taking courage, did as she was bidden, and Constable, searching her soul with his wise eyes, admitted her to his friendship.

From that time she looked forward to her casual meetings with the dog, although she always felt a certain awe at his strength and bulk, even when he allowed her to be most familiar. And he was invested with a human significance that also made for reverence. Gambol though he might, like the friskiest and least responsible of lambs, he filled, in the workaday hours of life, a post of extraordinary honour and responsibility. He had his being in that inner shrine of mystery where the fairy-princess dwelt; he guarded her most sacred body; he was her most intimate friend and servant. Sometimes, holding the dog's face between her hands, she would ask a child's question.

"What does she talk to you about? Why don't you tell me?" And she would whisper messages in his ear. Once she stuck a dandelion in his collar, and bade him give it to his mistress with her love. Then frightened at her own temerity, she took it back. The dream did not come true, but Constable became a very substantial and comforting part of its fabric.

Then there was Walter Herold. He had the faculty of getting through the deep-encrusted shell of apathy which baffled her other friends. His quick, laughing eyes and sensitive face compelled confidence. He did not wrap himself in the gloomy majesty of her protector, nor was he abrupt and disconcerting like Sir Oliver. The iron repression of her life had kept her dumb. Even now, when she took the initiative in conversation, making a statement or asking a question instead of answering one, instinct jerked her eyes from her interlocutor to space around, as though in apprehension of the fall of an audacity-avenging thunderbolt. Ignorant and inarticulate, she now had unjustly a reputation for sullenness in the household. Keen and sympathetic as were Lady Blount and the nurse, who had undertaken to give her elementary instruction in personal and table manners, they could elicit nothing but commonplaces from the chaotic mind. To Herold alone could the child that she was chatter freely. She told him of her life at the orphanage, the daily routine, the squabbles with schoolmates. She spoke of her five-months' inferno.

"But why did n't you run out into the street and tell the first policeman you met?"

"I was always 'fraid of p'licemen. And 'ow was I to know that was n't the regular thing in service? Where I came from, before I went to the orphanage, everybody used to knock each other about. And sometimes they used to beat us at the orphanage, but more often they put us in the cell on bread and water. Most of the girls 'drather to be licked. When I was at Smith Street, I thought the cell heaven." She paused for a moment, and her eyes hardened evilly. "I'm jolly glad she's in quod, though. Will they beat her there?"

"No, my dear," said Herold; "they 're trying to make her good."

She laughed scornfully. "'Er good? If I 'd known then what I know now, I 'd 'ave poured scaldin' water over her. S'welp me!"

"I'm very glad you did n't, for you and I would n't be sitting here now by this beautiful sea." He put his hand gently on her head. "Do you know how you can repay all these people who are so kind to you?"

"No," said Unity.

"By trying to forget everything that happened to you in the past. Don't think of it."

"I must," she replied in a dull, concentrated tone. "I should like to have her 'ere now and cut her throat." Herold remonstrated, and talked perhaps more platitudinously than was his wont. When he reported this interview to John, for it was from Herold that he learned most of the psychology of Unity Blake, John frowned.

"That's a bad trait."

"It will pass," said Herold. "She has come from the dungeons into the garden of life. She is for the first time just beginning to realize herself as a human being. Naturally the savage peeps out. That will be tamed. She has wonderful latent capacities for good. Already she has invented a kind of religion with Stellamaris as divinity."

"What does she know about Stella?" John asked roughly.

"Virtually everything," laughed Herold. "We talk Stella interminably. When she spoke of throat-cutting, I brought in Stella with great effect. I made her go down on her knees on the big rock and look up at the window and say, 'Princess Stellamaris, I am a bad and wicked girl, and I am very sorry.' She looked so penitent, poor little kid, that I kissed her."

John laughed half contemptuously and then looked glum. "I can never get a word out of her."

"That's not her fault," said Herold. "She confuses you, in some way, with God. And if you stand over her like an early Hebrew Jah in his most direful aspect, you can't expect the poor child to chirrup like a grasshopper."

"I 'll be glad when I get her under my own control," said John.

And all this time, while she was being deified, Stellamaris remained tranquilly unaware of the existence of her new devotee. The discipline of the house was so rigid that not a hint or whisper reached the sea-chamber. Perhaps Constable in his wistful, doggy way may have tried to convey Unity's messages, but how can a whine and a shake of the head and a touch of the paw express such a terribly complicated thing as the love of one human being for another? If only Unity had let the dandelion remain, or had slipped a note under his collar, Constable would have done his best to please. At any rate, as the days went on, he showed himself more and more gracious to Unity.

Now it happened one Saturday morning that Stellamaris was wearing a brand-new dressing-jacket. It was a wondrous affair of pale, shot silk that shimmered like mother-of-pearl, and it had frills and sleeves of filmy old Buckingham lace. More than ever did she look like some rare and sweet sea-creature. The jacket had come home during the week, but though it had been the object of her feminine delight, she had reserved the great first wearing for Saturday and the eyes of her Great High Belovedest. Her chances for coquetry were few. She surveyed herself in a hand-mirror, and saw that she was fair.

"Constable," she said, "if he does n't think it perfectly ravishingly beautiful, I shall die. You think it beautiful, don't you?"

Constable, thus appealed to, rose from the hearthrug, stretched himself, and, approaching, laid his head against his mistress's cheek. Then, a favourite habit, he put his forepaws on the edge of the bed, and stood towering over the sacred charge and gazed with wrinkled brow across the channel, as though scanning the horizon for hostile ships. He had done this a thousand times with no mishap. He would as soon have thought of biting her as of putting a heavy paw on beloved body or limb. But on this particular occasion the edge of the bed gave treacherous footing. To steady himself, he shifted his left paw an inch nearer her arm, and happened to strike the Buckingham lace.

"Down, Constable!" she cried.

He obeyed; but his claw caught in the lace, and away it ripped from the shoulder.

"Oh, darling, you 've ruined my beautiful jacket!"

Constable wagged his tail, and came up to be petted. A man would have confounded himself in apologies, and made matters worse. In such a circumstance the way of the dog may be recommended.

Stella rang the bell. The maid entered. Her Serene High-and-Mightiness the nurse was summoned. Dismay reigned in the sea-chamber. The dressing and undressing of Stellamaris was a tragic matter.

"If it 's not mended before Mr. Risca comes, my heart will break," she said.

The maid took the dressing-jacket and the torn lace down-stairs. Inspecting them, she found the damage not irreparable. The rents might be temporarily concealed from the unseeing eyes of man. But it would take time. She was busy, in the midst of some work for her mistress. Human nature asserting itself, she dratted Constable. On her way to her room she glanced out of a window that overlooked the lawn. There, in the May sunshine, sat Unity, hemming dusters. Now, Unity was made for higher things of the needle than dusters. She had a genius for needlework. The maid knew it. In a few moments, therefore, Unity had exchanged the dull duster for the exquisite and thrilling garment, warm from the sweet body of the Lady of Mystery herself. The maid brought the necessary battery of implements with which such delicate repairs are executed, and left an enraptured orphan on a rustic bench.

Unity set to work. The mending of torn lace is a ticklish affair under the most prosaic of conditions: when goddesses and fairy-princesses and Stellamarises are mixed up in it, the occupation absorbs mind and soul. Unity's first awakening to the fact of an outside world was effected by a huge, grayish blue head thrust between her face and her needle. It was Constable, who had been let loose for his morning frisk. She pushed him away. Even the most majestic of Great Danes is moist about the jowl. Suppose he dribbled on the sacred vesture! Marrow-freezing possibility! She held his head at arm's length, and bade him begone. But Constable broke through her puny restraint and sniffed at the dressing-jacket. He sniffed at it in so insistent and truculent a manner that Unity grew frightened. She held the dressing-jacket high in the air.

"Just you clear out!" she cried and jerked the arm in an indiscreet gesture. Whimsical fate decreed that it should slip through her fingers. It fell on the lawn. She pounced. Constable pounced. He pounced first, caught the jacket in his mouth, and trotted across the lawn. She pursued. The trot became a loping gallop. She ran, she called. The gutter child's vernacular came to her aid; she called him unrecordable things. Constable, whose ears had never been so shocked before, galloped the faster. He bolted into the house, head erect, the body of the jacket in his mouth, and a forlorn sleeve trailing on the ground. Unity pursued breathless, in the awful excitement of despair. She had no idea of place. Here was a horrible dog —he had lapsed utterly from grace—robbing her of the only thing in her life that had been precious. Her childish soul was concentrated on the rescue of the holy garment. Constable darted with scrabbling pads up the stairs. On the landing he halted for a moment, and, panting, looked down on her at the bottom of the flight. She crept up slowly, using hypocritical terms of endearment. He cocked derisive ears. When she had reached half way, he tossed his head and loped on down a corridor, up more stairs. In the house not a soul was stirring, not a sound was heard save the dull thud of the dog's pads on the carpet. Outside a cuckoo expressed ironical views on the situation. Once Unity nearly caught the robber, but he sprang beyond her grasp.

At last he butted a door open with his head, and vanished. Unity followed blindly, and stood transfixed a yard or two beyond the threshold of the room.

It was a vast chamber, apparently all window and blue sky, and on a bed by a window was a face framed in a mass of brown hair—the face of a girl with beautiful eyes that looked at you like stars. To Unity it seemed two or three miles from where she stood to the bedside. Constable was there already, and he had surrendered the jacket. His tail wagged slowly, and his head, with cocked ears, was on one side.

"Oh, Constable, it 's very good of you, but now you've done for my jacket altogether! Why will you try to be a lady's maid?"

It was the most exquisite voice in the world. Unity stood spellbound. She realized that she had unwittingly penetrated into the Holy of Holies. It was the princess herself.

"Who are you, my dear?" asked Stellamaris.

Unity's heart was beating. Her lips were dry; she licked them. She made the orphan's bob. Something stuck in her throat. Her head was in a whirl.

"Unity, m' lady," she gasped.

A peal of little golden bells seemed to dance from corner to corner of the vast room: it was Stellamaris laughing.

"I'm not 'my lady.' Only Aunt Julia is 'my lady.' But I've never seen you before, dear. Where do you come from?"

Unity pointed. "Constable—the jacket—I was mending of it."

Stellamaris at once appreciated the theatrical side of the situation. She gripped the Great Dane by the dewlap in her fragile fingers.

"Oh, you silly dear Lord High Constable! It's his scent," she explained. "Anything he finds in the house that I've worn, he always brings me. Susan has to lock her door against him. You were mending my lace?"

"In the garden."

Stella laughed again. "Foolish Constable, I can see it all. What did you say your name was, my dear?"

"Unity, m' lady."

"Then come here, Unity, and let us see whether Constable has utterly ruined the jacket. I did so want to wear it this afternoon."

Unity walked the two or three miles to the bedside, and took the jacket, and held it up for the inspection of four rueful eyes. There were great wet marks on it, of course, but these would dry. Otherwise no damage was done, Constable having carried it as tenderly as a retriever does a partridge.

"How old are you, Unity?" asked Stella.

"Nearly sixteen, m' lady."

"So am I. But how clever you must be to mend this! Now, when I try to sew, I make great big stitches that every one laughs at." She examined the repairs that Unity had already executed. "I don't know when I've seen such beautiful work."

Unity's cheeks burned. Her heart was full. She could utter no word of reply to such graciousness. Tears started into her eyes. Her nose began to water; she wiped it with the back of her hand.

There was a swish of stiff skirts at the door. Unity turned guiltily and beheld the nurse. Then, losing her head, she grabbed the dressing-jacket and bolted like a frightened hare.

"What was that child doing in your room, darling?"

Stellamaris explained more or less to the nurse's satisfaction.

"But who is she?"

Faithful to the Unwritten Law, the nurse lied.

"Just a little girl from the village who has come in for the day to help with the sewing."

"I should like to see her again," said Stella.

"I'm sorry you can't, darling."

"Why?"

"She is going to London for good this afternoon."

"I'm sorry," said Stella.

And the word of the lie went forth, and to it were bound the entire household from Sir Oliver to the kitchen-maid and John and Herold, when they arrived for the week-end. Herold had no choice but the bondage, but he sighed. It would have been better, he said, to bind Unity herself to silence. Any fabric built of lies offended his fine sense. Beauty was beauty, the highest good; but it must have truth as its foundation. Beauty reared in falsehood was doomed to perish. The exquisiteness of the Trianon ended in the tumbrils. The Tuileries fell in the cataclysm of Sedan. Sometimes Herold played Cassandra, and on such occasions no one paid any attention to his prophecies. He was disregarded now. For the rest of her stay at the Channel House, Unity, as far as Stella was concerned, had vanished into the unknown. No summons came to her from the sea-chamber; but she had met her goddess face to face for a few throbbing moments, and she fed on the blissful memory for many a long day afterwards.

# CHAPTER IX

MISS LINDON moved her goods and chattels, together with Dandy, Dickie, and Phoebe, into the little house at Kilburn. John and Unity followed with the furniture he had procured on the hire-purchase system for their respective rooms, and the curtain was rung up on the comic opera.

Herold had vainly tried to guide his friend in the matter of furnishing; but their ideas being in hopeless conflict, he had given up in despair. John, by way of proving how far superior his methods were to Herold's, rushed into a vast emporium, selected the insides of two bedrooms and a library complete (as per advertisement), and the thing was done in a couple of minutes. He girded triumphantly at Herold, who would have taken two years. Miss Lindon approved his choice, everything was so clean and shiny. She especially admired the library carpet (advertised as Axminster), a square of amazing hues, mustard and green and magenta predominant, the ruins of an earthquake struck by lightning. It gave, she said, such brightness and colour to the room. To the bedrooms she herself added the finishing touch and proudly led John up-stairs to inspect them. He found his bed, wash-stand, toilet-table, and chairs swathed in muslin and pink ribbon. His heart sank. This was a mania. If she had owned a dromedary, she would have fitted it out with muslin and ribbon. He glanced apprehensively at the water-jug; that alone stood in its modest nudity. Miss Lindon beamed. Was n't the room more homelike? He had not the heart to do otherwise than assent.

"There 's one thing, my dear Miss Lindon, that John 's very particular about," said Herold, gravely, when he, in his turn, was shown over the premises, with pomp and circumstance; "you must n't put ribbons in his pyjamas."

Unity, whose early-discovered gift of the needle was requisitioned for this household millinery, thought it all mighty fine. It had been impressed upon her that she was no longer a guest, as at Southcliff, but an inmate of the house, with a definite position. She had passed from the legal guardianship of the Sisters of Saint Martha to that of Mr. Risca. The house was her home, which she shared on equal terms with him and Miss Lindon. She was no longer to call them "Sir" and "Ma'am." Miss Lindon took the child to her warm heart and became "Aunt Gladys." She suggested the analogous title for her nephew; but he put his foot down firmly and declined to be called "Uncle John." He said it was farcical, subversive of the tragic dignity of the situation. She yielded complacently without in the least understanding what he meant.

"But you must have some name, dear," she pleaded. "Suppose she found that the house was on fire: it might be burned to the ground before she could settle how to call you."

"Oh, let her call me Demosthenes," he cried in desperation, taking up his pen,—he had been interrupted in the middle of an article,—"and also tell her, my dear aunt, that, fire or no fire, if she comes into this room while I 'm writing, I 'll make her drink the ink-pot."

It was eventually decided that to Unity he should be "guardian." The sacrosanctity of his library was also theoretically established. Unity, accustomed to discipline, paid scrupulous observance to the taboo; but Miss Lindon could never understand it. She would tap very gently at John's door, sometimes three or four times before he heard. At his "Come in," she would enter, manipulating the door-knob so as to make no noise, and would creep on tiptoe across the resplendent carpet.

"Now, I'm not going to disturb you, dear. Please go on writing. I only want to say that I'm ordering some tooth-stuff for Unity, and I don't know whether to buy paste or powder."

"Give her what you use yourself, my dear aunt."

Then would follow a history of her dentist. Such a gentlemanly man; in great trouble, too; he had just lost his fourth wife. John glared at his copy. "Careless fellow!" he growled. Many of his witticisms were at second hand.

"Indeed he's not. He's most careful, I assure you. I would recommend him to anybody."

And so forth and so forth, until John would rise and, taking her by her plump shoulders and luring her across the threshold, lock the door against her.

"She will drive me into a mad-house," he complained to Herold. "I want to murder her and hug her at the same instant."

In its primitive essentials, however, the comic-opera life was not impossible to the man of few material demands: he slept in a comfortable bed, his bath was filled in the mornings, wholesome food, not too fantastic, was set before him. The austere and practical Phoebe saw to these important matters. It was in the embroidery of life that the irresponsible grotesque entered. It took many weeks to persuade Miss Lindon that it was not her duty, if he was out of an evening, to wait up until his return. It was for her to look after his well-being. Before going to bed he might want hot cocoa, or bread and milk, or a cheery chat. How could he, in loneliness, procure these comforts at three o'clock in the morning? It was no trouble at all to her to sit up, she pleaded. When Dandy was ill, she had sat up whole nights together. John prayed to Heaven to deliver him from illness. Another feature of the masculine existence that passed her understanding was the systematic untidiness of the library. Books, papers, pipes, pens, paper-clips, and what not seemed to have been poured out of a sack, and then kicked in detail to any chance part of the room. When she restored order out of chaos, and sat with a complacent smile amid her prim gimcrackeries, John would be dancing about in a foaming frenzy. Where were his long envelopes? Where had that dear magpie of a woman secreted them? Her ingenuity in finding hiding-places amounted to genius. Then in impatient wrath he would take out drawers and empty their contents on the floor until the missing objects came to light. Miss Lindon sighed when she tidied up after him, not at the work to do all over again, but at the baffling mystery of man.

For a long time Unity regarded the feckless lady with some suspicion, sniffed at her, so to speak, like a dog confronted with a strange order of being. For the first time in her young life she had met an elder in only nominal authority over her. Of Phoebe, stern and Calvinistic, with soul-searching eye, who by some social topsyturvydom was put into subjection under her, she lived in mortal terror; but for "Aunt Gladys" she had a wondering contempt.

"Unity," said Miss Lindon one morning, in the early days, "when you've finished writing your copy for your guardian, you had better learn a chapter. Bring me your Bible, and I 'll find one. In my time all young ladies learned chapters,"—so do orphans still in convents, until orphans hate chapters with bitter hatred; but this the good lady did not know,—"and then you might, like a dear girl, run off the hems of the new sheets on the sewing-machine."

"I dunno 'ow to work a sewing-machine."

"Then tell Phoebe to give you a lesson at once. It's a most useful accomplishment. You have such a tremendous lot to learn, my dear. There's the piano and French, and embroidery and drawing, and nowadays I suppose young ladies must learn politics. Perhaps you had better begin. There 's a leading article on free trade—or the Young Turks, I forget which—in the 'Daily Telegraph.' I'm sure it must be very clever. You had better take away the paper and read it carefully,"—she handed the paper to the bewildered child,—"and when you 've read it, come and tell me all about it. It will save me the trouble of going through it, and so both of us will be benefited. And, Unity dear," she added as the girl was leaving the drawing-room, "it's such a beautiful day, so in an hour's time be ready to come out with me. We 'll take the omnibus to the Marble Arch and walk in the park."

Unity went into the dining-room, where in working-hours she was supposed to have her being, and stared at her avalanche of duties: her copy and the one or two easy lessons set by John; the chapter of the Bible; the instruction on the sewing-machine, involving the tackling of a busy and irritable Phoebe; the long column of print in the newspaper; and the preparation of herself for walking abroad—all to be accomplished within the space of one hour. For the first time in her life she encountered orders which had not the doomful backing of the world authorities.

The copy and the lessons for her guardian were, however, matters of high import. They filled her hour. At the end of it she put on her hat. A ride in an omnibus was still novelty enough to be a high adventure. On the way to the Marble Arch, Miss Lindon in her amiable way asked how she had spent her morning, and hoped that she had not been getting into mischief. Of Bible chapter, sewing-machine, or leader on free trade (or Young Turks) she appeared to have remembered nothing. The result of this flabbiness of command was lamentable. The next time Miss Lindon dismissed her to the execution of certain behests, Unity, after closing the door behind her, stuck out her tongue. It was ungenteel, it was ungrateful, it was un-anything-you-like, but the act gave her a thrill of joy, a new sensation. It was the first definite assertion of her individuality. The red tongue thus vulgarly flaunted was a banner of revolt against the world authorities.

It was a long time before she could accustom herself to taking her meals at the table with Miss Lindon and her guardian. Such table manners as had been inculcated at the orphanage had been lost in Smith Street, and the chief point of orphanage etiquette was not to throw food about, a useless injunction, for obvious reasons. Accordingly, despite her probationary period at the Channel House, Unity regarded the shining knives and forks and china and glass with malevolent dislike. The restrictions on so simple a matter as filling herself with nourishment were maddening in their complexity. Why could n't she bite into her hunk of bread instead of breaking off a mouthful? Why could n't she take up her fish in her fingers? Why could n't she spit out bones without the futile intermediary of the fork? Why could n't she wipe the gravy from her plate with soft crumb? Why could n't she use her knife for the consumption of apple tart? And how difficult the art of mastication with closed lips! She did not revolt. She humbly tried to follow the never-ending instructions; but their multiplicity confused her, making her shy and painfully nervous. Drink had a devilish habit of going the wrong way. It never went the wrong way with her two companions. Unity wondered why.

Then at the table sat her guardian, gloomy, preoccupied, Olympian in the eyes of the child; and Aunt Gladys, weaving corrections, polite instructions, reminiscences, and irrelevant information into an inextricable tangle of verbiage; while Phoebe hovered about, fixing her always, no matter what she was doing, with a relentless, glassy eye which no solecism escaped.

There were also a myriad other external matters which caused her great perplexity—the correct use of a handkerchief (one's sleeve was so much handier when one's nose watered), a tooth-brush, nail-scissors. The last she could not understand. Why, then, did God give people teeth to bite with? The question of speech presented extraordinary difficulties. It was months before her ear could even distinguish between O and aow, between a and i, between ou and ah; and the mysteries of the aspirate became a terror. She grew afraid to speak. Thus her progress in the graces of polite society was but slow.

John, not fired by enthusiasm, but intent on working out his scheme of indemnification, gave up an hour or so a day to her mental culture. He was not an unskilful teacher, but her undeveloped mind had to begin at the beginning of things. She learned painfully. The great world had revealed itself to her with blinding suddenness. For months she was simply stupid.

"How are things shaping?" asked Herold one day. He had been lunching at Kilburn, and Unity, feeling, that she was expected to be on her very best behaviour before him, had been more than usually awkward and ungenteel. This time a fish-bone had stuck in her throat.

John frowned. "You saw. Shapelessly. It's hopeless."

"You 're absolutely wrong," said Herold. "There are vast possibilities in Unity."

"Not one," said John.

"Are you trying the right way? Do you remember what the old don said when he came across two undergraduates vainly persuading the college tortoise to eat lettuce: 'Gentlemen, are you quite sure you are trying at the right end?' "

"What do you mean?"

"Can't you try by the way of the heart?"

John flared up. "You 're talking rot. The child has n't had a harsh word since she has been here. I'm not honey-tongued as a rule, but to her I've been a female saint with a lily in my hand. And my aunt, with all her maddening ways, would not hurt the feelings of a black beetle."

"Quite so," said Herold. "But all that's negative. Why can't you try something positive? Give Unity love, and you 'll be astonished at the result."

"Love," said John, impatiently. "You 're a sentimentalist."

This time Herold flared up. "If I am," he cried, "I thank the good God who made me. This affectation of despising sentiment, this cant that a lot of you writing fellows talk, makes me sick. If a bowelless devil makes a photograph of a leprous crew in a thieves' kitchen, you say: 'Ha! Ha! Here 's the real thing. There 's no foolish sentiment here. This is LIFE!' Ugh! Of all the rotten poses of the superior young ass, this is the rottenest. Everything noble, beautiful, and splendid that has ever been written, sung, painted, or done since the world began, has been born in sentiment, has been carried through by sentiment, has been remembered and reverenced by sentiment. I hate to hear an honest man like you sneering at sentiment. You yourself took on this job through sentiment. And now when I tell you in a few simple words, 'Love that child whose destiny you 've made yourself responsible for,' you pooh-pooh the staring common sense of the proposition and call me a sentimentalist—by which you mean an infernal fool."

John, who had bent heavy brows upon him during this harangue, took his pipe from his mouth.

"It's you who are feeding the tortoise at the wrong end," he said unhumorously. "This is not a matter of sentiment, but of duty. I do my best to be good to the child. I 'll do the utmost I can to make reparation for what she has suffered. But as for loving her—I suppose you know what love means? As for loving this poor little slut, with her arrested development and with the torture the sight of her means to me, why, my good man, you 're talking monkey gibberish!"

Herold lit a cigarette with nervous fingers. The animation in his thin, sensitive face had not yet died away.

"I'm not talking gibberish," he replied; "I'm talking sense."

"Pooh!"—or something like it—said John.

"Well, super-sense, then," cried Herold, who did not quite know what he meant, but felt certain that for the instant the term would floor his adversary. "And you 're as blind as an owl. Deep down in that poor little slut is a spark of the divine fire—love in its purest, the transcendental flame. I know it 's there. I know it as a water-finder knows there's water when the twig bends in his hands. Get at it. Find it. Fan it into a blaze. You 'll never regret it all your life long."

John's frown deepened. "If you 're suggesting the usual asinine romance, Walter, between ward and guardian—"

Herold caught up his hat.

"Of all the dunderheaded asses! You ought to be ashamed of yourself. I can't talk to you."

And in a very rare fury he sped from the house, slamming doors after him, leaving John foolishly frowning in the middle of the violent Axminster carpet.

Unity, for all her fingers' nimbleness with needle and thread, was clumsy with her hands. Glasses, bowls, vases, whatever she touched, seemed to be possessed by an imp of spontaneous disruption. Hitherto her code of morals with regard to breakage had been, first, to hide the pieces; secondly, to deny guilt if questioned; thirdly, if found out, to accept punishment with sullen apathy: for chastisement had followed discovered breakage as inevitably as the night the day. Accordingly when she broke a bowl of gold-fish in the drawing-room, she obeyed ingrained tradition. She threw the fish out of the window, mopped up the water, put a hassock on the wet patch on the carpet, and threw the shards of the bowl into the dust-bin. Miss Lindon, entering soon afterward, missed her gold-fish, bought only a few days before from an itinerant vendor. Unity disclaimed knowledge of their whereabouts. Phoebe, being summoned, took the parts of principal witness, counsel for the prosecution, judge, and jury all in one. Unity stood convicted. The maid was sent back to her work. "Now," thought Unity, "I'm going to catch it," and she stood with her eyes on the floor, stubbornly awaiting the decree of doom. An unaccustomed sound met her ear, and looking up, she beheld the gentle lady weeping bitterly.

"I should n't have minded your breaking the bowl, though I should like to know what has become of the poor little fishes,—they must be real fish out of water, poor dears! and one of them I called Jacky was just beginning to know me,—but why did you tell me a story about it?"

Unity, not having the wit to retort truthfully that it seemed the natural thing to do, maintained a stolid silence.

Miss Lindon, profoundly upset by this depravity, read her a moral lecture on the sin of lying, in which she quoted the Book of Revelation, related the story of George Washington and an irrelevant episode in her far-away childhood, and finally asserting that John would be furiously angry if he heard of her naughtiness, bade her go and find the gold-fish, which must be panting their little hearts out. And that was the last Unity heard of the matter. She thought Aunt Gladys a fool. Thenceforward she felt cynically indifferent toward accidental breakages of Aunt Gladys's property.

But one day during John's absence she upset a Dresden china shepherd, —such a brave, saucy shepherd,—that stood on his writing-desk, and, to her dismay, the head rolled apart from the body. It was one of his few dainty possessions. She knew that he set an incomprehensible value on the thing. Even Aunt Gladys touched it with extraordinary reverence. She turned white with fear. Her guardian was a far different being from Aunt Gladys. His wrath would be terrible. Herold was not far wrong in likening John Risca, as conceived by the child, to a Hebraic Jehovah. His dread majesty overwhelmed her, and she had not the courage to face his anger.

With trembling fingers she stood the poor decapitated shepherd on his feet and delicately poised the head on the broken neck. She gazed at him for a moment, his sauciness and bravery apparently unaffected by the accident, and then she fled, and endured hours of misery.

The inevitable came to pass, John discovered the breakage, instituted an elementary court of inquiry, and summoned the delinquent into his presence.

"Did you break this, Unity?"

"No," said Unity.

The lie irritated him. He raised his fist in a denunciatory gesture. With a cry of terror, like a snared rabbit's, she clapped her hands to her face and shrank, cowering, to the farther corner of the room.

"My God!" cried John, aghast at the realization of what had happened. "Did you think I was going to hit you?"

He stood staring at the little, undeveloped, rawboned, quivering creature. Her assumption of his right to strike her, of his capability of striking her, of the certainty that he would strike her, held him in amazed horror. The phantasmagorical to him was the normal to her. He had to wait a few moments before recovering command of his faculties. Then he went up to her.

"Unity, my dear—"

He put his arm about her, led her to his writing-chair, and kept his arm round her when he sat down.

"There, there, my child," said he, clutching at her side nervously in his great grasp, "you misunderstood entirely." In his own horrified dismay he had forgotten for the moment her wickedness. He could find no words save incoherences of reassurance. She made no response, but kept her hands before her face, her finger-tips pressed with little livid edges of flesh into her forehead. And thus for a long while they remained.

"I was n't going to punish you for breaking the figure," he explained at last. "You did n't do it on purpose, did you?"

She shook her head.

"What made me angry was your telling me a lie; but I never dreamed of hurting you. I would sooner kill myself than hurt you," he said, with a shudder. Then, with an intuition that came from the high gods, he added, "I would just as soon think of hurting Miss Stella, who gave me the little shepherd you broke."

To John's amazement,—for what does a man know of female orphans, or of female anything, for the matter of that?—Unity tore herself away from him and, falling in a poor little lump on the floor, burst into a wild passion of tears and sobs. John, not knowing what else to do, stooped down and patted her shoulders in an aimless way. Then with a vague consciousness that she were best alone, he went softly out of the room.

It was thus that, in the unwonted guise of ministering spirits, shame and remorse came to Unity Blake.

She had broken a sacred idol. He had not been angry. She had told a lie, and instead of punishing her,—of his horror-stricken motives she had no idea,—he had held her tight in kind arms and spoken softly. He had not actually wept, but he had been sorry at her lie, even as Aunt Gladys had been. Now he, being what to her mind was a kind of fusion of Jah and Zeus and Odin,—three single deities rolled into one,—was not a fool. Dimly through the mists of her soul dawned the logical conclusion: perhaps Aunt Gladys, in her sorrowful and non-avenging attitude towards her mendacities and other turpitudes, was not a fool either.

The bewildering truth also presented itself that lies, being unnecessary as a means of self-protection, were contemptible. In the same way she realized that if folks had no intention of punishing her for destroying their valuable property, even sacred gifts of fairy-princesses, but, instead, smiled on her their sweet forgiveness, they must have in them something of the divine which had hitherto been obscured from her vision. She had proved to herself that they could not be fools; rather, then, they were angels. They certainly could not enjoy the destruction of their belongings; therefore her clumsiness must cause them pain. Now, why should she inflict pain on people who were doing their utmost to make her happy? Why?

She began to ask herself questions; and when once an awakening human soul begins to do that, it goes on indefinitely. Some of the simplest ones she propounded to Miss Lindon, who returned answers simple in essence, though perhaps complex in expression; some her growing experience of life enabled her to answer for herself; some of the more difficult she reserved for her rare talks with Herold. But although the awfulness of John's majesty was mitigated by the investiture of an archangel's iridescent and merciful wings, she could never go to him with her problems. Never again since that memorable occasion did he put his arm around her; he held her gently aloof as before. But he had put his arm around her once, and the child's humility dared not hope for more.

Thus in a series of shocks, bewildering flashes of truth, followed by dark spaces of ignorance, was Unity's development initiated, and, indeed, continued. Her nature, deadened by the chill years, was not responsive to the little daily influences by which character is generally moulded. Only the great things, trivial in themselves, but great in her little life—for to an ant-hill the probing of a child's stick means earthquake, convulsion, and judgment-day cataclysm—only the great things, definite and arresting, produced perceptible change. But they left their mark. She was too dull to learn much in the ordinary routine of lessons; but once a fact or an idea could be made to appeal to her emotions or her imagination, it was there for all time. Not all the pains and teaching of her two protectors, for instance, could alter one inflection of her harsh cockney twang.

But one day after luncheon, Herold being present, Miss Lindon ordered her to recite "The Wreck of the Hesperus," which artless poem she had learned unintelligently by heart, at Miss Lindon's suggestion, in order to give pleasure to her guardian. To give him pleasure she would have learned pages of the army list or worn tin tacks in her boots. After a month's vast labour she had accomplished the prodigious task.

Very shy, she repeated the poem in the child's singsong, and ended up on the "reef of Norman's Waow".

John, not having been made a party to the "surprise" eagerly contrived by Miss Lindon, nodded, said it was very good, and commended Unity for a good girl. Herold kicked him surreptitiously, and applauded with much vigour.

"By Jove!" said he, impelled by queer instinct, "I used to know that. I wonder if I could recite it, too."

He rose and began; and as he continued, his wonderful art held the child spell-bound. The meaningless words resolved themselves into symbols of vast significance. She saw the little daughter, her cheeks like the dawn of day, a vision of Stellamaris, and felt the moonless dark of the stormy night and the hissing snow and the stinging blast, and she shivered at the awful sight of the skipper frozen at the wheel, and a hush fell upon her soul as the maiden prayed, and the tears fell fast from her eyes as the picture of the fisherman finding the maiden fair lashed to the drifting mast was flashed before her by the actor's magic.

"Now, Unity dear, don't you wish you could say it like that?" Aunt Gladys remarked.

Unity, scarcely hearing, made perfunctory answer; but as soon as she could, she fled to her bedroom, her ears reverberating with the echoes of the beautiful voice, and her soul shaken with the poignant drama, and crudely copying Herold's gestures and intonations, recited the poem over and over again.

The result of this was not a sudden passion for romance or histrionics, but it was remarkable enough. It awoke her sense of vowel sounds and aspirates. Henceforward she discriminated between "lady" and "lidy," between "no" and "naow," and although she never acquired a pure accent, her organs of speech refusing to obey her will, she was acutely aware of the wrong sounds that escaped from her lips.

As with this, so with other stages of development, both in things external and things spiritual. Scales had to be torn from her eyes before she saw; then she saw with piercing vision. Plugs had to be wrenched from her ears before she heard; then she heard the horns of Elfland. Her heart had to be plucked from her bosom before she felt; then her whole being quivered with an undying emotion.

So the weeks and the months passed and grew into years, and Miss Lindon said that she was a well-behaved and Christian child, and that it was a pity she was so plain; and Risca, forgetful, after a while, of her agony of tears and of Herold's angry diagnosis, retained his opinion that she was just dull and stupid, though well-meaning, and, having his head full of other things, took her at last for granted, together with his Aunt Gladys, as a normal feature in his sometimes irritating, though on the whole exceedingly comfortable, comic-opera household.

# CHAPTER X

ONE evening by the last post John received a letter bearing the prison stamp and addressed to him under the care of the firm of solicitors who had defended his wife. It ran:

I am coming out on Wednesday, the thirteenth. I suppose I shall have somewhere to go to and not be expected to walk the streets. Louisa Anne Risca.

That was all—neither ave nor vale. It was the only letter she had written. She knew well enough that the house in Smith Street was being maintained and that her allowance would be resumed as soon as she regained her freedom, having been so informed by the solicitors, on John's instructions; but a reference to this explicit statement would have discounted the snarl. Prison had not chastened her.

John sat back in his writing-chair, the ignoble letter in front of him. He made a rapid calculation of dates. It was two years and three months since the trial. She had worked out three fourths of her sentence, the remaining fourth evidently having been remitted on account of good conduct, in the ordinary course. Two years and three months! He had scarcely realized the swift flight of time. Of late his life had been easier. Distracted London had forgotten the past. He had sought and found, at his club, the society of his fellow-men. His printed name no longer struck horror into a reader's soul. At times he himself almost forgot. The woman had faded into a shadow in some land beyond the tomb. But now, a new and grim Alcestis, she had come back to upper earth. There was nothing trans-Stygian about the two or three cutting lines. She was alive, luridly alive, and on Wednesday, the thirteenth, she would be free, a force let loose, for good or evil, in the pleasant places of the world. At the prospect of the prison doors closing behind her, however, he felt great relief. At any rate, that horror would soon be over and done with. The future must take care of itself.

Presently he wrote:

Dear Louisa:

I am unfeignedly thankful to hear your news. I shall be waiting for you at the gate on the morning of the thirteenth and shall take you to Smith Street, which you will find quite ready to receive you.

Yours,

John Risca.

Then he went out and posted the letter.

"I'm glad you're going to meet her yourself instead of sending a solicitor's clerk," said Herold, when they discussed the matter next day.

"I'm not one to shirk disagreeable things," replied John.

"It may touch some human chord in her."

"I never thought of that," said John.

"Well, think of it. Think of it as much as you can."

"'You may as well use question with the wolf,'" growled John.

"I don't believe it," said Herold. "Anyhow, try kindness."

"Of course I'm going to do so," said John, with the impatience he usually manifested when accepting a new point of view from Herold. "You don't suppose I'm going to stand outside with a club!"

On the appointed day he waited, with a four-wheeled cab, by the prison gate. The early morning sunshine of midsummer flooded the world with pale glory, its magic even softening the grim, forbidding walls. A light southwest wind brought the pure scents of the down from many a sleeping garden and woodland far away. The quiet earth sang its innocence, for wickedness was not yet abroad to scream down the song. Even John Risca, anti-sentimentalist, was stirred. What sweeter welcome, what gladder message of hope, could greet one issuing into the upper air from the gloomy depths of Hades? How could such a one help catching at her breath for joy?

The gate swung open, casting a shadow in the small yard beyond, and in the middle of the shadow a black, unjoyous figure stood for a moment irresolute. Then she slowly came out into sunshine and freedom. She was ashen-coloured, thin-lipped, and not a gleam of pleasure lit her eyes as they rested with hard remorselessness on the man who advanced with outstretched hand to meet her. Of the hand she took no notice.

"Is this my cab?"

"Yes," said John.

She entered. He followed, giving the address to the driver. She sat looking neither to left nor right, staring stubbornly in front of her. The sunshine and the scent of summer gardens far away failed to bring their message. Though it was high summer, she wore the heavy coat which she had worn in the wintry weather at the time of her trial.

"I am very glad indeed to see you, Louisa," said John. "'Unfeignedly thankful!'" She chewed the literary phrase and spat it out venomously. "You—liar!"

John winced at the abominable word; but he spoke softly.

"You can't suppose it has been happiness for me to think of you in there."

"What does it matter to me? What the hell are you to me, anyhow?"

"I 'm your husband in the eyes of the law," said John, "and I once cared for you."

"Oh, stow that!"

"I will. But I want you to believe that I am utterly thankful that this—this unhappy chapter is closed—"

She interrupted him with a swift and vicious glance.

"'Unhappy chapter!' Get off it! You make me sick. Talk English, if you must talk."

"Very well," said he. "I 'm glad my legal wife is not in gaol. I want her to believe that I 'll do my best to forget it; also, that, as far as my means allow, she will have comfort and opportunity to try to forget it, too."

Not a muscle of her drawn face relaxed.

"I'm not going to have you or any one else fooling round where I live," she said. "I'm not going to be preached to or converted. I've had enough of it where I've come from. As for you, I hate you. I've always hated you, and if you have any decency, you 'll never let me see your face again."

"I won't," said John, shortly, and with this the edifying conversation came to an end.

The cab lumbered through the sunny thoroughfares of the great city, now busy with folks afoot, in trams and omnibuses, going forth to their labour; and John, looking out of the window, fancied they were all touched by the glamour of the summer morning. Every human soul save the woman beside him seemed glad to be alive. She sat rigid, apart from him—as physically apart as the seat would allow, and apart from the whole smiling world. She had her being in terrible isolation, hate incarnate. When by any chance their eyes happened to meet, he turned his aside swiftly and shivered with unconquerable repulsion.

When the cab drew up at the house in Smith Street, the door was opened, and a pleasant-faced woman and a man stood smiling in the passage. Mrs. Risca brushed past them into the dining-room, bright with daintily laid breakfast table and many flowers. The latter, John, at Herold's suggestion, had sent in the evening before.

"You see," said John, entering, "we've tried to prepare for you."

She deigned no glance, but slammed the door.

"Who are those people?"

"A married couple whom I have engaged to live here. The woman, Mrs. Bence, will do for you. The man goes out to his work during the day."

"Warder and wardress, eh? They can jolly well clear out. I'm not going to have 'em."

Then John's patience broke. He brought his fist down on the table with a crash.

"By heavens," he cried, "you shall have whomever I put here. You 've behaved yourself for two years, and you 're going on behaving yourself." He flung open the door. "Mrs. Bence, help Mrs. Risca off with her coat and bring in her breakfast."

Cowed, she submitted with malevolent meekness. Prison discipline does not foster the heroic qualities. Mrs. Bence took hat and coat and disappeared.

"Sit down at the table."

She obeyed. He laid some money beside her.

"This is your allowance. On the thirteenth of every month you will receive the same amount from my bankers. If you prefer, after a time, to live in the country, we may be able to arrange it. In the meanwhile you must stay here."

She neither touched the coins nor thanked him. There was a silence hard and deadly. John stood in the sunshine of the window, bending on her his heavy brows. Now and then she glanced at him furtively from beneath lowered eyelids, like a beast subdued, but not tamed. A dominant will was all that could control her now. He thanked an unusually helpful Providence that had sent him the Bences in the very nick of his emergency. Before marriage, Mrs. Bence had been under-attendant at a county lunatic asylum, and John had heard of her through Wybrow, the medical superintendent, a club friend, who had helped him before when the defense had set up the plea of insanity, and whom, with an idea of trained service in his head, he had again consulted. No more torturing of Unitys, if he could help it. Wybrow spoke highly of Mrs. Bence and deplored the ruin of a great career as a controller of she-devils; but as a cat will after kind, so must she after an honest but impecunious plumber. John had sought her and come to terms at once. For once in their courses, he thought grimly, the stars were not fighting against him. He had not told Herold of this arrangement. Herold had counselled kindness. The flowers, for instance, would be sure to make their innocent appeal. Tears could not fail to fill her eyes. Tears of sentiment in those eyes! Little Herold knew of the world of realities with which he was at death-grips.

Presently Mrs. Bence came in with coffee, hot rolls, a dish of bacon and eggs. The fragrant smell awakened the animal instinct of the woman at the table. She raised her head and followed the descent of dish and plate. Then a queer noise broke from her throat, and she fell upon the food. John left her.

Mrs. Bence followed him into the passage and opened the front door. "I've been used to it, sir."

"She must never guess that," said he.

He walked homeward through the parks, breathing in great gulps of the sweet morning air. He felt that he had been in contact with something unclean. Not only his soul, but his very body, craved purification. In the woman he had left he had found no remorse, no repentance, no sensibility to any human touch. Prison had broken her courage; but in its sunless atmosphere of the underground, all the fungoid growths of her nature had flourished in mildewed exuberance. He shuddered at the thought of her, a poisonous thing, loathsome in its abnormality. As some women dwell in an aura of sweet graciousness, so dwelt she in mephitic fumes of devildom. Implacable hatred, deadly venom, relentless vengeance, were the constituents of her soul. Relentless vengeance—He sat for a moment on a bench in Hyde Park, feeling chilled to the bone, although the perspiration beaded on his forehead. She would not strike him, of that he was oddly assured. Her way would be to strike at him through those near and dear to him. In the full sunshine of gay midsummer, with the trees waving their green and lusty bravery over his head, and the flower-beds rioting in the joy of the morning, he was shaken by an unreasoning nightmare terror. He saw the woman creep with snaky movements into the sea-chamber at Southcliff, and a pair of starry eyes become wells of awful horror as the murderous thing approached the bed. And he was held rigid by dream paralysis.

After a second or two—it had seemed many minutes of agony—he sprang to his feet with what he thought was a great cry, and looked dazedly about him. A nurse-maid, undistracted from her novelette, and wheeling a perambulator in which reposed an indifferent infant, passed him by. He shook himself like a great, rough dog, and went his way, ashamed of his fears. It was a practical world, he told himself, and he was a match for any mad-woman.

Unity was watering flowers in the tiny patch of front garden where he swung through the iron gate. She had grown a little during the last two years, but still was undeveloped; a healthier colour had come into her cheeks and a more confident expression into her common, snub-nosed face. Her movements were less awkward, and as she was eighteen, she wore her hair done up with a comb and the long skirts appropriate to her age.

She set down her watering-pot and stood at a kind of absurd attention, her usual attitude in the presence of John.

"Please, guardian," she said,—she could never rid herself of the school-child's exordium,—"have you had your breakfast?"

"No," said John, realizing for the first time that emptiness of stomach may have had something to do with his momentary faintness in the park.

"Aunt Gladys has been in such a state," said Unity. "She has made Phoebe cook three breakfasts already, and each has been spoiled by being kept in the oven, and I think now she is cooking the fourth."

In this announcement rang none of the mischievous mirth of eighteen over an elder's harmless foibles. Humour, which had undoubtedly presided at her birth, for like many another glory-trailing babe, she had crowed with glee at the haphazard coupling of which she was the result, had fled for good from her environment ever since the day when, at a very tender age, she had seen her mother knocked insensible by a drunken husband and had screamed single-mindedly for unobtainable nourishment.

She had no sense of glorious futility, of the incongruous relativity of facts. Each fact was absolute. Three breakfasts had been cooked and spoiled. The fourth was in the cooking. She narrated simply what had taken place.

"Run and tell Phoebe I'm hungry enough to eat all four," said John.

They entered the house. Unity hurried off on her errand. The meal was soon served. Miss Lindon, with many inquiries as to the reason for his early start, which he answered with gruff evasiveness, hovered about him as he ate, watching him in loving wonder. His big frame needed much nourishment, and now sheer hunger was being satisfied. To her acquaintance she spoke of his appetite with as much pride as of his literary achievements. It was Unity, however, who took charge of the practical service, removed his plates and poured out his tea, silent, submissive, and yet with a subtle air of protection. There were certain offices she would not allow Aunt Gladys or even Phoebe to perform for her guardian. She was jealous, for instance, like a dog, of any one touching the master's clothes. This morning, when Miss Lindon absent-mindedly grasped the handle of the teapot, the faintest gleam of anger appeared in her eyes, and her lips grew instinctively tense, and with a quick, authoritative gesture she unloosed the fat, helpless fingers and took possession of the sacred vessel. John liked her to wait upon him. She was deft and noiseless; she anticipated his wants in an odd, instinctive way and seldom made suggestions. Now, of suggestions his aunt was a living fount. They poured from her all day long. He had a vague consciousness that Unity, by tactful interposition, dammed the flood, so that he could go on his way undrenched. For this he felt grateful, especially this morning when his nerves were on edge. Yet this morning he felt grateful also to Miss Lindon, and suffered her disconnected ministrations kindly. To-day the queer home that he had made assumed a new significance.

When Miss Lindon fluttered out of the room, bound on a suddenly remembered duty—fresh groundsel for Dickie—John looked up from the newspaper which Unity had silently folded and laid beside him.

"Come here, my child," he said, after a few moments' thought.

She approached and stood dutifully by his chair.

"Unity, I don't think it right for you to remain in ignorance of something that has happened. I don't see how it can really affect you, but it 's better that you should learn it from me than from anybody else. Do you remember—" he paused—"that woman?"

It was the first reference he had ever made to her. Unity drew a quick, sharp breath.

"Yes, guardian."

"She was let out of prison this morning."

She kept her eyes full on him, and for a while neither spoke.

"I don't care," she said at last.

"I thought it might cause you some anxiety."

"What have I to be afraid of when I've got you?" she asked simply.

John twisted round in his chair and reached out his hand—a rare demonstration of affection—and took hers.

"It's to assure you, my dear, that you've nothing to fear that I've told you."

"She can't hurt me," said Unity.

"By heaven, she sha'n't!" he cried, unconsciously wrenching her arm so that he caused her considerable pain, which she bore without the flicker of an eyelid. "You 're a fine, brave girl, Unity, and I'm proud of you. And you 're a good girl, too. I hope you 're happy here; are you?"

"Happy?" Her voice quavered on the word. Her mouth twitched, and the tears started from her eyes. He smiled on her, one of his rare smiles, known to few besides Stellamaris, which lit up his heavy features, and revealed a guardian far different from the inaccessible Olympian.

"Yes, my dear, I hope so. I want you to be happy all your life long."

She uttered a little sobbing laugh and fell crouching to his feet, still clinging to his hand, which she rubbed against her cheek. How could she tell him otherwise?

"I think you are," said John.

"I 've just remembered I put the groundsel—" began Miss Lindon, coming into the room. Then she stopped, petrified at the unusual spectacle.

John laughed rather foolishly, and Unity, flushing scarlet, rushed out.

"I was only asking her whether we were treating her nicely," said John, rising and stretching his loose limbs.

"What a question to ask the child!"

"Well, she answered it like that, you see," said John.

"But what a way to answer a simple question! She forgets sometimes that she is a young lady of eighteen, an age when manners ought to be formed. But manners," she continued, hunting about the room, "are not what they were when I was young. I declare, I sometimes see young women in the streets with woollen caps and hockey-sticks—"

John took a salad-bowl from the mantelpiece. "Is that Dickie's ground-sel?"

"Oh, how clever of you! Where did you find it? Dickie has been so angry. He's just like a man when his dinner's late. I don't mean you. You 're a perfect saint, dear."

"Which reminds me," said John, with a laugh, "that I've mislaid my halo and I must go and find it."

With an exultant sense of comfort he went into his library. The women-folk of his household had never before seemed so near to him, so dependent on him, such organic factors of his life. He stood for a long time on his hearth-rug, scowling terribly, with the air of a wild beast standing at the entrance to its lair in defiant defence of the female and whelps within.

# CHAPTER XI

JOHN RISCA, at thirty-four, with a ward of twenty, and with the normal hope of a man's life withered at the root, regarded himself as an elderly man. He looked older than his years. Ragged streaks of gray appeared in his black hair, and the lines deepened on his heavy brow. There are some men who, no matter what their circumstances may be, never take themselves happily. To do so is a gift; and it was denied to John Risca.

Two years had passed since his wife's release. During the years of their separation before her imprisonment, she had counted for little in his thoughts save as a gate barring the way to happiness. She had never molested him, never stood in the way of his ordinary life. In her prison she had begun by being a horror haunting his dreams; gradually she had dwindled into a kind of paralyzed force, had faded into a shadow incapable of action. But since her return to the living world he had felt her hatred as an influence, vague, but active, let loose upon the earth. He dreaded contact with her, however indirect, and through whatever agency; but contact was inevitable. Whereas formerly she had been content to live according to the terms of their agreement on separation, now she made demands. One of them, however, he considered reasonable. In Smith Street, the scene of her misdeeds, she led the life of a pariah dog. She was friendless. Her own relatives had cast her off.

The tradespeople round about supplied her reluctantly with necessaries and refused to exchange words with her when she entered their shops. Children hooted her in the streets. John, foreseeing unpleasantness, had offered to find her a home in the country. But this, being town-bred, she had declined. Let her change her name, she urged, and seek other London quarters. He agreed. She adopted the name of Rawlings and moved to a flat off the Fulham Road. To the suggestion of a different part of London altogether she turned a deaf ear. She had lived in that neighbourhood all her days and would feel lost elsewhere. The common

Londoner has almost the local instinct of a villager. She would also, she said, be near her mother, who still let lodgings in Brompton.

"If your mother refuses to see you," said John, when they were discussing the matter, "I see no reason for your being near her."

She counselled him, in her vernacular, to mind his own business.

"So long as I don't come and live next to you, what have you got to do with it?"

"I certainly am not called upon to protect your mother," said he. He smiled grimly, remembering the hard-bitten veteran of a thousand fights with impecunious and recalcitrant lodgers. She could very well look after herself.

The Bences, much against her will, though she dared not openly rebel, accompanied her to the flat. Her installation was expensive. He paid readily enough. But then came demands for money, insidious enough at first for his compliance, then monstrous, vindictive. She incurred reckless debts; not those of a woman who desires to make a show in the world by covering herself with costly dresses and furs and jewels or by dashing about in expensive equipages.

That side of life was unfamiliar to her, and class instinct quenched the imagination to crave it. She had been bred to regard cabs as luxuries of the idle rich, and it never occurred to her to travel in London otherwise than by omnibus or rail. Her wilful extravagance was of a different nature. She ran up bills with the petty tradesmen of the neighbourhood for articles for which she had no use; for flowers which she deliberately threw into the dust-bin; for ready-made raiment which she never wore,—jackets at three pounds, ten and six, and hats at ten shillings—cheap jewelry, watches, and trinkets which she stored away in boxes. There was a gaudy set of furniture with which she bought a kind of reconciliation with her mother. When county-court summonses came in, she demanded money from John. When he refused, she posted him the summonses.

Meanwhile he found that she had struck up acquaintance with some helter-skelter, though respectable, folks in the flat below. The discovery pleased him. It is good for no human being, virtuous or depraved, to sit from month's end to month's end in stark loneliness. She forced him to the threat of revealing her identity to her new friends if she did not mend her ways. She mended them; but he felt his hands soiled by the ignoble weapons with which he had to fight.

After that she was quiet for months. Then one rainy afternoon, as he was walking downward with bent head, he ran into her in Maida Vale, the broad thoroughfare that merges into Kilburn. She started back with a quick gasp of fear.

"What are you doing in this part of London?" he asked angrily.

She plucked up courage. "I'm free to walk where I like, and just you jolly well don't try to stop me."

"You were going to my house."

"I wasn't. But supposing I was. What have you got to hide from me? My successor? Some little tuppenny-ha'penny piece of damaged goods you've picked up cheap? Think I want to see her? What do you suppose I care? Just let me pass."

He thrust aside the wet umbrella which she pushed rudely into his face.

"First tell me what you are doing here. Fulham people don't come to Maida Vale just to take a walk in the rain."

"I was going to see some friends," she replied sulkily.

A motor-omnibus came surging down toward them. At his hail it stopped.

"Get into that at once, or it will be the worse for you."

He took her arm in his powerful grip and dragged her to the curb.

"You bullying brute!" she hissed through her thin lips.

But she entered the 'bus. John watched it until it whizzed into space, and then retracing his steps, he went home and mounted guard by the window of his aunt's gimcrack drawing-room, to the huge delight of its unsuspecting mistress. But his wife did not double back, as he anticipated; nor did he see her again in the neighbourhood.

Thenceforward, save for irritating pin-pricks reminding him of her existence, such as futile revolts against the supervision of the Bences and occasional demands for money, she ceased to worry him. But since the day when he caught her about to spy on his home-life, her shadow, like that of some obscene bird, hovered over him perpetually. What she had tried to do then she might have already done, she might do in the future. The horrible sense of insecurity oppressed him: it is that which ages a man who cannot take himself happily.

Otherwise the two years had passed with no great stir. The recurrence of seasons alone surprised him now and then into a realization of the flight of time. He had succeeded to the editorship of the weekly review of which he had been assistant editor; he had published a little book on the "Casual Ward of Workhouses," a despised hash of journalistic articles which had brought him considerable recognition; leader writers had quoted him flatteringly, and his publishers clamoured for another book on a cognate subject; the President of the Local Government Board had invited him to a discussion of the matter, with a view to possible legislation; honours fell thick upon him; but, if it had been a shower of frogs, his disgust could not have been greater. For about the same time he had published a chunky, doughy novel destined to set the world aflame, which sold about a couple of hundred copies. He had cursed all things cursable and uncursable without in any way affecting the heartless rhythm of life. The world went on serenely, and in his glum fashion he found himself going on with the world.

Unity mended his socks and poured out his tea day after day, unchanging in her dull and common scragginess. Neither fine clothes, nor jewels, nor Aunt Gladys's maxims could turn her into a young lady. Miss Lindon sighed, Unity's inability to purr genteelly at tea-parties, the breath of female autumn's being, was the main sorrow in the mild lady's heart. She used to dream of the swelling pride with which she might have listened to Unity playing the "Liederohne Worte" or Stephen Heller or "The Brook" (such a pretty piece!), before the ladies purring on the gim-crack chairs. But the dream was poignantly vain. She had striven with vast goodness to teach Unity to play the piano, and the girl had honestly tried to learn; but as her brain could not master the mystery of the various keys, and as her ear was not acute enough to enable her to sing "Sun of my soul, thou Saviour dear," in tune, the study of music had to be struck out of her curriculum. And she could not talk to the faded gentlewomen who came to the house, and to whose houses Miss Lindon took her. The ordeal always made her perspire, and little beads settled on her snub nose, and she knew it was not ladylike. Such a thing, said Miss Lindon, ought never to happen. But it did, in defiance of all the laws of gentility. So Miss Lindon sighed. But none of these things wrecked the peace of the home. Uneventful serenity reigned in the little house at Kilburn.

Walter Herold went on playing his exquisite miniatures of parts, and, in theatrical terminology, he became very expensive, and prospered exceedingly in his profession; his relations with John remained unaltered;

Miss Lindon loved him, first because he was John's intimate, secondly (and here was a reason which she did not avow) because he had the gift of making her feel that, despite seven and fifty years of spinsterhood, she was still the most fascinating of her sex, and thirdly because he reminded her of poor Captain Featherstone, killed in the Zulu War, who was such a very clever amateur conjurer, and could act charades in a way that would make you die of laughing. And Unity came to him with her problems; and, as they both loved John Risca and Stellamaris, of whom (a thing undreamed of by John, for he rarely mentioned the fairy princess's name to Unity) they talked inordinately, the bond between them was strengthened by links ever freshly forged. And finally, in the sea-chamber at Southcliff, Herold maintained his rank of Great High Favourite, and companioned his august mistress on her fairy vagabondage along the roads that led no whither in the Land That Never Was.

And Stellamaris herself? She was twenty. John, still Great High Belovedest, still finding his perfect rest from care, his enchanted haven, in the great, wide-windowed room looking out to sea, wondered at the commonplace fact. Not long ago, it seemed to him, she had been but the fragile wraith of a child, with arms that you might pass through a signet-ring, and hands no bigger than an acacia-leaf. He had sat but yesterday full on the bed, without danger to the tiny feet which were far away from him. And now the little child had passed into the woman. Thanks to devotion, the world's learning, the resources of the civilized earth, the life-giving air of the sea, her malady had scarcely interfered with bodily growth. And the child's beauty had not been fleeting. It had remained, and matured into that of the woman. Unconsciously John had drifted away from childish things in his long and precious talks with her.

One day she rebuked him.

"Great High Belovedest," she said, "you have n't told me of the palace and Lilias and Niphetos for months and months. Or is it years?"

He laughed. "It must be years. You don't realize that you 're grown up."

"So every one says. I often wonder what it really means."

"You 've developed," said he.

"How?" she persisted.

"You've got longer and broader and—"

She laughed to hide a swift, pink confusion. "I know that, you silly dear. The doctor's always taking measurements of me and making funny calculations—cubing out the contents, as Mr. Wratislaw used to say. I know I'm enormous. That's an external matter of yards and feet,"—she spoke as if her proportions were Brobdingnagian,—"but I 'm referring to inner things. How am I different, in myself, from what I was four years ago?"

John scratched a somewhat puzzled head. How could he explain to her that of which he himself was not quite certain? In the normal case the phenomenon of manhood or womanhood, apart from the physical side,—allowing for the moment that the physical side can be set apart,—is a matter of a wider experience of life, of a million observations unconsciously correlated by a fully developed brain. It implies a differentiation between the facts and fancies of existence. The adult of twenty-one who takes seriously the make-believe of the dolls' house, and, sticking a paper crown on her head, asks you to recognize her as a queen, is merely an imbecile. The sane adult plays at mock tea-parties and crowns itself monarch in obedience to a different set of impulses altogether, either through sheer gaiety of heart, frankly making unto itself no illusions, or using make-believe as a symbol of the highest expression of life— videlicet, art—of which the human mind is capable. And, although we know very well that there are adults, many of advanced years, whom circumstances have so perverted that the Alpha and Omega of their lives is the pursuit either of a little ball or of a verminous animal over the surface of God's arresting earth, or else, it may be, a series of conjectures as to the comparative velocities of unimportant quadrupeds, yet none of them (at loose on society) would have the lunacy or the depravity to maintain that such pursuit or conjecture is a vital element in the scheme of existence. Even these who appear still to dwell in the play-world of the child have the essential faculty of discrimination. They have, in dull intervals between round or ride, encountered sorrow and pain and passion and wickedness and fierce struggle and despair. To them the sordid tragedies of criminal courts, the bestial poverty of slums, are commonplaces of knowledge. Any one of them can reel off a dozen instances of the treachery of false friends, the faithlessness of women, the corruption of commercial or political life. To them are also revealed splendours of heroism and self-sacrifice. They have a million data whence to deduce a serviceable philosophy. They are beyond all question grown up. But what wider experience of life had Stellamaris gained in the four years between the ages of sixteen and twenty?

What fresh facts of existence had been presented to her for observation and correlation? What data had she for that deduction of a philosophy which marks the adult? Neither harm nor spell nor charm had come the lovely lady any nearer during the last four years than during those of her childhood. The Unwritten Law had prevailed as strong as ever. The routine of the sea-chamber had remained unchanged. Her reading, jealously selected, had brought her no closer to the sad core of many human things. The gulls and the waves and the golden sunset clouds were still her high companions. What did people mean when they said she had grown up? John continued for some time to scratch a puzzled head.

"Are you not aware of any change in yourself?" he asked.

She reflected for a moment. "No," she replied seriously. "Of course I know more. I can speak French and Italian—" Professors of these tongues, duly hedged about with ceremonial, had for a long time past attended in the sea-chamber—"and I know lots more of history and geography and geology and astronomy and zoology—oh, Belovedest dear, I 'm dying to see a giraffe! Do you think if he stood on the beach he could stick his head through the window and look at me? And a hippopotamus—can't you bring one in on a string? Or do you think Constable would bite him?"

John expounded the cases of the giraffe and the hippopotamus with great gravity. Her eyebrows contracted ever so little, and a spark danced in her eyes as she waited for the end of the lecture.

"Oh, dear, can't you see a joke?"

"Joke?"

"Why, yes. Don't you think I know all about hippopotamuses?"

"Four years ago," said John, "if I had told you that a wyvern and a unicorn were coming to tea, you would have believed me. Now you would n't. You've grown up. That's what I meant."

"I see," said Stellamaris.

But she didn't; for she turned the conversation back to the palace.

"I'm afraid, dear," said he, "that the cats are dead and Arachne has married a stock-broker, and I've been so busy that the palace has run to seed."

"I thought she was going to marry a duke," said Stella, whose memory for unimportant detail was femininely tenacious.

"The duke was caught by Miss Cassandra P. Wurgles," said John, once more launched on the sea of romance.

"What a funny name," said Stella.

"It's the kind of name," he replied, "always given in English fiction to the heiresses of the Middle West of America."

"Was she an heiress?"

"Worth billions. After they were married they do say she would n't let the duke wipe his razor on anything less valuable than a thousand-dollar bill."

"I don't think that's quite true," laughed Stella.

"I don't know," said John. "Anyhow, Arachne fell back on a stock-broker named MacIsaac, and now there's no one to look after the palace."

"No one at all?" Her voice was full of pity.

"Not a soul," said he.

A tragic pause followed this forlorn declaration. "Dear Belovedest," said Stella, very seriously, "I do wish I could come and set it right for you."

Their eyes met. John sighed.

"I wish you could," said he. "There 's a fairy wand standing in the corner which no one but you can touch. It gives every one else an electric shock that sends them head over heels. But if you could get it and wave it about the place, you would make all sorts of dead things come to glorious life, and fill all the garden walks with flowers, and make the waters live again in the fountains."

It was the John Risca whom she had always known that spoke, the John Risca of whom Herold had occasional flashes, so that he could discount his usual gloomy petulance and love the essential man, the John Risca whose hand poor dumb, little Unity Blake had laid against her cheek—the best and purest John Risca, a will-o'-the-wisp gleam to all his nearest save Stellamaris; but to Stellamaris just the ordinary, commonplace, unaltering, and unalterable John Risca, the Great High Belovedest of her earliest memories. He had said things like this a hundred thousand times before. Yet now the colour rose once more into her cheeks, and a mist such as might surround a dewdrop veiled her eyes.

"What makes you think I could do all that for you?" she asked.

"I don't know, my dear," said John. "You seem to belong to another world." He stumbled. "You 're just a fairy sort of creature."

The answer did not satisfy the instinctive innermost whence sprang the question; but it served. Woman since the beginning of things has had to content herself with half-answers from man, seeing that she vouchsafes him scarcely any answers at all. She smiled and stretched out her hand.

John took it in his clumsy fingers. It was whiter than any hand in the world, veined with the faintest of faint blue.

"Anyhow," she said, "you ought n't to have neglected the palace."

"What was I to do?" he asked whimsically. "You 've been so busy growing up that you've had no time to help me to run it."

"Oh!" she said. She withdrew her hand. "Oh, Belovedest, how can you say such a thing!"

"You yourself," laughed John, "asked whether it was months or years since we talked of it."

"I 've never stopped thinking about it," she protested, and she went on protesting. But, like the Shakspearian lady, she protested too much.

"You've grown up, Stellamaris," said John.

But how much of the old fairy-tale she still believed in he could not gauge. He went away, man with the muck-rake that he was, with the uncomfortable conviction that the roots of her child's faith survived.

And yet she had grown up, and John, for the life of him, could not understand it. He was puzzled, because the sweet reverence of the man for the thing of sea-foam and cloud mystery that she had been to him all his man's life could not dream of physiological development. She was longer and broader; that met the eye. Living in her extraordinary seclusion from the multitudinous winds of earth, she could feel no breath of the storms that shake humanity into the myriad moulds of character. The physical side (other than mere linear and cubical expansion) apart, there was no possibility of change from childhood to womanhood. But John counted without his host—Nature, the host who claims reckoning from us all, kick though we may against her tyrannies; Nature, with her frank indecencies, her uncompromising, but loving, realism. The physical side in the development of any human being cannot be set apart. That passage of every maiden across the ford where brook and river meet is accomplished without a good, careless man's knowledge or conjecture. He kisses her to-day, as he has kissed her since she toddled with bare legs, and she responds, and it means little more to her than an acidulated drop. He shall kiss her to-morrow, and she shall grow as red as any turkey-cock, and cast down her eyes, and go through all the pretty antics characteristic, since the beginning of time, of a self-conscious sex. And the man shall go away scratching his head in a deuce of a puzzle.

Another year passed. Stella was twenty-one. The routine of the Channel House, of the house at Kilburn, of the Fulham flat, went on unchanged and unchanging. Time seems unimportant as a positive agent in human affairs. It is the solvent of sorrow, but it cannot create joy. From its benumbing influence no drama seems to spring. It is events—and events, too, no matter how trivial—that have their roots mysteriously deep in time that shake the world and make the drama which we call history. And it was an event, apparently trivial, but sudden, unlooked for, amazing, that shook the lives whose history is here recorded.

One morning, in obedience to a peremptory telegram from Sir Oliver Blount, John Risca met him at the Imperial Club. The old man rose from his seat near the entrance of the smoking-room into which John was shown, and excitedly wrung both his hands. "My dear boy, you must come to Southcliff at once." Two or three times before he had been brought down post-haste by Sir Oliver, only to find himself needed as a mediator between husband and wife. He shook himself free.

"Out of the question, Oliver. I 'm overwhelmed with work. I 've got my syndicate article to do, and the review goes to press to-night."

"You don't understand. It 's our darling Stella. This morning she lifted her head from the pillow."

"But that's her death-warrant," cried John, quickly. "It's her life-warrant. The fatal thing we've been warned against all these years is no longer fatal. She can move her head easily, painlessly. Don't you see?" The weak old eyes were wet.

"My God!" said John. His breath came fast, and he clapped his great hand on the other's lean shoulders. "But that means—great God in heaven!".—his voice shook—"what may it not mean?"

"It may mean everything," said Sir Oliver.

From time to time throughout Stella's life the great magicians of science had entered the sea-chamber and departed thence, shaking sad and certain heads. With proper care, they said, Stellamaris might live—might live, indeed, until her hair turned white and her young cheeks shrivelled with age; but of leaving that bed by the window and going forth into the outer world there was no hope or question. Still, Nature, the inscrutable, the whimsical, might be cozened by treatment into working a miracle.

At any rate, no harm would be done by trying, and her guardians would have the consoling assurance that nothing had been left undone. They prescribed after their high knowledge, and pocketed their high fees, and went their way. Dr. Ransome, Stella's lifelong doctor and worshipper, carried out each great magician's orders, and, as prophesied, nothing ever happened either for good or harm.

But, six months ago, a greater magician than all, one Wilhelm von Pfeiler of Vienna, who by working miracles on his own account with newly discovered and stupendous forces had begun to startle scientific Europe, happened to be in England, and was summoned to the sea-chamber. He was a dark, silky-bearded man in whose eyes brooded perpetual melancholy. He, too, shook his head and said "Perhaps." Ransome, who had seized with high hopes on the wandering magician, found him vastly depressing. His "Perhaps" was more mournfully hopeless than the others' "No." He spoke little, for he knew no English, and Ransome's German, like that of Stella's household, was scanty; but Ransome understood him to croak platitudes about time and youth and growth and nature being factors in the case. As to his newly discovered treatment, well, it might have some effect; he was certain of nothing; as yet no sure deductions could be drawn from his experiments; everything concerning the application of these new forces was at the empirical stage. So profound a melancholy rang in his utterances that he left Lady Blount weeping bitterly, and convinced that he had passed death-sentence on their beloved being. Then a near-sighted, taciturn young man, a budding magician who had sat at Von Pfeiler's feet in Vienna, came down from London with apparatus worth a hundred times its weight in gold. And nothing happened or seemed about to happen. Stella called him the gnome.

All this John knew. Like the rest of Stella's satellites, accustomed for years to the unhesitating pronouncements of the great specialists and to their unhealing remedies, he had little faith in Von Pfeiler. The taciturn young surgeon who had been administering the treatment kept his own counsel and gave no encouragement to questioners. John had agreed with Sir Oliver that it was a waste of time and money—a fabulous amount of money; but the treatment amused Stella, and she liked the gnome, whom every one else detested, because he loved dogs, and cured Constable, now growing old and rheumatic, of a stiff leg. So every one suffered the gnome patiently.

And now the miracle had been worked. Stella had lifted her head from the pillow. The two men sat tremulous with hope.

"I've been so upset," said Sir Oliver, "and so has Julia. We had words. Why, I don't know. I love our darling quite as much as she does; but Julia is trying. Waiter! Get me a brandy and soda. What will you have? Nothing? I don't usually drink spirits in the morning, John; but I feel I need it. I'm getting old and can't stand shocks."

"What does Ransome say?"

"He 's off his head. Every one 's off his head. The very dog is rushing about like a lunatic. Nearly knocked me down in the garden."

"And Cassilis?"

Cassilis was the gnome.

"Ransome has telegraphed him to come down at once. But I thought I'd run up and tell you. We might go together to see him and fetch him back with us. You 'll come, won't you?"

"Come? Why, of course I'll come. What do you think I 'll do? Stay in London at such a time and send her a post-card to say I'm glad?"

"You said something about seeing your review through the press."

"Oh, confound the review! It can go to the devil!" cried John.

London ablaze with revolution would have been a small matter compared with this world-shaking event, the lifting of a girl's head.

"It will be such a comfort to me," said the old man. "I don't know what to do. I can't rest. My mind's in a maze. It's like the raising of Jairus's daughter."

"Let us do some telephoning," said John.

They went out together. John rang up Cassilis. He had been out all the morning and would not be returning for another hour. John rang up Herold at a theatre where he knew him to be rehearsing, and gave him the glad news. They returned to the smoking-room. Sir Oliver drank off his brandy and soda at one gulp.

"And Stella herself? What does she make of it?"

"The only one not upset in the house. That little girl 's an angel, John." He blew his nose violently. "It appears she was stretching out her arm to pat the old dog's chaps, overreached herself a bit, and mechanically her head came away from the pillow. She called out to nurse, 'Nurse, I 've lifted my head.' Nurse flew up to her. 'What do you mean, darling?' She showed her. She showed her, by God! Nurse forbade her to do it any more, and flew down-stairs like a wildcat to tell us. Then we telephoned to Ransome. He saw her; she did it for him; then he came to us white and shaking all over. Naturally I wanted to see the darling child do it, too. Julia interfered. Stella must n't do it again till Cassilis came. Then we had the words. She said I was eaten through with egotism—I! Now, am I, John?"

Presently Herold dashed, in, aflame with excitement. The story, such as it was, had to be told anew.

"I 'll come with you to Cassilis, and then on to Southcliff."

"But your rehearsal?" said John.

Herold confounded the rehearsal, even as John had confounded his review. In the presence of this thrilling wonder, trivialities had no place.

Cassilis received this agitated and unusual deputation without a flicker of surprise. He was a baldheaded, prematurely old young man, with great, round spectacles. He gave one the air of an inhuman custodian of awful secrets.

"I presume you have called with reference to this," said he, indicating a telegram which he held in his hand. "I've just opened it."

"Yes," said Sir Oliver. "Is n't it wonderful? You must come down with us at once."

"It's very inconvenient for me to leave London."

"My dear sir, you must throw over every engagement."

The shadow of a smile passed over the young man's features.

"If you press the point, I'll come."

"But are n't you astounded at what has occurred? Don't you understand Ransome's message?"

"Perfectly," said Cassilis. "I 've already written to Dr. von Pfeiler—a week: ago—detailing the progress and full success of the case."

"Then you know all about it?" asked John. "Naturally. I've been practising her at it for the last fortnight, though she did n't realize what I was doing."

"Then why on earth did n't you tell us?"

"I had arranged to tell you to-morrow," said Cassilis.

"I don't think you've acted rightly, sir," cried Sir Oliver.

"Never mind that," said Herold. "Mr. Cassilis doubtless has his excellent reasons. The main thing is, Will her cure go beyond this? Will she get well and strong? Will she be able to walk about God's earth like anybody else?"

The little gnome-like man straightened with his toe a rucked corner of the hearth-rug. He paused deliberately before replying, apparently unmoved by the anxious eyes bent on him. There was a span of agonized silence. Then he spoke:

"This time next year she will be leading a woman's normal life."

The words fell clear-cut on the quiet of the room. The three men uttered not a word. Cassilis, asking their leave to make some small preparations for his journey, left them. Then, relieved of his presence, they drew together and pressed one another's hands and stood speechless, like children suddenly brought to the brink of some new wonderland.

# CHAPTER XII

Thenceforward a humming confusion reigned in the Channel House. The story of the miraculous recovery spread through Southcliff. Sir Oliver and Lady Blount held a little court every day to receive congratulations. A few privileged well-wishers were admitted to the sea-chamber, where Stella still lay enthroned by the window. She had not realized the extent of her fame among the inhabitants until a garrulous visitor told her that she was one of the pet traditions of the place and that her great-windowed room at the top of the house on the cliff was always pointed out with pride to the tourist.

In her mysterious seclusion she had become a local celebrity. This interest of the little world grouped about the Channel House added a joy to her anticipation of mingling with it. The affection in which she was held by butcher and baker, to say nothing of the mayor and corporation, cemented her faith (in which she had been so jealously bred) in the delightful perfection of mankind.

Meanwhile she progressed daily towards recovery, very slowly, but with magical sureness. Cassilis continued his treatment. Queer apparatuses were fitted to her so that she could go through queer muscular exercises. She was being put into training, as it were, for life. Every new stage in her progress was marked by fêtes and rejoicings. The first time that her bed could be wheeled into a room on the other side of the house was a solemn occasion. It was July, and the rolling hills, rich in corn-fields and forest greenery, were flooded with sunlight. The earth proclaimed its fruitful plenty, and laughed in the joy of its loveliness.

That which to those with her was a commonplace of beauty stretched before Stellamaris's vision as a new and soul-arresting wonder. She had only elusive, childish memories of the actual earth; for before she had been laid upon her back never to rise again, she had been a delicate, invalid child. She had seen thousands of pictures, so that she was at no intellectual loss to account for the spectacle; but, for all her life that counted, sea and sky in their myriad changes had been her intimate conception of the world. And it had been her world—the only world that her eyes would ever rest upon; and as it had never entered her head to hope for another, it had sufficed her soul's needs. Indeed, it had overwhelmed them with its largess, until, as Herold declared, she herself had become a creature of cloud and wave. This sudden presentation of a new and unrealized glory set her heart beating madly; her cheeks grew white, and tears rolled down them.

"Now, is n't that a beautiful view?" said Lady Blount.

"Soon we 'll hire a motor, until you can buy one for yourself, and go and explore it all, my dear," said Sir Oliver.

"Southcliff lies just below there on the left," said the nurse.

"See that red roof there between the trees? That's where our old friend Colonel Dukes lives. Devilish good house; though, if he had taken my advice when he was building it, it would have been much better."

"And just over there," said Lady Blount, pointing-, "is the railway that takes you to London."

"You 're quite wrong, Julia," said Sir Oliver; "that's a bit of the south coast line. Is n't it, John?"

"Oliver is right. You can't see the London line from here," said John.

They went on talking, but Stella, in a rapture of vision, heeded them not. Herold, who stood quite close to her, was silent. She held his hand, and gripped it almost convulsively. John, with rare observation, noticed that her knuckles were white. Her face was set in an agony of adoration too poignant for speech. John, curiously sensitive where Stella was concerned, realized that these two hand in hand were close together on a plane of feeling too high for the profane. With a little movement of deprecation which neither Herold nor Stella perceived, he pushed the others toward the door and, following them out of the room, closed it behind them.

"Better leave her alone with Walter," said he.

"Quite so," said Sir Oliver. "Just what I told you, Julia. We must let her go slow for a bit and not excite her."

"I don't remember you ever saying anything of the kind," retorted Lady Blount. "It was Walter."

"Well, Oliver agreed with him, which comes to the same thing," said John, acting peacemaker.

But they wrangled all down the corridor, and when the two men were left alone, Sir Oliver shook his head.

"A trying woman, John; very trying."

Meanwhile Stella and Herold remained for a long time in the quiet room without the utterance of a word. As soon as the others went, her grasp relaxed. Herold drew a chair gently to her side and waited patiently for her to speak; for he saw that her soul was at grips with the new glory of the earth. At last a quivering sigh shook her, and she turned her wet eyes away from the window and looked at him with a smile.

"Well?" said he.

"I feel that it is all too beautiful."

"It makes you sad."

"Yes; vaguely, but exquisitely. How did you guess?"

"Your eyes have been streaming, Stellamaris."

"Foolish, is n't it?"

"I suppose it 's the finite realizing itself unconsciously before the infinite. Is it too much for you?"

She shook her head. "I should like to stay here and gaze at this forever till I drank it all, all in."

"Have you ever read the life of St. Brigit?" he asked. "There's one little episode in it which comes to my mind."

"Tell me," said Stella.

"She founded convents, you know, in Ireland. Now, there was one nun dearly loved by St. Brigit, and she had been blind from birth; and one evening they were sitting on one of the Wicklow Hills, and St. Brigit described to her all the beauties of the green valleys below, and the silver streams and the purple mountains beyond, melting into the happy sky. And the nun said, 'Sister, pray to God to work a miracle and give me sight so that I can see it and glorify Him.' So St. Brigit prayed, and God heard her prayer, and the eyes of the nun were opened, and she looked upon the world, and her senses were ravished by its glory. And then she fell to weeping and trembling and she sank on her knees before St. Brigit and said, I have seen, but I beseech thee pray that my sight be taken again from me, for I fear that in the beauty of the world I may forget God.' And St. Brigit prayed again, and God heard her, and the nun's sight was taken from her. And they both lifted their voices to heaven and glorified the Lord."

Stella sighed when he had ended, and quiet fell upon them. She looked dreamily out of the window. Herold watched her face, with a pang at his heart. It was as pure as a little child's.

"It's a lovely legend," she said at last. "But the nun was wrong. The beauty of this world ought to bring one nearer to God instead of making one forget Him."

Herold smiled. "Certainly it ought to," said he.

"Why did you tell me the story?"

"Because it came into my head."

"There was some other reason."

He could not deny, for in her candid eyes he saw assurance; yet he dared not tell her that which dimmed the crystal of his gladness. He saw the creature of cloud and foam gasping in the tainted atmosphere of the world of men; the dewdrop on the star exposed to the blazing sun. What would happen?

"I am going to get well," she continued, seeing that he did not answer, "and walk out soon into the gardens and the streets and see all the wonderful, wonderful things you and Belovedest have told me of. And"—she pressed her hands to her bosom—"I can't contain myself for joy. And yet, Walter dear, you seem to think I should be better off if I remained as I am —or was. I can't understand it."

"My dear," said Herold reluctantly, wishing he had never heard of St. Brigit, "so long as you see God through the beauties and vanities of the world, as you've seen Him through the sea-mists and the dawn and the sunset, all will be well. But that takes a brave spirit—braver than St. Brigit's nun. She feared lest she might see the world, and nothing but the world, and nothing divine shining through. People who do that lose their souls."

"Then you think," said Stellamaris, wrinkling her smooth brow—"you think that the blind have the truer vision."

"Truer than that of the weak, perhaps, but not as true as the strong spirits who dare see fearlessly."

"Do you think I am weak or strong?" she asked, with a woman's relentless grip on the personal.

"What else but a strong spirit," he replied half disingenuously, "could have triumphed, as you have done, over a lifelong death?"

"Death?" She opened her eyes wide. "Death? But I've lived every hour of my life, and it has been utterly happy."

"The strong spirit, dear," said Herold.

"Great High Favourite dear, what else could you say?"

She laughed, but the tenderness in her eyes absolved the laugh and the feminine speech from coquetry.

"I might talk to you as John Knox did to Mary, Queen of Scots."

Just as life had been translated to the hapless Miss Kilmansegg of the Golden Leg into terms of gold, so had it been translated to Stella into terms of beauty. History had been translated, accordingly, into terms of romance. She had heard, indeed, of Mary Stuart, but as a being of legendary and unnaughty loveliness. At the stem image of the grave Calvinist she shrank.

"John Knox was a horrid, croaking raven," she emphatically declared, "and nobody could possibly talk like that nowadays."

Herold laughed and turned the conversation into lighter channels. The Unwritten Law prevailed over his instinctive impulse to warn her against the deceptive glamour of the world. Then the hour struck for an item in the invalid's routine, and the nurse came in, and Stella was wheeled back to her high chamber.

Many days of her convalescence after this were marked with red stones. There was the first day when, carried down-stairs, she presided from her high couch at a dinner-party given in her honour, the guests being John Risca and Walter Herold, Wratislaw and the nurse, Dr. Ransome and his wife, and the gnomeheaded and spectacled Cassilis.

It was a merry party, and towards the end of dinner, when the port went round, Stella's own maid coached for the part, at a sign from Sir Oliver who commanded silence, spoke in a falsetto voice sticking in a nervous throat the familiar words: "Miss Stella's compliments, and would the gentlemen take a glass of wine with her." And they all rose and drank and made a great noise, and the tears rolled down John Risca's cheeks and fell upon his bulging shirt-front, and Sir Oliver blew his nose loudly and made a speech.

A great day, too, was her first progress in her wheel-chair about the grounds of the Channel House. All was wonder and wild delight to the girl who had never seen, or had seen so long ago that she had forgotten, the velvet of smooth turf; the glory of roses growing in their heyday insolence; the alluring shade of leafy chestnuts; the pansies clinging to dear Mother Earth; the fairy spray of water from a hose-pipe over thirsty beds; the crisp motion, explaining the mysterious echo of years, of the grass-mower driven over the lawn; the ivy tapestry of walls; the bewildering masses of sweet-peas; the apples, small and green though they were, actually hanging from boughs; the real live fowls, jaunty in prosperous plumage, so different from the apologetic naked shapes—fowls hitherto to her, which Morris, the maid, had carved for her meals at a side table in the sea-chamber, the cabbages brave in crinkled leaf, unaware of their doom of ultimate hot agglutination, the tender green bunches of grapes in glass-houses drinking wine from the mother founts of the sun, the quiet cows on the gently sloping pasture-land.

At last she put her hands over her eyes, and Herold made a sign, and they wheeled the chair back to the house; and only when they halted in the wide, cool drawing-room, with windows opening to the south, did she look at outer things; and then, while all stood by in a hush, she drew a few convulsive breaths and rested her overwrought spirit on the calm, familiar sea.

A day of days, too, when, still in glorious summer weather, they hired an enormous limousine from the great watering-place a few miles off, and took her all but prone, and incased in the appliances of science, through the gates of the Channel House into the big world. They drove over the Sussex Downs, along chalk roads, between crisp grass-lands dotted with sheep, through villages,—gleams of paradises compact of thatched roof, rambler roses, blue and white garments hung out on lines to laugh in the sunshine, flashing new stucco cottages, labelled "County Police" (a puzzle to Stellamaris), ramshackle shops, with odd wares, chiefly sweets, exposed in tiny casement windows, old inns flaunting brave signs, "The Five Alls," "The Leather Bottell," away from the road, with a forecourt containing rude bench and table and trough for horses, young women, with the cheeks of the fresh, and old women, with the cheeks of the withered apple, and sun-tanned men, and children of undreamed-of chubbiness. And to Stellamaris all was a wonderland of joy.

During most of the month of August the rain fell heavily and outdoor excursions became rare events, and the world as seen from windows was a gray and dripping spectacle. But Stella, accustomed to the vast dreariness of wintry seas, found fresh beauties in the rain-swept earth. The patter of drops on leaves played new and thrilling melodies; a slant of sunshine across wet grass offered magical harmonies of colour; the unfamiliar smell of the reeking soil was grateful to her nostrils. And had she not the captivating indoor life among pleasant rooms in which she had hitherto dwelt only in fancy? Hopes in the process of fulfilment gilded the glad days.

She talked unceasingly to those about her of the happy things to come.

"Soon we 'll be teaching you to walk," said John.

She glowed. "That's going to be the most glorious adventure of my life."

"I've never regarded putting one foot before another in that light," he said with a laugh. Then suddenly realizing what he had said, he felt a wave of pity and love surge through his heart. What child of man assured of a bird's power of flight would not be thrilled at the prospect of winging his way through space? It would be indeed a glorious adventure.

"My poor darling!" said he, very tenderly.

As usual, she disclaimed the pity. There was no one happier than herself in the wide universe.

"But I often have wondered what it would feel like."

"To walk?"

"Yes. To have the power of moving yourself from one place to another. It seems so funny. Of course I did walk once, but I've forgotten all about it. They tell me I shall have to learn from the beginning, just like a little baby."

"You 'll have to learn lots of things from the beginning," said John, rather sadly.

"What kind of things?"

"All sorts."

"Tell me," she insisted, for ever so small a cloud passed over his face.

"Taking your place as a woman in the whirl of life," said he.

She turned on him the look of untroubled sapience that proceeds from the eyes of child saints in early Italian paintings.

"I don't think that will be very difficult, Belovedest. I'm not quite a little ignoramus, and Aunt Julia has taught me manners. I have always been able to talk to people when sick, and I don't see why I should be afraid of them when I'm well. I 've thought quite a lot about it, and talked to Aunt Julia."

"And what does she say?"

"She assures me," she cried gaily, "that I am bound to make a sensation in society."

"You 'll have all mankind at your feet, dear," said John. "But," he added in a change of tone, "I was referring to more vital things than success in drawing-rooms."

She laid her hand lightly on his..

"Do you know, Belovedest, what Walter said some time ago? He said that if I looked at the world and saw God through it, all would be well."

"I can add nothing more to that," said John, and, thinking that Herold had been warning her of dangers, held his peace for the occasion.

Then there came a day, not long afterward, when she made the speech which in some form or other he had been expecting and dreading.

"The next glorious adventure will be when you take me over the palace."

He laughed awkwardly. "I remember telling you that the palace has run to seed."

"But you still live in it."

"No, dear," said he.

"Oh!" said Stellamaris in a tone of deep disappointment. "Oh, why, why?"

John felt ridiculously unhappy. She believed, after all, in the incredible fairy-tale.

"Perhaps it was n't such a gorgeous palace as I made out," he confessed lamely. "As the cooks say, my hand was rather heavy with the gold and marble." She laughed, to his intense relief. "I have felt since that there was a little poetic exaggeration somewhere. But it must be a beautiful place, all the same." His spirits sank again. "I could walk about it blindfold, although we have n't talked of it for so long. Who is living there now?"

"I've sold it, dear, to some king of the Cannibal Islands," he declared in desperate and ponderous jest.

"So there's no more palace?"

"No more," said he.

"I 'm sorry," said Stellamaris—"so sorry." She smiled at him, but the tears came into her eyes. "I was looking forward so to seeing it. You see, dear, I've lived in it for such a long, long time!"

"There are hundreds of wonder-houses for you to see when you get strong," said John, by way of consolation, yet hating himself.

"Westminster Abbey and Windsor Castle, and so on. Yes," said Stella, "but they've none of them been part of me."

So he discovered that, at one-and-twenty, on the eve of her entrance into the world of reality, the being most sacred to him still dwelt in her Land of Illusion. Two or three frank words would have been enough to bring down to nothingness the baseless fabric of his castle in the air, his palace of dreams; but he dreaded the shock of such seismic convulsion. He had lied for years, putting all that was godlike of his imperfect humanity into his lies, so as to bring a few hours' delight into the life of this fragile creature whom he worshiped, secure in the conviction that the lies would live for ever and ever as vital truths, without chance of detection. And now that chance, almost the certainty, had come.

John Risca was a strong man, as men count strength. He faced the grim issues of life undaunted, and made his own terms. He growled when wounded, but he bared his teeth and snarled with defiance at his foes. In a bygone age he would have stood like his Celtic ancestors, doggedly hacking amid a ring of slain until the curtain of death was drawn before his blood-shot eyes and he fell, idly smiting the air. In the modern conflict in which, fortunately, human butchery does not come within the sphere of the ordinary man's activities, he could stand with the same moral constancy. But here, when it was a mere question of tearing a gossamer veil from before a girl's eyes, his courage failed him. Such brute dealing, he argued, might be salutary for common clay; but for Stellamaris it would be dangerous. Let knowledge of the fact that there had never been a palace come to her gradually. Already he had prepared the way. Thus he consoled himself, and, in so doing, felt a mean and miserable dog.

# CHAPTER XIII

S TELLA loved the garden, even when autumn came and flowers were rare; for still there was the gold and russet glory of the trees. Also the garden was a bit of her Promised Land; the road beyond the gate ran into the heart of the world. And the open air brought strength. On sunny days her wheel-chair was brought down and set on a gravel path, and there, wrapped in furs, she sat, generally alone save for the old hound always on guard beside her. She read, and dreamed her innocent dreams, and looked up at the ever-novel canopy of the sky, exulting quietly in her freedom. Those around her knew her needs and gave her at such times the familiar solitude which she craved.

"Don't be left alone, darling, a moment longer than you want," said Lady Blount. "Too much of that sort of thing is n't good for you."

And Stella, trying to interpret herself, would reply, "I just want to make friends with nature."

"I wish I could understand you, dear, like Walter," said Lady Blount. "What exactly do you mean?"

Stella laughed, and said truthfully that she did not know. Perhaps, it was that, the sea having taken her to its heart, she feared lest earth might not be so kindly, and she sought conciliation. But such flutterings of the spirit are not to be translated into words. A day or two before she had driven through a glade of blazing beech, carpeted deep brown, and the shadows twisted themselves into dim shapes, stealing through the mystery of the slender trunks, and the longing to be left alone among them and hear the message of the woodland had smitten her like pain.

One morning she sat warmly wrapped up, a fur toque on her head, in the pale autumn sunshine, with Constable by her side, when a draggled-tailed woman, carrying a draggled-bodied infant, paused by the front gate, taking stock of the place in the tramp's furtive way; and, spying the gracious figure of the girl at a turn of the gravel path, walked boldly in. Before she had advanced half-way, Constable, hidden by Stella's chair, rose to his feet, his ears cocked, and growled threateningly. The woman came to a scared halt. Stella looked up and saw her. Quickly she laid her hand on the dog's head, and rated him for a silly fellow and bade him lie down and not move till she gave the order. Constable, like an old dog who knew his place, but felt bound to protest, grumblingly obeyed. He had lived for eleven years under the fixed conviction that though female tramps with babies were permitted by some grotesque authority to wander on sufferance along the road, they could enter the gates of the Channel House only under penalty of instant annihilation. His goddess, however, through some extraordinary caprice ordaining them to live, the matter was taken out of his hands. Let them live, then, and see what came of it. It was beyond his comprehension.

"Don't be afraid," cried Stella in her clear voice. "The dog won't hurt you."

"Sure, Miss?"

"Quite sure." She smiled bountiful assurance. The draggled-tailed woman approached. "What do you want?"

The woman, battered, dirty, and voluble, began the tramp's tale. She had started from Dover and was bound for Plymouth, where she was to meet her husband, a sailor, whose ship would arrive to-morrow. What she had been doing in Dover, except that she had been in 'orspital (which did not account for the child's movements), she did not state. But she had slept under hedges since she had started, and had no money, and a kind gentleman, Gawd bless him! had given her a hunk of bread and cheese the day before, and that was all the food they had had for twenty-four hours.

As she talked, Stella's unaccustomed eyes gradually took in the scarecrow details of her person: the blowzy hat, with its broken feathers; the greasy ropes of hair; the unclean rags of raiment; the broken and shapeless boots; the huddled defilement of the staring, unwholesome child; and she began to tremble through all her body. For a while the sense of sight was so overwhelming in its demands that she lost the sense of hearing. What was this creature of loathsome ugliness doing in her world of beauty? To what race did she belong? From what planet had she fallen? For what eccentric reason did she choose to present this repulsive aspect to mankind?

At last, when her sight was more or less familiarized with the spectacle of squalor, the significance of the woman's words came to her as to one awaking from a dream.

"Not a bit of food has passed my lips since yesterday at twelve o'clock, Miss, and Gawd strike me dead, Miss, if I ain't telling the blessed truth."

"But why have n't you bought food?" asked Stella.

The woman stared at her. How could she understand Stellamaris?

"I have n't a penny in the world, Miss. The day afore yesterday a lady give me twopence, and I spent it in milk for the child. S'welp me, I did, Miss."

"Do you mean to tell me," said Stella, whose face had grown tense and white, "that it's impossible for you to get food for yourself and your baby?"

"Indeed I do, Miss."

"That the two of you might die of starvation?"

"We 're a-dying of it now, Miss," said the woman.

God knows that she lied. The tramp's life is not a path of roses, and it is not one suitable for the rearing of tender babes, and the fact of its possibility is a blot on our civilization; but the hard-bitten vagabond of the highroad has his or her well-defined means of livelihood. This was a mistress of mumpery.

She had passed the night in the comfortable casual ward of a workhouse five miles away, and had slept the dead sleep of the animal, and she and her baby had started the day with a coarse, though sustaining, meal. She was wandering on and on, aimlessly from workhouse to workhouse, as she had wandered from infancy, begging a sixpence here, and a plate of victuals there, impeded in her stray-cat freedom only by the brat in her arms, yet fiercely fond of it and regardful of its needs. She was a phenomenon that in our civilization ought not to exist. She was acquainted with hunger and thirst and privation; she was anything of misery that you like to describe; but she was not dying or likely to die of starvation.

The sociology of the tramp, however, was leagues outside the knowledge of Stellamaris. She looked at the woman in awful horror until her delicate face seemed to fade into a pair of great God-filled eyes.

"And you have no roof to shelter you from the cold and rain?"

After the manner of her kind the woman assured her that such was the fact. She put her head on one side, wheedling in the time-honoured way.

"If you would help a poor woman with a shilling or two, kind lady—"

"A shilling or two?" Stella's voice broke into a cracked falsetto. "You shall have pounds and pounds. I'll see that you don't die of starvation. I have no money to give you,—I've scarcely ever seen any,—but I have thousands of pounds in the house, and you shall have them all. If I could only walk, I would ask some one to fetch them to you. But I can't walk. I've never been able to walk all my life. You see, I'm tied here till my maid comes for me. What can I do?" She wrung her hands, desperately, stirred to the roots of her being.

"Never walked?" said the woman, taken aback, the elementary human fact appealing more to her dulled senses than the phantasmagorical promise of wealth. "Lor'! Poor young lady! I'd sooner be as I am, Miss, than not be able to walk. And such a sweet young lady!" Then the gleam of the divine being spent, she said, "Can't you call anybody, Miss?"

But there was no need to call anybody; for one of the maids, having caught sight of the intruder through a window of the house, came flying down the path, a protecting flutter of apron-strings.

"What do you mean by coming in here? Go away at once! We have nothing to do with tramps. Be off with you!"

She was breathless, excited, indignant.

"Hold your tongue, Mary!" cried Stella in a tone so unfamiliar that it petrified the simple maid. "How dare you interfere between me and the person I am talking to?" It must be remembered that Stella was of mortal clay. She had her faults, like the rest of us. She was born and bred a princess, an autocrat, a despot, a tyrant. And here was one of the white-hot moments of life when the princess was the princess and the tyrant the tyrant. The new commotion brought the old dog again to his feet. For the only time in her life she struck him in anger, though physically he felt it as much as the fall of an autumn leaf.

"Down, Constable, down!" And turning to the maid: "Wheel my chair into the drawing-room and ask Lady Blount to come to me. You follow us!" she commanded the tramp.

The bewildered Mary obeyed. The procession was formed: Stella, in her chair; Mary; Constable, head down, wondering like an old dog at the queer, newfangled ways of the world; and the bedraggled woman, with her pallid and staring baby.

The chair was wheeled across the threshold of the drawing-room. The tramp paused irresolute. Bidden to enter and sit down, she chose a straight-backed chair near the door. Mary sped to fetch her mistress to deal with the appalling situation. In a moment or two Lady Blount hurried in. The woman rose and sketched a vague curtsy.

Lady Blount began:

"My darling Stella—"

But Stella checked her, stretching out passionate hands.

"Aunt Julia, give me two or three thousand pounds at once, please, please!"

"My dear, what for?" asked the amazed lady.

"To give to this poor woman. She and her baby are dying of starvation. They are dressed in rags. They have no home. It 's dreadful, horrible! Can you conceive it?"

Lady Blount turned to the woman.

"Go round to the kitchen entrance, and they will give you some food. I 'll see you myself later."

The woman thanked her and blessed her, and disappeared.

"My dearest," said Lady Blount, gently, "you can't give such people vast sums of money."

"Why not? She has none. We have a lot. How can we live in comfort when she and her baby are wandering about penniless. They will die. Don't you understand? They will die."

"We can't provide for them for the rest of their lives, dear."

"But we must," she cried. "How can you be so cruel?"

"Cruel? My dearest, if I give her a plate of food, and some milk for the baby, and send her away with a shilling, she will be hugely delighted. A woman like that is not a very deserving object for charity."

Stella's bosom rose and fell, and she regarded Lady Blount in sudden, awful surmise.

"Auntie darling, what do you mean? Why are n't you horrified?"

"She's only a tramp. Neither she nor the baby is going to die of starvation. And, darling, you must n't let folks like that come near you. Goodness knows what horrible diseases they may be suffering from."

"But that makes it all the worse. If she is ill, we must help her to get well."

"My poor innocent lamb," said Lady Blount, "there are thousands like her. They are the dregs of our civilization. We could n't possibly keep them all in luxury, could we? Now, don't be distressed, dear," she added, bending down and kissing the girl's cheek.

"I 'll go and have a word with the woman. I 'll treat her quite generously, for your sake, you may be assured."

She smiled, and went out of the room, leaving Stella crushed beneath an avalanche of knowledge. Filthy, starving shreds of humanity were common objects in the beautiful world—so common as to arouse little or no compassion in the hearts of kind women like the maid Mary and her Aunt Julia. All they had thought of was of her, Stella, her danger and possible contamination. Toward the woman they were callous, almost cruel. What did it mean? Her chivalrous anger died down; reaction came. She looked about her beautiful world piteously, and then for the first time in her life she wept tears of bitter sorrow.

They told her afterward of the tramp's wayward, wandering life, of the various charities that existed for the regeneration of such people, of the free hospitals for the sick, of the workhouse system, and they gave her John Risca's famous little book to read. Eventually she was convinced that it was quixotic folly to bestow a fortune on the first beggar that came along, and she acquitted her aunt of cruelty. But a cloud hung heavy for a long time over her spirits, and a stain soiled the beauty of the garden, so that it never more was the perfect paradise. And, henceforward, when she drove through the streets of the great watering-place near by, and through the villages which still held something of their summer enchantment, her eyes were opened to sights of sorrow and pain to which they had been happily blind before.

Winter came, and the routine of her life went on, despite revolutionary changes of habit. Her heart had learned not to be affected by the transition from the prone to the sitting posture. No longer did beholders realize her as nothing but a head and neck and graceful arms, and no longer was a dressing-jacket the only garment into which she could throw her girlish coquetry. Her hair was done up on the top of her head in the manner prescribed by fashion, and she wore the whole raiment of womankind.

John, when he first saw her reclining in her invalid chair, dressed in a soft gray ninon gown, a gleam of silk stocking peeping between the hem and a dainty-shoe, hung back for a second or two from a feeling of shyness. It was a shock to find that Stella had feet like anybody else, and very prettily shaped, adorable little feet. It seemed almost indelicate to look at them, as it would be to inspect too curiously the end of a mermaid's tail. She held out both hands to greet him, laughing and blushing.

"How do you like me?" she asked.

The lights of the drawing-room were dim, and the firelight danced caressingly over her young beauty.

"I've never seen anything so lovely," said John, looking at her in stupid admiration until her eyes dropped in confusion.

"I did n't mean me, you silly Belovedest. I meant my new dress, my general get-up. Don't you think it's pretty?"

"I do," said John, fervently.

But what cared he, or what would have cared any man worth the name of man, for the details of her feminine upholstery, when the revelation of her complete deliciousness burst upon him? It was then that he realized her as woman. It was from that moment that she haunted his dreams not as Stellamaris, star of the sea, child of cloud and mystery, but as a sweet and palpitating wonder in a marvel of flesh and blood.

Despite dangers, and through the stress of tradition, the Unwritten Law still prevailed. The episode of the tramp caused her to ask many questions; but they answered them discreetly. Even when she grew strong enough to take her active share in the world's doings her life would still be a sheltered one. Knowledge would come gradually and unconsciously. Why wantonly give her the shocks of pain? But even a guarded house and garden could not be the sanctuary of the sea-chamber. Breaths of evil and sighs of sorrowful things come on the winds of the earth into most of the habitations of man. The newsboy alone flings into every household his reeking record of sin. This last did not penetrate into the sea-chamber; but lying about the rooms, it could not escape a girl's natural curiosity.

"Young ladies don't read newspapers, dear," said Lady Blount, asking Heaven's forgiveness for her lie.

"Why?" A natural question.

"They contain accounts of things which are not fit reading for young girls."

Stella pondered over this reason for some time; but one day she said:

"I am no longer a young girl. I am a grown-up woman. I want to know what the world is like. I hear every one talking of parliament and politics and foreign countries, and I am ignorant of it all, my dear Exquisite Auntship. I have a right to know everything about life. You must let me read the newspapers."

"Well, wait just a little, dearest," said Lady Blount.

And the next time John Risca and Walter Herold came down, she took counsel of them, and they reluctantly agreed that no longer could the old régime of the Unwritten Law be enforced. Stella must have her newspaper. Thenceforward, every morning, the portentous package of "The Times" (none of your sensational half-penny shockers!) was laid upon Stella's lap, and she read, poor child, the foreign news, and the leaders, and all the solemn and harmless and unimportant matters in big print until she yawned her pretty head off, in vast disappointment with newspapers. It all seemed to her ingenuous mind such a wordy fuss about nothing. Still, she read conscientiously about tariff reform and naval armaments and female suffrage and the pronouncements of the German Emperor and home rule for Ireland, in the puzzled assurance that thereby she was fitting herself for her future place in the great world.

But one day Lady Blount, going into the pleasant morning room where Stella now usually had her being, found her sitting with tragic face, staring out of the window, the decorous "Times" lying a tousled, crumpled mass on the floor. She was alarmed.

"Darling, what's the matter?"

"Oh, it's hateful! It's unthinkable! Why did n't you tell me that such things happened nowadays?"

"What things?"

Stella pointed to the outraged organ of British respectability.

"A day or two ago—it 's all true that 's in the newspaper, is n't it? It's not made up? It all happens?—a day or two ago, while we were laughing here, a man took a knife and killed his wife and three children. It's incredible that there can be such monsters in the world."

"My darling, when you know a little more," faltered Lady Blount, "you will learn that there are abnormal people who do these dreadful things and get reported in the newspapers. But they have nothing to do with us. You must n't be frightened. We never come across them. Our life is quite different."

"But what does that matter?" cried the girl, with agonized eyes. "They exist. They are among us, whether we happen to meet them or not. They are like the tramps."

The world-worn woman, lined and faded, her red hair turned almost gray now, put her arms around the girl, and sought physically to bring the comfort that her intelligence was not acute enough to convey in speech. Stella hid her face against the kind bosom and sobbed.

"Auntie dear, I'm frightened, so frightened!"

"Of what, darling?"

"Of ugliness and wickedness and horror."

"Nothing of that, dear, can ever come our way. It does n't come the way of decent folk. People like us don't have anything to do with that side of life."

Stella still sobbed. The words brought no conviction. Lady Blount continued her unenlightened consolation. Let the precious ostrich stick her head in a bush, and that which she could not see could by no chance happen.

"But men are out there—" she waved her arm vaguely—"who kill women and little children."

"But we never meet the men," cried poor Lady Blount, insistently. "Our lives are free from all that."

She preached her narrow gospel. There was a class of beings in the world who did all kinds of ferocious, criminal, cruel, mean, and vulgar things; but they were a class apart. In the world in which she herself and Stella and John and Walter dwelt all was beauty and refinement. Stella dried her eyes. At one-and-twenty one cannot weep forever. She allowed herself to be half persuaded of the truth of her Aunt Julia's sophistries. But the little, impish devil who stage-manages the comedies of life arranged a day or two afterward a sardonic situation.

It was the mildest of December mornings. Old Autumn humped a brave and kindly shoulder against Winter's onrush. A faint south-west wind crept warmly over the Channel, and sweet odours came from the moist, unsmitten earth. A pale sun clothed the nakedness of the elms and chestnuts in the garden, and brightened to early spring beauty the laurels and firs. Stella, with Constable near by, sat in the sunshine, by the ivy-clad north-eastern front of the old Channel House, and her chair was beneath the window of the morning-room. Now that she could sit upright, she had learned to use her hands in many ways. She could knit. She was knitting now, vaguely and tremulously hoping that the result might be a winter waistcoat for her Great High Belovedest, intent on her counting, one, two, three, four, pearl one, when suddenly voices in altercation broke upon her ear.

It was merely an unhappy, ignoble quarrel such as for many years had marred that house of sweet-seeming. Fierce hatred and uncharitableness were unchained and sped their clamorous and disastrous way. Bitter words uttered in strident and unnatural tones wounded the quiet air. The woman lost her dignity in vain recrimination. The man snarled savage and common oaths. Suddenly the door slammed violently, and there was the silence of death. The scene had lasted only a few moments. Sir Oliver, in his foolish anger, had evidently followed his wife into the morning room and left her abruptly. But the few moments were enough for Stella, who had heard everything. Her heart seemed frost-bitten, and her blood turned to ice.

The cruel, vulgar, and hideous things of life were not the appanages of a class apart. They entered into her own narrowed world. Her beautiful world! Her hateful, horrible terror of a world!

# CHAPTER XIV

I N midwinter the shadow that hung over John gathered into storm-cloud.

Miss Lindon, in pathetic despair, had abandoned her notion of turning Unity into a young lady of young-ladylike accomplishments. She could perform whatever marvels of exquisite sewing Miss Lindon could imagine, but there her proficiency in the elegances came to an end. The girl's tastes, Miss Lindon lamented, were so plebeian! She would sooner make puddings than afternoon calls; she would sooner sweep and dust and polish than read instructive or entertaining literature. In her child-of-the-people's practical way, she had ousted Miss Lindon from the management of the household, thereby coming into conflict with the stern Phoebe, no longer feared, who hitherto had carried out, according to her own fancy, the kind lady's nebulous directions. Miss Lindon sighed, and surrendered her keys, inwardly thankful to be relieved of crushing responsibilities. She had never known how to order dinner for John. If, after agonized searching, she had decided on lamb, and sweet peas and grouse and asparagus, it was only to be told that some or all of them were out of season. And she could never check the laundry-list, so eternally mysterious were the garments worn by man.

Unity was a born economist. As soon as she took over the seals of office, she abolished the easy and expensive system of tradesmen calling for orders. She herself marketed, and that was her great joy. Every day she took her market-bag and busied herself among the shops in the Kilburn High Road, choosing her meat with an uncanny sureness of vision, knocking extortionate pennies off the prices of vegetables, and seeing generally that she had good value for her money. Miss Lindon, accompanying her on one or two of these excursions, was shocked and scared at her temerity. How dared she talk like that to the greengrocer? Unity replied that she would talk to him until he did n't know himself if he gave her any more of his nonsense. She was n't going to allow her guardian to be robbed by any of them, not she; she was up to all their tricks.

"I suppose you thought that was a good lettuce, Auntie?"

"I am no judge, dear," said Miss Lindon; "but surely you ought n't to have hurt his feelings by saying that its proper place was the dust-bin, and not a respectable shop."

"He understands me all right," laughed Unity.

All the tradesmen did, and they respected the shrewdness of the businesslike little plebeian, whom they recognized and treated as one of their own class; and Unity saved her beloved guardian many shillings a week, which was a matter of proud gratification. She held her head high nowadays. She had found herself.

Once chatting casually with Herold, John said with the air of Sir Oracle:

"Unity has got quite a strong character."

Herold laughed. "Did n't I tell you so nearly three years ago? You would n't believe me."

"You talked some nonsense about love," growled John.

"Well, have n't you given it to her in your bearish way? What would you do in this house without her? You'd be utterly miserable."

"I suppose I should," said John. "But I wish you would get out of the infernal habit of always being in the right."

One afternoon—it was the Saturday before Christmas—Unity took the market-bag and went out to do her shopping. Evening had fallen on a thin, black fog. The busy thoroughfare was a bewildering fusion of flare and gloom. The Christmas crowd, eager to purchase or to gladden their eyes with good things unpurchaseable, thronged the pavements—an ordinary, crowd of middle-class folk, careless of the foggy air, enjoying the Christmas promise in shops almost vulgarly replete. A hundred rosetted carcasses in a butcher's shop where ten hung the day before is marvel enough to attract the comfortable loiterer, and the happy butcher's "Buy! Buy!" as he stands in a blaze of light sharpening his knife, is an attraction peculiarly fascinating. What with the stream entering and issuing from shops, the wedges of loiterers glued to shop windows, the two main currents of saunterers, progress was difficult. In the murky roadway motor-omnibuses and carts flashed mysteriously by in endless traffic. All was uproar and ant-heap confusion.

Unity, resolute, squat little figure, made her purchases, and, having made them, lingered, joyously in the throbbing street, her hereditary element. She was never so happy as when rubbing shoulders with her kind. The whistling shop-boy and the giggling work-girl were her congeners. For the sake of her guardian and Aunt Gladys she never spoke to such ungenteel persons, but in their swiftly passing company she had a sense of comfort and comradeship. Often she went out without knowing why. The street called her.

The sights and sounds of it provided an ever-changing, ever-exciting drama. A street accident, a fallen horse, a drunken man, held her fascinated. And tonight the abnormal life of the street afforded an extra thrill of exhilaration; there was so much to see. At last she found her progress blocked by a crowd hanging about a confectioner's window. She wormed her way through, and was rewarded by the enthralling spectacle of a huge clock-work figure of Father Christmas, who drew from his wallet the shop's special plum-pudding at ninepence-halfpenny a pound. It was mighty fine, and Unity never heeded the tossing and buffeting of the admiring crowd..The light shone hard on the ring of pink faces framed by the blackness beyond. Then eager sight-seers jostled her into the background.

Suddenly she felt a sharp and awful pain in her side. She shrieked aloud and turned. The baffling figure of a woman in black hurrying into the maw of the darkness met her eyes before the startled crowd closed about her. She put her hand instinctively to the tortured spot, and drew out from her flesh a long hat-pin; then she fainted.

An assistant in the shop, coming out to know the cause of the hubbub, recognized her and had her brought indoors. The policeman on the beat soon shouldered his way in. They put poor Unity on a shutter, covered her with rugs, and, followed by a tail of idlers, bore her to the house.

John came home soon afterwards and found an agitated Aunt Gladys in process of being reassured by a kindly doctor that Unity was not dead. The wound, though ugly and painful, was little more than flesh deep. The hat-pin had glanced off a corset bone and penetrated obliquely. Straightly driven, however, it would have been a deadly thrust. Of the murderous intent there could hardly be any doubt. A sergeant of police was also waiting for John; but John let him wait, and rushed in his bull-like way upstairs.

Unity, who had long since recovered consciousness, lay in bed, her wound tended, a cheerful fire lit, and Phoebe in attendance. John dismissed the latter with a gesture and flung himself on his knees by the head of the bed.

"'My God! child, what has happened?"

For all the difference of surroundings,—the pretty room and fine linen,—the common little face on the pillow was singularly like that which he had seen in the orphanage infirmary. But there was a deeper trust in the girl's eyes, for they were lit with a flash of joy at his great distress.

She recounted simply what had occurred.

"You saw the woman disappear?"

"I think so. It was all so quick."

It was a woman's stab. What man would use a hat-pin? And there could be only one woman alive who would stab Unity.

"Did you recognize her?"

His voice was hoarse, and his rugged face full of pain. She regarded him steadily.

"No, Guardian."

"It was not—she?"

"No," said Unity.

"Are you sure?"

Unity clenched her hands and turned away, and her eyes grew hard.

"If it was, I should have known her."

John rose to his feet and stood over her, his arms folded, and looked at her from beneath his heavy brows. Unity met his gaze. And so they remained for a second or two, and each knew that the other knew who had dealt the blow.

"It was n't her," said Unity.

The words were stamped with finality. John, meeting the girl's set gaze, had a glimpse of rocky strata far beneath. No process of question invented by man would induce her to unsay the words.

"There's a police sergeant downstairs," said he.

"I did n't see no woman either," said Unity, significantly.

And John did not notice her unusual relapse into orphanage speech.

Soon afterward he left her and joined the sergeant in the hall. The policeman asked the stereotyped questions. John replied that Miss Blake

—it was, as far as he knew, the first time he had given Unity her full style and title, and the name sounded odd in his ears—that Miss Blake had seen nothing of her assailant and could give no information whatever.

"You suspect nobody?"

"Nobody at all," said John, decisively. "You need n't trouble to pursue the matter any further, for the wound luckily is trifling, and in any case I should not prosecute."

"As you please, sir," said the Sergeant.

"Good evening, and thank you," said John.

"This is the hat-pin, sir."

"You can leave it with me," said John.

He went into his study and examined the thing. It was of common make, the head being a ball of black glass. A million such are sold in cheap shops.

He had no doubt as to the owner. She had spied upon him craftily, bided her time, and had then struck. He had not seen her since the day they had met in Maida Vale and he had unceremoniously packed her home, and for the last few months she had not molested him. Now came this unforeseen, dastardly attack.

He rang for Phoebe, gave a message for Miss Lindon, and went out with an ugly look on his face. A taxicab whirled him swiftly across London to Amelia Mansions in the Fulham Road. Mrs. Bence answered his ring. He stepped into the hall, and in his blundering way strode down the passage. The woman checked him.

"Mrs. Rawlings is n't in, sir. She is with Mrs. Oscraft, the lady downstairs."

He turned abruptly.

"Has she been out this afternoon?"

"She went out to lunch with Mrs. Oscraft and came back with her an hour ago."

He drew the hat-pin from the inside of his overcoat, where he had stuck it. "Do you recognize this?"

The woman looked puzzled. "No, sir," she said. "Mrs. Rawlings has n't any like it?"

Mrs. Bence inspected the pin. "No, I'm sure. If she had, I would have known." She saw the trouble in his face. "What has happened, sir?"

He told her briefly. The woman knitted a perplexed brow.

"I don't see how it could have been her, sir," she said. "She's nearly always with Mrs. Oscraft, and very seldom goes out by herself, and to-day, as I've said, she went out and came back with her. And I'm sure she has n't had a hat-pin like that in use."

"What exactly is this Mrs. Oscraft?" he asked. Mrs. Bence added to his vague knowledge. Her husband was a book-maker, very often absent from home, having to frequent race-meetings and taverns and other such resorts of his trade. She had many friends, male and female, of the same kidney, a crew rowdy and vulgar, but otherwise harmless. She and Mrs. Rawlings had become inseparable.

"I'll go down and see her," said John.

Mrs. Oscraft, an overblown blonde, floppily attired, opened the door of her flat.

"Hello! Who are you?" she asked.

He explained that he was the husband of Mrs. Rawlings.

"So you are. She 's got a portrait of you. Besides, I've seen you here. She 's in the drawing-room. Come along in and have a whisky and soda or a glass of champagne."

He declined. "I owe you a thousand apologies for intruding," said he, "but if you would answer me just one question, I should be greatly obliged."

"Fire away," said the lady. "Won't you really come in?"

"No, thank you," said John. "Will you tell me where my wife has been this afternoon?"

"With me all the time," said Mrs. Oscraft, promptly. "We've been doing Christmas shopping in Kensington High Street, and only just got back."

"She did n't go near Kilburn?"

"Lord bless you, no!" said the lady. "Look here, would you like to see her?"

"No," said John. He apologized again, and bade her good evening. He descended the stone stairs with a bewildered feeling that he had made a fool of himself; and Mrs. Oscraft, as soon as the door was shut, put her thumb to her nose and twiddled her fingers in the traditional gesture of derision.

John went away sore and angry, like a bull that, charging at a man, unexpectedly butts up against a stone wall. He had no reason for disbelieving Mrs. Oscraft, and the hat-pin was not his wife's. Yet who but his wife could have been the aggressor? It might have been an accident. It might have been a man—such cases are not uncommon—with the stabbing and cutting mania. Unity's fleeting glimpse of the woman in black might have been a trick of shadow in the lamplit fog. Yet in the deed he felt the hand of the revengeful and cruel woman. He was baffled.

On his way home he called on Herold, whom he found at dinner.

"I shall never know a moment's peace of mind," he said gloomily, after they had discussed the matter, "until she is put under restraint. If she did n't do it, as you make out—" Herold held to the theory that a person could not be in two places, Kensington and Kilbum, at the same time—"she is quite capable of it."

"It's a mercy," said Herold, "that you did not see her and tax her with the offence, and so put the idea into her head."

"I believe she did it all the same," said John, obstinately.

"But why should Mrs. Oscraft have lied? Mrs. Bence saw them go out and come in together. You can't suppose the other woman was an accomplice. It's absurd."

"I know it is," said John. "But the absurd often turns up in a churchwarden's unhumorous kit of reality in this Bedlam of a world."

They argued until it was time for Herold to go to his theatre, when John went home and ate a belated dinner in such a black mood that Miss Lindon dared not question him.

And that was the end of the matter. Unity's wound healed after a few days, and sturdily refusing Phoebe's protection on her walks abroad, she resumed her marketing in the Kilburn High Road. John called on the district inspector of police and obtained the ready promise that folks running amuck with hatpins should be summarily arrested and that his house and ward should be placed under special supervision.

It was characteristic of the terms of dumb confidence on which John and Unity lived together that neither of them referred again to the possible perpetrator of the outrage. When she became aware that the policemen in this district always kept her respectfully in sight and, on passing her, saluted, she knew that her guardian had so ordained things. One day in the New Year she entered his study, and stood at attention.

"Please, Guardian, may I have half-a-crown?"

He fished the coin out of his trousers' pocket and handed it to her.

"I don't want it for myself," she said.

She had her allowance for pin-money, which she was too proud to exceed. As a matter of fact, she hoarded her pennies in the top of an old coffee-pot and out of her savings bought not only finery for herself, but startling birthday and Christmas presents for her guardian and Aunt Gladys. It was astonishing what Unity could do with elevenpence three farthings.

John, knowing her ways, smiled.

"What do you want it for, then?"

"I'm going to give it to my best policeman," she said, and marched out of the room.

That was her only acknowledgement of her appreciation of the measures he had taken to ensure her safety. He understood, and, when telling Herold of the incident, called her, after the loose way of man, "a rum kid." Of the obvious he was aware, and it pleased him; but subtler manifestations escaped his notice. It never occurred to him that it was more than a pleasing accident of domestic life when, on letting himself into the house with his latch-key, he should find Unity, drab and stolid, her cheeks and snub nose and prominent forehead shining in the unladylike way deplored by Miss Lindon, as if polished with yellow soap, and her skimpy hair bunched up ungracefully, with patient, unchanging eyes, awaiting him in the little hall, her hands already outstretched to take hat and stick and to help him off with his overcoat. Yet ninety-nine times out of a hundred it happened. He did not notice the orderly confusion wrought by the ingenuity of sleepless nights out of the chaos of his study. Wishes—just the poor, commonplace little wishes of household life—what could poor, commonplace little Unity, with her limited soul-horizon, do more for him? wishes vaguely formulated in his mind he found quickly and effectively realized, and worried, hard-working, honest man that he was, he took the practical comforts sometimes as a matter of course, now and then with a careless word of thanks, and never dreamed—how could he? —of the passionate endeavour whereby these poor, commonplace little things came to pass.

There can be as much beautiful expenditure of soul—as beautiful in the eyes of God, to whom, as to any philosopher with a working idea of infinity, the fall of a rose-petal must be as important as the fall of an empire—in the warming of a man's slippers before the fire by the woman who loves him as in all the heroisms of all the Joans of Arc and the Charlotte Cordays and the window-breaking, policeman-scratching, forcibly fed female martyrs of modern London that have ever existed. It is a proposition as incontrovertible as any elementary theorem of Euclid you please; but so essentially unphilosophic is man, to say nothing of woman,—for a man would sooner break stones, play bridge, go bankrupt, slaughter his wife and family, or wear a straw hat with a frock-coat than brace his mind to think—that this self-evident truth passes him by unrecognized, unperceived, unguessed.

The volcanic forces of life—essentially such as act and react between man and woman—lie hidden deep down in the soul's unknown and unsuspected cauldron, and their outward manifestations are only here and there a puff of smoke so fine and blue that it merges at once into the caressing air. The good, easy man plants his vines on the mountainside. The sky is serene, the sun fills his grapes with joyousness. Then comes eruption, and the smiling slope is smitten into the grin of a black death's-head.

# CHAPTER XV

**W**INTER came and melted into spring. Physically Stella had progressed beyond all hopes. Like the Lady in "The Sensitive Plant," she walked a ruling grace about the garden of the Channel House, and nursed the daffodils and narcissi and tulips with tender hands. In these she took a passionate joy curiously exceeding that in other revelations of the great world. Indeed, during most of the winter, she had shrunk from mingling with humanity. Her zest for the new life had been dulled. She found excuses for not going beyond the garden gate, and of her own free will did not seek the society of those dear to her. The windows of her sea-chamber once more afforded her the accustomed outlook, and the gulls wheeling high in the wintry gusts again became her companions.

The Blounts let her have her way,—was she not autocrat?—putting down her hesitations and cravings for solitude to a young girl's delicate whimsies of which they could not divine the motive; for she, who had once been expansive, now had grown strangely reticent. Even Herold, who used to accompany her into the Land That Never Was, did not gain her confidence. Into those mystic regions she could admit him freely; but the Threatening Land that lay beyond the threshold of her sea-chamber a heart-gripping shyness forced her to tread alone.

"Life has frightened you," he said one day.

"How do you know that?" she asked, with a quick glance.

He smiled.

"You are like an Æolian harp set in the wind, my dear."

"Only you can hear it."

"Every one hears it."

She shook her head.

"No; only you."

"That's as may be," he said, with a laugh. "Anyhow, something has frightened you. What is it?"

Stella rose—she had learned to walk; the hours of her exercises had been the gayest in her day—and touched him lightly with her fingers on the shoulder, and went and stood by the great window of the drawing-room and looked out at her sky and sea. The Great High Favourite, with his uncanny insight, had read her truly. Womanlike, she did not know whether to resent his surprising of her innermost secret or to love him for it. She was understood; that was balm. Yet what right had he to understand? The question was a drop of gall. The pure spirit of her flew to the chosen companion of her dreams; something—the nature of which she was unaware—sex-instinct—forbade too close an intimacy in things real and tangible. And there was a touch of resentment, too, in an outer circle of her mind. Why had he given her no warning of the Threatening Land? He had allowed her to step ignorantly upon its thorns, and her feet still bled.

Herold turned in his chair and glanced at her slim figure framed by the window. Then he went softly to her side.

"Stellamaris, you are dearer to me than anything on God's earth. Tell me what frightens you. Maybe I can help you."

But Stella shook her head. She had been accustomed from childhood to lavish terms of endearment from her little band of intimates, and her woman's nature was as yet not enough awakened to catch the new and subtle appeal. A girl's pride froze her. The wounds that he had allowed her to receive she would cure by herself. She touched his hand, however, to show that she appreciated his affection. The touch sent a thrill to his heart.

"Stella, dear!" he whispered.

Then, as a note struck on a piano causes the harmonic on the violin to vibrate, so did his tone stir a chord in the girl's nature, occasioning an absurd little flutter of trepidation. She laughed, and threw wide the folding-doors that opened upon the lawn.

"Don't let us talk of bogies on such a beautiful day. I want to show you my crocuses."

It was her sovereign pleasure to break off the conversation. He dared not press her. She took him out among her crocuses and daffodils, and became the Stella he had always known, with the exception that now she dwelt in a spring flower's bloom instead of in a bit of silver in the flying scud. They talked eternal verities concerning the souls of flowers.

After this unsatisfactory and, to, a certain extent, baffling visit, Herold went back to London with a heartache, which induced an unaccustomed moodiness. At the theatre that night, Miss Leonora Gurney took him to task. Now, Miss Gurney (Mrs. Hetherington in private life; she had divorced the disreputable Hetherington years ago, and had not remarried) was a very important and captivating person. She was a woman of genius, a favourite of the London public, a figure of society, in management on her own account, wherein she showed shrewd business ability, and very much in love with Walter Herold, wherein she showed much of the weakness of Eve. This season Herold was her leading man.

To say that Herold had wrapped himself up in his Joseph's garment (not the one of many colours, but the other one equally famous) during all his stage career would be mendacious folly. Many a ball had come to him at the bound, and he had returned it gaily. He had laughed an honest way through innumerable love-affairs—things of the moment, things of the fancy, things of no importance whatsoever. Many maidens, and some matrons, had wept for him, but none bitterly. He had established a reputation for lack of seriousness in matters of the heart. His bright, blue eyes would flash at you, and his low, musical voice would murmur no matter what, even were it the Lord's Prayer backward, and you caught your breath, and lost your head, and were perfectly ready to say if he asked you, and sometimes even if he did n't ask you: "Take me, I am yours." But whatever he did, he never rose to the passionate height, or sank to the unromantic depth, of the situation. Which things were a mystery.

To qualify what might appear to be a sweeping proposition, it may be stated that there are certain phases in certain women's lives when they make straight for the mystery surrounding a man, as moth does for candle, and singe their wings in so doing. Thus singed were the chaste and charming wings of Leonora Gurney. Herold, no more aware of an aura of mystery than of a halo, received the lady's advances in his frank, laughing way. She had the raven hair, dark, blue eyes, and white skin of an Irish ancestry. She was exceedingly attractive. She played her love-scenes with him—his part in the piece was that of a broken-down solicitor's clerk who entertained an angel unawares—with an artistic sympathy that is the rare joy of the actor, when he feels, like one who has the perfect partner in a waltz, that he merges his own individuality into a divine union. At the end of the third act the curtain came down on the angel bending over his chair, her hand in his. It remained there, a warm and human thing, and her breath was on his cheek, for a long time, while the curtain went up and down. It was by no means disagreeable to hold Leonora's hand and feel her breath on his cheek, after the common emotion of the swinging scene. Hundreds of men would have given their ears to have done the same without any swinging scene at all.

Herold certainly took the lady by the tips of her fingers and adventured with her into the Land of Tenderness—the Pays du Tendre of the old French romanticists. How could mortal man help it? The theatre and the theatrical world clacked with gossip. The unapproachable Leonora, the elusive Herold: it was brilliant high-comedy marriage. Already those not bound by romance criticized the possibilities of a joint management. Could he always play lead to her? Was not his scope, exquisite in it though he was, too limited? She was the Juliet of her generation. Would he be content to play the Apothecary? Sooner or later there would be the devil to pay. To the onlookers who see most of the game and to the overhearers who hear ever so much more, the affair between the two was a concluded matter; but the parties to the supposed contract still wandered in the sweet pastures of the indefinite. And this was through no fault of the lady. She did her best, as far as lay in the power of modest woman, to lead him to the precise highroad; but Herold remained as elusive as a will-o'-the-wisp.

"You're not very responsive to-night, Walter," she said during a wait in the first act, which they generally spent on the stairs leading from stage to dressing-rooms.

In the intimate world of the theatre the use of the Christian name is a commonplace signifying nothing; but a trick of voice may make it signify a great deal. Herold, sensitive, caught her tone and bit his lip.

"The actor's Monday slackness," said he.

"Where have you been week-ending?"

"Nowhere in particular."

"And you refused Lady Luxmore's invitation, knowing that I was to be there, in order to go nowhere in particular?"

"The floor of that house is littered with duchesses," said he. "Its untidiness gets on my nerves."

"That's too flippant, Walter. Why not say at once that you went to Southcliff?"

"That's nowhere in particular," said he. "It's my second home."

"And you come back from it as merry as a young gentleman in a Hauptmann play. You are barely civil."

"My dear Leonora!" he protested.

She looked him straight in the eye and shook her head.

"Barely civil. What have I done to you?"

"You have always shown yourself to be the sweetest of women," said he.

"Then why not treat me as such?"

She stood near him on the narrow stair, alluring, reproachful, menacing, yet ready to be submissive. Despite her make-up, her proud beauty shone replendent. If she had been a wise woman, she would have let him answer the challenge. But a woman in love is an idiot; Heaven forbid that she should be otherwise! So is a man, for the matter of that; but he obeys an elementary instinct of self-protection. Woman essentially disobedient (cf. Rex Mundi vs. Eve) does not. Hence storms and tempests and cataclysms. Seeing him hesitate, she added jealously:

"I believe there is more attraction in the shadow-child at Southcliff than I have been led to suppose." A man of the world, he ignored the challenge, and turned off the innuendo with a laugh.

"Who can say what is shadow and what is substance here below? Kant will tell you that nothing exists save as an idea in our minds."

"I don't seem to exist in yours at all."

"There you wrong me," he cried.

They fenced as they had fenced before; but on her mention of Stellamaris, Herold had closed against her the outer court of his heart into which she had stepped, and, looking at her, had become frozenly aware that the dark Irish eyes, and the raven hair on a stately head, and the curved, promising lips, and the queenly figure, and the genius and rich womanhood of which these were the investiture of flesh, meant to him nothing and less than nothing. The woman read her sentence in his eyes, and abruptly left him, and stood in the wings until her entrance. And Herold, manlike, gave her no thought; for his head was in a whirl, and his heart afire, with a new and consuming knowledge. The splendour of all the Leonora Gurneys, of all the splendid women of the earth, faded into a pale glimmer before the starry eyes of one girl.

As a wonder-child, as a thing of sea-foam and sunset cloud, she had crept into his soul and had taken up therein her everlasting habitation. She was the very music of his being, an indissoluble essence of himself.

He wondered, as men untouched by love do wonder, why no woman had done more than stir the surface of emotion. Now he knew. He had loved her in her exquisite ideality with a love that was more than love. Now, in her magical transformation, he loved her with love itself.

Stella Maris, star of the sea! Stella Herold, star of that which is greater than all the multitudinous seas of earth, the soul of a man!

He dreamed his dreams, and gave that evening an exceedingly bad performance.

Soon afterwards, with drums playing and colours flying, Stella came with her retinue to London. She had rooms in a magnificent hostelry, a magnificent hired motor-car to transport her, and as magnificent raiment, chosen by her own delicate self, as any young woman could desire. But despite all this magnificence, she wept over many a lost illusion. Where were the music-haunted streets, the golden pavements, the gorgeous castles, the joyous throngs of which John, years ago, had fed the swift imagination of the child?

On their way from Victoria' Station they passed through St. James's Park.

"That's Buckingham Palace," said Sir Oliver, with more pride than if he owned it.

"That?"

Her heart sank like a stone dropped down a well: That dingy, black barrack the stately home of the king? And when they swung up Constitution Hill and lined up in the traffic by Hyde Park Corner, "This," said Sir Oliver, "is Piccadilly."

What she had expected, poor child, to find in Piccadilly, she scarcely knew; but from infancy, the name had a sweet and mystic significance. It connoted beauty and grandeur; it was associated in her mind with silk and gold and marble. It was what a street in the New Jerusalem might have been had John of Patmos had the training of a star reporter. Poor Piccadilly! To the Englishman the most beauteous, the most seductive, the fullest of meaning of all the thoroughfares of the cities of the world, to the disillusioned girl it was only a dismal, clattering, shrieking ravine. Why had they lied to her? She could not understand.

The first evening she was overstrained, and went to bed early; but the next night they took her to see the play in which Herold was acting.

"I 'll bring her round between the acts," said John to Herold, during a discussion of the adventure.

"You 'll do nothing of the sort," said Herold.

"It will interest her tremendously to go behind."

"And see all the tinsel and make-believe? What a fool you are, John!"

"Well, anyhow, we 'll come and see you in your dressing-room," said John, who recognized some reason in his friend's objection. "We can get round without crossing the stage."

Herold put his hands on John's great shoulders.

"My dear John," said he, "I love my profession very dearly, but there's one thing in it which I loathe, and that is having to paint my face."

He said no more; but John understood, though he thought it somewhat finicking of Herold to shrink from meeting Stella in his make-up. He had seen him talk thus to dames and damsels of the most exalted station without a shadow of false shame.

So Stella went to the play without peeping behind the scenes; and then, indeed, she once more lived in her Land of Illusion. The hushed house, spectral in the dim light, seemed part of a dream-world. On the stage, life real and vibrating passed before her enraptured eyes. During the first part of the play she squeezed John's hand tight, and during the intervals said very little. She did not question the means by which Herold transformed himself into the broken-down solicitor's clerk. He was the solicitor's clerk, and no longer Herold. His love for the beautiful woman, at first so hopeless, wrung her heart. Then the response of the woman set her pulses throbbing. The third act, an admirable piece of crescendo, reached a height of passion which held her tense. Love the Conqueror, the almighty, spread his compelling pinions over the breathless house. It was a revelation. She had never suspected the existence of such a tumultuous phenomenon. Love she had heard of, the love of Prince Charming for Princess Rose; but it had meant no more to her than the loves of butterflies. This was different. It explained things she had not understood in music. It opened up the world that had lain hidden beyond the crimson of her sunsets.

When the curtain came down on the end of the great love-scene she was too much overwrought to applaud. She sat pale, shaken, limp, with only one great desire—that all surroundings would vanish and that she could find herself by her window looking out over the moonlit sea. There, she felt, she could weep her heart out; here her eyes were intolerably dry.

Sir Oliver rose and stretched himself at the back of the box.

"Devilish good! Splendid! Never thought Walter could touch it. Miss Gurney, too, immense. Puts one in mind of Adelaide Neilson. Best Juliet there has ever been. Before your time, John. Jolly good job, however, people don't go on like that in real life."

Stella turned her head quickly.

"What do you mean, Uncle?"

"People go a bit quieter, my dear," he laughed.

"Gad! If that sort of thing became popular, it would tear us all to bits."

He went out to smoke, dragging John with him. Stella put a wistful little gloved hand on Lady Blount's knee.

"Is that true, Auntie?"

Lady Blount sighed. Such storms of emotion had not come her way. She looked backward over the dreary vista of sixty barren years. One such hour of madness, and what a difference in her memories!

"I can't tell you, darling. Perhaps not, if two people love each other very, very dearly; but they must do that—and love is n't given to every one."

An ingenuous question rose to the girl's lips, but it died there, poisoned by the remembrance of vile words of hatred. Instead, she asked:

"How many people, then, love like those two in the play?"

"About one in a million," replied Lady Blount.

And Stella, with the young girl's sweet and natural wonder whether she might possibly be one of the million, felt the hot blood rise to neck and cheek. Ashamed, she held her fan before her face and, leaning over the front of the box, watched the shimmering stalls.

The play over, they drove home in the magnificent motor-car. Supper awaited them in their sitting-room, where Herold was to join them later. Stella lay back on the luxurious seat, nestling by Lady Blount, languid, with closed eyes. The others, thinking that she was physically fatigued, said little. They did not realize the soul-shaking effect of the revelation of human passion on their pure star of the sea. It was not given them to divine the tempest—such a one, perhaps, as that which rocks the bee on its flower, though a storm all the same—that raged beneath the mask of the delicate face. They thought she was fatigued, and because they loved her they did not weary her with speech.

She was indeed tired, desperately tired, by the time they arrived at the hotel. She could scarcely walk up the steps. John supported her to the lift. When they reached their landing, he took her bodily in his arms and carried her down the corridor, Sir Oliver and Lady Blount hurrying on in front, so as to open the sitting-room door and turn on the lights. Stella's head lay on John's shoulder, an arm, for security's sake, instinctively round his neck. The way was long, the lift serving the wing wherein their apartments were situated being out of working order, and John lingered on the delicious journey.

"Poor darling! We 've exhausted you," he whispered.

She shook her head and smiled wanly. "It was wonderful." And after a second she said: "And this is wonderful, too. How strong you are, Belovedest."

"Do you like me to carry you?"

She opened her eyes and they looked dreamily into his. He laughed, and bent his head, and kissed her. He had kissed her thousands of times before, but this time her soft lips met his for an instant, and when they parted, her eyes closed again, and she lay back very white in his arms. And John, too, was shaken, and held the delicate body very tight against him and quickened his pace.

He laid her gently on a couch in the sitting-room. Lady Blount was all for her going then and there to bed; but she pleaded for a sight of Herold. He came in a few moments afterwards. She roused herself, thanked him in her gracious way for the evening of delight.

"To-morrow, dear, I 'll tell you all about it. I am just a little bit dazed now."

"Has it been a great adventure?" he asked, with a laugh.

Involuntarily she glanced at John and saw his eyes fixed on her. She flushed slightly.

"Perhaps the greatest of all," she said.

The men walked together the common part of their homeward journey. John slipped his arm through his friend's, a rare demonstration of affection.

"Wallie, old man," said he, "I 'm in hell again. I 've got to get out. I must n't see any more of Stella."

"Why not?"

"Just that. I must get out of her life somehow. Things have changed. It's too horrible to think of." Herold shook himself free and halted.

"My God!" he cried, "you?"

John threw up his arms in a gesture of despair. "Can I help it? It is n't given to man to help these things."

"And Stella?"

"I must get out of her life," said John.

"It will be difficult."

"What can you suggest?"

"Nothing," said Herold—"nothing now."

They moved on, and walked in dead silence to the parting of their ways.

# CHAPTER XVI

THE making and the executing of a good resolution are two entirely different actions. The former is a process as instantaneous as you please—one born of passion, heaven-sent inspiration, alcohol, or New Year hysteria; the latter one of practical handling conditioned by the entanglement of a thousand circumstances. If a man carried out with lightning rapidity every good resolution he formed, he would inevitably make marmalade of his affairs, and clog therein the feet and bodies of many innocent people as though they were wasps. With evil resolutions it is another matter. You want to play the devil, and the sooner and more completely you do it, the nearer do you approximate to your ideal. But it is very dangerous to do good, and involves a vast amount of weary thought and trouble.

It was all very well for John Risca to resolve to go out of the life of Stellamaris, but how could he do so without committing the manifest absurdity of taking a ticket for equatorial Africa? He was beset by forbidding circumstances. There was his work; there was Unity; there was his aunt; there was Stellamaris herself; and, chief of all, there was the baleful figure of the woman who went about with murderous hatpins. Thus in an ironical way did history repeat herself. Six years before he was all for flying to the antipodes on account of his wife, and was restrained by consideration of Stellamaris; and now, when it would be the heroical proceeding to fly to the ends of the earth from Stellamaris, he was restrained by considerations in which his wife was a most important factor.

He lay stark awake all night, wondering how he could carry out his resolve. At dawn he came to the only sane conclusion. He could not carry it out at all, at least in no desperate or brutal fashion. When he got up and faced the daylight world, he scorned himself for a fool. The soft clinging of her lips had transmuted the worship of years into the fine gold of love. That was true, maddeningly true. His being was aflame with the new and wondrous thing. But Stellamaris? To her the kiss that she gave had been one of gratitude, affection, trust, weariness. She had lain in his arms and had felt safe and sheltered, and so had kissed him, the Great High Belovedest of her childhood. To her the kiss had meant nothing. How could it? How could passion touch the creature of sea-foam and cloud? And even allowing such an extravagant possibility, how could he, great, rough, elderly, ugly bear that he was, inspire such a feeling in a young girl's heart? He a romantic figure! He, with the pachydermatous mug that offended his eyes as he shaved! He denounced the monstrous insolence of his overnight fancy. He would keep tight grip on himself. She should never know. As far as the infinitely precious one was concerned, all would be well. So argued the human ostrich.

After his morning's work at the office of the weekly review, he went to the Carlton, where the party of intimates had arranged to lunch. He arrived early, but found Herold, who was earlier, waiting in the palm court.

"Look here, old man," said he as he sat down by his side, "forget the fool nonsense I talked last night."

"Did n't you mean it?" asked Herold.

"Yes," said John, bluntly. "I did n't sleep a wink. But forget it all the same. Things have got to go on outwardly just as they are."

"As you like," said Herold. He lit a cigarette, and after a whiff or two, added: "I must repeat what I hinted at and what you seemed to reply to. What about Stella?"

"It's absurd to think of her suspecting," said John.

Herold's nervous fingers snapped the cigarette in two.

"She must never suspect," said he.

"Do you think I'm a devil?" said John.

"No. You 're a good fellow. Who knows it better than I? But you 're passionate and impulsive. You must be on your guard—not for the next two or three days, but for ever and ever."

"All right," said John. "Now put the matter out of your mind."

Herold nodded, squeezed the burning end of his broken cigarette into an ash-tray, and lit another.

"You 're looking fagged out, Wallie," said John, after a while. "What have you been doing?"

"Nothing in particular. This part is rather trying, and I've not had a holiday for a couple of years. I want one rather badly. I don't complain," he added, with a smile, glad to get away from the torturing talk of Stellamaris. "During the two years I've been working, scores of better actors than I have n't been able to get an engagement. I'm a spoilt child of fortune. My time will come, I suppose, when they no longer want me."

The talk drifted to the precariousness of the actor's calling. Even men in demand from every management found a difficulty in making a living. Herold instanced Brownlow, one of the few jeunes premiers of the stage, who had slaved every day for a year, and having been in four or five successive failures, found himself, at the end of it, the recipient of three months' salary. Six weeks' slavery at rehearsal for nothing, and a two weeks' run! The system ought to be changed. John agreed, as he had agreed to the same argument a thousand times before.

"But I don't like to see you so pulled down," said he, affectionately.

Herold smiled and shrugged his shoulders. He, too, had not slept; but he did not inform John of the fact. It was a significant aspect of their friendship, if not of their respective temperaments, that John received few of Herold's confidences. The essential sympathizers among men are mute as to their own cares. Divine selfishness or a pride equally noble seals their lips. John Risca, with a cut finger, would have held it up for the commiseration of Herold, cursing heft and blade, and everything cursable connected with the knife; but Herold, with a broken heart, would have held his smiling peace.

For a moment he was convinced of John's faith in Stella's ignorance; but only for a moment. When she entered the palm court with Sir Oliver and Lady Blount, and he saw her eyes, dewy with a new happiness, rest on John, he felt that, awakened or unawakened, Stellamaris loved not him, Herold, but his friend. And when she came up to him in her frank, gracious way, and let her gloved little hand linger in his, he laughed and praised her radiance with a jest, and not one of the four dreamed of the pain in the man's heart.

They took their seats in the gay and crowded restaurant.

"This is really a palace!" cried Stella, in great delight. "Why can't every place be as beautiful as this?"

She had recovered from the emotional fatigue of the night before, having slept the sound sleep of happy girlhood, and awakened to the shy consciousness of impending change. The pink of health was in her cheeks.

Sir Oliver replied to her question.

"It takes a deuce of a lot of money to run such a concern."

"But why has n't every one got money?"

"That's what these confounded socialist fellows are asking," replied Sir Oliver, helping himself largely to anchovies and mayonnaise of egg.

But Stella scarcely heard. She remembered the tramp who had not a penny and the misery that had met her eyes during her rides abroad, and a momentary shadow fell on her.

"I think there 's a great deal to be said for the socialists," remarked Lady Julia.

Sir Oliver laid down his fork and stared less at his wife than at the blasphemy.

"There 's nothing to be said for 'em; nothing at all."

"You 'll admit the uneven distribution of wealth," said Lady Blount, drawing herself up. She was rather proud of the phrase.

"Lazy dogs—all to get and nothing to do. You ought to be ashamed of yourself, Julia."

"Oh, darlings, don't get cross with me!" cried Stella, in distress. The observance of the Unwritten Law had imperceptibly grown less strict as the influence of the sea-chamber had waned, and the poor quarrelsome pair were not at their old pains to hide their differences. "I never meant to talk socialism."

"My precious dove!" cried Sir Oliver, "who in the world said you did? It was your aunt."

"I believe it's John who is at the bottom of it, because he 's wearing a red tie," Herold interposed, with a laugh. "Oh, John, where did you find it?"

"I think it suits him beautifully," declared Stella, quick to follow the red herring of a cravat. "It 's when he wears mauve or light blue or green striped with yellow that he goes wrong. Belovedest,—" she turned to him tenderly; she was placed between him and Sir Oliver,—"now that I am like everybody else,"—her favorite euphemism,—"do let me choose your ties for you."

"Of course, dear; of course," said John, who had been eating hors d'ouvre in glum silence. "Who is there with taste like you?"

It would be entrancingly delectable to wear ties chosen by Stellamaris. Why, it would be coiling her sweet thoughts about his neck! This concession at least was harmless. Then suddenly he remembered that for the last two or three years Unity had taken charge of such details of his wardrobe, and he had sufficient glimmering of insight into feminine nature to know that between Unity with her domestic rights and a tigress with cubs there was remarkably little difference. How was he to abrogate one of her privileges? The gadfly question worried him. With such trumpery concerns are the deepest emotions of human life complicated. He who does not recognize them has no sense of values.

The conjugal wrangle having been checked, the meal proceeded gaily enough. Stella spoke of the play and praised Herold's acting, but with curious shyness avoided discussion of the theme. Herold noticed her adroit detours. He also noticed, with a sensitive man's pain, many other little things indicative of the awakening of Stellamaris. Once he saw her lay her hand impulsively on John's, as she had been wont to do since her childhood, and draw it quickly away, while a flush, like a rose-edged fairy cloud, came and went in her cheek. He also caught her glancing covertly at John, her brow knitted in a tiny frown, as though she wondered at his unusual silence.

When the party broke up, John leaving early, owing to pressure of work at the office, she said:

"I shall see you to-night, of course?"

"I'm afraid not. I have to see the review through the press."

Her face fell piteously.

"Oh, Belovedest!" she cried. "And I can't have Walter, because he's tied to his theatre."

But the disappointment was on account of John, not on account of Herold.

"You 'll have Walter most of the afternoon," remarked Lady Blount.

Stella laughed. "But I want everybody always," she said disingenuously.

It had been arranged that while Sir Oliver should go to his longed-for and seldom-used club, and Lady Blount visit certain cronies, Herold should take Stella to the Zoological Gardens.

She turned to John.

"Are you quite sure you can't come too, dear?"

He shook his head. "A newspaper office is a remorseless machine—just like a theatre. I must work."

"I'm beginning to be frightfully jealous of work," she said, with a laugh.

"It 's the noblest thing a man can do," said Sir Oliver.

At the zoo, Stella found a world of wonder, which drove disappointment from her mind, and in her childlike gaiety and enthusiasm Herold forgot his heartache for a while. Sufficient for the moment was the joy of her exquisite presence, of her animated cheeks and dancing eyes, of her beautiful voice rippling into exclamations of rapture at monkey or secretary-bird or hippopotamus.

"These are springbok," said Herold, in front of an inclosure.

Stella's brows knitted themselves into their customary network of perplexity.

"But I've read that men go out to shoot springboks."

"I'm afraid they do," said Herold.

"Men deliberately kill these beautiful, harmless things, with their melting eyes?" Her own filled with moisture. "Oh, Walter! How can men be so vile?" She knelt on the ground, and spoke to one, which poked its sensitive nose through the railing. "Oh, you dear! Oh, you perfectly lovely dear!"

Then she rose and took Herold by the arm, and a little shiver ran through her shoulders. "I suppose men kill everything. I 've found out they even kill one another. Would you or John kill creatures that did you no harm?"

She looked at him straight, with the searching candour of a spotless soul.

"I've shot birds which were afterwards eaten," he replied uncomfortably. "You see, dear, you eat partridges and pheasants, don't you? Well, they have to be killed, just like sheep or oxen. Often in South Africa men's lives depend on the supply of springbok meat they can obtain."

"And does John shoot little birds?"

"John has n't had the opportunity of going about to shooting parties. All his life he has had to work too hard."

"I'm glad," said Stella, curtly, and for a while she walked on in silence, and poor Herold felt like an unhanged wallower in innocent gore.

At last she said, "Are n't there any lions and tigers?"

"Of course."

"Why have n't we seen them?"

"They roar dreadfully, and they're rather fierce and terrible, Stella-maris."

"Are you afraid of them?"

He noted the feminine, quasi-logical touch of scorn, and laughed with a wry face.

"They're behind bars, dear. But I thought they might possibly frighten you."

"Frighten me? Let us go and see them."

So, seeing that Stellamaris was a young woman of intrepid and imperious disposition, Herold dutifully took her to the Great Cat's House, where again the child in her was enraptured by the splendour of the striped and tawny brutes. She lingered in front of the lion's cage. The four-o'clock meal was over. The lioness lay asleep in the corner, but her mate sat up, with his head near to the bars, an enormous, cleaned bone between his paws. The absurd and useless animal had struck a photographic pose at which Herold, with a more sophisticated companion, would have laughed. But Stellamaris took the lion too seriously. He fulfilled all her dreams of a lion. She looked in breathless admiration at the lion, and the lion, choke-full of food, regarded her with grave benevolence. Again she pressed Herold's arm.

"How noble! How kingly!"

He assented. The lion was certainly doing his best to warrant the impression.

"He is just like John," said Stellamaris.

"Something," said Herold, leading her out into the fresh air and sunshine.

"That fearless, royal look," said Stella—"don't you think so?"

Before replying, he took her to a shady bench where they both sat down.

"John's the finest and the best and the bravest fellow in the world," said he, loyally.

Her eyes shone. She put out her gloved little hand in her familiar, caressing way and pressed his gently. Her maidenhood did not glow at the sisterly touch.

"I'm so happy, my Great High Favourite, dear," she said.

"Why? Why now more than usual?" He smiled wistfully.

The sky was blue, and the trees were heavy with leafage, and she had just seen the king of beasts in his most kingly aspect, and he reminded her of the man she loved, and her heart was young and innocent. Herold once more became her chosen companion in the Land That Never Was. She dropped her voice to a whisper, for staring people strolled along the path ten yards away. Besides, there are times when the sound of one's own voice is embarrassing.

"You love John, don't you, dear? You love him dearly, dearly, dearly, as he deserves to be loved?"

"I would lay down my life for him," said Herold, gravely.

She gripped his hand. "I know. He would do the same for you. Do you think, Walter dear—" she paused and lowered her eyelids, "do you think there's a more splendid man than John in the world?"

"I am his friend, Stellamaris, and I'm prejudiced,—Love is blind, you know,—but I don't think so."

She leaned back in her seat and meditated. Then she said:

"I wish you and I were sitting by my window. You and I understand each other, but I miss the sea. You and I and the sea understand one another better. Can't you see it this lovely afternoon? It 's quite calm, but there 's a little kissing breath of wind, which makes it dance and sparkle in the sun. It 's laughing with gladness. Trees are beautiful, but they don't laugh."

"They whisper eternal things," said Herold.

"What?"

"The rhythm of life—fulfilment, as now, winter's decay, and the everlasting rebirth of spring."

"They don't tell me that. I don't understand their language," replied Stella. "To-day I want the sea, just with you—just you and I and the sea."

"And then you think I should understand all that the pink sea-shell that is you is trying to tell me?"

She laughed. "I could tell the sea, and the sea could tell you."

Secret de Polichitielle! Had she not been telling him all the time, as implicitly as maidenhood could tell man, of the great and wonderful adventure of her soul? He was exquisitely near,—that he knew,—nearer, indeed, to the roots of her being than the leonine hero of her dreams. He alone of mortals was privileged to receive and treasure the overflow of her heart. With him as joint trustee was the eternal ocean. He winced at the irony of it all.

Presently she asked:

"Have you ever loved any one?"

He answered as he had done years before:

"I have loved dreams."

She retorted in his own words:

"One can't marry a dream." He shrugged his shoulders.

"You will love some one some day, and then you will want to marry her," she continued, with her direct simplicity. "And when you do, you 'll come and tell me, dear, for I shall understand."

"I'll tell you, Stellamaris," he promised. Then he sprang to his feet. The pain had grown intolerable, "We have n't seen the giraffes," said he.

The child in her once more came to the surface. "I've longed to see a giraffe all my life," she cried, and she accompanied him blissfully.

After leaving her at the hotel, Herold went home and suffered the torments of a soul on fire. Tragedy lay ahead. Stellamaris, star of the sea, steadfast as a star—he knew her. Love had come to her not in the fluttering Cupid guise in which he visits most of the sweet maidens among mortals, but in the strong, godlike essence in which alone he dare approach the great ones. The sea-foam and mist formed but a garment for this creature of infinite sky and eternal sea. They but shrouded or touched to glamour the elemental strength.

She had given her love to John Risca, her Great High Belovedest. God knows what dreams she had woven about him; the man's fine loyalty asserted his friend's worthiness of any woman's dreams. The only, and the hideous, consideration was the fact of John being tied for life to the unspeakable. Himself and the pain of his love he put aside. What were the unimportant sufferings of a thousand such as he compared with one pang that might shoot through the bosom of Stellamaris? What could be done to avert the tragedy? His faith in John Risca was absolute. But John had shut his eyes to the glory shimmering in front of them. His eyes must be opened. Stellamaris must be told. All foundations of the Unwritten Law would have to be swept away, and she would survey in terror the piteous wreckage of the whole fabric of her life.

How could he save her? How could he save her from inevitable pain?

# CHAPTER XVII

THE next morning Stella was putting on her hat, a foamy thing of white tulle and pink roses, before her mirror, when an audacious thought came dancing into her head. It dizzied her for a moment, and took away her breath. With throbbing heart, she stood looking into her own wide eyes, which were filled with delicious excitement.

It would be a great adventure. Why should she not embark on it? She was free till luncheon, her uncle and aunt having gone out on their own errands and left her to the rest they supposed she needed. But she felt strong, pulsatingly strong. She looked out of the window. The June sunshine allured her. Why should she sit indoors on such a morning? There was not the faintest shadow of a reason. But how should she reach her destination? Her mind worked swiftly. Sir Oliver had set out on foot, bound for Bond Street and Piccadilly. Lady Blount had declared her intention to renew the joys of her youth, and go about in a hansom, which had been procured for her with some difficulty by the magnificent commissionnaire. The motor was at Stella's service. She had only to order it, and it would come to the front door and carry her whithersoever she desired.

It would be a wild adventure to feel herself alone and independent in this welter of London, and then, more thrilling still, to burst in upon her Great High Belovedest, not in his palace,—that, alas! he had given, up,—but in his Great High Mansion at Kilburn.

Where Kilburn was she had not the remotest idea; but it was somewhere in Fairy-land. The chauffeur would know; he seemed to know everything. The temptation overpowered her. She yielded. Orders were given to a bewildered and protesting maid. What would Lady Blount say?

"That 's a matter between Lady Blount and myself," said Stella.

"Can't I come with you, miss?"

"I am going alone, Morris." She had the gracious, but imperative, way of princesses. Morris dared argue no more. She attended her mistress to the door of the motor, and saw her driven away in prodigious state.

It was a glorious adventure. How could she have spoiled it by allowing the protection of a prosaic serving-maid? Hitherto she had not strayed alone beyond the confines of the gardens of the Channel House. Now she had the thrill of the first mariner who lost sight of land. She was on an unknown sea, bound for a port of dreams. Of the port she knew nothing definite. Since the dispersion of the apocryphal palace household, John had told her little of his domestic life. The old habit of deception had been too strong, and her other intimates had entered into the conspiracy of silence. Why trouble her with accounts of his Aunt Gladys, of whom she had never heard; of Unity, of whom it were best that she should not hear; of the poor, little, economical establishment,—Unity at the head, watching the pennies—which, together with the one in Fulham, was all that his means allowed him to maintain? All her life he had been to Stella-maris the prince eating off gold plate. Cui bono, to whose advantage and to what end, should he break the illusion and confess to chipped earthen-ware? Although she now recognized (to her sadness) the palace story as overlapping the fable, and set Lilias and Niphetos side by side with the cat Bast and the dog Anubis in the shrine of myth, yet her ingenuous fancy still pictured Risca as the writer of compelling utterances which caused ministers of state to clutch their salaries with trembling fingers and poten-tates to quake on their thrones. And she still imagined a fitting environ-ment for such a magnifico. On his private life during the week, outside his work, she scarcely speculated. For her it was spent at Southcliff from Saturday to Monday. It was difficult to realize that Southcliff was not the world.

The car sped like an Arabian-Nights carpet through wide thorough-fares thronged with traffic, up the wider, more peaceful, and leafy Maida Vale, passing broad avenues to right and left, and then, making a sudden turn, halted before the shabbiest of a row of shabby, detached little villas. The chauffeur descended, and opened the door of the car.

"Why have you stopped here?"

"It's the address you gave me, miss."

"Are you sure?"

"Quite sure, miss," smiled the chauffeur. "Fairmount, Ossington Road, Kilburn, London, NorthWest."

Fairmont had been to her a mount of beauty on the summit of which stretched the abode of her Belovedest. The chauffeur, still smiling,—for who could talk sour-faced to Stellamaris?—pointed to the gate.

"There it is written, miss,—'Fairmont.'"

She alighted, tears very near her eyes, and passing through the gates and tiny front garden, rang the bell. The door was opened by a common-looking, undersized girl of about her own age, dressed in a tartan blouse and a brown stuff skirt. Her nose was snub, her mouth wide, her forehead bulged, and her skimpy hair was buckled up tight with combs on the top of her head. There was a moment's breathless silence as the two girls stared at each other. At last Unity's face broke into a miracle of gladness, which transfigured her plain features. She retreated a step or two along the passage.

"Miss Stella! Miss Stella!" she gasped, and as Stella, still more amazed and bewildered, said nothing, she drew nearer. "It is Miss Stella, is n't it?" she asked.

"Yes," Stella answered. She paused; then, recovering herself, went on rather hurriedly: "I 've seen you before. You are the girl who came once into my room—I remember—Constable tore my jacket—you were mending it—"

"Yes, miss," said the other, forgetful, in the sudden excitement of again seeing her goddess face to face, of the precepts of gentility in which Miss Lindon had trained her.

"It all comes back, though it was long, long ago—ever so many years ago. Your name is Unity."

"Yes, Miss Stella."

"But what in the world are you doing here?"

"Mr. Risca is my guardian. I keep house for him—I and Aunt Gladys."

"Aunt Gladys?"

"Mr. Risca's aunt, Miss Stella." It was sweet to pronounce the beautiful name.

Stella's knees grew weak, and she leaned against the wall. Here were mysteries of which John had left her in ignorance. She felt guilty of unwarrantable intrusion. The joy of her adventure was blotted out. The shabby villa; the poverty-stricken passage; the glimpse through an open door into a gimcrack parlour, all bamboo and ribbons; Unity, the little sewing-girl who was John's ward; the unheard of Aunt Gladys—all was shock, sending dreams into limbo, startling an unready mind into a whirling chaos of conjecture. Too late she realized that, had he wanted her there, he would have invited her. He would be vexed at her coming. Her cheeks burned.

"Is he at home?" she faltered.

She heard with incredible relief that he had gone into town on business. Miss Lindon happening to be in bed with a slight cold, the duties of hospitality devolved on Unity.

"Won't you come in and sit down for a minute, Miss Stella?"

"I am afraid I must n't."

"Oh, why? Do come."

Unity stretched out her hand timidly. The gesture and the pleading in the girl's eyes made a strong appeal. Youth also called to youth.

"Just for a minute. It would make me so happy."

Stella could not refuse. They entered the little drawing-room. Stella had never seen such a funny, prim room before. She sat down on the slippery sofa. Unity fixed on her the eyes of a spaniel brought into the presence of a long-lost mistress.

"I think you 're even more beautiful than when I saw you before," she said, abruptly.

Somewhat confused, Stella smiled. "I am well now, like other people, so that's perhaps why I look better."

"When I heard of it, I cried with joy."

"You, my dear? Why?"

"I 'd been thinking of you all the time—all the time."

And Stella had never given a thought to Unity, though dramatic incidents at the Channel House had not been so frequent that the sight of Unity had not, brought back to her mind the circumstances of the episode. Stay, had she remembered all the circumstances?

"My dear," she said, moved by the girl's almost passionate sincerity, "I remember you well. I wanted you so much to come back and talk to me, and I asked for you; but they told me that you went away that afternoon. What were you doing at the Channel House?"

"I had been ill, and my guardian asked her ladyship to let me stay there for a bit."

"But they told me," cried Stella, the missing circumstance coming in a flash, "that you were a village girl who had been brought in for a day's sewing."

Unity flushed brick-red, realizing her indiscretion. She knew well enough now why she had been forbidden the sea-chamber.

"I was a noisy, horrid, badly-brought-up child," she said, "and they were afraid I should worry you. That was why," she said, with a slight air of defiance.

Stella was not convinced; the story lacked the ring of truth that characterized Unity's other statements. She felt that for some unknown reason they had lied to her, and that in order to bear them out Unity was lying. Her loyalty and delicacy forbade her questioning Unity further.

"If you were horrid, you would n't have remembered me all this time," she said, with a smile.

"That 's just how you looked when I called you 'my lady,' "said Unity. "How do you think one could forget you? Besides, Mr. Herold is always talking about you."

Stella opened her eyes. "Do you know Mr. Herold, too?"

"Of course. He's my guardian's dearest friend."

Stella's heart sank lower. Her Great High Favourite, too, was in this conspiracy of concealment.

"Does—does your guardian ever speak of me?"

"Why should he?" asked Unity.

The queer retort puzzled Stella.

The other, seeing the implied question in her glance, continued: "I should n't dare to ask him. He's too great and wonderful." Again the transfiguring light swept over her coarse features. "It 's beautiful of him to let me do things for him."

"What do you do?"

"I look after his clothes, mend and darn and buy things for him, and I dust his books and see that he has what he likes to eat and, oh, hundreds of things—just so that he sha'n't have any worry at all."

A new pain began to creep round Stella's heart, one she had never felt before, one that frightened her.

"Tell me some more," she said.

And Unity, her tongue loosened as it was with no one else in the world save Walter Herold, talked of the trivial round of her days and the Olympian majesty of John Risca.

"You must love him very much," said Stella.

A glow came into her patient eyes as she nodded and fixed them on Stellamaris; and then a tear started.

"Does n't everybody love him?"

She rose abruptly. "Would you like me to show you his room, Miss Stella—the room he works in?"

Stella rose, too. "He might not like it," she said.

This was a point of view incomprehensible to Unity. Even the all-great master must bow to the sanctification brought into the house by Stella's feet. She said softly:

"He worships the ground you tread on. Don't you know that?"

Stella flushed, and evaded the question.

"You think that if I'm afraid to go into his room, I don't care for him? It is n't that. I—I love him more than anything else in the world. I—" she stopped short, and the flush deepened, for she realized what she was saying. "It is something I can't quite explain to you," she continued, after a pause. "In fact, I ought n't to stay any longer."

Despite unregenerate Fatima temptation, despite a girl's romantic desire to see the table at which the dear one writes his immortal prose, she could pry no further into her Great Belovedest's home. She had pried too much already for her peace of mind.

She put out her hand. Unity took it, and, holding it, looked up into her face. She was squat and undersized; Stella was slim and tall.

"I thought I should never see you again," she said, in a low voice.

"I hope now we shall see each other often," replied Stella, and drawn toward the girl by the magnetism of her love, she kissed her on both cheeks.

But she drove away in the magnificent limousine very heavy-hearted, out of tune with life. She seemed to be living in an atmosphere of lies, from which her candid soul passionately revolted. She met them at every turn. Once more the world became the Threatening Land full of hidden ugliness, only awaiting opportunity to be revealed. The glamour of the last day or two in London had gone. When John Risca, truly her belovedest, when Walter Herold, whom in her simplicity she had regarded all her life less as a man than as a kind of Adonaïs spirit, when all, all she loved had lied to her persistently for years, to whom and to what could she pin her faith? Who would guide her through this land of which she was so ignorant, this land so thickly set with cruel traps?

John was poor and struggling and lived in a shabby little house. Had she known it, the fact would have made him all the dearer. But why had he given her to believe that he lived in fantastic luxury? Why had he lied? Why had he not told her of Unity—Unity who was so interwoven in his life, Unity who looked after his very clothes? A sudden thought smote her, and a scalding wave of shame lapped her from head to foot. She had proposed to buy his ties. She hated herself for the proposal, and she hated herself for starting on this lamentable adventure of indiscretion. She became aware that the new, frightening pain that had crept round her heart was jealousy, and she hated herself for the ignoble passion. She felt it like a stain upon her.

A slight smirch upon a gown of gray (such as most of us wear) escapes notice; but on a robe of white it stands out in hideous accusation.

The butterfly that had left the hotel so gaily returned with sorry wings from which the gossamer had been rubbed. She crept into her bedroom, where Lady Blount, coming in a while later, found her lying somewhat feverish on the bed. At the sight of her aunt, she sprang up to make instant and spirited confession.

"Do you know what I've done this morning? I thought I would give John a surprise and I took the car to Kilburn. He was not at home, but I saw the girl Unity, his ward."

Lady Blount looked at her in terrible dismay.

"My darling, you ought n't to have done it."

"I know, Auntie. And when you see John, will you tell him how sorry I am, and give him my apologies."

"Apologies?"

"Yes. It was ill-breeding on my part. He has a perfect right to keep his home affairs to himself, and I should not have intruded. You must apologize for me."

It was a very proud and dignified Stella that spoke, a spot of red burning on each cheek, and her slim figure held very erect.

"I hope, my darling," said Lady Blount, longing to ask a more direct question—"I hope that girl was n't rude to you."

"Unity rude?" Stella knitted her brow. The idea was ludicrous. "On the contrary, like the rest of you, she is far too fond of me. I don't know why;

it 's very odd. And she is devoted body and soul to John. She has a fine, great, generous nature."

The stain of jealousy should be wiped away, if she could possibly manage it.

"I believe she is a very good girl, though I have n't seen her—"

"Since she stayed at Southcliff?" said Stella with steady eyes.

"I—I was just going to say so," Lady Blount stammered. The situation was perplexing. "And John does n't often speak of her." She made rather a failure of a smile. "And what did the two of you talk about?"

The bitter knowledge of good and evil was coming fast to Stellamaris. A little while ago her innocence would have taken the question at its facevalue; now, perhaps for the first time in her life to suspect disingenuousness, she penetrated to the poor little diplomacy lying beneath.

"Chiefly of John and myself—of nothing very particular," she replied. "I did n't stay long."

She saw the repression of Lady Blount's sigh of relief. Swiftly she drew her deductions. They were all concealing something from her, and the fact of their concealment proved it to be something shameful and abominable. Her bosom rose in revolt against the world. Lift but a corner of the fairest thing in life, and you found the ugliness below.

She sat on the bed by the foot-rail, and rested her throbbing head on her hand.

"Your little escapade has upset you, darling," said Lady Blount, weakly; "but it was nothing very serious, after all. If John's furious when he hears of it, it 'll only be because he was not there to welcome you himself."

"I 'm not afraid of John being furious, Auntie," said Stella. "It 's not that at all. You don't understand."

"I don't think I do, dear," said poor Lady Blount. She sat down beside the girl and put a loving arm round her. "Tell me what it is."

But this was more than Stella could do. To speak would be to accuse and reproach, and she could not accuse or reproach any of her dear ones. Yet she needed the comfort like any other young and suffering soul. She surrendered to the elder woman's caress, feeling very weary.

"Perhaps I 'm not as strong as I thought I was, Auntie," she said.

The confession stirred all the mothering instincts in Lady Blount. With physical things she could grapple. She tended her with her thin, deft hands and persuaded her to lie down.

"My poor lamb, London is too much for you. Never mind. We 're going home to-morrow."

"I shall never want to leave home again," said Stella.

It was half-past one. Sir Oliver was lunching and spending the afternoon at his club. A tray was brought to Stella's bed, and Lady Blount pecked at a flustered woman's meal in the sitting-room.

"What about John and the pictures, darling?" she asked when she rejoined Stella. It had been arranged for John to call for them at three o'clock and take them to the Royal Academy.

"I don't think I feel equal to it," said Stella, truly. She was not yet quite "like every one else." Her sensitive nature also shrank from meeting John. Before him she would shrivel up with shame. "You go with him, Auntie; I 'll rest here and read."

On the stroke of three came John, who, having been detained on his business in town, had not gone home for luncheon. It was therefore from Lady Blount that he heard of Stella's adventure. He listened with his heavy frown, moving restlessly about the room, his hands in his pockets.

"I would give a thousand pounds for it not to have happened," said he.

"It's done now. We must make the best of it."

"Unity was discreet? Are you sure?"

"Quite sure."

He walked about for a while in silence.

"Perhaps it's just as well Stella should know so much," he conceded, "though I would rather she had learned it differently. I suppose she was somewhat upset?"

"She's still delicate," said Lady Blount, "and she's all sensitiveness— always has been, as you know. I have made her lie down."

He swung round sharply.

"She's not ill?" he asked.

"No, not ill; but exertion easily tires her. And she's afraid you 'll be angry with her, and miserable because she thinks she did an ill-bred thing in intruding on your privacy. She 's deeply ashamed; she feels acutely. She's not like other girls. We've got to realize it. She wants me to apologize to you—"

"Stella apologize to me! Stella!" he shouted in amazement and indignation. "We 'll soon see about that!"

He strode toward the door leading into Stella's room. Lady Blount checked him.

"Don't, John. I would n't see her now."

"Do you think I 'd leave her a minute to suffer fear and misery and shame?"

"You exaggerate, dear."

"Those were your words. No, Julia. I must set this right."

Stellamaris suffering, afraid of him, miserable, and ashamed! As well say Stella beaten, Stella thumb-screwed, Stella thrown to wolves! It was intolerable. He forgot his resolutions.

With rough gentleness he thrust Lady Blount aside and, opening the door, slightly ajar, caught sight of Stella lying, wrapper-clad, upon the bed. He entered in his impetuous fashion and slammed the door behind him.

"Darling, don't worry. Julia has told me. It 's only you that could have had the beautiful idea of coming to see me. I love you for it, and I could kick myself for not being at home."

Instinctively and unthinkingly, as if he had been in the sea-chamber, he sat down heavily beside her and took her two hands. Her brown eyes looked piteously into his.

"Stella, darling, it 's I that must ask for forgiveness for not having prepared you. Years ago, when you were little, I began the silly story of the palace to amuse and interest you; and I had a lot of troubles, dear, and it helped me to bear them to come to you and live with you in a fairy-tale. And then it was so hard to undeceive you when I found you believed it. I tried—you must remember."

"Yes, dear," she said, feeling very weak and foolishly comforted by the nervous grasp of his great hands. "Yes, I remember."

"You were there on your bed by the window," he continued, "and every one thought you would never rise from it. So what was the good of telling you just the weary prose of life? What place could it have in the poetry of yours? And I was selfish, Stella darling; I used to come to you for something sweet and pure and lovely that the wide wide world could n't give me. And I got it, and it sent me away strong for the battle; and I 've had to fight, dear—to fight hard sometimes. And when you got well and came out into the world, I felt it was necessary to tell you something more about myself—that there never had been a palace; that I was just a poor, hard-working journalist; that I had adopted a little girl called Unity, whose life had not been of the happiest; that she and an old aunt of mine kept house for me: but our old life went on so smoothly, and I still got the help and courage and faith I needed from you, that I put off telling you from week to week. That's the explanation, darling. And now I'm glad, more than glad, you came to-day. Don't you believe me?"

"Yes, Belovedest," she sighed. "I believe you."

He went on, finding in her presence his old power of artistic expression. In the overwhelming desire to bring back the laughter to those wonderful eyes that met his he forgot prudence, forgot the fact that he was making a passionate appeal. He was pleading her cause with happiness, not his own. It was the purest in the love of the man that spoke. Again he wound up by claiming her faith. And again, this time with soft, melting eyes, she said, "Yes, Belovedest, I believe you."

What else could she say, poor child? Here was her hero among men belittling himself just for her glorification. Here was his strong, beloved face wrought into an intensity of pleading. Here he was using tones of his deep voice that made every chord in her vibrate. Cloud-compeller, he cleared her overcast horizon to radiance. Is there a woman breathing, be she never so cynical, who, in the sunshine of her heart, does not believe in the sun?

She laughed and drew his hands to her face. "So you think I've been making mountains out of molehills?"

"Out of molecules," said he.

She laughed one of her adorable, childish little laughs. But the woman whispered, "Forgive me, Belovedest."

Time has invented but one proof of forgiveness in such a case, and eternity will not find a substitute. Obeying the everlasting law, he proved his forgiveness; but he mastered himself sufficiently to draw back the moment their lips had touched. He rose to his feet.

"Now we 're quite happy, aren't we?"

A little murmur signified assent. Then she sat up, and swung her legs daintily over the side of the bed, and, flushed, happy, and adorably dishevelled, looked at him.

"And now," she cried gaily, "if you 'll let me put on my frock, I 'll come with you and auntie to see the pictures."

He remonstrated. She was tired out; she must rest. But she stood up and faced him.

"I want to be happy to-day. Tiredness does n't count. I shall be at the Channel House to-morrow, and I can rest for a month."

She put her hand on his shoulder and led him to the door. In the next room Lady Blount was anxiously awaiting him. He took her lean shoulders in his bear's hug.

"All right, Julia. She's perfectly happy, and she's coming with us to the Royal Academy."

So once more that day was the limousine ordered to the hotel entrance, and once more Stellamaris entered it with a sense of high, but now delectably safe, adventure, this time helped in by John as tenderly as though she were a thing of spun glass and moonbeams. And they drove away joyously to see one of the most beautiful, but at the same time, one of the saddest sights of the world—the aspiring, yet fettered, souls, the unrealized dreams, the agonized hopes, individually concrete, of thousands of God's elect on this imperfect earth.

John Risca, absorbed in the laughter he had brought back to precious eyes, did not see a thin-lipped woman dressed in black slip behind one of the porphyry columns of the portico as they drove out. And the woman meant that he should not see, as she had meant it hundreds of times before during the last six years. Had he done so, there would have been an end to the intense, relentless, and diabolically patient purpose of her life.

# CHAPTER XVIII

CONSTABLE, dragging the feet of an old hound, mounted the stairs behind Stellamaris and followed her into the sea-chamber, and to the south window, whither she went instinctively to gaze out over her beloved sea, now gray and choppy, as the sky was overcast and a fresh breeze was blowing. He had been the most unhappy dog alive, they told her, during her absence. Since his dim, far-away puppy-hood not a day had passed without his spending hours in her company. She had been the reason of his existence. The essential one gone, there was nothing to live for; so at first he had wandered round in a bewildered way looking for her, and then, not finding her, he had refused food and pined, and, had she stayed away much longer, would have died of a broken heart, after the manner of deep-natured dogs. When she arrived, he was at the gate to meet her. At her magical appearance he tried to prance as in his youthful days, and lashed the whip of his tail against the iron railings so that it bled. Sobered by age, he had not had what Stella used to call a "bluggy" tail (the disability of his race) for years. But as prancing and tail-lashing and whinnying do not accord with the muscles and wind of an old dog, and as his heart was full, he had lain down at her feet, his snout beyond his paws, trembling all through his great bulk. And it was only after she had knelt on the ground beside him, thereby blocking the path to Sir Oliver and Lady Blount, to say nothing of Morris, the maid, and Simmons, the gardener, and the hand luggage, and had caressed and kissed him, that he had found strength to stagger to his feet and make way for his fellow-humans. After that he had not left her for a second. Who could tell but that she might vanish again into thin air, this time not to be reincarnated? Descartes, who said that the lower animals were automata, could never have known the wonder of a dog's love.

Constable followed Stella to the window and snuggled his great head into the curve of her waist. Her arm, soft and precious, drooped about his neck. Constable and the sea and herself had been secret-sharing companions since the world was young. So she stood for a long time by the open window, drinking in the salt of the sea-breeze, and communing, in her own way, with the elemental spirit of the waters. Presently she turned with a sigh, bent down, and took the old hound's slobbering chaps between her hands and looked into his patient eyes.

"Are you glad I'm back, dear High Constable darling? Very glad? Not gladder than I am, dear. No; you can't be. You've never been to London. Oh, you would hate it. It pretends to be a beautiful place, but it is n't. It 's a sham, dear. I'm sure you've never heard of a whited sepulchre; but that's what it is. And London's the world, my precious, and the world isn't a bit like what you and I were led to expect. It 's full of ugliness and wickedness, and nobody can get at the truth of anything." Still fondling him, she sat on the window-seat. "Yes; you and I are very much better off here. If you went abroad, you 'd be such a miserable Constable. You would, darling." She looked tragically at him, and he, responsive to the doleful tones of her voice, regarded her in mournful sympathy.

Then she laughed, and kissed him between the eyes.

"But I do so want to be happy. I'll tell you a secret—oh, a great, great secret—that no one knows." She lifted the velvet flap of his ear and whispered something below her breath, which Constable must have understood, for he laid his cheek against hers; and so they stayed until Morris, intent on unpacking, disturbed their peace.

Then came a day or two of rest during which she strove to reconcile the irreconcilable,—her dreams in the sea-chamber and the realities outside,—using her newly found love for talisman. And just as she was trying to forget the ugliness of the world, a domestic incident cast her back into gloom and doubt.

One morning she entered the morning-room on a scene of tragedy. Sir Oliver stood with his back to the fire, looking weakly fierce and twirling his white moustache; Lady Blount sat stern and upright in a chair. A bulky policeman, bare-headed, stood at attention in the corner,—there is something terrifically intimate about an unhelmeted policeman,—while, in front of them all, a kitchen-maid in a pink cotton dress sobbed bitterly into a smudgy apron.

Stella paused astonished on the threshold. "Why—" she began.

"My dear," said Sir Oliver, "will you kindly leave us?"

But Stella; advanced into the room. "What is Mr. Withers doing here?"

Mr. Withers was the policeman, and a valued acquaintance of Stellamaris.

"Go away, darling," said Lady Blount. "This has nothing to do with you."

But Stella had been accustomed to rule in that house. Anything that happened in it was her concern. Besides, she would have ugly things hidden away from her no longer; and here was obviously an ugly thing.

"No, my dears," she said in her clear voice; "I must stay. Tell me, why is Eliza crying?"

"She's a wicked thief," said Lady Blount.

Then Stella caught sight of a couple of rings and a brooch and a five-pound note lying on a table.

"Did she steal those?"

Sir Oliver explained. The articles had been stolen during their absence in town. He had applied to the police, with the result that the theft had been traced to Eliza.

So that was a thief—that miserable, broad-faced girl. Stella looked at her with fearful curiosity. She had heard of thieves and conceived them to be desperate outcasts herding in the sunless alleys of great cities, their hideous faces pitted with crime, as with smallpox; she never imagined that they came into sheltered homes.

"What is Mr. Withers going to do with her?"

"Take her to prison," said Sir Oliver, whereat the culprit wailed louder.

"What is prison?" asked Stella.

"A place where they lock you up for months, sometimes for years, in a stone cell, and make you sleep on a plank bed, and you have to pick oakum all day long, and are known by a number, and—er—"

"Please, Oliver!" remonstrated Lady Blount.

"I want to know, Auntie," said Stella, a gracious, white-clad figure standing in the midst of them. She turned to the policeman.

"Are you going to take her to prison?"

"If Sir Oliver charges her, miss."

"Of course I 'm going to charge her," cried Sir Oliver. "It 's my duty." He drew himself up. "I should be failing in it if I did n't."

"Then it depends on you, Uncle, whether she is locked up or goes free?"

"That's so, miss," replied the policeman. "I can't arrest her unless some one charges her."

"What do you say, Auntie?"

"It's very painful, dear. That is why I did n't want you to come in. But people who do these things have to be punished."

"But why have they to be punished?" Stella asked, feeling curiously calm and remote from them all.

"They must be made examples of, dear. They must n't be let loose on society," said Sir Oliver. "It's a duty to one's country, a duty to one's neighbours. I'm afraid you don't understand, Stella. I implore you to leave this matter in our hands."

It was strange how the girl whom they had reared in blank ignorance of life remained supreme arbiter of the situation. She said:

"You are afraid that if she were set free, she would rob somebody else?"

"Of course she would," said Sir Oliver, testily.

"Would you, Eliza?" asked Stellamaris.

Thus appealed to, the guilty little wretch threw herself on the ground, in horrible abasement, at Stella's feet.

"Oh, Miss Stella, don't let them put me in prison! For God's sake! don't let them put me in prison! I'll never do it again. I swear I won't. Save me, Miss Stella!"—She clutched the white skirts—"Don't let them send me to prison."

She continued in terrified reiteration. Stella felt an icicle in her bosom in place of a heart. She had never before seen humanity lowered to the depths.

"Why did you do it?"

The crouching thing did not know. The drawer of the dressing-table had been left unlocked. She had been tempted. It was the first time she had stole anything. She would never do it again. And then she cried again, "Don't let them send me to prison!"

"Julia, can't you prevent her making such a noise?" said Sir Oliver.

The bulky policeman, desiring to carry out Sir Oliver's wishes, came forward and laid his hand on the girl's shoulder. She screamed. Stella touched him on the arm, and he stood up straight. Then she opened the door.

"Thank you very much, Mr. Withers, for your trouble; but we are not going to have this girl put in prison."

The kitchen-maid lay a huddled, sobbing mass on the floor.

"You 're doing a very foolish thing, Stella," said Sir Oliver.

"You had much better let your uncle and me deal with this," said Lady Blount.

"My dears," said Stella, very white, very dispassionate, cold steel from head to foot, "if you put this girl in prison, I shall go mad. All the things you have taught me would have no meaning. We say every day, 'Forgive us our trespasses, as we forgive them that trespass against us.' "

"But, my darling child, that's quite different," said Sir Oliver. "That 's a form of words referring to spiritual things. This is practical life."

"Is that true, Auntie?"

"No, dear, not quite. It's most difficult to know how to act," replied Lady Blount, resting her weary old head on her hand. "Do as you like, child. What you do can't be wrong."

Stella turned to the policeman, who had been looking from one to the other and wondering from whom he should take his final instructions.

"We sha'n't need you any more, Mr. Withers."

"Very good, miss."

He saluted and went away. Stella shook the girl by the arm.

"Get up," she commanded, "and go to your room. Don't speak. I can't bear it. Go."

The maid picked herself up and rushed out of the room. Stella confronted the two old people. The morning sun streamed through the casement window, and the light fell full on Sir Oliver's wrinkled old face and spare form, and Stella, through the semi-military jauntiness and aristocratic air of command produced by the thin features and white moustache and imperial, saw, as by means of X-rays, all the weakness, the foolishness, the pomposity, the vanity, that lay beneath. And yet she knew that he loved her more dearly than any one in the world. She looked at her aunt, and, in the awful flash of revelation that at times sweeps through the young soul, she knew her to be a woman of little intelligence, of narrow judgment, of limited sympathies; and yet, she, too, loved her more dearly than any one in the world. Over them, she, Stella, had achieved a tranquil victory. Ashamed and hurt to her inmost heart by the stabbing consciousness of the humiliation she must have brought on these two poor ones so dear to her, she had not a word to say. Nor could they speak a word. There was a tense silence. Then reaction came. All the love of a lifetime flooded Stella's heart, and she threw herself by the side of Lady Blount and, her head in the old woman's lap, burst into a passion of tears. Sir Oliver, with a palsied gesture of his hand, left the women to themselves.

Once more poor Lady Blount, with her commonplace little platitudes, preaching obedience to the law, tried to comfort Stellamaris, whose intelligence had been scrupulously trained to the understanding of nothing but obedience to the spirit. And once more Stellamaris went away uncomforted. Guilt must be punished—a proposition which she found it hard to accept; but, accepted as a basis of argument, was it not punishment enough to reduce a human being to such grovelling degradation? Did not the declared intention of sending that wretched girl to prison imply pitilessness? Thenceforward hardness and suspicion began to creep into Stella's judgments. Dreams of evil began to haunt her sleep, and brooding by her window, she began to lose the consolation of the sea.

Three week-ends passed, and John did not come to the Channel House, making varied excuses for his defection. He wrote cheerily enough, but Stella, with poor human longing for the magic word that would set her heart beating, found a lack of something, she scarce knew what, in his letters. Her own, once so spontaneous, so sparkling with bubbles of fancy, grew constrained and self-conscious. John seemed to be eluding her. One of the Sundays Herold came down. The Blounts told him of the episode of the kitchen-maid and of the way in which Stella had taken the law into her own hands.

"I never imagined she had such a spirit," Sir Oliver declared. "Egad! she stood up against us all like a little reigning princess."

"But she broke down afterward, poor darling!" said Lady Blount.

Herold tried to question Stella on the subject, but met with no response.

"Let us talk of pleasant things," she pleaded.

He went away sorrowful, knowing the conflict in her soul—knowing, too, that the strong soul has to fight its battles unaided.

Meanwhile Stella put on a smiling face to the world,—for, after all, the world smiled on her,—and she was gentle with Sir Oliver and Lady Blount. She mingled in such social life as the neighbourhood afforded—a luncheon party, a garden party, where young men fell at her feet in polite adoration, and young women put their arms round her waist and talked to her of hats. She liked them all well enough, but shyly evaded intimacy. They belonged to a race of beings with whom she was unfamiliar, having passed their lives in a different spiritual sphere. They frightened her ever so little; why, she did not know, for her unused power of self-analysis was not sufficiently strong to enable her to realize the instinctive shrinking from those, strangers to her, who had been drenched from childhood in the mysterious and dreadful knowledge of evil. She met them only on the common ground of youth and talked of superficial things, fearing to inquire more deeply into their thoughts and lives.

"I love to see her enjoying herself," said Lady Blount.

Sir Oliver rubbed his hands, and agreed for once with his wife.

"There's nothing like a little harmless gaiety for a girl," said he. "She has been shut up with us old fogies too long."

"She's beginning to realize now," said Lady Blount, "the happiness that lies before her in the new condition of things."

ONE day when Stella was returning, unattended, from a small shopping excursion in the village, a thin-lipped woman in black crossed the road just before the turn that led to the gate to the Channel House and accosted her.

"Miss Blount?"

"Yes," said Stella, coming to a halt.

She had noticed the woman for some little time walking on the opposite side of the way, and had been struck by a catlike stealthiness in her gait. Now, face to face with the woman, she met a pair of pale-green, almost expressionless eyes fixed on her with an odd relentlessness. The woman's lips were twisted into the convention of a smile.

"Could I have the pleasure of a few words with you?"

"Certainly," said Stella. "Will you come into the house with me? We are almost there."

"If you will excuse me, Miss Blount," said the woman, holding up a deprecating hand,—she was well-gloved and was dressed like a lady,—"I would rather not go in with you. I have my reasons. I must speak with you entirely in private. If we go round here, there is a comfortable seat."

Near the point at which they were standing the road up the cliff diverged into two forks. The upper fork led to the gate of the Channel House. The lower one was a pathway round the breast of the cliff. The woman pointed to the latter. Stella hesitated.

"What have you so private to tell me that we can't talk in the garden?"

"It's something about John Risca," said the woman with the thin lips.

Stella put her hand to her heart. "John—Mr. Risca? What is the matter? Has anything happened to him?"

"Oh, he's in perfect health. Don't be alarmed. I only don't want us to be interrupted by Sir Oliver or Lady Blount. Do come with me. I assure you it's something quite important."

She moved in the direction of the lone path, and Stella, drawn against her will, followed. They, reached the seat. Below sank sheer cliff to the rocks on the shore. Above sheer cliff rose to the crest on which stood the Channel House. The sea sparkled in the sunshine. In the far distance a great steamer, her two funnels plumed with gray, sped majestically down Channel. The woman looked about her with nervous swiftness. They were out of sight of human creature. Then she turned, and the cold face changed, and Stella shrank from its sudden malignity. The woman clutched the girl by her arm.

"Now, my lady, do you know who I am?"

"No," said Stella, shrinking back terrified, and striving to wrench herself free.

"I am John Risca's wife."

Stella looked at her for an agonized moment, then, as white as paper, collapsed on the seat, the woman still gripping her arm.

"John—married—you—his wife!" she stammered incoherently.

Louisa Risca bent down and scrutinized the white face.

"Do you mean to say you didn't know?"

Stella shook her head in frightened negation. Her ignorance was obvious, even to the criminal woman now on the point of carrying out the fixed idea of years. Gradually the grasp on her arm relaxed, and the woman stood upright.

"You did n't know he was a rotter, did you?"

The word smote Stellamaris like a foul thing. She shivered. Mrs. Risca kept her eyes fixed on her for a few seconds until, as it were, some inspired thought flashed into them a gleam of joy.

"It 's jolly lucky for you that you did n't know. There 's a nice little drop from here down to the rocks. I've been here often before."

Stella sprang to her feet and thrust her hands against the woman's breast. .

"Let me pass! Let me pass!" she cried wildly.

But the woman barred the downward path. A few steps beyond the bench it narrowed quickly upward until it merged into the cliff-side.

"I'm not going to. You've got to stay here," said Mrs. Risca, seizing Stella's wrists in a grip in which the girl's frail strength was powerless. "If you struggle and make a fuss, you 'll have us both chucked over. Don't be silly."

Then Stella, calling to her aid her pride and courage, drew herself up and looked the evil woman in the face.

"Very well. Say what you have to say. I will listen to you."

"That 's sensible," said Mrs. Risca, dropping her wrists. "I don't see why you should have gone on so. I only wanted to speak to you for your good and your happiness. You sit down there, and I 'll sit here, and we 'll have a nice, long talk about John."

Stella sat on the extreme upper edge of the bench, Mrs. Risca on the lower, and smiled on her victim, who drew a convulsive breath.

"He has been making love to you, has n't he?" she asked, enjoying the flicker of pain that passed over the delicate features.

"Go on, if I must hear," said Stella.

"And all the while he's been a married man, and I'm his shamefully neglected and deserted wife."

"How am I to know that you 're his wife?" said Stella.

"I thought you'd ask that, so I've brought proof."

She drew two papers from a little bag slung over her arm, and handed one to Stella. It was a certified copy of the marriage-certificate. Stella glanced over it. Ignorant as she was in things of the world, she recognized the genuineness of the official document. Her eyes were too dazed, however, to appreciate the date. She passed the slip of blue paper back without a word.

"Here's something else."

Mrs. Risca gave her a discoloured letter, one which she had kept, Heaven knows why, perhaps in the vague hope that it might one day be turned into an instrument against her husband. It was an old, old, violently passionate love-letter. Stella's eyes met a few flaming words in John's unmistakable handwriting, and with a shudder she threw the letter, like something unclean, away from her. Mrs. Risca picked it up from the path and restored it, with the marriage-certificate, to her bag.

"He 's a pretty fellow, is n't he? Fancy his kidding you all the time that he was a single man. And you believed him and thought him such a noble gentleman. Oh, he can come the noble gentleman when he likes. I know him. I 'm his wife. He wants to be taken for a rough diamond, he does. And he's never tired of showing you what a diamond he is. And for all his rough diamondness, he 's as vain as a peacock. Have n't you noticed it, darling?"

She paused, and smiled horribly on Stellamaris. Stellamaris, from whose brown pools of eyes all translucency had gone, looked at her steadily. The girl's face was pinched into a haggard mask.

"I don't think you need tell me any more. Will you please let me go."

"I have n't nearly finished, darling," replied Mrs. Risca, finding a keener and purer delight in this vista of exquisite torture that in the half-confessed intention of throwing the innocent interloper over the cliff. "I want to be your friend and warn you against our dear John. He 's the kind of male brute, dear, that any silly young girl falls in love with. I know I did. He has a way of putting his great arms around you and hugging you, so that your senses are all in a whirl and you think him some godlike animal."

Stella shuddered through all her frame at a memory hitherto holy, and clenched her teeth so that no cry could escape. But the woman gloated over the setting of the jaw and the tense silence.

"That 's John, my pretty pet. And he likes us young. He took me young, and because I would n't hear of anything but marriage, he married me, and then threw me over, and deserted me, and brought me into terrible trouble, and all that he or any one else may say against me is a lie. Oh! I know all about you. This is n't the first time I've been to Southcliff. And as soon as you could get up and go about,—he knew all along that you would n't lie on your back forever—trust him,—he comes and makes love to you and kisses you, does n't he? And he can't marry you, because he's already married."

Stella rose, and straightened her slim figure, and threw up her delicate head.

"I have heard enough. I order you to let me pass." But the woman laughed at the childish imperiousness. She knew herself to be of wiry physical strength. To catch up that light body and send it hurtling into space would be as easy as kicking a Yorkshire terrier over the edge of a pier. She had once done that.

"You 'd make your fortune as a tragedy queen. Why don't you ask Mr. Herold to get you on the stage? Sit down again, darling, and don't be a little fool. I've got lots more to tell you."

"I prefer to stand," said Stella.

"It does n't matter to me whether you stand or sit, my precious pet," said Mrs. Risca. "I only want to tell you all about your dearly beloved John. Oh, he 's a daisy! They 'll tell you all sorts of things about me— about me and Unity—"

"Unity?" cried Stella, taken off her guard.

"Yes, darling. You went and saw her the other day, did n't you? Oh, no matter how I know. I only mention it to let you see that I 'm telling the truth. They 'll tell you all sorts of things about me and her; but they 're all lying. What do you think of our friend John's relations with Unity?"

"Mr. Risca is Unity's guardian," said Stella in a cold voice.

The woman laughed again. "You little fool! She's his mistress."

Unity again, with the baffling mystery surrounding her! The woman spoke directly, as if in complete revelation. Yet Stella was still in darkness, and the uncontrollable feminine groped toward the light.

"I don't understand what you mean," she said haughtily.

"You mean to tell me you don't understand what a man's mistress is?"

It took her a few moments to appreciate the virginal innocence of the white and rigid thing in woman's guise. When she did appreciate it, she laughed aloud.

"You pretty lamb, don't you know what a wife is?"

Stella stood, the cliff above her, the cliff below, midway between her sky and her beloved and dancing sea, a hard-eyed statue. The supreme and deliciously unexpected moment of the criminal woman's life had come. She rose and held Stellamaris with her pale-green eyes, and in a few brutal words she scorched her soul.

# CHAPTER XIX

A WHISTLING youth who lumbered up the path saved Stellamaris. There was nothing about him suggestive of the dragon-slaying and princess-rescuing hero of the fairy-tale, nor did he at any time thereafter dream that he had played the part of one; but at the sight of him the she-dragon fled, her ultimate purpose unfulfilled. Stella sank quivering on the bench. The knight-errant touched his cloth cap, and, unaccustomed to the company of princesses, lounged in awkward self-consciousness a few yards away, with his hands in his pockets and pretended to admire the view. Stella, aware of deliverance from physical danger, drank in the unutterable comfort of his presence. After a while he turned and was moving off, when a cry from her checked him.

"Please don't go!"

He advanced a step or two. "Is anything the matter, miss?"

She reflected for a moment. "I came over rather faint," she said. "I don't know whether I can get down to the house alone." She was too proud to confess to fear of the evil woman. . .

The youth offered help. He could easily carry her home. To have carried the mysterious lady of the Channel House would make him the envy of the village. Such aid, however, she declined.

"Shall I tell them at the house, miss?"

She sprang to unsteady feet.

"No, don't do that! See, I can walk. You go in front, and if I want you, I 'll tell you."

The youth, somewhat disappointed, lounged ahead, and Stella followed, with shaking knees; so had she progressed during her early lessons in the art of walking. At the turn of the path Stella held her breath, dreading to come upon the woman; but no woman was in sight. She walked more freely. At last they reached the gate of the Channel House, which the youth held open for her. She thanked him, and once within the familiar shelter of the garden she sped into the house and up the stairs into her room, where she fell exhausted on the bed.

The sensation of physical peril was gone,—of that she felt only the weakness of reaction,—but the woman had scorched her soul, shrivelled her brain, burnt up the fount of tears. The elfin child of sea-foam and cloud lay a flaming horror.

They found her there, and saw that she was suffering, and tended her lovingly, with many anxious inquiries; but she could not speak. The touch of ministering hands was torture, almost defilement. All humanity seemed to be unclean. Dr. Ransome, summoned in haste, diagnosed fever, a touch of the sun, and prescribed sedatives. For aught she cared, he might have diagnosed a fractured limb. Of objective things she was barely aware. Figures moved around her like the nightmare shapes of a dream, all abhorrent. She heard their voices dimly. If only they would go! If only they would leave her alone!

Her High-and-Mightiness, the nurse, long since relieved of her occupation, was telegraphed for from London. She came and bent over the familiar bed and put her hand on the hot forehead. But Stella withdrew from the once-cooling touch, and closed her ears to the gentle words, for they seemed to be the touch and the words of the woman with the pale, cruel eyes and the thin lips. All night long she could not sleep, tormented by the presence of the watcher in the room. Outside the night was dark, and a fine rain fell. Within, the lamp of Stellamaris burned in the western window of the sea-chamber. For the first time in her life she longed for the blackness; but she could not speak to the watching shape, and she clenched her teeth. Her brain, on fire, conceived the notion that she was caught in one of the Cities of the Plain, and far above her floated a little, dazzling, white cloud, which mockingly invited her to mount on its back and soar with it into the infinite blue.

After the dawn had broken, she fell asleep exhausted, and the sun was high when she awoke.

The nurse, who had been watching her, bent down.

"Are you feeling better, dear?"

She smiled at the well-known face.

"Yes, High-and-Mightiness," she said. They were the first words she had spoken since the day before.

She raised her head, and suddenly memory awoke, too, and the horror swooped down upon her like a vast-winged, evil bird. She sank again on the pillow and hid her eyes with her hand.

"The light too strong, dear?"

Stella nodded. Words and shapes were now clearly defined. The nurse took her temperature. It was virtually normal.

"It must have been a touch of the sun, darling, as the doctor said," remarked the nurse. "But, thank heavens! you 're better. You gave us all such a fright."

"I'm sorry," said Stella. "It was n't my fault."

IT was a new and baffling Stellamaris that entered the world again. She went about the house silent and preoccupied. Joy was quenched in her eyes, and her features hardened. The lifelong terms of endearment from the two old people met with no response. Their morning and evening kisses she endured passively. They had become to her as strangers, having gradually undergone a curious metamorphosis from the Great High Excellency and Most Exquisite Auntship of her childhood into a certain Sir Oliver and Lady Blount, personages of bone and flesh of an abominable world, in whom she could place no trust.

One evening before going up-stairs, she picked up a French novel which Sir Oliver had left in the drawing-room.

"Don't read that, Stella dear," said Lady Blount.

"Why?" asked Stella.

"I don't think it's suitable for young girls."

"Is it unclean?"

"My darling, what an extraordinary word!" said Lady Blount.

"Is it unclean?" Stella persisted.

"It deals with a certain side of life that is not wholesome for young girls to dwell upon."

"You have n't answered my question, Auntie."

"The fact that your uncle and I have read it is an answer, dear," said Lady Blount, with some dignity.

"Then I will read it, too," said Stella.

She took it up to her room and opened it in the middle; but after a few pages her cheeks grew hot and her heart cold, and she threw the book far out of the window.

It was a foul, corrupt world, and all the inhabitants thereof save herself gazed upon its foulness, and took part in its corruption, not only without a shudder, but positively with zest. In the sane lucidity of her mind, humanity was scarcely less intolerable than in the nightmare of her day and night of horror.

To perform an act of ethical judgment, no matter how rough and elementary, one must have a standard. The fact, too, of ethical judgment being inherent in the conditions of human existence, implies faultiness in those conditions. In an ideal state of being, such as the evangelical heaven, where there is no faultiness, there can be no possible process of judgment, and thereby no standard whereby to measure right and wrong. If a dweller about the Throne were to visit the earth, and even limit his visit to Cheltenham or a New England township, the record of his impressions would be, from our point of view, both grotesque and unjust. He would have no standard, save the infinite purity of the Godhead (and an infinite standard is a contradiction in terms) whereby to measure human actions. He would be a lost and horrified seraph. His opinions would not be a criticism, but an utterly valueless denunciation of life.

Stellamaris, for all the imperfections inseparable from humanity, had been a dweller about the Throne in her mystical Land of Illusion. Evil, or the whisper of evil, or the thought of evil, had, by the Unwritten Law, never been allowed to enter the sea-chamber. She issued therefrom, like the unfortunate seraph, without a standard. Her impressions of life (from our worldly point of view) were grotesque and unjust. John was condemned by her unheard. Like the seraph, she was lost and horrified. But, unlike the seraph—and here lies the tragedy, for no one of us would break his heart over the horrification of a seraph, as he has only to fly back whence he came to be perfectly happy—unlike the seraph, Stellamaris was just poor human clay, and she could not fly back to her Land of Illusion, because it did not exist. It was her fate to lead the common life of imperfect mortals, feeling the common human physical and spiritual pangs, with all the delicate tendrils of her nature inextricably intertwined in human things, and to focus the myriad sensations afforded by the bewildering panorama of life from the false and futile point of view of the seraph. In consequence, she suffered agonies inconceivable—agonies all the more torturing because she could not turn for alleviation to any human being. She shrank from contact with her kind, wandered lonely in the garden, save for the attendance of the old dog, and sat for hours by the window of the sea-chamber looking with yearning eyes at sea and sky.

But no more could sea and sky, cloud and sunset, foam and mist, take Stellamaris into their communion. She had put on mortality, and they had cast her out from their elemental sphere. The sea-gulls flashed their wings in the sun and circled up the cliff and hovered at her window, fixing her with their round, yellow eyes, but they were no longer the interpreting angels of wind and wave. The glory of all the mysteries had faded into the light of common day, and the memory of them was only the confused and unrecallable tangle of a dream. And Stellamaris cried passionately in her heart for the days when she had not set foot in the world of men, and when she lived somewhere out there in the salt sea-spray, and felt her soul flooded with happiness great and exquisite. But such days could never dawn again. She, too, had become bone and flesh of an abominable world.

Herold came down again, and found her white and pinched, with dark lines beneath her eyes. She scarcely spoke, replied in monosyllables, only made such appearances as the conventions of life demanded, and craftily avoided meeting him alone. She was no longer Stellamaris.

"What 's the matter with her, for pity's sake?" asked Herold.

"She has not yet got over that touch of the sun," said Sir Oliver.

"This has nothing to do with the sun," Herold declared.

Lady Blount sighed. "Perhaps it 's a phase. Young girls often pass through it, though earlier. But Stella is different."

Herold saw that they did not understand, and, knowing their limitations, felt that even if they were enlightened, they would do more harm than good. As soon as he returned to town he tracked John to his office. John looked up from proof-sheets.

"Just back? I nearly ran down yesterday. I should have done so if I had n't promised my aunt to go to church with her."

"You've quite taken to church-going lately," said Herold, dryly.

John laughed. "It pleases the old soul."

"And keeps you in Kilburn," said Herold.

"It might be something worse," John growled. Then he banged the table with his fist. "Can you realize what it means to keep away from her? I think of her all day long, and I can't sleep at night for thinking of her. It 's idiotic, weak, disgraceful, wicked, any damned thing you like, but it's so." And he glowered up into Herold's face. "I am eating myself out for her."

"What about Stella?" Herold asked.

"That you can tell me. You've just come from her. I don't know. I 've kept away scrupulously enough, Heaven knows, and my letters are just footling things. But I've not heard from her for over a week. I waylay the postman and look over my letters like a silly ass of a boy."

"Have you told her about your marriage?"

"Not yet."

Herold drew a deep breath and turned away and pretended to study a proof of the contents-bill of the next number of the Review that was pinned against the wall. He had come there to ask that question. He had half expected and wholly hoped for an answer in the affirmative. Stella's knowledge might have accounted for her metamorphosis.

"She must be told at once," he said, returning to the table.

"Why?"

"Because she loves you. You fool!" he exclaimed, "have n't I seen it? Has n't she all but told me so herself? And she has told you, in some sort of way, only you have made up your mind not to listen. Let me put matters plain before you. She says good-bye to you here in London, and goes home full of happiness and looks forward to your coming down invested in a new halo, and to your letters,—you know what sort of letters a man writes to the woman he loves,—and instead of all that you never go near her and you write her footling notes. What do you imagine she's thinking and feeling? What do you think any ordinary decent girl would think and feel in the circumstances?"

"Stella is n't an ordinary girl," said John, leaning back in his writing-chair and looking at Herold from beneath his heavy brows.

"For that reason she thinks and feels a thousand times more acutely. She's ill, she's changed, she's the shadow of herself," he went on fiercely, "and it's all through you."

He broke off and, as John said nothing, he put both hands on the table and leaned over and looked into John's eyes.

"I 'll tell you another thing. The whole lot of us have caused her endless misery. We 've fed her all her life on lies. God knows how I hated them! Her coming out in the world has been a gradual discovery of them. She has had shock after shock. She has n't told me,—she's too proud,—but I know, I can read it in her face, in her eyes, in the tone of her voice. And now she's going through the biggest disillusion of all—you."

"Do you mean," said John, frowning heavily, "that she thinks I'm a blackguard because I seem—you put the phrase in my head by talking of the ordinary young woman—because I seem to have thrown her over?"

"She's wondering whether you are a lie, like most other things. And it's killing her."

"What am I to do?"

"Tell her straight. You ought to have done so from the first."

"If she feels it as deeply as you say, it might kill her outright."

"It won't," said Herold. "She 's made of metal too fine. But even if it did, it were better so, for she would die knowing you to be an honest man."

John put his elbows on the table and tugged at his hair with his big fingers. He could not resent Herold's fiery speech, for he felt that he spoke with the tongue of an archangel. Presently he raised a suffering face.

"You 're right, Wallie. It has got to be done; but I feel as if I'm taking a knife to her."

He rose and pushed away the pile of proofs. "All this," said he, "is going to the devil. I 've got to work through it over and over again, because I can't concentrate my mind on anything." He walked about the room and then came down with both hands on Herold's shoulders.

"For God's sake, Wallie, tell me that you understand how it has all come about! Heaven knows she has had the purest and the highest I've had to give her. I 'm a rough, selfish brute, but for all those years she stood to me for something superhuman, a bit of God fallen on the earth, if you like. And then she came out in woman's form and walked about among us —I could n't help it. Say that you understand."

"I can quite understand you falling in love with her," said Herold, quietly.

"And you 'll help to set me right with her—as far as this damnable matter can be set right?"

"You two are dearer to me than anything in life," said Herold. "There is nothing too difficult for me to undertake for you; but whether I succeed is another question."

"I wish I were like you," said John. He shook him with rough tenderness and turned away. "God! It is n't the first time I've wished it."

"In what way like me?"

"You've kept your old, high ideals. She's still to you Stellamaris—the bit of God. You have n't wanted to drag her down to—to flesh and blood —as I have."

Herold grew white to the lips and took up his hat and stick. "Never mind about me," he said, steadying his voice. "I don't count. She's all that matters. What are you going to do? See her or write?"

"I 'll write," said John.

Herold went out, carrying with him the memory of words he had spoken to John many years before—words of which afterwards he had been ashamed, for no man likes to think that he has spoken foolishly, but words which now had come true: "I have walked on, roses all my life; but my hell is before me... my roses shall turn into red-hot ploughshares, and my soul shall be on fire." And he remembered how he had spoken of the unforgivable sin—high treason against friendship. But in one respect his words had not come true. He had said that in his evil hour he would have a great, strong friend to stand by his side. He was walking over the ploughshares alone. And that evening, in their wait on the stairs during the first act, in retort to some jesting reply, Leonora Gurney said:

"I believe you 're the chilliest-natured and most heartless thing that ever walked the earth, and how you can play that love-scene in the third act will always be a mystery to me."

"Perhaps that's the very reason I can play it," said Herold.

His heart wrung in a vice, John wrote the letter to Stellamaris. He was "killing the thing he loved." Good men, and even some bad ones, who have done it, do not like to dwell upon the memory. He posted the letter on his way home from the office. It dropped into the letter-box with the dull thud of the first clod of earth thrown upon a coffin. At dinner Miss Lindon talked in her usual discursive way on the warm weather and sun-spots and the curious phenomenon observable on the countenance of a pious curate friend of her youth, who had spots, not sun-spots, but birth-marks, on brow, chin, and cheeks, making a perfect sign of the cross. But the dear fellow unfortunately was afflicted with a red tip to his nose, wherefore a profane uncle—"your great-uncle Randolph, dear"—used to call him the five of diamonds.

"But he was a great gambler—your uncle, I mean. I remember his once losing thirty shillings at whist at a sitting."

To all of which irrelevant chatter John made replies equally irrelevant. And Unity dumbly watched him. She had been at great pains to prepare a savoury dish that he loved. He, ordinarily of Gargantuan appetite, as befitted the great-framed man that he was, scarcely touched it. Unity was distressed.

"Isn't it all right, Guardian?" she asked.

"Yes, dear; delicious."

Yet he did not eat, and Unity knew that his heart was not in his food. It was elsewhere. He was unhappy. He had been unhappy for some time. Two lines had come between the corners of his lips and his chin, and there was a queer, pained look in his eyes. A far lesser-hearted and weaker-brained thing in petticoats than Unity would have known that John loved the radiant princess of Wonderland. Unity dreamed of it—the love between her king and her princess. Of herself she scarcely thought. Her humility—not without its pride and beauty—placed her far beneath them both. Her king was suffering. The feminine in her put aside such reasons as would have occurred to the unintuitive male—business cares, disappointed ambition, internal pain, or discomfort. He was suffering; he went about with a mountain of care on his brow that made her heart ache; he answered remarks at random; he had no appetite for the dish he adored—lamb-chops en casserole, which she had learned to make from a recipe in "The Daily Mirror." He was pining away for love of Stellamaris.

So deeply engaged was Unity with these thoughts that it was not until she had switched on the light in her bedroom and was preparing to undress that she remembered, with a pang of dismay, that the Olympian tobacco box (old pewter, a present years ago from Herold), one of her own peculiar and precious cares, was empty. She went down-stairs to the store-cupboard, where she hoarded the tobacco and, with it in her hand, she proceeded to the study, and opened the door softly.

Her guardian, her king of men, her beginning and end of existence, sat in his writing-chair, his head bowed on his arms, folded on the table. A blank sheet of paper lay on the blotter. She saw that his great shoulders shook. As he did not hear her enter, she stole on tiptoe to the table, and laid the packet of tobacco on the corner. She tiptoed back to the door, and turned and stayed there for a moment, watching him, soul-racked with futile longing to bring him comfort.

She caught muffled words. She knew in her heart that nothing she could do would be of any avail. In an instinctive gesture she stretched out her hands piteously toward the bowed head and went out of the room, noiselessly closing the door behind her.

That night, she cried as she had never cried before, not even when hot irons had seared her flesh.

An hour or so afterwards John Risca put out the lights in his study and went up-stairs to bed. He could not sleep, and he thought, after the poor, but human, manner of men, not so much of the killing of the thing he loved, as of the unimaginable, intolerable blank in his own life when the thing he loved should be killed.

In the morning he said to himself, "She has got my letter," and fell into a frenzy of speculation.

That day he watched the post for an answer, and the next day and the next and the next; but no answer came. For the irony of fate had so ordained that, as with the other unanswered letters, Stellamaris, her finger-tips quivering with shame and horror at contact with the envelope, had destroyed it unopened.

# CHAPTER XX

UNITY watched the beloved being as only a woman can watch man or a sailor can watch sea and sky. To each, signs and portents are vital matters. She noted every shadow on his face, every deepening line, every trick of his eyes, every mouthful that he ate, and the very working of his throat as he swallowed. She noted the handwriting on envelopes and unfinished manuscript, the ashes knocked out of pipes, the amount of evening whisky consumed, and the morning muddle of pillow and bedclothes. She was alive to his every footstep in the house. She knew, without entering the study, whether he was working, or sitting morose in his old leather arm-chair, or pacing the room. She knew whether he slept or was restless of nights.

One day she made a discovery, and in consequence took the first opportunity of private use of the telephone, and rang up Herold. She was anxious about her guardian. Could she see Herold as soon as possible without Aunt Gladys or guardian knowing? They arranged a meeting just inside the park, by the Marble Arch.

Herold, who knew Unity to be a young woman of practical common sense, had readily assented to her proposal, and in considerable perturbation of mind started from his home in Kensington. He arrived punctually at the Marble Arch end of the park, but found her already there, a patient, undistinguished little figure in her tartan blouse and nondescript hat adorned with impossible roses. The latter article of attire was her best hat. She had bought it already trimmed for seven-and-six, which had seemed a reckless expenditure of her guardian's money.

She was sitting on a bench of the broad carriage-drive, watching with a London child's interest, despite her preoccupation, the gorgeous equipages, carriages, and automobiles transporting the loveliest ladies (save one) in the world, ravishingly raimented, from one strange haunt of joyousness to another. For it was half-past three of the clock on a beautiful day in the height of the London season, and, as everybody knows, Hyde Park is a royal park, and along that stretch of road from Hyde Park Corner to the marble arch no cart or omnibus or hackney cab or pretentious taxi is allowed under penalty of instant annihilation. Only the splendour (in eyes such as Unity's) of plutocratically owned vehicles meets the enraptured vision. Pedestrian fashion, however, does not haunt that end of the road, which is mostly given up to nurse-maids and drab members of the proletariat; but the flowerbeds make compensation by blazing with colour, and the plane-trees wave their greenery over everything.

Herold raised his hat, shook hands, and sat down by Unity's side.

"It was good of you to come, Mr. Herold. I scarcely dared ask you, but —"

"What's gone wrong?" he asked, with a smile.

She began her tale: how her guardian neither ate nor slept, how he tore up page after page of copy,—he who used to write straight ahead; she found the pieces in the waste paper basket,—how he was growing gloomy and haggard and ill. Her woman's mind laid pathetic stress on these outward and visible signs.

"You must have noticed the difference in him, Mr. Herold," she said tearfully.

He nodded. John took trouble badly, which was one of the reasons that endeared Herold to him. In some aspects he was nothing but a Pantagruelian infant; but it was no use discoursing on this to Unity.

"He feels things very deeply," he said instead.

"Would n't you, if you loved Miss Stella, and never saw or heard from her?"

"I should," said he, with a smile.

"And she loves him. I know it. And she feels deeply, too."

He acquiesced. "She, too, is very unhappy."

"And they 're separated forever because they can't marry?"

"That is so, Unity," said he.

"Why can't he get rid of her—the other woman I mean?" cried Unity, fiercely.

"She has given him no grounds for divorce."

Unity twisted her handkerchief in her hands. "I suppose there comes a time," she said, "when people can't stand any more suffering, and they break down or do something dreadful."

"Your guardian is too strong for that," replied Herold.

"I don't know. I don't know." The mothering instinct spoke. "That 's what I 've come to ask you about. I'm frightened."

She turned on him a miserable, scared face and told him of her discovery. She had gone into her guardian's study that morning in order to tidy up, and had seen that he had left the key in the lock of his private drawer, with the rest of the bunch hanging from it. She had opened the drawer and found, lying on top of some documents one of which was a sealed envelope endorsed "My Will," a loaded revolver and a case of cartridges. She knew that the revolver was loaded because she had examined it. Then, hearing his step, she had shut the drawer, and gone on with her dusting. He had entered, locked the drawer, put the bunch in his pocket, and gone out without a word.

Herold looked grave. More in order to gain time for reflection than to administer a moral lesson, he said:

"You should n't have searched his private drawer, Unity."

"I'd search anything, if only I could find a way of helping him," she replied impetuously. "When I see him suffer and can't do anything for him, I feel crazy. I can't sleep sometimes, and stand outside his door in the middle of the night. It does n't matter whether I ought n't to have done it or not," she cried with an awkward and impatient gesture; "I did it, and I found what I found. What I want to know is, Why should my guardian make his will and keep a loaded revolver in his room unless he thought that—that he was going to die?"

Her eyes filled with tears. Herold, alarmed by her news and touched by her devotion, took her cheap-gloved hand and pressed it. Occupants of the dazzling equipages stared at the elegantly attired gentleman and the dowdy little girl love-making on the public seat. He tried to reassure her.

"Every man with folks depending on him makes a will, so we can dismiss that; and I know heaps of men who keep revolvers."

"But why should the will be dated two days ago?" asked Unity.

"Was it?"

"The date was written on the envelope, with 'My Will' and his name."

"In all probability," said Herold, "the cloud that has come between him and Stellamaris has made him decide to make a fresh will. I know he made one some years ago."

"But why the revolver?"

"He spoke to me, also some years ago, about getting one. There had been one or two burglaries and an ugly murder—don't you remember?—in the neighbourhood. He must have got it then."

"It looks too new," said Unity.

"Those things keep new for ever so long, if they 're not used," he argued.

"Then you think there 's no danger?" she askeds with both her hands on his wrist.

"Not at present," he said, with a smile. "Look after him as closely as you can and keep up your brave little heart, or we 'll have you too going about with hollow eyes and gaunt cheeks, and we can't afford it."

"Me?" She sniffed derisively. "I'm as tough as a horse. And what do I matter?"

"Your guardian would have a pretty poor time of it if he had only Aunt Gladys to look after him."

The shadow of a grin flickered over Unity's face.

"I suppose he would," she said.

She went away half-comforted. She had shared her terrifying secret with Herold, which was a good and consoling thing; but she had not been quite convinced by his easy arguments. And Herold went away entirely unconvinced. He knew John as no one, not even Unity, who had made him the passionate study of her life, could know him. It was his peculiarity to pursue his right-headed ideas with far less obstinacy than his wrong-headed ones. In the former case he had a child's (and sometimes a naughty child's) hesitations, and was amenable to argument; but when bent on a course of folly, he charged blindly, and could be stopped only with great difficulty. Herold walked through the park in anxious thought, and, at a loose end for an hour or two, took a taxi to the club to which both he and John belonged. Avoiding the lounge and its cheery talk, he mounted to the deserted morning-room, and, having ordered tea, settled down to an evening newspaper, the pages of which he stared at, but did not read.

Presently, to his surprise, John, who had avoided the club for some little time, burly and gloomy, entered the room.

"I thought I'd come in for a quiet talk with somebody; but there's that ass Simmons down-stairs. He makes me sick."

Simmons was the wit and brilliant raconteur of the club.

"You can have a quiet talk with me, if I'm good enough," said Herold. "I've been wanting to see you. What line are you going to take in the 'Review' on this latest freak of the censor?"

The prohibition of a famous Continental play had aroused the usual storm in the theatrical and journalistic world. Every one who wrote turned his back on the harmless and ridiculously situated man, and in cut-tlefish fashion squirted ink at him. But John Risca took no interest in the question, and stated the fact with unnecessary violence. He, on his side, had wanted to see Herold. He had taken his advice and written to Stella and had received no reply. More than a week had passed. The whole thing was driving him mad.

Herold made a proposal which had been vaguely in his head for some days, and to which Unity's communication had given definiteness.

"Come away with me on a sea-voyage—a couple of months—South Africa, anywhere you like. I'm tired out. As for the piece, it's near the end of the run, and it 'll hurt no one if I go out and let Brooke play my part. I have n't had a holiday for two years. It would be an act of charity. You can get away; no man is indispensable, and you can afford it. If you stay here, you 'll lose your balance and very likely commit some act of idiotic folly. By our return, time will have done its soothing work, and the relations between Stella and yourself will have been readjusted."

Such was the substance of that which for a solid hour he strove to nail into John's armour-clad mind. His efforts were vain. In the first place, John was not going to accept such a quixotic sacrifice of professional interests from any man, even from Herold; secondly, he could n't get away from London, and did n't want to; thirdly, if he were being driven mad within a journey of an hour or so from Stellamaris, he would become a raving maniac if he were separated from her by half the length of the earth; fourthly, he was in perfect health and perfect command of his faculties, and the only meaning he could attach to Herold's insinuation regarding idiotic folly was that he might forget himself so far as to go down to Southcliff and make a scene with Stellamaris, thereby acting with insensate cruelty toward her: all of which was ludicrous, and it was insulting on Herold's part to make such a suggestion.

Herold called him a fool and said that he did not mean that at all.

"Then what did you mean?"

"When a man loses control over himself and lets himself be obsessed by a fixed idea, his brain 's not right, and he's capable of anything. The only chance for him is change of scene and interests, and that's why I've been imploring you to come away with me."

"And that's why I'm going to do nothing of the kind," said John, rising and looking down upon his friend with blood-shot eyes. "I'm pretty miserable, I own. Lots of men are, and they have to keep their mouths shut, because they have n't any one before whom they 're not ashamed to let off steam. I've got you. I've had you all my man's life. I've told you everything. Somehow I've not been ashamed to tell you things I would n't dream of breathing to any other man living. There 's a kind of woman, I believe, whom I might have talked to as I do to you. I've not met her, so I've got into the habit of coming to you with whatever worries me; and you 've never failed me. And I've come to you now. But there are limits beyond which even a friend like you has no right to go. You've no right to tell me I'm going out of my mind and to warn me against behaving like the inmate of a lunatic asylum. You've no right. I resent it. I'm not going to stand it."

Herold's reply was checked by the creaking of the door and the entrance of the bent figure of an old member, a county court judge who, on his way to a writing-table by the window, nodded courteously to the two younger men and remarked that it was a fine day.

"I suppose most people would call it so," said John.

"Don't you?"

"I hate it," cried John. "I wish it would rain. I wish it would rain like the devil. I would give my ears for a pea-soup fog. Sunshine is too blightingly ironical in this country."

The old judge lifted his eyebrows. "The metaphysics of meteorology are beyond me," he said, with a smile and a bow, and sat down to write.

John lingered for a second or two by the side of his friend, tracing the pattern of the Turkey carpet with the toe of his boot; then he swung round abruptly.

"Excuse me," said he. "I've got to look at Baxter's imbecile article in 'The Contemporary.' "

He went to the table where the current magazines and reviews were tidily displayed, and Herold, sitting in an arm-chair some distance away, with his back to the table, pondered over the discussion that had just taken place. But for the rumble and clatter of London that came through the open windows, the ceaseless choric ode to all the drama of the vast city, there was silence in the spacious room, broken only by the scratching of the old judge's quill pen. Herold resumed his aimless skimming of the evening newspaper. What further appeal could he make to John in his contradictory and violent mood?

At last the old judge, having scribbled his note, got up and left the room. Herold turned and found himself alone. John had gone without drum or trumpet. In the lounge down-stairs there was no John, and in the hall the porter told him that Mr. Risca had left the club.

He went home to his actor's six o'clock dinner, and found a letter from Lady Blount imploring him to come to Southcliff at once. Stella was getting worse day by day. Sir Oliver and she were in despair, Dr. Ransome was at his wits' ends. In a woman's frantic helplessness she adjured him to come and work a miracle. Now, it so happened that on the early afternoon of the next day he had a very important appointment. It was a question of his going into nominal management in the autumn. Suitable pieces, a theatre, and financial backers, obscure but vital elements in theatrical business, had been found, and it was with these last that the morrow's all-important interview was to take place. He turned up the railway time-table, and saw that by leaving London by the first train in the morning, and probably skipping lunch, he could spend a couple of hours in Southcliff and get back in time for his engagement. He telegraphed to Lady Blount, dined, and went to the theatre. For perhaps the first time in his pleasant life he was overwhelmed that evening by the sense of the futility of his work, which every artist, actor, painter, and poet is doomed to feel at times. The painted faces of his colleagues, the vain canvas of the sets, the stereotyped words, gestures, inflections, repeated without variation for more than the two hundredth time, the whole elaborate make-believe of life that at once is, and is not, the theatre,—all this oppressed him, filled him with shame and disgust. It had no meaning. It was an idle show. He had given to inanity a life that might have been devoted to the pursuit of noble ideals.

Folks are apt to imagine that, when the pains of the actual world get round about an artist's soul, the supreme moment has arrived for him to deliver himself in immortal utterances. This is untrue. He does n't so deliver himself. On the contrary, he cuts up his canvas, smashes his piano, and kicks his manuscript about the room. What interpretation of life, however celestially inspired, can have the all-annihilating poignancy of life itself? Your poet may write an immortal lyric by the death-bed of his mistress; but it is a proof that he did not care a brass farthing for the lady: he is expressing the grief that he might have felt if he had loved her. For the suffering artist, at grips with the great realities, art is only a trumpery matter. It is only when he is getting, or has got, better, that he composes his masterpieces working

... the world to sympathy
With hopes and fears it heeded not.

So Herold, instinctively obeying the common law, as all poor humans in one way or another have to do, grew heartsick at the vanity of his calling, and, after a mechanically perfect performance, wondered how an honest man could live such a life of shameless fraud.

After a night and dawn of rain the sun shone from a blue sky when he reached the Channel House next morning. Sir Oliver and Lady Blount received him in the dining-room. They looked very old and careworn. Like Constable, they had nothing to live for save Stellamaris; and now Stellamaris, stricken by an obscure but mortal malady, was dying before their eyes. So, antiphonally, and at first with singularly little bickering, they told Herold their story of despair. It added little to his knowledge. The symptoms of which he was already aware had intensified; that was all. But the two guardians had altered their opinion as to the cause. Sir Oliver ruefully discarded the theory of the touch of the sun, and his wife now realized that the state of Stellamaris was not merely the morbid phase through which most maidens are supposed to pass. Dr. Ransome, with intuition none too miraculous, had emitted the theory that she had something on her mind. "But what could the poor darling innocent child have on her mind?" cried Sir Oliver.

"What, indeed," echoed Lady Blount, "unless her mind is affected?"

"Don't be a fool, Julia," said Sir Oliver.

"I'm not such a fool as you think, Oliver. Stella has n't lived a normal life, and who knows but what the change of the last year may have done harm? Dr. Ransome himself said that if we could cure the mind, we could cure the body, and advised us to take her abroad so that she could be distracted by fresh scenes."

"He hinted nothing about insanity. You ought to be ashamed of yourself," said Sir Oliver, with querulous asperity.

Then Herold saw that the truth must be told.

"Has it never struck you that John may be the cause of it all?"

Sir Oliver jerked himself round in his chair. "John? What do you mean?"

"Why, I wrote to John at the same time that I did to you," said Lady Blount, "begging him to come down in almost the same words; for you know, dear Walter, I'm not a clever woman and can't say the same thing in two different ways. She does n't know I did so, for she's so strange and won't talk to any one alone, if she can help it. I thought John and you might succeed in getting something out of her. But John has n't replied at all. I can't understand it."

"Does n't that bear out what I say?" asked Herold.

"But John—what do you mean?" Sir Oliver repeated.

"Yes, dear, what do you mean? Of course John has behaved in an extraordinary way lately. He has n't been to see us for ever so long. But the dear fellow has explained. He is overwhelmed with work, especially at week-ends. He writes me charming letters, and he corresponds regularly with Stella. I don't see—".

"Oh, for heaven's sake, Julia, let Walter put in a word!" cried Sir Oliver, rising and throwing his cigarette-end into the bank of flowering-plants that filled the summer fireplace, a domestic outrage that always irritated Lady Blount, and even now caused her to wince and dart an angry glance at the perpetrator. "Go on. Tell us what you mean."

"Has it never occurred to you that Stella and John may have fallen in love with each other—with the ghastly barrier of the wife between them?"

The two old people looked at him wide-eyed and drooping-mouthed. That Stellamaris, their fragile, impalpable child of mystery, more precious to them than a child of their own bodies, over whom they might have quarrelled—that Stellamaris should be a grown woman, capable of a grown woman's passions, was a proposition bewilderingly preposterous. Sir Oliver found speech first.

"Stella in love with John? It's absurd; it's ludicrous. Why, bless my soul! you might just as well say she was in love with me! It's nonsense—ridiculous nonsense."

He walked up and down beside the dining-room table, with arms out-stretched, shaking his thin hands in protest.

Lady Blount, her elbow resting on the table, looked at Walter.

"The barrier of the wife? Who could have told her?"

"John himself."

"How much?"

"I don't know."

Sir Oliver brought himself to an abrupt standstill by the side of his wife.

"He ought n't to have done anything of the kind. Such things are not fit for her to hear."

"That's the dreadful mistake we've made all along, my dear Oliver," said Herold, sadly; and he disclosed to them probabilities of which they had not dreamed.

Lady Blount began to cry silently, and her husband laid his hand on her shoulder. She put up her own and clasped it. They looked very forlorn, robbed of the darling they loved. The new Stellamaris was alien to their conservatism. They did not know her. They were lost. Like children they clasped hands, and their hearts were united at last in common dismay.

Herold turned and looked out of the window. Presently he said:

"She's in the garden. I'll go and talk to her, if she will let me."

"Do, Walter dear. Try to make her speak. It's that awful silence that we can't bear."

"She has always been devilish fond of you," said Sir Oliver.

Herold went out and came upon her, escorted by Constable, in a path bordered on each side by Canterbury bells and fox-gloves and sweet-william. She drew herself up as he approached, and looked at him like some wraith or White Lady caught in the daylight, with no gleam of wel-come in her glance. The old dog, however, pushed by her to greet Herold, whom he held in vast approbation. Then, aware of being relieved from duty, he wandered down the path, where he lay down and, like a kindly elder, suffered the frisky impudence of a stray kitten of the household.

"I suppose they've sent for you because they think I am ill," Stella began suspiciously.

"You are ill, dearest," he replied in a quiet voice, "and it's causing us all very deep grief."

"I'm not ill," she retorted. "But every one's worrying me. I wish you would tell them to leave me alone."

He took a nerveless, unresponsive hand and put it to his lips. "Stella-maris, Stella darling, don't you know how we all love you? How we would give everything, life itself, to make you happy?"

She withdrew her hand. "Don't talk of happiness. It's a delusion."

"Every living thing can be happy after its kind," said Herold. "Look at this great bumble-bee swinging in the campanula."

"You were n't sent here to talk to me about bumble-bees," she said with an air of defiance.

"No. I came to speak to you about John."

It was a thrust of the scalpel. It hurt him cruelly to deal it, but it had to be dealt. He closely watched its effect. Her wan face grew even whiter, and her lips grew white, and she held herself rigid. Her eyes were hard.

"I forbid you to mention his name to me."

"I must disobey you. No, my dearest," said he, gently barring the path, "you must listen. John is as unhappy and as ill as you yourself. He is suffering greatly. I don't know what to do with him. He 's going on like a madman. You must not be unjust."

"I'm not unjust. I know the truth at last, and I judge accordingly."

"You are hard, Stella. Perhaps that's the first unkind word anybody has ever spoken to you—and I've got to speak it, worse luck! John would have told you long ago of the unhappy things in his life if he had thought they could possibly concern you. As soon as he found that they might do so, he told you frankly."

"He has told me nothing," said Stella, icily.

"He wrote to you about his marriage over a week ago."

"I did n't read the letter. I never read his letters. I don't take them out of the envelopes. I destroy them."

Herold stared in amazement. "Then how," he cried, "do you know what you call the truth? What do you know?"

"He married a woman who is still alive. I know a great deal more," she added, ingenuous still in her cold disdain.

"More?" His brain worked against baffling conjecture. Who could have told her? Suddenly his eyes caught the shadow of tragedy. He made a step forward and closed his hands on her arms, and even then he felt the shock and pain of their fragility. In London, a short time ago, they were round and delicately full.

"Stellamaris darling, tell me. It is I, Walter, who have loved you all your life, and to whom you have always told everything. Something none of us know has happened. What is it?"

She swayed back from him, and half closed her eyes.

"Let me go," she said faintly. "Such things are not to be spoken of. They are not to be thought of. They only come in horrible dreams one can't help."

He put an arm round her instinctively to save her from falling.

"Who told you? You must speak."

She wrenched herself free and stood rigid again.

"She told me, his wife herself."

"His wife!" His head reeled.

"His deserted wife, a woman with green eyes and thin lips. I suppose you know her. She came down here to tell me."

"My God!" cried Herold. "My God in heaven!"

And for the first time Stella saw a man in white, shaking anger, showing his teeth and shaking his fists.

"When was it?"

She told him. He controlled the riot within him and questioned her further, almost hectoringly, masterfully, and she replied like a woman compelled to obey, yet flinging her answers defiantly. And he went on unrelenting, fighting not her, but the devil that had got possession of her, until she told him all, even the final horror, as far as he could wring confession from her virgin fierceness; for, in the white-hot passion of his anger he had challenged her knowledge of evil almost as directly as the woman had done.

"And you believe her?" he cried. "You, Stellamaris, believe that murderous thing of infamy, when you've known John Risca and his love and his tenderness all your life? You believe it possible—John and Unity? Good God! It 's monstrous! It's hellish!"

He planted himself on the path before her, hands on hips, his sensitive face set, his blue eyes aflame, and looked at her as no man or woman had ever yet looked at Stellamaris. And she met his look, and her eyes, despite the battle her proud soul was fighting, lost their hardness, and new light flashed into them, as though they had changed from agate to diamond.

"She loves him, body and soul," she said. "I ought to have recognized it in London. I did n't know the meaning of things then. I do now."

"Yes, she does love him; she loves him as I love you,"—and, unrealized by him, there came into his voice the vibrating notes of passion that had stirred Stellamaris to the depths at the theatre,—"with every quivering fibre, heart and spirit, body and soul." He flung both hands before his face, —these were words of madness,—and went on hurriedly: "She loves him as John loves you, as the great souls of the earth can love, without thought of hope, just because they love."

She looked at him, and he looked at her, and they stood, as they had been standing all the time, in the pathway, between the gay borders of flowers; and the sky was blue overhead, and the noonday sun caressed the ivy and lichens on the Georgian front of the Channel House, which basked peacefully on the farther side of the lawn. The kitten had frisked away with feline inconsequence, and Constable sprawled stiffly asleep on the gravel, like a dead dog.

"You say you love me like that?" said Stellamaris.

"You command love. Unity herself loves you like that," replied Herold, loyally.

"What reason should she have for loving me? She should be jealous of me, as I was of her. And who is she? Who is Unity?" she asked with an imperious little stamp. "I 've been lied to about her for many years. She too lied. Will you explain her? If she's not what that woman said, what is she?"

"I 'll tell you," he said.

He spared her nothing. It was not the hour for glossing over unpleasant things. Let her judge out of the fullness of knowledge. At his tale of the torturing—he gave her the details—she shrank back, covering her eyes and uttered a sobbing cry.

"It 's too horrible! I can't bear it; I can't believe it."

He waited a while to give her time for recovery.

"It's true," said he.

"I don't believe it," she cried, facing him again. "The woman warned me against lies that were being told about her—lies to screen Unity."

"It 's true," he repeated. "If you want proofs, I could get you the newspaper reports of the trial. She was put into prison for three years. Then John swore that Unity should never suffer again, and, by way of reparation, adopted her as his own daughter. He came like a god and lifted her from misery to happiness. That 's why she loves him, as you say, body and soul."

"And he loves her."

Her tone staggered him. "He loves her as a father loves a daughter."

"And she as a woman loves a lover. I'm no longer a child. I know what I 'm talking about."

Then he saw how deep the poison had gone. It was a ghastly travesty of Stellamaris that spoke.

"You are talking wickedness, Stellamaris," he said sternly. "Go on your knees and pray to God for forgiveness."

She threw back her head. "There is n't a God, or He would not allow such foulness and horror to be on His earth. I believe in nothing. I believe nobody. I would just as soon believe that woman as you. At least she did n't pretend to be good. She rejoiced in her vileness. She hid nothing, as every one else hides things. And now—" her voice dropped to a tone of great weariness—"don't you think you've tortured me enough?"

The word was a sword through his heart. He stretched out reproachful hands.

"Stella, dearest, dearest—"

"Forgive me," she said. "Sometimes I hardly know what I'm saying."

"If you would only trust me!"

She shook her head sadly.

"I can trust no one, not even you. Let me go now."

He saw that she was at the end of her strength. Any concession that she might make now would be for him a Pyrrhic victory. And it was true that he had tortured her—tortured her, as his whole being asserted, for her soul's welfare. But he could probe her no further.

They walked in silence toward the house. Constable, as soon as they had passed, rose and followed them. It is for the greater happiness of big-hearted dogs that they do not understand all things human.

At the foot of the staircase leading to Stella's wing they parted.

"Stella, darling," said he, taking her hand, "if you will believe nothing else, believe this: all our hearts are breaking for you."

She looked at him for a long, odd moment, with the diamond glitter in her eyes.

"Mine is broken," she said.

He stood and watched her wearily mounting the stairs until she disappeared at the turn of the landing, the old hound scrabbling up behind her.

# CHAPTER XXI

HEROLD caught his train. He had accomplished his mission; Stella had spoken. In a few words he had enlightened Stella's unhappy guardians.

"Be gentle with her," he had recommended. "Don't try to force her confidence. Don't let Ransome feel her pulse too often or give her physic. Talk about the tropics, and try to stimulate her interest and make her think she would like to go on a sea-voyage. Or, if you can get hold of a lost baby, stick it in the garden where she can find it."

He had talked bravely to the old people, who would have cut off each other's heads—and their own, for the matter of that—to bring back the Stellamaris of a year ago. They clung to him pathetically. If he had counselled them to shut Stella in a room and read the minor prophets aloud to her, they would have obeyed him with unquestioning meekness. With a smile on his lips, he had put heart into them. Lady Blount had kissed him, and Sir Oliver, watery-eyed, had wrung his hand.

In the empty carriage of the train he gave way, as your highly strung, sensitive man must do, if he would avoid disaster. He did not think. To think implies an active process. But thoughts came tumultuous, and without a struggle he let them assail him. He felt that if he attempted to put into logical order the intricacies of passionate emotion in which he and John and Stella and Unity were involved, if he attempted to gage the effect on all their lives of this new horror brought therein by the murderous devil-woman, if he allowed himself to think of Stella's challenge, "You say you love me like that?" he would go mad. Let the burning thoughts sear his brain as they listed; his sanity demanded passive surrender.

At Victoria Station he collected his wits so as to deal with the commonplace routine of life. He looked at the clock, rapidly calculating. He would have time to go home, bolt some food and drink, and go off to keep his appointment with the men of money. He drove to his house in Kensington in a taxicab, and, telling the driver to wait, let himself in with his latchkey. His man met him in the hall.

"A lady waiting to see you, sir."

"I have no time to see ladies. Tell her I'm very sorry, and bring me a sandwich and a whisky and soda."

He thought she was some persistent actress in search of an engagement. Such phenomena are not infrequent in the overcrowded theatrical world.

"It 's a Miss Blake, sir, Mr. Risca's ward. She telephoned this morning, and asked when you would be likely to be in—"

"Miss Blake?"

He stood amazed. What was Unity doing in his house? It was only yesterday that he had seen her. What had happened?

"Where is she?"

"In the library, sir."

He ran up the stairs. As he entered the room, Unity rose from the straight-backed chair in which she had been sitting and rushed to meet him. She was an eager and anxious Unity, still wearing the tartan blouse, but not the gorgeous hat of yesterday. A purple tam-o'-shanter hastily secured by a glass-headed pin, had taken the place of that extravagant creation.

"Oh, Mr. Herold, do you know anything about guardian?"

The eagerness faded from her face as she saw the perplexity on his.

"What do you mean, dear?"

"He went out last night about seven o'clock, and has n't come back since." She wrung her hands. "I thought you might be able to tell me something."

He could only look at her in blank dismay, and question her as to John's latest known movements. There was very little to tell.

"He had an appointment in town after lunch, which was the last time I saw him. I heard him come in about a quarter to seven and go straight into his study—"

"He left me about half-past five—at the club," said Herold. "He was all nerves and crazy-headedness. He almost quarrelled with me. He said he had n't slept for weeks."

"He has n't," said Unity. "That's what makes me so frightened."

"Well, go on."

"I heard him come in. I was in the kitchen helping Phoebe. A few minutes afterward I heard him walk down the passage—you know his quick, heavy tread—and go out again, slamming the street door. We waited dinner for ever so long, and he did n't come. And then it was bedtime. Aunt Gladys was n't anxious, because nothing that guardian did now would surprise her. She's like that, you know. And I did n't think very much about it at first, because he's always irregular. But when it came to two and three and four o'clock in the morning—I can never go to sleep till I hear him come in, you know," she explained simply—"then I was terribly anxious —"

"Why did n't you ring me up during the night?" Herold asked.

"I thought of it; but I did n't like to disturb you. I did early this morning, but your servant said you had already gone down to Southcliff. Oh, I was so hoping," she sighed, "that he had gone to Southcliff, too! There was a letter waiting for him—"

"Good Lord!" cried Herold, with a flash of memory, "so there was! From Lady Blount."

"Do you know what was in it?" she asked quickly.

"Lady Blount told me. She said that Stellamaris was very ill, going to die,—an alarming letter,—and begged him to go down at once."

"And he went out, but he did n't go down," said Unity.

Their eyes met, and the same fear froze them. "Did you look—"

"No; how could I? The drawer was locked."

"It must be broken open," said Herold.

The man-servant came in to ask whether he should pay and dismiss the waiting driver of the taxi.

"Yes," said Herold, after a moment's reflection. "And, Ripley, you might telephone to Mr. Bowers of Temple Chambers and say that I'm detained; that I don't know whether I 'll be able to come at all."

It was impossible to transact business beneath this lowering cloud of tragedy. The men of money could wait till John was found, dead or alive. Suddenly he remembered that a taxicab was the one thing necessary. He recalled Ripley.

"Let the cab wait." He turned to Unity as soon as the man had closed the door.

"It must be broken open, and at once. I 'll come with you and do it. I 'll take the responsibility."

"Yes," said Unity. "Let us know the worst."

"I 'll go and fetch a couple of bunches of keys. We may find one to fit."

He went out and soon afterward returned, the keys jingling in his pocket. Ripley was at the hall telephone as they passed.

"I 'm going up to Mr. Risca's," said Herold.

In a few moments they were speeding across London. Unity sat very tense, her red hands clenched together till the knuckles showed white.

"The house first, and then Scotland Yard," he said.

"We must know first," she assented.

He glanced at her admiringly.

"You 're one of the bravest girls I've ever met."

She shrugged her shoulders. "It is n't a time for playing the fool and going into hysterics," she said bluntly.

Many girls of her mongrel origin would have broken down under the strain, shed wild tears, uttered incoherences of terror. Not so Unity. "She is the kind that walks through fire," thought Herold.

They spoke little. He grew sick with anxiety. Lady Blount's letter had been the determining cause of John's flight from home. Of this there could be no question. It had not been a sane man who raved at him yesterday. He was primed for any act of madness. The letter was the spark. Stella ill, fading away to a ghost and as silent as one, victim to an obscure and wasting disease that baffled them all; Stella dying before their eyes —the unhappy picture of the beloved was poignant in its artlessness. It would have stirred to grief any friend of Stellamaris. What emotions, then, had it not aroused in the breast of the man who loved her desperately, and whose very love had brought her to this pitch of suffering, to this imminence of dissolution? And the appeal for help, for the immediate presence of the rock and tower of strength of the household, with what ironic force had that battered at the disordered brain? There were only three courses for a man situated like Risca, and gifted or afflicted with Risca's headstrong and gloomy temperament, to pursue: to surrender to the appeal, which he had not done; to find his friend and bid him stand by while he cursed the day he was born and the God who made him and the devil-ruled welter of infamy which called itself a world, which likewise he had not done; or, in a paroxysm of despair and remorse, to fling himself beyond reach of human touch and seek a refuge for himself in the darkness. The conclusion that he had taken this last course forced itself with diabolical logic on Herold's mind. The very key to the door of darkness had lain ready to his hand, hidden in the study drawer. Before the eyes of the imaginative man, strung tight almost to breaking-point by the morning's emotions, flashed vivid pictures of tragic happenings—so vivid that they could not but be true: the reading of the letter; John standing by the study table; the letter dropping from his hands, which, in familiar gesture, went to the crisp, grizzly hair; the bloodshot eyes,—he had noted them yesterday,—the heavy jaw momentarily hanging loose, then snapping tight with a grating of the teeth; the unlocking of the drawer; the snatching up of the evil, glittering thing; the exit along the passage, with "his quick, heavy tread."

Did he remember to lock the drawer again? The vision was elusive. The question became insistent.

"Did you try the drawer?" he asked suddenly.

"No," said Unity.

It was unlocked. He felt sure that it was unlocked. He recalled the moving picture, bade it stay while he concentrated his soul on the drawer. And one instant it was shut, and another it did not seem flush with the framing-table and a crack, a sixteenth of an inch, was visible.

He strove to carry on the vision beyond the house-door; but in vain. He saw John Risca going out grim into the soft and clouded summer evening, and then the figure disappeared into lucent but impenetrable space.

Unity gripped his hand. Her common little face was like marble.

"Supposing he's dead!"

"I won't suppose such a thing," said Herold.

"You must. Why not face things?"

"All right. Let us face them."

"Supposing he's dead. Do you think he 's wicked?"

"Certainly not. Do you?"

"You know I don't," said Unity.

"Of course I know," said Herold.

"I could die for her myself, and I'm not a man," said Unity.

"Is n't it best, however, to live for those one loves, even at the cost of suffering?"

"Not if you can do them good by dying."

"Supposing he 's dead," asked Herold,—clean direct souls can ask each other such questions,—"what will you do?"

Her grip grew fierce as she turned up to him her snub-nosed little cockney face. "There 'll be no need for me to kill myself. I 'll die all right. Don't make any mistake about that."

"But supposing he is alive, and supposing the barrier were removed— I mean, supposing the woman—you know whom—were no longer there, and he married—what would you do?"

"What would you?"

"I?"

"You don't think you can fool me," said Unity. "You love Miss Stella as much as he does."

"How do you know?"

Unity flung her hand to the outer air. "How do I know that's an omnibus?"

"You 're right, my dear, I do love her. You 're one of the few human beings in this world who know what love means, and I 've told you what I 've told to no one living. But if she married John to-morrow, I would strangle everything wrong in me and devote my life to watching over their happiness."

"Don't you think I'd do the same?"

"I know you would."

"Then what 's the good of asking me what I 'd do?" said Unity.

"Talk like this helps."

Unity sought his hand again.

"It does," she said gently.

There was silence for a while. The white, wall-inclosed houses of Maida Vale, gay in the sunshine, flashed by them. She gripped his hand harder.

"But supposing he 's dead, supposing he 's dead."

"Let us suppose nothing, my dear," said Herold.

The cab stopped at Fairmont, Ossington Road. Herold gave Unity his hand to alight, and together they went through the tiny front garden, now bright with geraniums and petunias and pansies, into the house.

Miss Lindon, who had been watching all day for John by the drawing-room window, greeted them in the passage, her eyes red, and her cap askew on her white hair.

"Oh, Mr. Herold, have you found him? Where is he? I 'm sure he 's been run over by a motor-omnibus," she continued, on learning that Herold brought no news. "The way they whizz upon you when you 're not looking is so bewildering. The old days of horses were bad enough, although I do remember his poor father being upset out of a rowing-boat at Ramsgate."

"You may be quite sure, dear Miss Lindon," said Herold, gently, "that John has n't met with a street accident. The police would have told us long ago."

"But what could have happened to him? I know I 've thought of everything."

"Very likely he went down to spend the night in the East End, so as to write a descriptive article for the review," said Herold. "You have n't thought of that."

Miss Lindon admitted she had not, but tearfully held to the motor-omnibus theory. He tried to reassure her. Unity clenched her teeth, half mad with anxiety to get to the fateful drawer. At last Herold led the dear but delaying lady into the drawing-room.

"I am going to examine John's papers. Very likely I shall find something to put me on the track. You don't mind if I go in alone—with Unity to tell me where things are?"

"I'm sure, if you really try, you 'll find him. You are so clever," she replied.

He kissed her hand and left her sitting by the window, the tears running down her cheeks. In the passage Unity caught him by the hand.

"Come along!"

They ran down the passage into the study and locked the door.

"Which is the drawer?"

"The writing-table—the one to the right."

Herold flew to it and tried it. His vision had been false: it was locked. He sat down in John's worn leather writing-chair and pulled out his bunches of keys. One after another he tried them. Some were too large, others too small. Now and then one fitted into the keyhole and turned slightly in the wards.

"It 's coming."

"Yes—no."

"Let me try; it won't do."

The perspiration streamed upon their faces, and their fingers shook.

Sometimes the tried keys slid back into the bunch, and all had to be tried over again. A piano organ which had been playing maddeningly in front of the house ceased suddenly, and there was the silence of death in the room, broken only by the rattle of the keys and the tense breathing of the two.

At last they assured themselves that none of the keys would fit. They tried to wrench the drawer open by the handles, but the workmanship was stout. It was clattering discord. They searched the room for some instrument to pick or break open the lock. They rummaged among unlocked drawers filled with papers, old letters, bits of sealing-wax, forgotten pipes thrown together haphazard after the fashion of an untidy man. They found many rusty keys, which they tried in vain.

"We must break it open," said Herold.

He sent Unity for a screw-driver, and during her short absence looked through the papers in the baskets on the table; but they gave no clue. Unity returned, and locked the door again behind her. Once more they wrenched and jerked the drawer, and this time it gave sufficiently for the edge of the screw-driver to be inserted. And at last the woodwork broke away from the lock and the drawer flew open, and there lay the bright revolver on the sealed envelope just as Unity had described.

Herold sank into the writing-chair, and Unity steadied herself, her hands behind her, against the table.

They regarded each other for a while, pale, panting, breathless.

"Thank God!" he whispered.

"Yes, thank God!"

# CHAPTER XII

S o they remained, recovering from their almost intolerable relief. John Risca had not killed himself. It was a conclusion logical enough. The probability was that he was alive. But where? What had become of him? With what frenzied intention had he fled from the house?

Presently Unity drew up her squat little figure and closed the mutilated drawer.

"Can she have anything to do with it?" she asked, looking at him steadily.

"She?"

"Yes."

There was no need of explanation. "She" was the incarnation in woman of all evil. He rose from the chair, putting his hand to his forehead. He had not thought of her in connection with John's disappearance; judged in the light of the morning's revelation, the connection was more than possible. Of no ingenuity of fiendishness was the woman incapable.

"What made you think of her?"

"How can I help thinking of her?" said Unity.

"It is the she-devil," he cried excitedly. "She has been at work already. My God! I have it!" He smote his palm with the fist of the other hand. "She has told him."

"What?"

"She went down to Southcliff and saw Stellamaris. She poisoned her ears with hideous things. She was going to throw her over the cliff."

Unity, a queer light behind her patient eyes, crept up close to him, and an ugly look accentuated the coarseness of her features.

"She dared? She dared to speak to my precious one? What did she say? Tell me."

"She told her she was John's deserted wife, and that you—" he hesitated for a moment, and saw that he was not dealing with a young girl, but with a tragic woman—"and that you were his mistress."

Unity closed her eyes for a moment and swallowed the horror. Then she looked at him again.

"And what else?"

"She gave to her innocent soul to understand what a mistress was. She taunted her and jeered at her. She had her at her mercy."

"When did you learn this?"

"This morning, from Stellamaris herself. I told her the whole truth from beginning to end, but, God help her! her soul is so poisoned that she does n't know whether to believe the woman or me."

"If he knew that—if he knew that," said Unity, slowly, "he would murder her."

"Would to God she were murdered!" cried Herold in a shrill voice. "Would to God she were dead! She should be killed outright like a wild beast. But not by him, oh, not by him! It would be whirling catastrophe and chaos." He walked wildly and uttered senseless things. Then he halted. "But why should he know? Why should she tell him? Why should she invite her own destruction? No, she can't have told him." He took her by her shoulders. "Unity, he must never know. He would kill her. It's a hanging matter. It's unthinkable. Swear you will never tell him."

"I'll never tell him," said Unity.

"He must be saved," continued Herold, on the same note, his sensitive face pinched and his eyes eager. "And she must be saved. All this is killing them both--both of those who matter all the world to you and me. This thing of infamy is standing between them and blasting their lives. She will live, and they will be destroyed."

"If she were dead, would they come together?" asked Unity.

"Why not? What's to prevent them? Time and love would clear up clouds. But she—the unutterable—she will live. She will work in the dark, as she did that night when she stabbed you."

"I'm not thinking of that," said Unity.

"But I am." He waved her disclaimer aside, not appreciating for the moment how immeasurably was she lifted above the plane of personal desire for vengeance. "I am," he repeated. "She is walking murder. She meant to murder you. She meant to murder Stellamaris. Think of it!" He threw out his arms in a wide gesture. "There's a path down there—round the face of the cliff—"

"I know it," said Unity. "There's a bench. I used to sit there."

"She lured her there. You know—it's sheer above and sheer below and rocks beneath. She played with her, cat and mouse, would have thrown her over, dashed her down, Unity—dashed that precious, beautiful body down on to the rocks! But she did n't. God sent somebody to save her— to save her life that time. But she failed. She will try again. She will work her devilishness against her—against him—against you."

"I tell you, I don't care what she does to me," she interrupted roughly. "What the hell does it matter what she does to me?" It was the aboriginal gutter transcendentalized that spoke. "Leave me and her out of it. I've nothing against her. I 'm not a silly fool. If it had n't been for her, I shouldn't be here living like a lady. I ain't a lady, but I'm supposed to be one. And I should n't have known him, and I should n't have loved him. And I should n't have known my precious one—and I should n't have known you. I should have scrubbed floors and washed up plates in a lodg-ing-house—all I was fit for. I 've nothing against her—nothing. She can do what she likes with me; but with him and her—" She broke off on the up-note.

"Yes, you and I don't matter. We can put our foot on the neck of our own little devils, can't we?"

Somehow he found his hands round Unity's cheeks and his eyes look-ing into hers; she suffered the nervous clasp gladly, knowing, in her pure girl's heart, that he was a good man, that he loved Stellamaris as she loved John, and that he loved John as she loved Stellamaris. Brother and sis-ter, in a spiritual relation singularly perfect in this imperfect world, they stood, the gentleman of birth and breeding, the artist, the finely fibred man of wide culture, and Unity Blake, whose mother had died of drink in a slum in Notting Hill Gate a year after her father had died in prison, and of whom Miss Lindon despaired of ever making a lady.

There came a twisting of the door handle. They fell apart. Then came a tapping at the door. Herold turned the key and opened. It was Phoebe, elderly and gaunt. She clasped her hands tight in front of her.

"Oh, sir! oh, sir!" she said.

"What's the matter?"

"Master—he's found. Your servant has just telephoned. Mr. Risca 's met with an accident and is at your house, and will you please go there at once?"

THEY found him lying on the sofa, a pitiable object, the whole of his head from the back of his neck to his eyebrows swathed in bandages. His clothes were mere limp and discoloured wrappings. They looked as though they had been wet through, for the red of his tie had run into his shirt-front and collar. The coarse black sprouts on pallid cheek and upper lip gave him an appearance of indescribable grime. His eyes were sunken and feverish.

Unity uttered a little cry as she saw him, but checked it quickly, and threw herself on her knees by his side.

"Thank God you 're alive!"

He put his hand on her head.

"I 'm all right," he said faintly; "but you should n't have come. That 's why I did n't go straight home. I did n't want to frighten you. I 'm a ghastly sight, and I should have scared your aunt out of her wits."

"But how, in Heaven's name, man," said Herold, "did you get into this state?"

"Something hit me over the head, and I spent the night in rain and sea-water on the rocks."

"On the rocks? Where? At Southcliff?"

"Yes," said John, "at Southcliff. I was a fool to go down, but I've been a fool all my life, so a bit more folly does n't matter." He closed his eyes. "Give me a drink, Wallie—some brandy."

Herold went into the dining-room, which adjoined the library, and returned with decanter, syphon, and glasses. He poured out a brandy and soda for John and watched him drink it; then he realized that he, too, would be the better for stimulant. With an abstemious man's idea of taking brandy as medicine, he poured out for himself an extravagant dose, mixed a little soda-water with it, and gulped it down.

"That 'll do me good," said John; but on saying it he fell to shivering, despite the heat of the summer afternoon.

"You've caught a chill," cried Unity. She counselled home and bed at once.

"Not yet," he murmured. "It was all I could do to get here. Let me rest for a couple of hours. I shall be all right. I'm not going to bed," he declared with sudden irritability; "I 've never gone to bed in the daytime in my life. I've never been ill, and I'm not going to be ill now. I'm only stiff and tired."

"You 'll go to bed here right away," said Herold.

John protested. Herold insisted.

"Those infernal clothes—you must get them off at once," said he. John being physically weak, his natural obstinacy gave way. Unity saw the sense of the suggestion; but it was giving trouble.

"Not a bit," said Herold. "There 's a spare bedroom. John can have mine, which is aired. Mrs. Ripley will see to it."

He went out to give the necessary orders. Unity busied herself with unlacing and taking off the stiffened boots. Herold returned, beckoned to Unity, and whispered that he had telephoned for a doctor. Then he said to John:

"How are you feeling, dear old man?"

"My head's queer, devilish queer. Something fell on it last night and knocked me out of time. It was raining, and I was sheltering under the cliff on the beach, the other side of the path, where you can see the lights of the house, when down came the thing. I must have recovered just before dawn, for I remember staggering about in a dazed way. I must have taken the road round the cliff, thinking it the upper road, and missed my footing and fallen down. I came to about nine this morning, on the rocks, the tide washing over my legs. I 'm black and blue all over. Wonder I did n't break my neck. But I 'm tough."

"Thank God you 're alive!" said Unity again.

He passed his hands over his eyes. "Yes. You must have thought all manner of things, dear. I did n't realize till Ripley told me that I had n't let you know. I went out, meaning to catch the 7:15 and come back by the last train. But this thing knocked all memory out of me. I'm sorry."

Herold looked in bewilderment at the stricken giant. Even now he had not accounted for the lunatic and almost tragic adventure. What was he doing on the beach in the rain? What were the happenings subsequent to his recovering consciousness at nine o'clock?

"Does it worry you to talk?" he asked.

"No. It did at first—I mean this morning. But I'm all right now— nearly all right. I'd like to tell you. I picked myself up, all over blood, a devil of a mess, and crawled to the doctor's—not Ransome; the other chap, Theed. He 's the nearest; and, besides, I did n't want to go to Ran-

some. I don't think any one saw me. Theed took me in and fixed me up
and dried my clothes. Of course he wanted to drag me to the Channel
House, but I would n't let him. I made him swear not to tell them. I don't
want them to know. Neither of you must say anything. He also tried to
fit me out. But, you know, he 's about five foot nothing; it was absurd. As
soon as I could manage it, he stuck me in a train, much against his will,
and I came on here. That 's all."

"If only I had known!" said Herold. "I was down there all the morning."

"You?"

"I had a letter from Julia, summoning me."

"So had I." He closed his eyes again for a moment. Then he asked,
"How is Stella?"

"I had a long talk with her. I may have straightened things out a bit.
She 'll come round. There's no cause for worry for the present. Julia is a
good soul, but she has no sense of proportion, and where Stella is concerned she exaggerates."

When a man has had rocks fall on his head, and again has fallen on
his head upon rocks, it is best to soothe what is left of his mind. And
after Walter had partly soothed it,—a very difficult matter, first, because it
was in a troubled and despairing state, and, secondly, because, John, never
having taken Unity into his confidence, references had to be veiled,—he
satisfied the need of another brandy and soda. Then Ripley came in to
announce that the room was ready.

"Ripley and I will see to him," said Herold to Unity. "You had better
go and fetch him a change of clothes and things he may want."

"May n't I wait till the doctor comes?" she pleaded.

"Of course, my dear. There 's no hurry," said Herold.

The two men helped Risca to his feet, and, taking him to the bedroom,
undressed him, clothed him in warm pyjamas, and put him into the bed,
where a hot-water bottle diffused grateful heat. Herold had seen the livid
bruises on his great, muscular limbs.

"Any one but you," said he, with forced cheeriness, "would have been
smashed to bits, like an egg."

"I tell you I'm tough," John growled. "It's only to please you that I sub-
mit to this silly foolery of going to bed."

As soon as Ripley was dismissed, he called Herold to his side.

"I would like to tell you everything, Wallie. I couldn't in the other room. Unity, poor child, knows nothing at all about things. Naturally. I had been worried all the afternoon. I thought I saw her—you know—hanging about outside the office. It was just before I met you at the club. I did n't tell you,—perhaps I ought to,—but that was why I was so upset. But you 'll forgive me. You 've always forgiven me. Anyway, I thought I saw her. It was just a flash, for she, if it was she, was swallowed up in the traffic of Fleet Street. After leaving the club, I went back to the office—verification in proofs of something in Baxter's article. I found odds and ends to do. Then I went home, and Julia's letter lay on my table. I've been off my head of late, Wallie. For the matter of that, I'm still off it. I've hardly slept for weeks. I found Julia's letter. I looked at my watch. There was just time to catch the 7:15. I ran out, jumped into a taxi, and caught it just as it was starting. But as I passed by a third-class carriage,—in fact, I realized it only after I had gone several yards beyond; one rushes, you know,—I seemed to see her face—those thin lips and cold eyes—framed in the window. The guard pitched me into a carriage. I looked out for her at all the stations. At Tring Bay the usual crowd got out. I did n't see her. No one like her got out at Southcliff. What 's the matter, Wallie?" He broke off suddenly.

"Nothing, man; nothing," said Herold, turning away and fumbling for his cigarette-case.

"You looked as if you had seen a ghost. It was I who saw the ghost." He laughed. And the laugh, coming from the haggard face below the brow-reaching white bandage, was horrible.

"Your brain was playing you tricks," said Herold. "You got to Southcliff. What happened?"

"I felt a fool," said John. "Can't you see what a fool a man feels when he knows he has played the fool?"

Bit by bit he revealed himself. At the gate of the Channel House he reflected. He had not the courage to enter. Stella would be up and about. He resolved to wait until she went to bed. He wandered down to the beach. The rain began to fall, fine, almost imperceptible. The beacon-light in the west window threw a vanishing shaft into the darkness.

"We saw it once—don't you remember?—years ago when you gave her the name—Stellamaris. I sat like a fool and watched the window. How long I don't know. My God! Wallie, you don't know what it is to be shaken and racked by the want of a woman—"

"By love for a woman, you mean," said Herold.

"It 's the same thing. At last I saw her. She stood defiant in the light. She had changed. I cried out toward her like an idiot,"—the rugged, grim half face visible beneath the bandage was grotesque, a parody of passion, —"and I stayed there, watching, after she had gone away. How long I don't know. It was impossible to ring at the door and see Oliver and Julia."

He laughed again. "You must have some sense of humour, my dear man. Fancy Oliver and Julia! What could I have said to them? What could they have said to me? I sat staring up at her window. The rain was falling. Everything was still. It was night. You know how quiet everything is there. Then I seemed to hear footsteps and I turned, and a kind of shape—a woman's—disappeared. I know I was off my head, but I began to think. I had a funny experience once—I 've never told you. It was the day she came out of prison. I sat down in St. James's Park and fell half asleep,—that sort of dog sleep one has when one's tired,—and I thought I saw her going for Stella—Stella in her bed at the Channel House—going to strangle her. This came into my mind, and then something hit me,—a chunk of overhanging cliff loosened by the rain, I suppose,—and, as I've told you, it knocked me out. But it's devilish odd that she should be mixed up in it."

"As I said, your brain was playing you tricks," said Herold, outwardly calm; but within himself he shuddered. The woman was like a foul spirit hovering unseen about those he loved.

Presently the doctor, a young man with a cheery face, came in and made his examination. There was no serious damage done. The only thing to fear was the chill. If the patient's temperature went down in the morning, he could quite safely be moved to his own home. For the present rest was imperative, immediate sleep desirable. He wrote a prescription, and with pleasant words went away. Then Unity, summoned to the room, heard the doctor's comforting opinion.

"I 'll be with you to-morrow," said John.

"You don't mind leaving him to Mrs. Ripley and me just for one night?" asked Herold.

"He 's always safe with you," Unity replied, her eyes fixed not on him, but on John Risca. "Good-bye, Guardian dear."

John drew an arm from beneath the bedclothes and put it round her thin shoulders. "Good-by, dear. Forgive me for giving you such a fright, and make my peace with auntie. You 'll be coming back with my things, won't you?"

"Of course; but you 'll be asleep then."

"I should n't wonder," said John.

She made him cover up his arm again and tucked the bedclothes snugly about him, her finger-tips lingering by his cheeks.

"I 'll leave you, too. Try and get to sleep," said Herold.

They went together out of the room and back to the library.

"Has he said anything more?"

He stood before her trembling all over.

"What is the matter?"

He burst into an uncontrollable cry. "It 's that hellish woman again! He saw her spying on him outside his office, he saw her in a railway carriage on the train he took. Because she disappeared each time, he thinks it was an hallucination; and somehow he was aware of her presence just before the piece of rock came down."

Unity's face beneath the skimpy hair and rubbishy tam-o'-shanter was white and strained.

"She threw it. I knew she threw it."

"So do I. He saw her. She disappeared as she did that night in the fog. A woman like that is n't human. She has the power of disappearing at will. You can't measure her cunning."

"What did he go down for?"

He told her. Unity's lips twitched.

"And he sat there in the rain just looking at her window?"

She put out her hand. "Good-bye, Mr. Herold. When you see Miss Stellamaris, you 'll tell her I'm a good girl—in that way, you know—and that I love her. She has been a kind of beautiful angel to me—has always been with me. It's funny; I can't explain. But you understand. If you'd only let her see that, I'd be so happy—and perhaps she'd be happier."

"I 'll do my utmost," said Herold.

He accompanied her down-stairs, and when she had gone, he returned to the library and walked about. The horror of the woman was upon him. He drank another brandy and soda. After a while Ripley came in with a soiled card on a tray. He looked at it stupidly—"Mr. Edwin Travers"—and nodded.

"Shall I show the gentleman up?"

He nodded again, thinking of the woman.

When the visitor came in he vaguely recognized him as a broken-down actor, a colleague of early days. As in a dream he bade the man sit down, and gave him cigarettes and drink, and heard with his outer ears an interminable tale of misfortune. At the end of it he went to his desk and wrote out a cheque, which he handed to his guest.

"I can't thank you, old man. I don't know how to. But as soon as I can get an engagement—hello, old man," he cried, glancing at the cheque, "you've made a funny mistake—the name!"

Herold took the slip of paper, and saw that he had made the sum payable not to Edwin Travers, but to Louisa Risca. It was a shock, causing him to brace his faculties. He wrote out another cheque, and the man departed.

He went softly into John's room and found him sleeping peacefully.

Soon afterward Ripley announced that dinner was ready. It was past six o'clock.

"Great Heavens!" he cried aloud, "I've got to play to-night."

After a hurried wash he went into the dining-room and sat down at the table, but the sight and smell of food revolted him. He swallowed a few mouthfuls of soup; the rest of the dinner he could not touch. The horror of the woman had seized him again. He drank some wine, pushed back his chair, and threw down his table-napkin.

"I don't want anything else. I 'm going for a walk. I 'll see you later at the theatre."

The old-fashioned Kensington street, with its double line of Queen Anne houses slumbering in the afternoon sunshine, was a mellow blur before his eyes. Whither he was going he knew: what he was going to do he knew not. The rigid self-control of the day, relaxed at times, but always kept within grip, had at last escaped him. Want of food and the unaccustomed drink had brought about an abnormal state of mind. He was aware of direction, aware, too, of the shadow-shapes of men and women passing him by, of traffic in the roadway. He walked straight, alert, his gait and general demeanour unaffected, his outer senses automatically alive. He walked down the narrow, shady Church Street, and paused for a moment or two by the summer greenery of Kensington Churchyard until there was an opportunity of crossing the High Street, now at the height of its traffic. He strode westward past the great shops, a lithe man in the full vigour of his manhood. Here and there a woman lingering in front of displays of millinery recognized the well-known actor and nudged her companion.

The horror within him had grown to a consuming thing of flame. Instead of the quiet thoroughfares down which he turned, he saw picture after shuddering picture—the woman and Stellamaris, the woman and John Risca. She attacked soul as well as body. The pictures took the forms of horrible grotesques. Within, his mind worked amazingly, like a machine escaped from human control and running with blind relentlessness. He had said years ago that he would pass through his hell-fire. He was passing through it now.

The destroyer must be kept from destroying or be destroyed. Which of these should be accomplished through his agency? One or the other. Of one thing he was certain, with an odd, undoubting certainty: that he would find her, and finding her, that he would let loose upon her the wrath of God. She should be chained up forever or he would strangle her. Shivering thrills diabolically delicious ran through him at the thought. Supposing he strangled her as he would a mad cat? That were better. She would be out of the world. He would be fulfilling his destiny of sacrifice. For the woman he loved and for the man he loved why should he not do this thing? What but a legal quibble could call it murder? Stellamaris's words rang in his ears: "You say you love me like that?"

"Yes, I love you like that. I love you like that," he cried below his breath as he walked on.

He knew where she lived, the name by which she passed. John had told him many times. There were few things in John's life he did not know. He knew of the Bences, of Mrs. Oscraft, the fluffy-haired woman who lived in the flat below. Amelia Mansions, he was aware, were in the Fulham Road. But when he reached that thoroughfare, he stood dazed and irresolute, realizing that he did not know which way to turn. A passing postman gave him the necessary information. The trivial contact with the commonplace restored in a measure his mental balance. He went on. By Brompton Cemetery he felt sick and faint and clung for a minute or two to the railings. He had eaten nothing since early morning, and then only a scrap of bacon and toast; he had drunk brandy and wine, and he had lived through the day in which the maddening stress of a lifetime had been concentrated.

One or two passers-by stared at him, for he was as white as a sheet. A comfortable, elderly woman, some small shop-keeper's wife, addressed him. Was he ill? Could she do anything for him? The questioning was a lash. He drew himself up, smiled, raised his hat, thanked her courteously. It was nothing. He went on, loathing himself as men do when the flesh fails beneath the whip of the spirit.

He was well now, his mind clear. He was going to the woman. He would save those he loved. If it were necessary to kill her, he would kill her. On that point his brain worked with startling clarity. If he did not kill her, she would be eventually killed by John; for John, he argued, could not remain in ignorance forever. If John killed her, he would be hanged. Much better that he, Walter Herold, whom Stellamaris did not love, should be hanged than John—much better. And what the deuce did it matter to anybody whether he were hanged or not? He laughed at the elementary logic of the proposition. The solution of all the infernally intricate problems of life is, if people only dared face it, one of childish simplicity. It was laughable. Walter Herold laughed aloud in the Fulham Road.

It was so easy, so uncomplicated. He would see her. He would do what he had to do. Then he would take a taxi-cab to the theatre. He must play to-night. Of course he would. There was no reason why he should n't. Only he hoped that Leonora Gurney would n't worry him. He would manage to avoid her during that confounded wait in the first act, when she always tried to get him to talk. He would play the part all right. He was a man and not a stalk of wet straw. After the performance he would give himself up. No one would be inconvenienced. He would ask the authorities to hurry on matters and give him a short shrift and a long rope; but the length of the rope did n't matter these days, when they just broke your neck. There was no one dependent on him. His brothers and sisters, many years his seniors,—he had not seen them since he was a child, —had all gone after their father's death to an uncle in New Zealand. They were there still. The mother, who had remained with him, the Benjamin, in England, had died while he was at Cambridge. He was free from family-ties. And women? He was free, too. There had only been one woman in his life, the child of cloud and sea foam.

Stellamaris, star of the sea, now dragged through the mire of mortal things! She should go back. She should go back to her firmament, shining down upon, and worshipped by, the man she loved. And he, God!—he should be spared the terrifying agony of it.

Thus worked the brain which Walter Herold told himself was crystal clear.

It was clear enough, however, to follow the postman's directions. He took the turning indicated and found the red-brick block, with the name "Amelia Mansions" carved in stone over the entrance door. The by-street seemed to be densely populated. He went into the entrance-hall and mechanically looked at the list of names. Mrs. Rawlings's name was followed by No. 7. He mounted the stairs. On the landing of No. 7 there were a couple of policemen, and the flat door was open, and the length of the passage was visible. Herold was about to enter when they stopped him.

"You can't go in, sir."

"I want Mrs. Rawlings."

"No one can go in."

He stood confused, bewildered. An elderly, buxom, woman, with a horrified face, who just then happened to come out of a room near the doorway, saw him and came forward.

"You are Mr. Herold," she asked.

"Yes; I want to see Mrs. Rawlings."

"It 's all right, constable," she said in a curiously cracked voice. "Let this gentleman pass. Come in, sir. I am Mrs. Bence."

He entered the passage. She spoke words to him the import of which he did not catch. His brain was perplexed by the guard of policemen and the open flat. She led him a short distance down the passage. He stumbled over a packed kit-bag. She threw open a door. He crossed the threshold of a vulgarly furnished drawing-room, the electric lights turned on despite the daylight of the July evening. There were four figures in the room. Standing and scribbling in note-books were two men, one in the uniform of a sergeant of police, the other in a frock-coat, obviously a medical man.

On the floor were two women, both dead. One was John Risca's wife, and the other was Unity. And near by them lay a new, bright revolver.

# CHAPTER XXIII

I n after-time Herold's memory of that disastrous night and the succeeding days was that of a peculiarly lucid nightmare in which he seemed to have acted without volition or consciousness of motive. He ate, dressed, drove through the streets on unhappy missions, gave orders, directions, consoled, like an automaton, and sometimes slept exhaustedly. So it seemed to him, looking back. He spared John the first night of misery. The man with his bandaged head slept like a log, and Herold did not wake him. All that could be done he himself had done. It was better for John to gather strength in sleep to face the tragedy on the morrow. And when the morrow came, and Herold broke the news to him, the big man gave way under the shock, and became gentle, and obeyed Herold like a child. Thereafter, for many days, he sat for the hour together with his old aunt, curiously dependent on her; and she, through her deep affection for him, grew singularly silent and practical.

In her unimaginative placidity lay her strength. She mourned for Unity as for her own flesh and blood; but the catastrophe did not shake her even mind, and when John laid his head in her lap and sobbed, all that was beautiful in the woman flowed through the comforting tips of her helpless fingers.

From Herold he learned the unsuspected reason of Unity's crime and sacrifice; and from Unity, too, for a poor little pencil scrawl found in her pocket and addressed to him told him of her love and of her intention to clear the way for his happiness. And when the inquest was over and Unity's body was brought to Kilburn and laid in its coffin in her little room, he watched by it in dumb stupor of anguish.

Herold roused him now and then. Action—nominal action at least —had to be taken by him as surviving protagonist of the tragedy. The morning after the deed the newspapers shrieked the news, giving names in full, raking up memories of the hideous case. They dug, not deep, for motive, and found long-smouldering vengeance. Unity was blackened.

John responded to Herold's lash. This must not be. Unity must not go to her grave in public dishonour; truth must be told. So at the inquest, John wild, uncouth, with great strips of sticking-plaster on his head, told truth, and gave a romantic story to a hungry press. It was hateful to lay bare the inmost sacredness and the inmost suffering of his soul to the world's cold and curious gaze, but it had to be done. Unity's name was cleared. When he sat down by Herold's side, the latter grasped his hand, and it was clammy and cold, and he shook throughout his great frame.

Then Herold, driven to mechanical action, as it seemed to him afterward, by a compelling force, dragged John to an inquiry into the evil woman's life. It was Mrs. Oscraft, the full-blown, blowzy bookmaker's wife, the woman's intimate associate for many years, who gave the necessary clue. Horrified by the discovery of the identity of her friend and by the revelation of further iniquities, she lost her head when the men sternly questioned her. She had used her intimacy with Mrs. Risca to cover from her own husband an intrigue of many years' standing. In return, Mrs. Risca had confessed to an intrigue of her own, and demanded, and readily obtained, Mrs. Oscraft's protection. The women worked together. They were inseparable in their outgoings and incomings, but abroad each went her separate way. That was why, ignorant of the truth, Mrs. Oscraft had lied loyally when John Risca had burst into her flat long ago. She had thought she was merely shielding her fellow-sinner from the wrath of a jealous husband. Thus for years, with her cunning, Mrs. Risca had thrown dust in the eyes both of her friend and of the feared and hated wardress whom John had set over her. Under the double cloak she had used her hours of liberty to carry out the set, relentless purpose of her life. To spy on him with exquisite craft had been her secret passion, to strike when the time came the very meaning of her criminal existence.

"And for the last two or three years she gave no trouble and was as gentle as a lamb, so how could I suspect?" Mrs. Bence lamented.

"It 's all over," said John, stupidly; "it's all over. Nothing matters now."

To Herold, in after-time, the memories of these days were as those of the doings of another man in his outer semblance. His essential self had been the crazy being who had marched through the mellow Kensington streets with fantastic dreams of murder in his head. At the sight of Unity and the woman lying ghastly on the floor something seemed to snap in his brain, and all the cloudy essence that was he vanished, and a perfect mechanism took its place. When John with wearisome reiteration said: "God bless you, Wallie! God knows what I should have done without you," it was hard to realize that he had done anything deserving thanks. He was inclined to regard himself—when he had a fugitive moment to regard himself—with abhorrence. He had talked; Unity had acted. And deep down in his soul, only once afterwards in his life to be confessed, dwelt an awful remorse for his responsibility in the matter of Unity's death. But in simple fact no man in times of great convulsion knows himself. He looks back on the man who acted and wonders. The man, surviving the wreck of earthquake, if he be weak, lies prone and calls on God and man to help him; if he be strong, he devotes the intensity of his faculties to the work of rescue, of clearing up debris, of temporary reconstruction, and has no time for self-analysis. It is in reality the essential man in his vigour and courage and nobility and disdain who acts, and the bruised and shattered about him who profit by his help look rightly upon him as a god.

It was only after John had visited the house of death, where, according to law, the bodies both of slayer and slain had to lie, and had seen the pinched, common face, swathed in decent linen, of the girl who for his sake had charged her soul with murder and taken her own life, and after he had driven away, stunned with grief and carrying with him, at his feet in the taxi-cab, the useless kit-bag packed by the poor child with Heaven knows what idea of its getting to its destination, and had staggered to the comfort of the foolish old lady's outstretched arms and received her benediction, futilely spoken, divinely unspoken—it was only then that, raising haggard eyes, all the more haggard under the brow-reaching bandage he still wore, he asked the question:

"What about Stella? She is bound to learn."

"I wrote to her last night," said Herold. "I prepared her for the shock as best I could."

A gleam of rational thought flitted across John Risca's mind.

"You remembered her at such a time, with all you had to do? You 're a wonderful man, Wallie. No one else would have done it."

"Are you in a fit state of mind," said Herold, "to understand what has happened? I tried to tell you this morning,"—as he had done fitfully,—"but it was no use. You grasped nothing."

"Go on now," said John. "I'm listening."

So Herold, amid the fripperies of Miss Lindon's drawing-room, told the story of his summons to the Channel House some time ago—Good God!—He caught himself up sharply—it was only yesterday! and of his talk with Stellamaris in the garden, and of her encounter with the evil woman, and of the poison that had crept to the roots of Stella's being.

John shivered, and clenched impotent fists. Stella left alone on the cliff-edge with that murderous hag! Stella's ears polluted by that infamous tale! If only he had known it! Why did she hide it from him?

It was well the murderess was dead, but, merciful Heaven, at what a price!

"Listen," said Herold, gravely, checking his outburst; and he told of his meetings with Unity,—it was essential that John should know,—of her almost mystical worship of Stellamaris, of their discovery of the revolver —

"Poor child!" cried John, "I bought it soon after I went to Kilburn. I took it out the other day and played with a temptation I knew I should n't succumb to. I should never have had the pluck."

Herold continued, telling him all he knew—all save that of which he stood self-accused, and which for the present was a matter between him and his Maker. And Miss Lindon, fondling on her lap a wheezy pug, the successor to the Dandy of former days who had been gathered to his fathers long ago, listened in placid bewilderment to the strange story of love and crime.

"I 'm sure I don't understand how people think of such things, let alone do them," she sighed.

"You must accept the fact, dear Miss Lindon," said Herold, gently.

"God's will be done," she murmured, which in the circumstances was as relevant a thing as the poor lady could have uttered. But John sat hunched up in a bamboo chair that creaked under his weight, and scarcely spoke a word. He felt very unimportant by the side of Unity—Unity with whose strong, passionate soul he had dwelt in blind ignorance. And Unity was dead, lying stark and white in the alien house.

After a long silence he roused himself.

"You wrote to Stella, you said?"

"Yes," replied Herold.

"What will happen to her?"

"I don't know."

John groaned. "If only I had protected her as I ought to have done! If only I had protected both of them!"

He relapsed again into silence, burying his face in his hands. Presently Miss Lindon put the pug tenderly on the ground, rose, and stood by his chair.

"My poor boy," she said, "do you love her so much?"

"She's dead," said John.

Herold shook him by the shoulder. "Nonsense, man. Pull yourself together."

John raised a drawn face.

"What did you ask? I was thinking about Unity."

That day, the day after the tragedy, Stellamaris faced life, in its nakedness, stripped, so it appeared to her, of every rag of mystery.

She had breakfasted as usual in her room, bathed and dressed, and looked wistfully over her disowning sea. Then, as she was preparing to go downstairs, Morris had brought in Herold's letter, scribbled so nervously and shakenly that at first she was at a loss to decipher it. Gradually it became terribly clear: Unity was dead; the woman was dead; Unity had killed the woman and then killed herself.

"Details of everything but the truth will be given in the morning papers," Herold wrote; "but you must know the truth from the first—as I know it. Unity has given her life to save those she loved—you and John—from the woman. She has laid down her life for you. Never forget that as long as you live."

She sat for some moments quite still, paralyzed by the new horror that had sprung from this false, flower-decked earth to shake her by the throat. The world was terrifyingly relentless. She read the awful words again. Bit by bit feeling returned. Her flesh was constricted in a cold and finely wrought net. She grew faint, put her hand to her brow and found it damp. She stumbled to her bed by the great west window and threw herself down. Constable, lying on the hearth-rug, staggered to his feet and thrust his old head on her bosom and regarded her with mournful and inquiring eyes. She caressed him mechanically. Suddenly she sprang up as a swift memory smote her. Once she lay there by the window, and the dog was there by the bed, and there by the door stood the ungainly figure of a girl of her own age. Was it possible that that ungainly child whom she had seen and talked to then, whom a few weeks ago she had kissed, could have committed this deed of blood? She rose again to her feet, pushed the old dog aside blindly, and hid her eyes from the light of day. The girl was human, utterly human at those two meetings. Of what unknown, devastating forces, were human beings, then, composed?

She took up the letter again. "Unity has given her life to save those she loved—you and John—from the woman. She has laid down her life for you. Never forget that as long as you live."

Walter Herold said that. It must be true. Through all of yesterday's welter of misery, after he had left her, she had clung despairingly to him. There was no God, but there was Walter Herold. Her pride had dismissed him with profession of disbelief, but in her heart she had believed him. Not that she had pardoned John Risca, not that she had recovered her faith in him, not that she had believed in Unity. Her virginal soul, tainted by the woman, had shrunk from thoughts of the pair; but despite her fierce determination to believe in neither God nor man, she had been compelled to believe in Herold. She had stood up against him and fought with him and had bitten and rent him, and he had conquered, and she had felt maddenedly angered, triumphantly glad. The whole world could be as false as hell, but in it there was one clear spirit speaking truth.

She went to the southern window, rested her elbows on the sill, and pressed the finger-tips of both hands against her forehead. The soft southwest wind, bringing the salt from the dancing sea, played about her hair. Unity had laid down her life to save those she loved. So had Christ done —given his life for humanity. But Christ had not killed a human being, no matter how murderous, and had not taken his own life. No, no; she must not mix up things irreconcilable. She faced the room again. What did people do when they killed? What were the common, practical steps that they took to gain their ends? Her mind suddenly grew vague. Herold had spoken of newspapers. She must see them; she must know everything. Life was deadly conflict, and knowledge the only weapon. For a few seconds she stood in the middle of the room, her young bosom heaving, her dark eyes wide with the diamond glints in their depths. Life was a deadly conflict. She would fight, she would conquer. Others miserably weaker than herself survived. Pride and race and splendid purity of soul sheathed her in cold armour. A jingle, separated from context, came into her mind, and in many ways it was a child's mind:

Then spake Sir Thomas Howard,

" 'Fore God, I am no coward."

"'Fore God, I am no coward," she repeated, and with her delicate head erect she went out and down the stairs and entered the dining-room.

There she found Sir Oliver and Lady Blount sitting at a neglected breakfast. The old faces strove pitifully to smile. Stella kissed them in turn, and with her hand lingering on the old man's arm, she gave him Herold's letter.

"Is it in the newspapers?" she asked.

"What, what, my dear?" said Sir Oliver, adjusting his glasses on his nose with fumbling fingers.

She looked from one to the other. Then her eyes fell on the morning papers lying on the table. They were folded so that a great head-line stared hideously.

"Oh, darling, don't read it—for Heaven's sake do n't read it," cried Lady Blount, clutching the nearer newspaper.

But Stella took up the other. "I must, dearest," she said very gently. "Walter has written to me; but he could not tell me everything."

She moved to the window that overlooked the pleasant garden, and with steady eyes read the vulgar and soul-withering report, while the two old people, head to head, puzzled out Herold's scrawl.

When she had finished, she laid the paper quietly at the foot of the table and came and stood between them, revolted by the callous publication of names, almost physically sickened by the realistic picture of the scene, her head whirling. She caught hold of the back of Sir Oliver's chair.

"The newspaper lies," she said, "but it does n't know any better. Walter tells us why she did it."

Sir Oliver, elbow on table, held the letter in his shaking grasp. It dropped, and his head sank on his hand.

"It's too horrible!" he said in a weak voice. "I don't understand anything at all about it. I don't understand what Walter means. And all that old beastly story revived. It's damnable!"

He looked quite broken, his querulous self-assertion gone. Lady Blount, too, gave way, and stretched out an imploring and pathetic arm, which, as Stella moved a step or two toward her, fell around the slim, standing figure. She laid her cheek against Stella and cried miserably.

"O my darling, my precious one, if we could only spare you all this!

Walter should n't have written. O my darling, what are we to do! What are we to do!"

And then Stellamaris saw once more that Great High Excellency and Most Exquisite Auntship, for all their love of her, were of the weak ones of the world, and she looked down with a new and life-giving feeling of pity upon the bowed gray heads.

Once,—was it yesterday or weeks or months or years ago? She could not tell,—but once, to her later pain and remorse, she had commanded, and they had obeyed; now she knew that she had to comfort, protect, determine. And in a bewildering flash came the revelation that knowledge was a weapon not only to fight her own way through the evil of the world, but to defend the defenceless.

"I wish Walter was here," she whispered, her hand against the withered, wet cheek.

"Why Walter, dear?"

"He is strong and true," said Stellamaris.

"Why not John, darling?"

Yes, why not John? Stella drew a sharp breath. Sir Oliver saved her an answer.

"John has enough to look to, poor chap. He has got everything about his ears. Stella's right. We want Walter. He's young. He's a good fellow, is Walter. I must be getting old, my dear,—" He raised his face, and, with a sudden forlorn hope of dignity, twirled his white moustache,—"A year ago I should n't have wanted Walter or anybody. It 's only you, my child, that your aunt and I are thinking of. We've tried to do our duty by you, have n't we, Julia? And God knows we love you. You 're the only thing in the world left to us. It is n't our fault that you are drawn into this ghastliness. It is n't, God knows it is n't. Only, my dear,"—there was a catch in his voice,—"you 're not able to bear it. For us old folks who have knocked about the world—well, we 're used to—to this sort of thing. I've had to send men to the gallows in my time—once twenty men to be shot. The paltry fellows at the Colonial Office did n't see things as I did, but that's another matter. We 're used to these things, dear; we 're hardened—"

"If I have got to live in the world, dear Excellency," said Stella, feeling that there were some sort of flood-gates between the tumultuous flow of her being and the still waters of pity in which for the moment her consciousness acted, "it seems that I must get used to it, like every one else."

"But what shall we do, darling?" cried Lady Blount, clinging pathetically to the child of sea foam, from whom all knowledge of the perilous world had been hidden.

"Anything but worry Walter to come down here."

"I thought you wanted him?"

"I do," said Stella, with her hand on her bosom; "but that is only selfishness. He is needed more in London. I think we ought to go up and see if we can help in any way."

"Go up to London!" echoed Sir Oliver.

"Yes, if you 'll take me, Uncle dear."

The old man looked at his wife, who looked helplessly at him. Through the open window came the late, mellow notes of a thrush and the sunshine that flooded the summer garden.

"I am going to send Walter a telegram," said Stella, moving gently away.

She left the room with the newly awakened consciousness that she was absolute mistress of her destiny. Love, devotion, service, anything she might require from the two old people, were hers for the claiming—anything in the world but guidance and help. She stood alone before the dragons of a world, no longer the vague Threatening Land, but a world of fierce passions and bloody deeds. Herold's words flamed before her: "Unity had given her life for those she loved." Had she, Stellamaris, a spirit so much weaker than Unity's?

She advanced an eager step or two along the garden walk, clenching her delicate fists, and the fiery dragons retreated backward. She could give, too, as well as Unity, her life if need be. If that was not required, at least whatever could be demanded of her for those she loved. Again she read the letter. Underlying it was tenderest anxiety lest she should be stricken down by the ghastly knowledge. With the personal motive, the intense and omnipotent motive of her sex, unconsciously dominating her, she murmured half articulately:

"He thinks I'm a weak child. I 'll show him that I am a woman. He shall see that I'm not afraid of life."

So when Walter Herold went home late that night,—the theatre being out of the question, he had stayed at Kilburn until John had been persuaded to go to bed,—he found a telegram from Stellamaris.

"Coming to London to see if I can be of any help. My dear love to John in his terrible trouble. Tell me when I had better come."

The next day, when they met before the inquest, he showed the telegram to John, who, after glancing at it, thrust it back into his hand with a deprecating gesture.

"No; let her stay there. What is she to do in this wilderness of horror?"

"I have already written," said Herold.

"To keep away?"

"To come."

"You know best," said John, hopelessly. "At any rate the news has n't killed her. I feared it would. I had long letters from Oliver and Julia this morning."

"What do they say?"

John put his hand to his head. "I forget," said he.

# CHAPTER XXIV

OUTSIDE the house in Kilbum were stationed a hearse and two carriages, stared at by a knot of idlers. Within was felt the pervasive presence of a noiselessly moving, black-attired man of oiled tongue. Upstairs in the little room rested on its trestles the flower-covered coffin wherein all that remained of Unity lay. The blinds of the gimcrack drawing-room were lowered, and the company sat waiting—John, Miss Lindon, and Herold, Sir Oliver, Lady Blount, and Stellamaris.

Although Stella had been in London for a day or two, this was the first time that John had seen her since the riotous June day when he had waved farewell to the train carrying her back to Southcliff. He had gone to the front gate to meet her in his ill-fitting, outgrown frock-coat, sticking-plaster still hiding the wounds on his scalp, and his heavy face white and drawn. She, in her black dress, looked a startling lily enveloped by night; her great eyes had softened from diamond into starshine. Behind her came the old people, attendant ghosts. John folded her hand in his.

"Stella dear, how good of you to come!"

She said in a low voice:

"It is to ask forgiveness from you and her."

He bowed over her hand. She passed into the house, where Miss Lindon received her.

"My dear," she said, holding Stella's hand. "I think our poor darling will go to her grave very happy. She was always talking of you, ever since she came to live here, and if you wonder what has become of the beautiful lilies you sent, it's because I have put them inside with her, knowing that there's where she would wish them to be. And now you 've come yourself, and I'm sure she would n't ask for more."

The weak mouth, set in the full, foolish face crowned with white hair, worked dolorously. Stella, with a sudden movement, threw her arm round her neck and broke into uncontrollable sobbing. A soul pure and beautiful beyond question spoke to Stellamaris in simple words and in silly yet exquisite sentiment. She clung very close,—why, the unsuspecting and innocent lady never guessed,—but it made her broad bosom swell with an emotion hitherto unknown to have a girl lay her head there and sob and seem to find comfort; and, as she clung, the lingering poison of the evil woman melted forever from Stella's heart, and she knew that the place whereon she stood, where Unity and she had talked, that gimcrack, tawdry, bamboo drawing-room, was holy ground.

She had come, poor child, full of her fierce and jealous maiden pride—she was only twenty, and life had been revealed to her of late as a tumultuous conflict of men with devils,—she had come highly wrought for battles with the Apollyons that straddled across the path; she had come with high hopes of bringing help to the faint-hearted, solace to the afflicted, of proving to her tiny world that she was the help-giver instead of the help-seeker; she had come on the wings of conquest; and she fluttered down like a tired bird to the surrender of herself on the bosom of the simplest and, in the eyes of men, the least important creature on God's earth.

She drew gently away and dried her eyes, and while Miss Lindon spoke a few words to Lady Blount, she went somewhat shyly up to John.

"You should have let me know Miss Lindon long ago," she said.

"I should have done many things long ago," he replied. "But I myself have known my aunt only the last few days."

She regarded him somewhat incredulously.

"Yes," he said, "it's true. The last few days have taught me all kinds of things. I never knew what she was"—he made a vague gesture—"until it was too late. I think, Stella dear, I have gone through life with my heart shut."

"Except to me," said Stellamaris.

"That's different," he said, with a turn of his great shoulders.

He left her abruptly and joined the group of the three elders by the window. She came to Herold, who had been standing with his back against the empty fire-place.

"You must be very tired."

He saw her brows knit in their familiar little fairy wrinkles as she anxiously scanned his face. Indeed, he was very weary, and his eyes and cheeks showed it.

"There has been a lot not only to do, but to feel of late," he said.

She put out a timid hand and touched his sleeve.

"You must n't do and feel too much, or you 'll break down."

"Why should I, if you have n't?" he asked with a faint smile.

"I think it cowardly to break down when one ought to be strong," she said.

"Are you afraid of my being a coward, Stella?"

She uttered a little cry, and her touch became a grasp.

"You! Oh, no! You? You've been strong. There 's no need for you to do any more. You 've got to live your own life and not that of other people—"

"The only life left to me," he said in a low voice, "is that of those dear to me."

John lumbered up gloomily. "You must persuade him to take a rest, Stella. He has been driving himself to death." He laid a heavy hand on his friend. "God knows what I should have done without him all this time. Wait," he said suddenly, with the other hand uplifted.

And all were silent when to a scuffle of feet succeeded a measured tramp of steps descending the stairs. The bearers passed along the passage by the door of the drawing-room. Unity was going forth on her last journey through the familiar Kilburn streets.

The little crowd on the pavement had swelled. The case and all about it had been manna to hungry July reporters, and all the world knew of Unity and judged her this way and that, according to individual prejudice. But the male part of the crowd uncovered as the coffin and afterward the little group of mourners passed through. John and Miss Lindon and Lady Blount went in the first carriage; Stella, Sir Oliver, and Herold in the second. Sir Oliver, as is the way of Sir Olivers all the world over, spoke of funerals he had attended in years and latitudes both remote. Poor Roddy Greenwood—best fellow that ever lived—it was in Berbice, Demerara—God bless his soul, it was in '68—he had left him at six in the morning after a night's loo—good game loo; no one ever played it these days—and he had followed him to his grave that day before sunset. Then there was Freddy Nicol—they brought it in accidental because he was cleaning his gun—there were the rags and oil and things about him; but it was odd, devilish odd, that it should have happened the day after Kitty Green married that fellow What 's-his-name? Tut! tut! he would remember it in a minute. Now, what the Dickens was the name of the fellow Kitty Green married? But as Kitty Green and her obscure and unremembered spouse were young in the days when Sir Oliver was young, and at the best and happiest were both wrinkled, uninteresting ancients, the baffling question did not stir the pulses of his hearers.

"Anyhow," said Sir Oliver, summing up, "death is a devilish funny business. I've seen lots of it."

"And you who have seen so much of it, dear," said Stellamaris, very seriously, "what do you think of death?"

"I've told you, my child; I've told you. It's devilish funny—odd—here to-day and gone to-morrow. Devilish funny."

They arrived at the cemetery. In the bare mortuary chapel Stella knelt and heard for the first time in her life the beautiful words of the service for the burial of the dead. And there in front of her, covered with poor, vain flowers, was the coffin containing the clay of one whom man with his opportunist laws against murder and self-slaughter was powerless to judge. At the appointed time they went out into the summer air and walked in forlorn procession behind the hearse, through the startling city in whose tenements of stone and marble no mortal could dwell; in which there was no fevered strife as in the cities of men; in which all the inhabitants slept far beneath their stately domes or humble monoliths, at peace with mankind, themselves, and God. And green grass grew between the graves, and sweet flowers bloomed and seemed to say, "Why weep, since we are here?" But for the faint grinding of the hearse wheels on the gravelled path and the steps of the followers all was still. Stellamaris clung to Herold's arm.

"I can't believe they are all dead," she whispered. "The whole place seems alive. I think they are waiting for Unity. They will take her by the hand and make her one of themselves."

"And bow down before her," said Herold. "It is only the dead that know the great souls that pass from the earth."

They reached the graveside. The surpliced chaplain stood a pace or two apart. The dismal men in black deposited the coffin by the yellow, upturned earth. The group of six gathered close together. The July sunshine streamed down, casting a queer projection of shadow from the coffin-end.

"Man, that is born of a woman, hath but a short time to live, and is full of misery. He cometh up, and is cut down, like a flower; he fleeth as it were a shadow, and never continueth in one stay."

Stella heard the chaplain's voice as in a dream. The rattle of the earth on the coffin-lid—"Earth to earth, ashes to ashes, dust to dust"—roused her with a shock. Below, deep in the grave, lay Unity—Unity, who had taken a human life, and had taken her own for the sake of those she loved; Unity, who in the approach to her murderous and suicidal end was all but unfathomable to her; Unity, whom she had read and thought enough to know to be condemned by the general judgment of mankind. There, in that oak coffin, lay all that remained of the common little girl, with the lilies she herself had sent on her bosom. The lilies she had seen, pure white, with their pistils of golden hope; the dead white face she had not seen. Yet her lilies were looking into the dead face, and the dead face was near the lilies, down there, underneath the baffling, oaken coffin-lid.... She became aware of words sharp and clear cutting the still air.

"Who shall change our vile body that it may be like unto his glorious body; according to the mighty working whereby he is able to subdue all things to Himself.... I heard a voice from heaven, saying unto me, Write, From henceforth blessed are the dead which die in the Lord: even so saith the Spirit; for they rest from their labours."

Stellamaris stood tense until the end. A great peace had fallen upon her. "Blessed are those that die in the Lord." The simple words held a mystic significance. They reiterated themselves in her brain. Young, emotional, inexperienced, overwhelmed by the shattering collapse of the exquisite, cloud-capped towers of her faith, she found in them an unquestioned truth. By that grave-side, in the sacred presence of the dead, not only of "the dear sister here departed," but of the inhabitants of all the gleaming stone and marble tenements around, there could be no lying; such was the unargued conviction of her candid soul. A voice, coming not from the commonplace, white-robed man, but from the blue vault of heaven, proclaimed that Unity had died in the Lord and that she was blessed. The message was one of unutterable consolation. Unity had died in the Lord. The comforting acceptance of the message indicated the restoration of Stella's faith in God.

The mind of the child-woman is a warp of innocence shot with the woof of knowledge, and the resultant fabric is a thing no man born can seize and put upon canvas, and, for the matter of that, no woman, when she has ceased to be a child.

John stood for a while looking down into the grave, and gently dropped a wreath which he held in his hand. Then he turned gloomily away, and the others followed him, and the grave-diggers' spadefuls of earth rattled down on the coffin with a sound of dreadful finality.

STELLA's heart had softened toward John. Herold had told her how he had nearly come by his death on the rocks below the Channel House. It had moved her to the depths. And now she saw that he was bowed down with grief for Unity. All resentment against him had died. She recovered her faith, not perhaps in the wonder of the Great High Belovedest of the past, but in the integrity of the suffering man. When they reached and had re-entered the house, she took an opportunity of being alone with him. The two elder ladies were up-stairs, and Walter and Sir Oliver had gone out to smoke in the little front garden. Then she said with shy gentleness:

"This must be very desolate for you, dear. Won't Miss Lindon and you come down with us to Southcliff? I have fallen in love with her. I wonder whether I dare ask her. The sea air would do her good."

"She would be delighted, I'm sure; but would you like me to come, too?" he said, bending his heavy brows.

"Of course," replied Stella. She flushed slightly and lowered her eyes.

"I'm afraid I'm not a very gay companion, Stella. In fact, I don't think I ever was one—except in the days when I used to tell you fairy-tales about the palace—"

"Oh, don't!" She could not restrain the quick little cry and gesture. "We must n't talk about that any more. We've got the future to think of. Reconstruction—is n't that what they call it? We have got to look at things as they are, and laugh sometimes."

"I feel," said he, "as though I could never laugh again."

"Yet Unity meant to make you happy and not miserable," said Stella.

"I know," said he, "and that's the devil of it."

He paused for a moment, his hands thrust deep in his trousers' pockets, and his heel on the fender. At last he said: "It would be the best thing in the world for the dear old lady. And God knows it will be good for me. So if you 'll have us for a week or two, we 'll be glad to get away from here."

"I 'll ask Miss Lindon when she comes down."

And Miss Lindon, coming down soon afterwards with Lady Blount, received and accepted the invitation. Sir Oliver, summoned from the garden, expressed his approval.

"My boy," said he, "we've been perfectly wretched without you. Make him put in a long time with us, Miss Lindon. We three old folks will join forces."

Stella slipped out by the front door and stood by Herold, who was leaning over the gate. Of course he too must come to the Channel House. He smiled rather wearily and shook his head.

"Not just now, dear," said he. "I have a week's business to do in London, settling my autumn arrangements—I'm going into management, you know—and then I must run away for a bit—abroad somewhere, a little mild climbing in Switzerland, perhaps."

Stella's face fell. "Going abroad?" she echoed. "For how long?"

"A month or so, if I can manage it. I want a rest rather badly."

"Of course you do; but I was hoping," she faltered, "that you could find rest at Southcliff."

"It's good of you, dear," said he, "to think of me. For Heaven knows how many years I've looked upon the Channel House as a second home; you can never realize what it has meant to me. But I need a complete change, a sort of medicine I must take, no matter how nasty it may be. Besides," he added with a smile, "you will have John now."

"John is John, and you are you," said Stella. There was a little pause. Then after a glance at his tired face, she said in a low voice: "You 're right, Walter; you must go away and get strong again. I spoke very selfishly. I've not been accustomed to think much of other people."

"Stellamaris dear," he said, "if I thought I could serve you by staying, I would stay. But there's nothing for me to do, is there? The—the what shall I say—the veil between John and you has been cut in twain, as it were, by a flaming sword. Perhaps Unity did it. But there's no veil now. The only thing that has to be done is to bring back the sunshine into John's life. That's for you to do, not for me."

She looked at him queerly. Her face was so white, her dress so black. The only gleam about her was in her eyes.

"I know that," she said. "But who is going to bring back the sunshine into your life?"

He leaned against the wooden gate and gripped the top bar tight.

What did she mean? Was she a woman or, after all, only the old fancied child of sea-foam and cloud?

"When I can eat like a pig and sleep like a dog," he said lightly, "and feel physically fit, I shall be all right." He smiled, and took her black-gloved hand. "And when I see the roses in your cheeks and hear you laugh as you used to laugh—that fascinating little laugh like a peal of low silver bells—that I 'll be the Princess Stellamaris's court jester again."

She smiled wanly. "You were never court jester; you were Great High Favourite." She sighed. "How far off those childish days are!"

"They 'll return as soon as you 're happy."

"Life is too full of pain for me to find happiness in superficial things," said Stella.

For all his wretchedness he could have laughed, with a man's sweet pity, at the tone of conviction in her philosophic but childish utterance.

"You must look for it and find it in the deep things," said he.

She made no reply, but stood thoughtfully by his side, and drew with her fingers little lines in the summer dust on the upper surface of the bar of the gate.

"There 's something silly I want to say to you, Walter," she murmured at last, "and I don't quite know how to say it. It 's about the sea. I think you can understand. You always used to. Our long talks—you remember? Since all this has happened, the sea seems to have no meaning for me."

"It will all come back, dear," said Herold, "with your faith in God and the essential beauty of the world."

"But what is the essential beauty of the world?"

"My dear," he laughed, "you must n't ask a poor man such conundrums and expect an instantaneous answer. I should say roughly it was strength and sacrifice and love." He took a cigarette from his case and lit it. "You 'll find the comfort of the sea again. I think it will have quite a new meaning for you, a deeper meaning, when you sit by it with the man whom you love and who loves you, as you know he loves you, and all the past has become sacred, and there's no longer a shadow between you."

"Are you sure?"

"Quite sure. You see, Stellamaris dear," he added after a second or two, "you don't need me any longer. Your happiness, as well as John's happiness, is in your own hands. I can go away with an easy mind. And when I come back—"

"Yes? And when you come back?"

Pain started through his eyes. When he came back? What would be left for him? His art, his ambitions? What were they? A child's vain toys cumbering his feet. His soul was set on the slip of pale girlhood, startlingly black and white, with her mass of soft hair beneath the plain, black hat, and her great pools of eyes, no longer agates or diamonds, but aglow with remote flames, who, in poor common earthliness, stood by his side, but in maddening reality was pinnacled on inaccessible heights by the love between her and the man they both loved. He felt that the pure had an unsuspected power of torture.

"When I come back? Well—" he broke off lamely. And they looked at each other without speaking until they became aware of a human presence. They turned and saw John, his huge bulk in the frame of the doorway, watching them dully beneath his heavy brows.

At the Channel House Stella's health began to mend. The black shadows disappeared from beneath her eyes, and her lips caught the lost trick of a smile. She no longer wandered desolate about house and garden, but sought the companionship of those about her. The old folks discussed and wrangled over the change.

"One would have thought," said Lady Blount, "that this terrible affair would have crushed her altogether."

"Any one who did n't know her might have thought so," replied Sir Oliver; "but I 've watched her. I sized her up long ago. It 's astonishing how little you know of her, Julia. She has lots of pluck—the right stuff in her. And now John 's free and he 's down here. What more can she want?"

"Poor fellow! He does n't seem to be much the happier for it."

"You don't expect him to go about grinning as if nothing had happened, do you?" said Sir Oliver. "Can't you understand that the man has had a devil of a shock? He 'll get over it one of these days."

"I don't want him to grin; but I'd like him to look a little more cheerful," said Lady Blount.

But cheerfulness and John Risca were strangers. Even when he and Stellamaris were alone together, looking at the moonlit sea from the terrace outside the drawing-room windows, or in the sunshine of the sweet cliff garden, the cloud did not lift from his brow. Unless they talked of Unity,—and it relieved his heart to do so, and Stellamaris loved to listen to the brave little chronicles of her life,—long silences marked their intercourse. To get back to the old plane was impossible. They could find no new one on which to meet. She gave him all her pity, for he was a man who had suffered greatly, and in a way it was she herself who had brought the suffering on him. Her heart ached to say or do something that would rekindle the old light in his rugged face; but an unconquerable shyness held her back. If he had thrown his great arm around her and held her tight and uttered broken words of love, pity would have flamed passionate in surrender. If he had pleaded for comfort, pity would have melted warm over his soul. But he made no appeal. Both were burningly aware that Unity had died so that they could be free, no barrier between them. Yet barrier there seemed to be, invisible, inscrutable.

Once Sir Oliver, who had joined them in the garden, asked:

"What are your plans for the future, my boy?"

"Plans? I have none. Just the same old round of work."

"I mean your domestic arrangements."

"I 'll go on living with my old aunt. We 're a queer couple, I suppose, but we understand each other."

"Humph!" grunted Sir Oliver, and he went away to tie up a drooping rose.

They walked on in dead silence, which was broken at last by John, who made a remark as to Constable's growing infirmities.

So the visit came to an end without a word having been said, and John went back to his desolate house, physically rested and able to take up the routine of his working life. Herold in Switzerland wrote letters about snows and glaciers and crystal air. The calm tenor of existence was resumed at the Channel House. Incidentally Stella found an occupation. Old Dr. Ransome, in casual talk, mentioned a case of great poverty and sickness in the village. Stella, followed by Morris bearing baskets of luxuries, presented herself at the poor house in the character of Lady Bountiful. At the sight that met her eyes she wept and went away sorrowful, and then it dawned upon her inexperienced soul that gifts costing her nothing, although they had their use, might be supplemented by something vastly more efficacious. She consulted the hard-worked district nurse, and, visiting the house again, learned how to tend the sick woman and wash the babies and bring cleanliness and air and comfort into the miserable place. And having made in this way the discovery that all through her life she had accepted service from all and sundry and had never done a hand's turn for anybody, she plunged with young shame and enthusiasm into the new work.

Afraid lest convalescence on the part of the patient would throw her back into idleness, she ingenuously asked the nurse if there were other poor people in Southcliff who needed help. The nurse smiled. Even at Southcliff there was enough work among the poor and needy for every day in the week the whole year round.

"I'm glad," said Stellamaris. Then she checked herself. "No, I can't be. I 'm dreadfully sorry." The little lines of complexity knit themselves on her brow. "It 's a confusing world, isn't it?"

The state of mind of Stellamaris at this period may be best described as one of suspended judgment. It was a confusing world. She could not pronounce a more definite opinion. The Land of Illusion was a lost Atlantis of which not a speck remained. On the other hand, the world was no longer the mere abode of sin and ugliness and horror to which she had gradually awakened. Unity had taught her that. What, then, was this mysterious complication of life in which she found herself involved? It no longer frightened her. It interested her curiously.

"Excellency dear," she said one day, "are there any books about life?"

He stared at her, covering his non-comprehension with the usual military twirl of his moustache.

"Millions. What kind of life?"

"Life itself. The meaning of it."

"Religious books? I'm afraid they're not in my line, my dear."

"I don't think it 's religious books I want," said Stella.

"Philosophy, then. Kant, Schopenhauer,—um—er,"—he hooked a name from the depths of his memory—"Bain, and all those fellows. I could never make head or tail of them myself, so I don't suppose you could, dear."

"Did you say Kant? I think I've seen a book of his in the library."

She pulled down a dusty volume of the "Critique of Pure Reason" from a top shelf and puzzled her young brains over it. It seemed to be dealing with vital questions, but, like Sir Oliver, she was hopelessly befogged. She asked the old doctor. He had a glimmering of her meaning. "The best book in the world, my dear,"—he waved a hand,—"is life itself."

"But I can't read it without a dictionary, Doctor," she objected.

"Your heart, my child," said he.

This was pretty, but not satisfactory. "Walter could tell me," she said to herself, and forthwith wrote him a long letter.

She lived in a state not only of suspended judgment, but also of suspended emotion. The latter hung in the more delicate balance. Her maidenhood realized it vaguely. She had half expected John to speak of his love for her; at the same time she had dreaded the moment of declaration; and, at the same time also, she had felt that beneath the shadow of the wings of death it behoved mortal passion to lie still and veiled. The anguish of the weeks preceding the tragedy had passed away. She had no pain save that of yearning pity for an agonized world. The old people in their dependence on her and in the pathos of their limited vision once more became inexpressibly dear. The childish titles were invested in a new beauty. Her pretty labours in sorrow-stricken cottages, amateurish as they were, held a profound significance. Unlike the thousands of sweet English girls up and down the land who are bred in the practice of philanthropy and think no more of it than of its concomitant tennis-parties and flirtations, she had come upon it unawares, and it had all the thrill of a discovery. It was one little piece fitted certainly into the baffling puzzle of life.

John came down again for the week-end. Stella found him gentle, less gloomy, but oddly remote from her—remoter even than when he lay crushed beneath the tragedy. Now and again she caught him looking at her wistfully, whereupon she turned her eyes away in a distress which she could not explain. Gradually she became aware that the Great High Belovedest of the past had vanished into nothingness, with so many other illusory things. The awakening kiss that he had given her as he carried her in his arms faded into the far-off dreamland. On the Sunday night they lingered in the drawing-room for a moment after the old people had retired to bed.

"I must be going back by the early train in the morning, and sha'n't see you," said he, "so I 'll say good-by now."

"I'm sorry, dear." She put out her hand. "I hope the little change has done you good."

For answer he bent down and touched her forehead with his lips. Then he held the door open for her to pass out.

"God bless you, dear," said he.

She went up-stairs, feeling in a half-scared way that something, she knew not what, had happened, and she cried herself to sleep.

# CHAPTER XXV

It was a sullen night in mid-August, following a breathless day and an angry sunset that had shed a copper-coloured glow above a bank of cloud. The great windows of the drawing-room of the Channel House were flung open wide, and on the terrace beneath the starless heaven sat the little group of intimates, which now included the placid lady of the little Kilburn house. Walter Herold, who had returned from Switzerland tanned and strong, told his adventures to Sir Oliver and Dr. Ransome, while John and Stella, a little way apart, listened idly. Lady Blount and Miss Lindon murmured irrelevancies concerning the curates of long ago and the present price of beef. They had many points at which the curves of their natures touched, such as mathematicians, with unique spasm of romance, call points of osculation.

But for the voices all was still. From below, at the base of the cliff, came the lazy lapping of the sea against the rocks. Outside the glow of light cast by the illuminated drawing-room the world was pitch black. The air grew more and more oppressive.

"I think there's going to be thunder," said Lady Blount.

"I hope not," said Miss Lindon. "I know John thinks it foolish, but I'm terribly afraid of thunder."

"So does Sir Oliver; but I don't care. Whenever there's a thunder-storm, I go up to my room and put my head under the bedclothes until it 's over."

"Now is n't that remarkable, my dear," said Miss Lindon—"I do exactly the same! I draw down the blinds, and hide scissors away in a drawer, and throw a woollen shawl over the steel fender, and then I put my head under the blankets. My Aunt Margery, I remember, invariably used to go and sit in the coal-cellar. But she was a strong-minded woman, and would put her foot on a black beetle as soon as look at it. I hope I'm fond of most of God's creatures, but a black beetle frightens me out of my wits."

"What do you think of thunder-storms, Stella?" John asked, knocking the ashes out of his pipe.

"I'm rather frightened," she confessed. "Not because I think they 'll hurt me." She paused and sighed. "I never could understand them."

"What do you mean by understanding a thunderstorm?" he asked.

"I don't know," she answered. "You either understand things or you don't."

Herold broke in to spare her further explanation. "There was a splendid one the week before last in the mountains—a real Walpurgisnacht. It seemed as though hell had broken loose."

He described it in his vivid way. The elderly ladies looked at the glimmer of white shirt-front and the glowing cigarette-end by which alone he was revealed, and wondered at the heroical, or, as it seemed in the unconfessed depths of their souls, the God-defying qualities of male humanity. A few resounding splashes fell from the sky. The party rose hurriedly.

"Gad! we 're in for it," cried Sir Oliver. "Let us get indoors."

A flash of lightning rent the southern sky, and a clap of thunder broke over the Channel, and the rain came down like a waterspout. In the drawing-room Lady Blount put her hand before her eyes.

"You must all forgive me. I can't stand it. I must go up-stairs. Besides, it 's late, very near bedtime, My dear Miss Lindon, shall we go?"

The two old ladies, after hasty good nights, retired to the protection of their respective bedclothes. A great wind arose and swept through the room, blowing over a vase of flowers on the piano. Dr. Ransome, who happened to be standing near, mopped up the water with his handkerchief. Herold sprang to the window and shut it. Stella was by his side. Another flash sped through the blackness, and the thunder followed. They drew near together and waited for the next.

Sir Oliver hospitably pushed John and the old doctor toward the drawing-room door. "There are drinks in the library. It 'll be cosier there, on the other side of the house, away from this confounded racket. Come along, Walter. Stella, darling, you had better go to bed. It 's the best place for little girls in a thunder-storm."

She turned, the breadth of the drawing-room separating Walter Herold and herself from the others.

"I 'll stay up a little longer and look at it, dear Excellency," she said, with a smile. "I 'll come into the library later and tell you all good night."

At this announcement, and Stellamaris's announcements had ever been sovereign decrees, John and Dr. Ransome, standing by the open door, obeyed the courteous wave of Sir Oliver's hand. The old man waited for Herold, who advanced a pace or two.

"I suppose you 're dying for whisky and soda," said Stella, resignedly.

He stopped short. "Not in the least. I would far rather look at this,"—he flung a hand toward the window,—"if you would let me."

"Only for five minutes, Favourite, dear; then I 'll send you away."

Sir Oliver went out, shutting the door behind him. Herold and Stellamaris were alone in the spacious room. There came another flash and the thunder peal, and the rain spattered hard on the stone terrace.

"Why should n't we sit down?" he asked, and drew a small settee to the window.

She stood, expectant of the lightning. It came and lit up a suddenly tempestuous sea. With her eyes straining at the blackness, she said in a low, voice:

"Turn out the lights. This is all that matters." He went to the door, snapped the electric switches, and the darkness was so absolute that he waited for the next flash to see his way across the room. They sat down together side by side. A flash of vehement and reiterated radiance revealed a God's wrath of spindrift scattered from mountainous waves that tossed in the middle distance the three-masted skeleton of a ship, and blasted the chalk-cliffed promontory to the west into a leprous tongue. They watched in silence for a long, long time. Save for the lightning, pitch blackness enveloped them. The rain swished heavily against the windows, and the surf roared on the rocks below. After a livid revelation of elemental welter and the deafening crash of cataclysm, she clutched his arm. When the peal had rolled away into an angry rumble, he whispered:

"Are you frightened?"

"No," she replied, also below her breath, "not frightened. It excites me, it makes me feel, it makes me think. I seem to be understanding things I never understood before. Don't let us speak."

To remove impression of rebuke, her hand slid down his arm, found his hand, and held it. Neither spoke. After a while he scanned her face by the lightning. It was set, as though she saw a vision, her eyes gleaming, her lips parted. At the thunderclap her grasp involuntarily tightened. Again and again her face was startlingly visible. Herold's mind went back down the years. He had seen that rapt expression times without number when she lay by the window of her sea-chamber and looked out into the mysteries of sea and sky; and times without number she had held his hand while her spirit, as he had loved fantastically to believe, went forth to dance with her sisters of the foam or to walk secure through the gates of the sunset. And he had loved to believe, too, that his own spirit, in some blind, attendant way, though lagging far behind, followed hers over the borders of the Land That Never Was. Sensitive to her moods, he felt now a strange excitement. She had become once more the Stellamaris of the cloudless and mystical years. The sea that had rejected her had again claimed her for its own, and was delivering into her keeping mysteries such as it had withheld from her even then; for she had found no message in the war of elements, mysteries deep and magnificent. He returned her tense pressure, and followed her spirit out into the vastness.

The storm grew fiercer. Every few moments spasms of livid daylight rent the darkness and dazzlingly illuminated the eager faces of the pair, the window-jambs and transoms, the terrace, the howling waste beyond, the skeleton ship tossing grimly, the promontory, the pitch black of the sky; and the thunder burst in awful detonations over their heads. Unconsciously and instinctively Stellamaris had drawn nearer to him, and her arm rested against his. After a long time, in the stillness of the dark, he spoke like one in a dream:

"The terrible splendour of life, that is the secret—the terrible splendour."

She awoke almost with a shock, and, turning round, shook him by the lapel of his coat.

"How did you know, Walter? How did you know?"

Her voice quavered; he felt that she was trembling. A flash showed her straining her eyes into his face. They waited for the thunderclap during a second of intensity.

"What?" he asked.

"Those words. Those very words had just come to me, the meaning of everything—The terrible splendour of life. How did you know?"

"It was our souls that were going together through the storm."

She released him, and withdrew a little.

"Did you know all that I was thinking?"

"Or all that the sea was telling you?"

"Did you feel that, too?" she asked breathlessly.

"I think so," he replied.

"It was strange," she said. "I hardly knew that I was here. I seemed to be away in the midst of it all, but I don't think I lost consciousness. I had adventures—curious adventures." She paused abruptly, then she continued: "They seemed to be definite then, but they are all a blur now. It was a kind of battle between man and evil forces, and I think I felt a voice speaking through it, and saying that the splendour of man would never be subdued; and the impression I've got is, that I saw something, whether it was a shape or a scene I don't know, but something great and grand and fierce and heroic, and the voice told me it was life. The only thing I have clear is the words, 'the terrible splendour of life,' the words you plucked out of me."

"It is the great secret," he said.

"Yes."

There was another silence. The storm began to pass gradually away. The lightning became rarer, and the intervals longer between flash and thunder.

"It is beginning to be clear," she said at last. "All that has troubled me. All that you guessed I was feeling, and that I told you of only when you compelled me. You have been right. Once—do you remember?—you said that if I saw God through the beauty and the vanity of the world all would be well."

"I ought to have told you to see Him through the pain of the world," said Herold.

"You have told me that, in other words, ever since; and I was deaf."

"Not I, dear," said Herold.

"Yes, you. Now I understand." She drew a deep breath. "Now, I understand. It's like an open book. That woman—Unity—wait," she paused, and put her two hands to her head in the darkness. "I have a glimmer of a memory—it's so illusive. It seems that I saw Unity just now. I understand all that she was, all that she meant." A flash showed the sea. "Yes, I was out there," she cried excitedly, and pointed. "Just out there." Darkness engulfed them. "I forget," she faltered, "I forget."

"But the sea has taken you back at last, Stellamaris," said Herold.

She seized his hand and held it during the peal. Then she cried in a tone of sudden terror:

"Walter!"

"Yes?"

"What you said—your prophesy—the comfort of the sea—the deeper meaning—"

He leaped to his feet.

"Don't think anything more of it. They were just foolish words to comfort you. You and I seem to have been on the Edge of Beyond and looked over, and we're not quite normal. We must get down now to practical things. I'm just what I always was, dear, a fantastic person who rode with you into fairyland. I am still. Nothing more."

"Are you quite sure?" suddenly asked a deep voice out of the blackness of the room.

Stella with a little cry of fright sprang to Herold for protection. For a second or two they were still. In their exaltation the question seemed to come from some vast depth of the abysm of time. Their hearts beat fast, and they clung together, listening, and there was not a sound. Then the lightning played its dancing daylight about the room, and they saw John Risca standing by the door. They sprang apart.

In another moment the room was flooded with electric light. The drawing-room, for all its beauty, looked mean and unimportant. The lights showed up glaringly an old Florentine tapestry over the chimney-piece. It seemed to have singularly little relation to life. It jarred impertinently.

"I came in to find Walter," said John; "I didn't think Stella was still up. It's late. You didn't hear me. I'm sorry I inadvertently overheard."

"There's nothing, my dear John, that you could not have heard," said Herold.

John came forward in his lumbering way.

"I know that, Walter."

For a minute or two no one spoke. The three stood stock-still, their hearts thumping. Outside, the rain fell pitilessly on the flags of the terrace, and the waning storm flashed and growled. John's burning eyes looked at Herold beneath heavy, knitted brows. At last he said:

"You love Stella. You have loved her always. You never told me."

"That is not so," said Herold. "You have found us in a foolishly false position. A thunder-storm is an emotional piece of business. My old intimacy with Stella has its privileges. I 'll leave you. Stella will speak for her-self."

John stretched out a detaining arm. "No, my friend; stay. We three must have a talk together. It was bound to come sooner or later. Let it be now." He spoke quietly, with dignity and authority. "There is nothing for us to talk about," said Herold,—Stellamaris stood clutching the back of an armchair, and looking from one man to the other,—"the words you overheard ought to tell you that. And in answer to your question, I can say that I am quite sure."

"You lie," said John, quietly. "You lie out of the loyalty of your heart—" he raised his great hand to check the other's outburst—"God Almighty in Heaven knows I'm not accusing you. If ever man had deep and devoted and unselfish love from another, I've had it from you. And I have it still. It's a matter not of reproach, but of reparation."

"Don't you think," said Herold, "we might continue this extraordinary conversation in the library—by ourselves?"

"No," said John in the obstinate tone that Herold had known for many years. "You and I are two men, and Stella is a woman, and a hell-mess just like that—" he pointed to the tempest—"has upset our lives. It's time to put them to rights again."

"I don't know what you 're talking about," said Herold. "It 's a pity you have chosen to-night. Things are a bit abnormal. Let us go to bed, and talk to-morrow, if you like, in the light of common sense."

John folded his arms. "I'm going to talk to-night. I want you calmly to consider the position."

"I do," said Herold. "Stop,"—-as John was about, to interrupt,—"let me speak."

"Yes," said Stella, breaking silence for the first time; "let Walter speak."

But she stood apart, fascinated by this strange duel, as her primitive ancestress might have done when two males fought for her with flint-headed axes.

"What I feel as regards Stella is neither here nor there. I 've never told her that I loved her. I 've never told you. Both you and she have told me that you love each other. That was enough for me. I joined with Unity in seeking to remove the obstacle in the path of your happiness. If Unity had not forestalled me, I—well, God knows what I should have done! I left you asleep that evening, and went, half crazy, to the flat, and there I found what I found. But, anyhow, Unity committed murder and suicide to set the two of you free. If you want strong, blatant words, there you have them. A girl, one of God's chosen, has laid down her life for the two of you." He stood between them and threw up his hands. "Take each other. It is a sacrament."

Stella, her arms still on the back of the chair, hung her head and stared downward. John cast a quick glance at her and then, a thing which he rarely did, drew his great frame up to its full height and challenged his friend.

"If you don't love her, she loves you. I know."

Herold said:

"You two belong to each other."

"Then Stella must decide," said John.

She threw out a flutter of delicate fingers and covered her face. "No, no!" she gasped.

The lightning flickered mildly in the well-lit room, and the eventual thunder reverberated in distant anger.

John again came close to Herold. "This may be an extraordinary conversation, but it has to be. If Stella loved me, do you think she would stand like that?"

Stella dropped to her knees, her face and arms huddled against the chair.

"My dear old man, I've learned many things of late. I can't tell you exactly. I'm not good at that sort of thing. But Unity has been too big for me."

Stella raised a white face.

"What do you mean? Say exactly what you mean."

"I mean—oh, God knows what I mean." He strode blindly across the room, returned, and faced the two, still near together. "Can't you understand?" he cried, with a wide gesture. "I'm infinitesimal sand beneath that child's feet. I'm a blind mole in comparison with her transcendent vision. I'm in the dust. Oh, God!" He turned away.

Stella rose, and, clasping hands to her bosom, went to him.

"Belovedest, for Christ's sake, what is the end of all this?"

He halted and took her hands.

"Not shadows, not lies. Once I thought—indeed, I knew—you loved me. That was when you were an ignorant child. You loved some one you thought was me. Now your eyes are opened. You have passed through flames. Knowledge has come to you. You see me as I am, and your love has gone. I know, too, what I am. Unity has taught me. You can't—you don't love me, Stella. That I know. I've known it ever since that day when we put her into her grave."

Herold came between them imploringly. "My dear man—my dear fellow—what is the use of this wild talk? You two love each other. Unity gave her life for the two of you. If you two don't come together, it 's all overwhelming, blasting irony. I could n't believe in God after it. It would be hellishly cynical. Stella, in God's name, tell him that you are bound by Unity's sacrifice—that you love him and will marry him and make his life happy!"

Stella, very pale, looked at John. "If you want me, I will marry you," she said in a clear voice.

John waved her aside. "I will not take you, my dear," said he.

Spurned sex winced involuntarily.

"If you have stopped caring for me—"

"I stopped caring? I? Merciful God, I've never loved you so much. But you love a better man. What's the good of saying the same things over and over again? But I 'll tell you this, both of you, that if Unity had not given her life, and if I had been free, I should have fought for you and had you despite everything. That 's my accursed nature. But Unity has not died in vain, and it's because of that child's death, the beauty and heroism of it, that I'm able to stand here and tear my heart out and throw it away. Don't make any mistake,"—he turned fiercely on Herold,—"it's not I who am giving her up. It's Unity."

"Very well," said Herold. "Let us put it at that. It's your point of view. You also force me to speak. It would be grotesque to keep silence any longer. Yes, I do love her. She is the beginning and end of life to me. If she had lain on her back all her days, I should never have married another woman. There! You have it now."

The two men's eyes held each other for a space. Stellamaris looked at the pair with a fearful admiration. They were men. Herold she had divined and known long ago; this, on his part, was only the supreme fulfilment of promise. But John Risca, who had passed through the illusion and disillusion of her soul, stood before her in new strength, a great and moving figure.

At last John drew a deep breath, turned to Stellamaris very gently, and smiled.

"And you?"

The smile sent swift pain through her heart. She made a step or two, and fell sobbing on his breast.

"O Belovedest, I am sorry! You have guessed right. Forgive me!"

He caressed the bowed head tenderly for an instant, then releasing himself, he clapped his hand on Herold's shoulder and shook it with rough affection.

"I 'm going to bed," said he. He moved to the door. There he paused to nod a good night; but at sight of them both looking sadly at him he walked back a couple of paces.

"Don't worry about me. I'm at peace with myself for the first time for years. There 's lots of happiness in the world left." He smiled again. "Enough for the three of us—and for Unity."

He left them, and went to bed in the room which Stellamaris had furnished for him long ago, and fell into the sleep of the man who has found rest at last in the calm and certain knowledge of spiritual things. Unity had not died in vain. And Stellamaris, sitting once more by Herold's side in the wide bay of the window, and talking with him in a hushed voice of the wondrous things that had come to.pass, knew that John Risca had spoken a great truth. It had been God's will that so should the terrible splendour of the world be made manifest.

Herold asked for the million-billionth time in the history of mankind:

"When did you first find that you loved me?"

She replied, perhaps more truly than most maidens:

"There was never a time when I did n't love you. I mean—I don't quite know what I mean," she said confusedly. "You see, I 've lived a strange life, dear," she went on. "You seem to have been a part of me ever since I can remember what is worth remembering. You have always understood things that went on inside me almost before I could tell them to you. I always wanted you to explain foolishness that I could n't speak of to any one else."

"That's very beautiful," Herold interrupted, "but love is a different matter. When did the real love come to you?"

"I think it was that morning in the garden when you almost whipped me," said Stella. She started an inch or two away from him. "And I 'm sure you knew it," she said.

And he remembered, as he had often remembered in his great struggle, her eyes, turning from agates to diamonds and her words, "Do you love me like that?"

"Heaven knows, Stellamaris dear; I did not mean to betray myself."

She laughed the enigmatic laugh of a woman's contentment, and Herold was too wise to ask why.

They spoke of deepest things. "There is something I must tell you," said he, "which up to now I have had to keep secret, and it is right that you should know."

And he told Her the story of Unity and himself—the revolver, their talk of the evil woman, their parting words, his crazed adventure through the sunny streets.

She listened, her body leaning forward, her hands clasped on her knee. When he had finished, she sat without change of attitude.

"You did that so that another man could marry the woman you loved. Unity did that so that the man she loved could marry another woman. John came in to-night to sacrifice himself and give us both happiness. The three of you have done terrible and splendid things. I am the only one of us four who has done nothing."

Herold rose, took a nervous pace or two. What she said needed more than a lover's sophistical reassurance. He could speak a thousand words of comfort; but he knew that her soul required a supreme answer, a clue to the dark labyrinth through which she had worked. What could he say? He looked through the window, and suddenly saw that which to him was an inspiration. He threw the folding-doors wide. It had stopped raining long ago, though neither had noticed.

"Come out on the terrace," said he.

She followed him into the gusty air. The sea still roared resentfully at the late disturbance of its quiet. The southwest wind that had brought up the storm had driven the great rack of black cloud above the horizon, and there below the rack was a band of dark but cloudless sky, and in it one star hung serene. Herold pointed to it.

"What have you done, dear?" His voice broke in a catch of exultation, and his usually nimble wit failed to grasp the lunatic falsity of the analogy.

"You have done what that has done—come through the storm pure and steadfast."

"Not I, dear," she said, "but my faith in the God we breathe."

"No; you yourself." He put his arm around her, and all his love spoke. "You. The living mystery of beauty that is you." He whispered into her lips. "You—Stellamaris—Star of the Sea."

## THE END

# ANSWERS

Unscramble:
Biblioklept

| | | | | | | | | |
|---|---|---|---|---|---|---|---|---|
| 4 | 2 | 6 | 8 | 1 | 9 | 7 | 5 | 3 |
| 7 | 9 | 5 | 3 | 6 | 4 | 2 | 8 | 1 |
| 1 | 3 | 8 | 7 | 2 | 5 | 9 | 6 | 4 |
| 3 | 8 | 2 | 1 | 7 | 6 | 5 | 4 | 9 |
| 5 | 4 | 7 | 9 | 3 | 2 | 6 | 1 | 8 |
| 6 | 1 | 9 | 5 | 4 | 8 | 3 | 2 | 7 |
| 8 | 7 | 3 | 2 | 5 | 1 | 4 | 9 | 6 |
| 9 | 5 | 4 | 6 | 8 | 7 | 1 | 3 | 2 |
| 2 | 6 | 1 | 4 | 9 | 3 | 8 | 7 | 5 |

*SUDOKU*

CPSIA information can be obtained
at www.ICGtesting.com
Printed in the USA
BVHW081103111022
649158BV00011B/1380

9 781950 464128